D0467501

THE WONDERFUL SIBLEYS

The
Wonderful Sibleys

BY WILLIAM MAIER

CHARLES SCRIBNER'S SONS

NEW YORK

© COPYRIGHT 1956 BY WILLIAM MAIER

All rights reserved. No part of this book
may be reproduced in any form without
the permission of Charles Scribner's Sons.

Printed in the United States of America

For Ellie and Ruth and Mort and Peter
and, of course, Cappy,
in memory of an afternoon on the terrace

THE WONDERFUL SIBLEYS

I

1 ·

As he paced the forward deck of this little island ferry that was more like a miniature seagoing ship than the Jersey Central ferries he had known all his life, Noah Sibley realized that people were staring at him. But he was too agitated to sit still, torn by too many conflicting feelings. Disregarding the stares, he walked with determination, a big man in white trousers and a gray coat, six feet and a hundred and ninety pounds of energetic and slightly awkward bone and flesh. He swung his soft Panama by the brim in his hand as he walked, and the wind danced through the blond fuzz on the top of his head and whipped the billowy white trousers around his legs.

Frowning into the wind through his glasses, he wondered again and again why he had come. Better, he would think for a moment, to have let the sleeping dog that had slept for fifteen years lie. But then he would remind himself that too often in his thirty-eight years he had, wittingly or unwittingly, avoided experience, and this would be an experience. It could be an excruciatingly embarrassing one. It could be a tremendous disillusionment too. Perhaps it was better to hold on to what illusions you had. It could even be a fairly jolly weekend, a weekend of laughing, weren't-we-young-in-those-days reminiscences. It could be. If only he had a little more confidence in his own ability to carry it off, to act the part that the script of his own imaginings called for.

As they left the mainland farther behind, the wind grew stronger. He stopped his pacing and took up a position behind the high railing in the bow. With the freshening of the wind, his spirits rose. This trip in this little vessel was, he decided, an experience in itself. Never an experienced salt-water man, he found the easy movement of the boat, the briskness of the wind, the flecks of whitecaps against the deep blue, the tumbling white thunderheads on the distant horizon freshly and surprisingly stimulating. If only they could go sailing on through this blue—but already they were swinging in toward the Island, and he could make out houses and trees along its shore. And once again, as they moved inexorably nearer, he was troubled by that funny breathlessness, a breathlessness that seemed to be located in a hollow somewhere deep in his stomach.

2·

HE saw Natalie before she saw him. She was standing there on the dock among all the laughing people and the scurrying children, looking very intense and alive and not quite so unbecomingly tanned as the rest of them. And Noah, who had burned the only picture he had ever had of her fifteen years before and had been unable for many years now to bring up in his mind any clear image of what her face had looked like, said to himself, "Of course that's what she looks like. How could I ever have forgotten that that's the way her face looked?"

She was wearing a square-necked, wide-skirted sun dress, pale tan and dark brown, and she seemed, if anything, slimmer than he remembered her. That was a surprise. Once he had thought that the girlish roundness of her shoulders and arms and legs might someday turn to plumpness. And her figure had not sagged, as Noah had always believed that women's figures inevitably do under the weight of years and child bearing.

Now she was walking along beside the boat, frowning as she looked up at the line of faces, and it was the same intense, strangely restrained walk that he remembered, as though all the muscles in her body were taut elastic bands.

There was a commotion among the children at the end of the dock, and he looked away for a moment. When he looked back, he saw that she had found him. She was smiling and waving, and he smiled and waved back. She said something, but the churning of the water around the piles and the dozens of shouted conversations drowned it out entirely. He put his hand to his ear and shook his head and smiled helplessly.

She nodded, smiling back at him, and for the embarrassingly long time it took to make the ferry fast and to clear a way through the hold, they stood, alternately smiling at each other and looking away.

Seeing her there as one of the crowd, looking at her as he might have looked at a stranger, he came to the conclusion—quite dispassionately, he felt—that she was, in her own highly individual way, beautiful. The gold still glinted in her brown hair, her skin still glowed with that same vital warmth, her mouth was still expressive, still a little too wide. Her face did seem a little thinner. That was the only change he could see: a suggestion of hollow cheeks, a new accentuation of the bony structure of the face, a hint, perhaps, that the fifteen years had not been soft ones.

The crowd had begun to move toward the stairway. He smiled at her once more and turned away. It occurred to him, as he moved along with the crowd, that with this opportunity to appraise her from a distance he had already had the part of the adventure that he had looked forward to most. He went on down the stairs, forced along by the crowd, feeling suddenly like a man who wonders, halfway, if he really wanted to be on the escalator.

3.

It seemed to Noah that the only civilized way to handle the embarrassments that were inherent in the situation was to cover them up with small talk, to act as though they were old acquaintances reunited after fifteen years, to inquire about brothers and sisters and fathers and mothers and jobs and places.

But Natalie was having none of such talk. She drove the station wagon slowly, as though she didn't want to get back to her cottage before a lot of things had been said. And she kept turning to look at him, smiling a searching, yet somehow timid, half smile. "You were very bad about Christmas cards, Noah, weren't you?"

"I suppose I was."

"Didn't you get my Christmas cards?"

"I got some—way back."

"Of course I finally took the hint and stopped. But you never sent me one, did you?"

"No, I never sent you one."

"And you didn't even write me when Pamela and Peter were born."

He remembered the first announcement, the one about the girl—Pamela Parkes Humeston. It had come from St. Paul, Minnesota, in

[3]

midwinter, and it had made the thing seem irrevocably final, final in a way that the wedding announcement never had.

They had left the harbor behind and reached the four corners of the little village. Natalie stopped for the traffic, then shifted gears and started on. Noah sat with his hat in his lap, staring straight ahead at the road. It was scrub country ahead, brown fields dotted with bayberry and beach plum, patchy woods of scrub oak and scrub pine.

He knew that she was looking at him again. "You never forgave me, did you, Noah?"

He glanced at her quickly. Apparently she had no thought of covering the embarrassments. He didn't answer, thinking that his silence might make her change to some easier subject. But she drove on at twenty miles an hour, waiting for his answer. Finally he said, "I stopped thinking about you—eventually."

"But you never stopped feeling resentful."

He sat still, drumming on his hat with his fingers. The best you could say for this was that it was bad manners. And the annoying thing about it was that just being near her, sitting beside her here in the seat of a car, was bringing back, not the old resentments, but the old excitement. The way her hand lay on the wheel, the firm line of her neck where it came up toward her chin, above all that sense of leashed vitality, that hunch you always had that she was feeling more intensely than she was acting—invariably in the old days, he remembered, being near her had started the stirrings of these long-forgotten unruly ferments. And now he was discovering that it was as though no years at all had intervened.

"Did you?" she asked.

"Did I what?"

"Ever stop feeling resentful."

"Yes, I stopped feeling resentful."

"Good," she said. "Did you ever fall in love with anybody else?"

He turned quickly again, scowling at her. Then suddenly he laughed, and when he laughed she turned and smiled at him.

"Let's talk about your children," he said. "How old would the little girl be now?"

"She's fourteen."

"Is she charming?"

"I haven't any idea." He knew that she was looking at him again. "You've changed, Noah," she said, "far more than I thought you would. I like the changes too."

"And the boy," Noah asked, "how old would he be?"

[4]

She laughed. "Did you ever fall in love with anybody else, Noah?"

She was watching his face. He looked back at her, keeping his face expressionless, and their eyes met.

"You're wishing you hadn't come, aren't you?" she asked.

"Yes."

"I'm sorry. I'm not trying to be nasty. But I'm anxious to know."

He laughed again, unhappily. "Why?"

"I can't tell you, exactly. Just answer me a few more questions and then I'll be nice. Did you ever fall in love with anybody else?"

A rabbit scurried down the ditch ahead of them, then leaped into the bushes and disappeared. Noah turned his head, watching it. There had been girls, of course, a few girls—surprisingly few, he guessed, if you figured how many nights there were in fifteen years. And he couldn't remember that he had ever quite thought that he was in love with any one of them. "Not very wholeheartedly," he said.

"Did you ever think of marrying anybody else?"

"Not very seriously."

"Because you were still thinking about me?"

"I stopped thinking about you—eventually."

"That's right. You told me that. And you stopped feeling resentful."

He nodded. "Up to a couple of minutes ago."

She chuckled. "You've gained a lot of self-confidence, haven't you? It's very becoming to you. It was what you always needed, you know."

"Was it?"

"Of course. Your father died, didn't he?"

He nodded, feeling more comfortable. At last she was getting around to the fathers and mothers and brothers and sisters. "Four years ago," he said, "in '49. Quite suddenly. A stroke."

"You always worshiped him, didn't you? Do you still worship him, now that he's dead?"

Noah frowned at the road ahead, annoyed that she, almost a stranger, should feel free to ask such a question in such a tone, touched where it hurt by a quick suspicion that she had seen, in one short summer, something that he was only now beginning to see dimly. But she could have no way of knowing how timely her question was. "He was a very remarkable man," he said defensively.

"Of course," she said in a tone that was far from convinced, and immediately Noah was furious with her. If he wanted to suspect that his father was a little less wonderful than he had once thought, that was his privilege. But it was not for Natalie to hint at. And knowing

[5]

that his family loyalty was an unreasoning thing did nothing to make his anger less.

Perhaps she sensed that he was provoked. She smiled at him. "Wasn't it nice that I saw that little article about you in your alumni magazine. I'd lost track of you entirely. And I had no idea that you were becoming famous."

"I'm not becoming famous."

"The article said so."

He wet his lips, still angry. "In the whole country there are maybe a hundred people who've ever heard of the work I'm doing. The guy who wrote that article happened to be one of them."

"It sounded very impressive," she said.

He shook his head. "Hack work. Second-hand work. The important contributions are all my father's."

"Oh," she said, and she sounded disappointed.

4·

THEY turned off the main road at a discreet little sign that said "J. R. Humeston." Now they were on a narrower road that wound through thicker pine woods. There were no open fields, no views, and no houses.

Natalie had become silent, and Noah sensed in her a tension, a repressed excitement that was something more than the restrained inner excitement that had always been a part of her. He kept his eyes on the road ahead, but he knew that she was turning now and then to look at him appraisingly, doubtfully, as though searching for something in him that she wasn't sure whether she was finding or not.

They came to the end of the road in a large parking area beside a low, wooden, three-car garage. There was a sedan in the garage. She drove in beside it and said, "Jeffrey's still on the golf course," and Noah thought he detected relief in her voice. "He should be back soon," she said. "You've never met him, have you?"

Noah looked at her. "Of course I haven't."

She laughed and opened the door beside her. "That's right. Of course you haven't."

Carrying his bags, he followed her across the corner of the parking area to the broad flight of stone steps that led up to the cottage. It was a two-storied cottage, white with green trim and shutters, very

[6]

broad across the back, with latticework hiding the kitchen. They went in at the back of a wide hall and along the side of the staircase to the front door. Through the open door and the wide windows of the dining and living rooms, which opened into the hall from left and right, Noah could see a veranda running the full length of the front, and through the railing of the veranda he caught glimpses of a spectacularly broad view of the Sound.

Natalie showed him to his room, and after he came down they sat on the veranda looking out at the water. Now she did ask him all the questions about his mother and his two older brothers and his two younger sisters that he had been expecting her to ask when he got off the boat. But in all her questions he felt a not quite disinterested meaningfulness, in each one a tiny barb that managed to prick at his family esteem.

He sat with his eyes on the railing, giving her factual, unelaborated answers. Yes, his mother was still living in the old house in New Jersey, still spending her summers up at the Lake in Vermont. Yes, of course she was much broken up by his father's death. Well, he supposed she did perhaps live a good deal in the memory of his fame, but no more, he said, feeling his face flushing, than was natural for a woman in her position.

Yes, Barrett had married that pretty blond girl he used to go around with at the Lake, but they'd been divorced during the war and he was married again now and had two children. He was back in Washington after a few years of private practice in New York. No, the change of administration hadn't affected his standing one way or the other, he thought. The kind of thing he did was a little above partisan politics.

"Of course," she said, again obviously unconvinced, and he knew that what she was suspecting was that Barrett was too clever to get caught out on any political limbs, which was ridiculous and completely unfair to Barrett. He looked at her sideways, tight-lipped.

Mark? Mark, he said evenly, watching his words, was doing magazine work. Book reviews, mostly, and critical essays. He had had two books of critical essays published. Well, yes, come to think of it, he *had* had a boyhood ambition to be a novelist. Noah was very sure that he was thoroughly happy now doing the sort of work he was doing. He didn't mention the fact that Mark had written two novels that had never been published.

She was listening to everything he said intently, studying him as he talked, and as fast as he got an answer out she was ready with another question. She kept glancing toward the door, obviously anxious to get through the whole of this unpleasant catechism before her husband arrived.

"Is Mark married?"

Mark was married, he told her, but his wife was in a sanitarium and he was back living with Noah and his mother. Yes, he agreed, tight-lipped again, it was very pleasant for the three of them to be together there.

And Kate? Yes, Kate was married. And she did have children. Six of them, and the seventh on the way. And when Natalie laughed and said, "How wonderfully predictable!" he did not laugh. "What do you mean, 'predictable'?"

"Even when she was twenty years old it was obvious that that was the one career she was cut out for."

"She's had another career," he said, pleased to prove her wrong, "in sculpture."

"Oh?"

"She exhibits pretty regularly in various shows around the country."

"You mean she still works at it? With six children?"

"She's doing some of the best work now she's ever done."

"Good heavens!"

It was only when she got to Connie that there seemed to be no hidden meanings in her questions, no hint of sarcastic reservations in her voice. When he told her that Connie was teaching in a private school for girls in Connecticut, Natalie wondered if she would enjoy having dinner with her in her apartment in New York sometime in the fall. Noah smiled at her, a little grimly, and said he was sure she would. Knowing Connie's unfailing curiosity, he felt confident that he was not lying.

He had been making no effort to hide his annoyance, and he knew from her expression that she was conscious of it. It was an odd expression, compounded of a sad sort of apprehension over his obvious anger and a determination to go on, to find out this something that she had to find out. "I'm not trying to be nasty," she had said in the car. "But I'm terribly anxious to know."

He scowled at the railing, as much annoyed with himself as with her. A cleverer man would see the purpose behind all this questioning. But he could see no way in which these sarcastic innuendoes about his family could have to do with any kind of purpose. He could see no justification for them at all. And to him no hurt could rankle so sorely as a hurt to his family pride. He turned and looked at her.

She was not through. "And you, Noah," she said, "are an historian."

[8]

He wet his lips. "Sort of."

"A statesman," she said, underlining Noah's appraisal of Barrett's work with her voice, "and a critic and an historian and a sculptress and a teacher. The distinguished children of a distinguished father."

She looked at him and smiled and raised her eyebrows, as though asking him to confirm the statement.

"You said it," he said. "I didn't."

She chuckled nervously. "All right." Then she returned to the attack. "You've had articles in some reviews and magazines I'd never heard of, and you're getting ready to write a great big book."

He nodded, holding himself alert, knowing that she was working up to something but unable to guess what. "Several volumes, probably," he said.

"It sounds very interesting, Noah—but—"

He glanced at her, waiting.

"It doesn't sound very profitable." She sat back, and he knew she was disproportionately relieved to have gotten it out—and still disproportionately anxious to hear what he was going to say.

He smiled at her. "What you want to know is where I get my money from. Is that it?"

She nodded, the curious, half-timid smile on her face.

He took a deep breath. "I'm paid a salary by the William Huntington Sibley Memorial Foundation."

"Oh," she said, and there was both disappointment and disgust in her voice. "So there's a William Huntington Sibley Memorial Foundation. And where did the money for *it* come from?"

"From a number of people," he said. It was a literal truth and a practical lie, and as soon as he had said it he wished he hadn't.

"A number of people—and I suppose in more or less equal proportions?"

He got to his feet, and she looked frightened. "Okay, Natalie," he said, "I'm paid a salary by my mother to edit and annotate my father's work. Is that what you want me to say?" He stared at her.

She looked away and waited before she said, "It was what I was hoping you wouldn't say."

"Why?" He stood over her, shaking his head. "What does all this mean to you? What does all this disagreeable business about my family mean, anyway?" He remembered that there was probably a maid somewhere and toned his voice down. "Did they ever hurt you? They never had anything against you."

He glared down at her, and then she was smiling up at him help-

[9]

lessly, pathetically, and suddenly he was remembering times when she had smiled up at him like that years ago. It was an expression, a mannerism, that he had forgotten, and at this instant his memory of it was so vivid that he was no longer seeing the woman he was talking to but the girl he had been in love with sixteen years before. "As I remember it," he went on with the speech he had started, but haltingly now, with all the fire gone from his voice, his mind filled with confusion, "as I remember it, they were always damned decent to you."

"Of course they were, Noah." Her voice was thin, a frightened little voice. "I'm sorry if I was nasty about them. But you, Noah—you're worth so much more than—well, than you think you are. I used to try to make you feel that, remember?"

He did remember, and it was like bringing a fuzzy image on a projection screen into clear focus. He nodded dumbly as a dozen memories, suddenly as clear as his memory of the ferry ride, came bubbling up from the pool where he had kept them submerged.

She stood up briskly. "I never quite succeeded, did I?" She smiled at him again, and there was something sad and final in the smile.

Then her manner changed abruptly. "Jeffrey doesn't seem to be coming," she said, self-possessed now, the hostess talking to her guest. "We're having some people in for cocktails and dinner, but they won't be here for an hour and a half. Perhaps you'd like a chance to rest and have a shower."

He nodded again, looking at and through her, still seeing the girl who had once smiled up at him helplessly and pathetically—in the exact way that she had smiled up at him the moment before. Seeing the girl with all the wonderful and silly enthusiasms, the girl who occasionally, in her enthusiasm, used to giggle a funny, incongruous little giggle. He was wondering if she ever giggled like that now and finding it hard to imagine that she could.

And as he walked up the stairs and into his room and sat down on the bed, only half conscious of the big bedroom with its wide windows and its chintz-covered furniture and its pattern of slanting sunlight on the floor and walls, all the memories that had become fuzzy and gray over the years were somehow, by the miracle of a chance expression on a woman's face, sharp and bright again. The memories of a few half-forgotten moments when he had felt in complete rapport with another human being, and that a lithe and almost beautiful girl, of a few weeks when Natalie Parkes had made him feel that he was not a clumsy oaf but a man as good as any other man.

II

1·

If the human race had never gotten up on its hind legs, Noah had sometimes reflected in his more humorous moods, he might have been a very fine fellow indeed. It was the agile moving about of the feet, the easy shifting of weight from one foot to the other, so essential in such glamorous sports as football and hockey and tennis, that had always been his downfall. That, combined with his nearsightedness, gave people the impression that he was an unco-ordinated fellow all around, but he knew in his own mind that that was not true.

Get his two feet firmly planted on the ground and his glasses on him, as for instance in casting a trout fly, and he could demonstrate not only normal co-ordination but very considerable skill. Or better yet, get him off his feet entirely, as around the water where he had spent so much of his boyhood, and he could, and did, earn his letter at Princeton in both swimming and crew, a fact which people always took with a certain incredulity.

It was while he was in the water, and thus very much at his best, that he had first seen Natalie Parkes—or, what was more to the point, that she had first seen him. He was, in fact, in the act of being something of a hero, all in the best tradition of the romantic stories they had both read back in their school days. Of course they and the times had outgrown the tradition by that time, it being the still disillusioned year 1937 and they having both been college graduates for over a month when the thing happened.

Perhaps some vestiges of the romantic tradition had been lingering in Noah's imagination, but he had learned largely to subdue them by that time. Anyway, it was a more auspicious way to meet a girl than at somebody's party or in somebody's night club.

It happened one summer forenoon at the Lake when Noah was

swimming off the Sibley raft with Kate, who was twenty then and already showing promise of what she was to become later, and Connie, who was seventeen. Outside the little town dock, which was a hundred yards up the shore, two little girls, seven or eight years old, had tipped out of a canoe.

There was nobody on the dock, and Noah had swum over there with his easy, powerful strokes, seen that one of the little girls was fairly successfully keeping her head above water, and swum around under water looking for the other one. He found her a few feet under the surface, sailing about very gracefully with her hair flowing away from her head as though she were running in a wind and her skirt billowing straight out from her waist like a ballet dancer's—a weird and beautiful sight that even today, sixteen years later, he could bring back as sharply as if he had seen it yesterday.

He got his two hands under her armpits and brought her in to the little beach beside the dock. And he was carrying her over to the dock when he saw a girl in a white bathing suit, standing there at the foot of the dock watching him.

Without his glasses and with the water still clouding his eyes, he saw her face as a misty and beautiful blur. Perhaps too his excitement and the manly exertion was having some sort of effect on his endocrines, heightening his appreciation of feminine beauty. At any rate this was another image he was to carry with him through the years: the image of a tall, slender, and beautifully molded girl with a skin that was not so much tanned as golden, standing like a poised statue, her short, light-brown hair gleaming in the sunlight.

And although he could not see her eyes, he could somehow sense, perhaps in her pose, perhaps in what appeared to be parted lips, admiration; and admiration from a golden girl was to Noah a novel and devastating experience.

He could never remember afterward that he had thought about the other little girl at all after he had seen this beautiful apparition. Possibly he had known that Kate and Connie had come around by the shore and were wading out from the beach toward her. He did remember, to his shame, that from then on, while he was laying his limp burden face down on the dock and applying artificial respiration, he was far more conscious of the big girl beside him than of the little ones and their plight.

"Is there anything I can do?" the big girl had asked in a voice that was just as Noah had known it would be, low and vibrant.

Noah straddled the child's slender hips and leaned back, his hands poised beside his shoulders. "You might rub her legs," he said, "toward the heart."

As he brought his weight forward, wrapping his hands around the child's rib cage, he was happy in the knowledge that he had a good tan and that four years of pulling a heavy oar had given him long sinewy muscles in his back and shoulders. He could feel the closeness of the girl behind him. When he leaned back the hair from her bent head brushed his back lightly. He never thought of it afterward as a time when a life was at stake. It was always an unbelievably thrilling moment.

The rest of the episode proved a little anticlimactic, but it could never dull the thrill of that memory. After a half dozen of Noah's mighty, muscular pushes, the little girl had said in a voice that was strong and clear, "Don't squeeze so hard, Noah."

Noah patted her little behind smartly and pulled her to her feet and sent her home. "The little brat," he said.

"Do you know her?" the big girl asked.

"Oh, sure," Noah said breathlessly, his voice sounding strangely hollow. "Everybody on this lake knows everybody. We've all been coming here summers ever since we can remember. Her father taught me to swim."

The girl smiled, and she had a nice smile. "That was a chicken that came home to roost for him, wasn't it?"

Noah tried to think of something casually brilliant to say to that, but nothing came. He stared at the vision of beauty.

"You made it all look very easy," she said, and it *was* admiration that was in her voice. Again Noah looked at her, smiling sheepishly this time, and said nothing. Everything he thought of sounded either theatrical or stupid. But he couldn't stand there staring forever, and he said, without getting any of the bantering lightness into his voice that he had hoped would be there, "You're one person on this lake I don't know." He wished the muscles in his back could have gone on speaking for him indefinitely.

"My name is Natalie Parkes. I'm visiting the Hendricks."

"Oh," he said. "I know. A college friend of Margy's."

"That's right."

"My name is Noah Sibley. Our place is over there behind that raft." Almost anybody else, it seemed to him, could have thought of something more inspired to say to her.

At this point Connie and Kate had appeared from somewhere, swinging their bathing caps in their hands. Noah watched them as

[13]

they stepped up onto the dock as though he had never seen them before, disappointed and at the same time relieved to have the conversation interrupted.

"Did you get her bailed out all right, Noah?" Kate asked in her rich, husky voice.

Natalie laughed, softly and appreciatively, and Noah realized later that it was the first time it had occurred to him that this golden girl might be something more than a vision of beauty, that she might be a person with traits and a personality just as other people were persons with traits and personalities. And he took a good deal of credit to himself for having guessed then, merely on the strength of that laugh and the few remarks she had made to him, that she was a person with an unusual capacity for enthusiasm, for appreciating things, a person who was always full of some sort of inner excitement.

Right then she was appreciating Kate, and Kate was looking at her through her ridiculously long lashes and smiling faintly. Rarely in history, Noah thought at the time, had one small dock accommodated two such strikingly impressive females.

Kate's career in fertility had not begun to unfold by then, of course, but her generous and firmly rounded muliebrity was already in full bloom, and her coloring seemed even more startling then than it was today: the occasional improbable streak of shiny copper through hair that otherwise was light like Noah's, the eyebrows that were much darker than the hair, the lashes that were so long and so dark that people always assumed they were false. A big girl, barely three inches shorter than Noah and, like him, built on an ample model, she was to bring appreciative gasps from many people with less of a gift for appreciation than Natalie's.

"I'll bet you're Mr. Sibley's sister," Natalie had said, and her manner of speaking seemed to hint that nothing could be more wonderful than being Mr. Sibley's sister.

Kate had never been one for girlish friendships, nor was she one for feminine jealousies. By and large, she was not interested in girls. She nodded, still looking amused but scarcely delighted, and sat down on the edge of the dock, moving with that lazy vitality of hers which men, perhaps rightly, always took to denote an excess of sexuality. She dangled her toes in the water.

"They're both my sisters," Noah had said, and to Connie and Kate, "This is Miss Parkes, Margy Hendricks' friend."

Connie had been eying Natalie curiously but not unsympathetically, looking slight and coltish and unimpressive beside the other two.

Her mustard-colored hair was dry on top and plastered to her head around the edges where she had failed to catch it in her cap. But, always loyal to Noah and always sensitive to his moods, she rose to the occasion as Kate never would have. "I'm Connie," she said, smiling her funny, reticent, enigmatic smile, "and this is Kate, and we're glad to know you, and won't you and Margy come over to dinner tonight?"

2 ·

THAT evening, as the dinner hour approached, Noah, in a clean pair of white flannels and a clean white shirt, had waited on the dock for Margy and her friend to come down the lake in the Hendricks' canoe. He idled about, going through the motions of inspecting the boat and the canoe and the dock itself.

He was, within the limits that he had learned that he dared to be, excited, partly because this new girl who was coming with Margy had appeared to him to be exceptionally pretty, partly because, for one of the few times in his life, it was he and not Barrett or Mark who had met the girl first. This gave him, temporarily at least, a certain proprietary interest in her. But he had only the vaguest hopes, and no real expectations at all, that he could keep his proprietorship for more than an hour or two.

Even so it was somehow pleasant, at that age, to know that she was about to be further impressed with him, that the brilliance of his family would, as always, lend him an additional luster. In his twenty-two years he had learned to take a real pride in this impersonal kind of second-hand, reflected glory. Few boys he knew could feel as sure as he that everyone would think better of him because of his membership in his family. And in his twenty-two years he had learned to accept the fact that he, with his clumsiness and his glasses and his gauche attempts at the light touch, would always be outshone by the brilliance and charm and easy gaiety of the rest of them. Only vaguely, in idle dreams, did he ever even hope that it might someday be otherwise.

He watched the canoe slide out from the shore and turn down along the lake toward him, and with a tolerant, delighted smile he watched the neophyte attempts of the new girl to paddle bow. When they finally got near and swung in toward him, he knelt on the dock and, catching only a glimpse of Natalie's face as she slid past, grasped the gunwale at the thwart and steadied the canoe as she got out.

Margy, as heavy-featured and plump and friendly as a Labrador puppy, a girl with whom Noah had always felt a bond of common experience, said from the stern seat, "Hi, Noah." There was a lilt of unusual excitement in her voice, and because of their common experience he sensed at once that she had come prepared to shine in the reflected glory of her college friend.

Noah acknowledged their common bond and their common excitement with a grin. "Hi, Margy."

And as he stood up, the girl who was standing beside him there said, "Good evening, Noah."

He glanced at her and smiled doubtfully and said, "Good evening —Miss Parkes."

She laughed with that easy poise that Noah had noticed that almost all girls who get to be seniors in college have. "Good heavens," she said. "Aren't you going to call me Natalie?"

Noah felt himself blushing. Summoning all the casual gallantry he could muster, he said, "Of course I am—Natalie."

He felt that he had carried it off rather well, and perhaps because he was more completely at home here around the dock and the front of the cottage than anywhere else in the world, he beached the canoe with practiced skill and guided them up the path and on up the steps and through the door with gratifying poise and gracefulness. But in all that time he had not dared to look directly at Natalie's face.

It wasn't until she was seated on the couch between his mother and Connie, and he was squatting on the stool beside the fireplace, that he got up the courage to take a good look at her. He had to admit to himself then that, seen through his corrective lenses and without the water clouding his eyes, she was not quite the magazine cover beauty he had imagined her at the dock. Her mouth was too wide, her face just a bit too broad. But her skin did have the glowing, healthy quality it had seemed to have then, and her eyes were a deep and lively blue. And as she smiled at something his mother said to her, it seemed to him that she had a lovely smile. Maybe not a magazine cover beauty, he told himself, but at any rate a very special-looking girl.

Proudly he looked around at Barrett and Mark, asking with his glance for their approval. All afternoon they had been joking him, with amused and affectionate condescension, about the "little girl" he had picked up at the dock, somehow pleased and proud that Noah had managed to find himself a girl on his own initiative, obviously sure that she would prove to be no great shakes of a girl. Why they had assumed that she was little he didn't know.

Now neither of them was even glancing in Natalie's direction. Barrett, tall and slender and self-assured, Barrett of the sternly thoughtful eyes and the wavy brown hair, was in a private conversation with Margy over by the window seat, bending over her in a pose of the gravest, the most concentrated, the most flattering attentiveness. It was a new mannerism, one that Noah had noticed before during the summer, one that he must have learned at law school, but, as with all of Barrett's accomplishments, he had mastered it so thoroughly, made it so completely his own, that from now on anyone else seen assuming that pose would be thought to be imitating Barrett.

Mark was over at the sideboard pouring the sherry. He was smiling to himself, as though amused at some little joke of his own, while he filled the glasses, studying each one with elaborate care. There was grace in every pose he struck, the almost unconscious grace of the natural athlete, and only those who knew him very well indeed, like Noah, could have guessed that there was anything conscious in the present pose that kept his classic Grecian profile to the couch where Natalie was sitting, so engrossed was he in the business of pouring the sherry. He was a little taller than average, a couple of inches shorter than Barrett and Noah, slender like Barrett and blond like Noah.

Neither of them was glancing toward Natalie, but Noah sensed from their manners that they had already done their glancing, that they had both been pleasantly surprised in her, that they were biding their time, waiting for the propitious moment to move in. And Noah, being what his life had made him, could take a grim and only mildly resentful pride in the knowledge that before the evening was over one of them would have her neatly hooked, so securely hooked that none of the other men around the Lake would have a chance at her so long as he wanted her. The only question was which one it would be, whether she would prefer the taller, darker Barrett or the shorter, blonder Mark, Barrett's grave-eyed flattering courtesy or Mark's quick-smiling gaiety.

Kate, having greeted Natalie with one brief, dazzling smile when she came in, was sitting at the piano, softly picking out tunes with one finger. And Dr. Sibley, in the mulberry smoking jacket with its silk facings which he wore every evening as the badge of his profession, sat in his big chair on the other side of the fireplace from Noah, smiling inclusively at his wife and Natalie and Connie on the couch.

His smile was modest and benign and patient. Noah could see that he too had been impressed by Natalie's girlish charm, and he smiled at his father affectionately, feeling, as so many of the people who knew him did, that nothing proved his greatness more than his refusal to hide his natural weaknesses, such as his very human—though never in the slightest degree lascivious—eye for a pretty girl.

At fifty-two he was still a remarkably handsome man, handsome in much the same way that Mark was, though heavier now and almost completely white-haired. Photographs of him in his mid-twenties bore an amazing resemblance to the Mark of today.

Mark brought the tray of sherry glasses over from the sideboard and solemnly, with exaggerated obsequiousness, passed them around. Dr. Sibley stood up, his glass raised, and waited, smiling patiently, for his wife to finish what she was saying to Natalie. Then, holding his glass out toward Natalie, he said, "We're going to drink, my dear, to a happy stay for you at our little lake colony. We hope you'll like us as well as I know we're all going to like you."

Natalie looked confused only momentarily. Then she smiled up at him very prettily and said, "Thank you very much, Dr. Sibley," and it was obvious to Noah that she was already captivated by his unassuming friendliness and his never-failing charm. It never, in all Noah's lifetime, had failed. And suddenly, unexpectedly, with a guilty sense of disloyalty, Noah wished that for once it would fail.

Natalie sipped her sherry and smiled first at one of his family, then at another. For a moment she would be smiling at his father, then at his mother, then at Mark, who had brought up a chair and now sat directly in front of her, looking into her face. She even smiled at Connie. But never once did she look in Noah's direction, and he sat staring, glowering, thoroughly miserable, angry with Natalie, angry with himself, angry with his whole wonderful family.

At dinner Natalie sat at Dr. Sibley's right. Noah was on the other side of her, but even if he could have thought of something to say to her, he wouldn't have had a chance to say it. Dr. Sibley was telling her about the Peace Conferences at Lake Mohonk that he and his wife had attended every year from 1910, the year they were married, through 1915—and managing to make what might have seemed a dull subject sound glamorous, romantic, and exciting. The breath-taking beauty of the famous resort, the distinguished, wealthy, and elegant people who attended the conferences, the rousing good tennis matches they used to have after the sessions, the times when he and his wife, still practically newlyweds, sneaked out from some of the most important speeches by world-famous diplomats and went swimming in a cove out of sight of the hotel.

He made no mention whatever of his own by no means inconsequential part in the conferences, of his position as secretary of what was at that time one of the country's greatest organizations for peace and arbitration, or, of course, of his own reputation, which grew up so rapidly between 1910 and 1916, as the boy wonder of the movement for world peace. And never once while amusing Natalie with his stories of the conferences did he let himself slip into the trick which so surely betrays the less than great, the trick of making casual references to his own friendship with the famous people who were gathered there.

Noah saw only the back of Natalie's head. It was lovely hair, light brown with a reddish glint, wavy, full of sparkle and life, cut short and neatly trimmed. He had never seen lovelier hair, and its loveliness suggested in a tantalizing way that the face on the other side of her head might be lovely too. Once, halfway through the main course, she did turn and smile at him, but at the moment he was scowling so fiercely, attacking his roast beef with such ferocity, that she merely looked dismayed and turned back to his father.

Then, over coffee, she turned and smiled at him again, this time with determination. Noah, taken aback, trying too abruptly to rise to the occasion, managed nothing better than a very sickly grin in return.

"Your father is one of the most fascinating men I've ever met," she said, "and your mother is a dear." Her face was flushed and her eyes had the sparkling look of excited enthusiasm that he was to know so well later. "It must be wonderful to live in such a—such a stimulating atmosphere."

Torn between the guilty, novel resentment that he had been feeling for the last hour and his lifelong habit of pride in his family, Noah tried again, as he had on the dock, to think of something casually brilliant to say in reply. And again nothing came. Finally, because he had to say something, he said, "It has its points," and she laughed delightedly, as though he had said something very brilliant indeed.

And when the meal was over and they moved into the living room, she very pointedly chose a seat beside him and leaned toward him and said in a voice that she apparently thought would be too low for the rest of the family to hear, "Tell me about yourself, Noah. Margy tells me that you're going to Columbia in the fall to do graduate work."

[19]

Confused and acutely conscious of the glances of the rest of the family, Noah said, "Yes, I am. In history."

"Oh," she said, full of delight, "I majored in history."

And while Barrett and Mark sat watching in bewildered consternation and Connie sat grinning with devilish delight in the corner, she continued her private conversation with Noah. Finally Mrs. Sibley, driven by her duty as a hostess, began a conversation with Margy, to which Mark and Dr. Sibley were forced to listen. Kate went back to playing softly on the piano. And Barrett, accepting the situation with an uncomprehending shake of the head, announced that he was going over to see Louise and tiptoed out of the door.

All through the evening, stopping to join the general conversation only when politeness seemed to demand it, Natalie forced Noah to monopolize her. And when she and Margy went home at the end of the evening, Noah, feeling as he had never felt before in his life, realized that he had, with almost no effort on his own part, made a date to take her canoeing the next morning, another one to take her to the dance at the Town Hall that night, and still another to take her trout fishing the day after.

3.

THE days that followed that night were as unlike any other days that Noah had known before or since as a dream is from waking—or an island from a mainland. And right now, as he lay in his bathrobe on the bed in Natalie's guest room, waiting for the time to take his bath and dress and go down to meet her husband, he was not only remembering them more clearly than he had ever remembered them before, but seeing in them a significance that he had never seen before.

Often since, he had gone over them in his mind in a vague and vaguely resentful way, but he was sure now that he had never, until this moment, realized just what they had done for him, how different a man he had been because of them, how unquestionably those weeks that had been filled with Natalie had completed for him the first cycle in the spiral of a young man's increasing awareness.

There had been distressing moments during those weeks, moments when Natalie had acted in ways that he still couldn't understand or find excuses for. But now, as all the memories came back so unexplainably clear, he was coming to see how inconsequential the distressing moments had been compared to the self-revealing ones, how essentially unimportant they were when weighed against the many times when he had begun to think of himself as he had never thought of himself before.

It was the times when they had been alone together that he now saw as the really significant ones. It was bright mornings when, with white puffy clouds floating across a deep-blue sky, they had explored the points and coves of the lake in Noah's canoe, rocky points covered with blueberries, dark amber coves where the firs hung breathlessly still out over the water. The evenings when they had watched the sunset together from Randolph's Hill as the shadows moved up the mountains and sometimes the calm pure note of a wood thrush had come up from the woods below. Noah could see her now, sitting there with her lips parted and her eyes shining, and he could feel again the breathless, agonized ecstasy of worship and self-doubt with which he had watched her.

It was the lazy hours they had spent swimming off the raft and basking in the sun together. The rainy afternoons when they walked the shores of the lake, he in his slicker and she in her hooded raincoat. The nights when they had drifted around the lake in the canoe, listening to the distant barking of dogs and the soft music of phonographs from open-windowed cottages.

The days when they had taken their lunch and Noah's fishing tackle and driven over to the Ledwick River, and Natalie had walked along the bank while Noah fished the stream down through the maple grove and on out into the open pastures and finally down into the dark piny gorge. He could see her so clearly, see how excitedly she would be smiling when he had approached a fresh pool and studied it and then, just before making his first cast into it, looked up at her.

Before the first of those trips she had never seen a fly rod, nor an artificial fly. When Noah made the long line straighten out over the water, as though by some power in his wrist he could make it stay there, and then when the fly dropped onto the water as lightly as a falling leaf, she had giggled her incongruous childlike giggle of delight, the giggle that was so unlike her normal voice and so unlike her normal manner.

It was, most particularly of all, it seemed to him now, that noon when he had stopped at the edge of the gorge, where the deep woods were on one side of them and the open fields of goldenrod and asters and devil's paintbrush on the other, and he had cleaned a half dozen of the fish and built a fire and fried them in cornmeal and salt pork.

They had turned a beautiful brown, and he had picked up the pan and stepped over to where she was sitting to show her how beautiful they were. And he had tripped on a protruding tree root and spilled the whole panful of fish onto the ground. They had dusted the dirt off and eaten them anyway, and he could remember now how grateful he had been to her for not trying to tell him that it was not clumsy of him.

That, he was thinking as he got up from the bed and went in to take his shower, was the key to this thing that she had given him. She had never protested that he wasn't, on occasions, awkward. She had never pretended that she hadn't noticed that he wore rather thick-lensed glasses. She had merely given him to feel that the awkwardness and the glasses were not all there was to him.

She had taken them as a part of him, along with his strong swimming and his deft handling of a canoe and his skill with a fly rod and his immense popularity with all the children around the lake. And she had given him to feel that the whole added up to a pretty satisfactory sort of man. Only Connie had ever given him the same sort of feeling about himself, and he had had to discount that as the affection of a sister.

Now he was understanding, more than he ever had before, how, under Natalie's unspoken encouragement, his confidence and his sense of humor had expanded, how it had even seemed that some of his clumsiness of foot had disappeared, how for the first time he had begun to feel that he was a part of life instead of an onlooker watching it move on around him.

III

1.

NOAH went down the stairs expectantly, eager to look at Natalie again, to see if he could find in her something more of the girl who had, long ago, done so much for him, the girl who had given him for the first time a suspicion that it might be all right for him to be Noah Sibley.

At the sound of his footsteps, she came out into the hall from the living room. She had changed into a pale yellow dress, very simply cut. Perhaps it was it, or perhaps the high heels, that made her seem taller and slimmer than he remembered her from the old days. She had put on rouge and lipstick—a little too much, he thought—and they accentuated the new hollowness in her cheeks that he had noticed at the ferry dock.

She smiled up at him as he came down the last few steps, holding out her hand. The mouth and chin were stronger than those of the girl he had been remembering—in a less sympathetic mood he might have called them harder—and in her eyes there was a misty guardedness that was unlike anything he remembered. It might be, he thought, that behind the guardedness he saw uncertainty, a suggestion of doubt or fear. But if it was there, there was also the strength to hide it.

She took his hand and led him into the living room. "This is Jeffrey," she said, and Jeffrey came across from the opposite corner of the room to greet him. The slanting rays of the lowering sun were reflected by a highly polished grand piano into Noah's eyes, and his first impression of Jeffrey was only of a man smaller and slighter than he had expected.

Jeffrey pumped his hand. "Glad to have you with us, Sibley," he said with a gusto that took Noah by surprise. "Natalie showed me the article about you."

"Oh, that," Noah said. He tried to make his smile friendly and casual as he glanced around the room, taking in its dimensions and furnishings. It was very large, large enough to take the grand piano without being overpowered by it. A very pleasant room, actually, airy and light, all grays and gray-greens and mulberry, but something about it a little disappointing, too, a little impersonal. Certainly nothing to suggest Natalie's personality. More likely a decorator's personality, he thought.

Jeffrey was still pumping his hand. Noah smiled at Natalie. "An article like that gives you a very cockeyed impression," he said modestly. "To tell you the truth, it's a job anybody could do if he chose to —only most people wouldn't choose to."

Jeffrey laughed heartily—a little more heartily, it seemed to Noah, than the humor of his remark called for. "You're not kidding us a bit, Sibley," he said, very friendly. "It read to me like an article about a man on his way up." He clapped Noah on the arm. "What do you say to a quick one before the crowd starts milling around here?"

"Fine with me," Noah said, trying to sound as friendly and enthusiastic as this surprisingly cordial host was acting.

Jeffrey rubbed his hands together, beaming. "What'll it be? Martini, old fashioned, Scotch, Bourbon?"

Noah hesitated, and Jeffrey took his arm and guided him over to the drink-mixing table in the corner. There was an impressive array of bottles and glasses and other tools of the bartender's trade. Jeffrey winked at him and waved at the table. "Look 'em over," he said, "and take your pick."

Pretending to look at the bottles, Noah looked sideways at his face. It was not like any of the faces that he had, at various times in the last fifteen years, imagined as the face of Natalie's husband. And the thought that came to him was that it was not quite the face that went with the extreme heartiness of manner. The features were chiseled and sharp, the mouth firm and tight-lipped, the hair dark and straight and carefully wet and combed, the eyes alert.

"I'll give you a tip, Sibley," he said, cocking his head humorously. "If I do say so myself, my martinis have quite a reputation."

Noah was conscious of Natalie standing behind them there. He turned and smiled at her. "A martini would be fine," he said.

"Thataboy," Jeffrey said. "Always glad to have somebody join me in one. My wife never drinks anything but Scotch and water, Scotch and water, Scotch and water. What a bore!"

[24]

The tone with which he spoke was jocular, but Noah caught a quick glance, first at Natalie's face, then at his own.

Jeffrey talked on as he mixed Natalie's drink. "So you're an old friend of Natalie's," he said.

"That's right," Noah agreed.

"From her college days."

It wasn't exactly from her college days, but it hardly seemed a point to quibble over and Noah nodded.

Jeffrey stirred Natalie's drink and turned and handed it to her. "There you are, beautiful," he said. "The good old Scotch and water."

He grinned at her and turned back to the table and began to manipulate the set of implements he used to mix martinis. He handled them with great deftness, talking and pausing and talking again as he worked. "A college training is one of the things I've had to get along without, Sibley . . . a great handicap." He smiled sideways at Noah, and Noah knew that he did not consider it a great handicap. "Of course I *hire* plenty of college graduates."

Noah stole a glance at Natalie, and her expression was one of resigned watchfulness, as though she knew that something unpleasant was about to happen and knew too that she could do nothing to stop it.

"Natalie's college training did a great deal for her," Jeffrey was saying. "She actually got her bank account to balance last April . . . first time in fifteen years . . . nothing like the trained mind." The mischievous glance he threw toward Noah was a comradely one, as though he were asking him to share his disdain for the trained mind, or the feminine mind, or perhaps with Natalie herself.

He had a special little pair of tongs with which he lifted onions from the special little bowl in which they sat. The cocktail glasses, unusually large ones, were nestled into a large bowl of ice. He lifted them out and ceremoniously filled them from the shaker. They came out exactly right, with the glasses filled to the brim and the shaker empty. He glanced proudly out of the corner of his eye at Noah. "There you are, Noah," he said, and Noah sensed that the shift from calling him "Sibley" to calling him "Noah" had been deliberate. "See what your taste buds have to say about that."

Noah took a sip. He shook his head, twisting his face into what he was afraid might be a somewhat exaggerated grimace of smacking his lips. "Swell," he said, wondering if Natalie was thinking, as he was, that he was making a fool of himself trying to play up to Jeffrey's cordiality. But, fool or no fool, he guessed it was what he had to do.

[25]

"Boy, that's the tops," he said, and Jeffrey smiled and nodded, accepting Noah's praise as nothing more than a just tribute.

"Well, I suppose we might as well sit down," he said, looking at his watch. "Betty is late, as usual."

Natalie led them back over to the chairs. Before she sat down she turned to Noah. "Betty is my sister. I don't believe you ever met her, did you?"

"No, I never did," Noah said, remembering vaguely that she had had a sister and wondering if he should have asked about her. "She was younger than you, wasn't she?"

"Much younger," she said, smiling, "and much lovelier."

Noah grinned at her. "I'll believe that when I see it."

She looked thoughtful for a moment, her head a little to one side, suddenly very feminine. Then she smiled at him. "That's nice of you, Noah." She looked thoughtful again, then suddenly shrugged and laughed. "You'll see it all right."

She and Noah sat down.

Jeffrey stood beside the piano, his cocktail in one hand and his watch in the other. "Very lovely," he said, "and always late—just like her sister. That's one of the great advantages of being married to one of the Parkes girls. You learn patience." Again his glance toward Noah was a comradely one, and again the expression in his eyes belied the jocular tone.

"So is everybody else late," Natalie said wearily.

Jeffrey bowed to her. "Thank you for telling me, my dear," he said. "I'm sure I'd never have guessed it otherwise." He looked at Noah with an expression of amused helplessness. "My wife always credits me with so much intelligence."

Noah wondered if these half-humorously intended digs at Natalie were Jeffrey's usual way of entertaining company, or if this might be a mood that his own presence had brought on. "This is a beautiful place you have here, Jeffrey," he said, feeling a little self-conscious about the "Jeffrey."

Jeffrey smiled at him; his manner toward him was still the epitome of hospitality. "Glad you like it, Noah. Some advantages to an island, we figure, even if everything does cost like hell out here. But it's the best way I know to keep away from—well, from all the undesirables, if you know what I mean." He sipped his drink, and the way he sipped it was cautious and precise, out of keeping with the hearty manner. "As for the location," he said with an amused gleam in his eye again, "that was the kind of compromise we make in the Humeston family.

[26]

Natalie likes views and being way the hell away from everybody. I like being around near people and handy to the yacht club and the golf course. So we compromised and built way the hell out here away from everything. And we have a lovely, lovely view."

Noah suddenly found himself annoyed, embarrassed for Natalie's sake. He took a big swallow of his drink and got to his feet and walked over to the window.

Jeffrey was quick to catch the implication of the change in his manner. He laughed, and for the first time Noah detected warmth and affection in his voice. "You don't want to take us seriously, Noah. We're all a great bunch of kidders out here. Natalie and I just have fun kidding each other. Don't we, honey?"

He stepped across the room and patted her gently on the cheek, and she smiled up at him with an expression which was, if not quite affectionate, at least intimate and personal.

Noah looked away quickly, embarrassed by this glimpse into their intimacy, disturbed by the necessity of changing his appraisal of the relationship between them. He felt confused and, for some reason, hurt. He turned his back to them and looked out at the Sound. With the changing light the water had become darker than it had been when he and Natalie were sitting on the veranda, darker with a weird purplish tinge, and the mainland, off there across the wide expanse, seemed more remote. As he looked, he had a sensation of isolation, of island remoteness, of being cut off, and he found himself wondering, stupidly, why he had ever come here.

He heard the voices of people coming up the steps at the back of the house, and he looked down at his glass and saw that it was empty. He had planned to make that drink last a long time. They were unusually large cocktail glasses. He turned to Natalie, and she was on her way out into the hall. Jeffrey was back at the drink-mixing table, and Noah wondered, embarrassed, if he had noticed that the glass was empty. He started to speak, then stopped himself and turned and looked out at the distant shore.

Now the people were coming in at the back door, and suddenly Jeffrey was at his elbow. "That's the way I like to see a man drink," he said with the same jovial heartiness.

Noah looked down at his glass and grinned sheepishly. "I'm afraid I did kind of gulp that one down, didn't I?"

Standing there beside him with the shaker in his hand, Jeffrey laughed a startlingly loud laugh and put his hand on Noah's shoulder. Still laughing into his face, he left it there until the guests came in from the hall. "That's what they're for, Noah," he said boisterously.

Awkwardly, Noah smiled at him. He realized that they presented a tableau of genial, man-to-man friendliness, and that Jeffrey had planned it that way. Now he was patting Noah affectionately on the back and calling to the man who was coming through the door, "Come here, Sid, I want you to meet my friend Noah Sibley, the author."

It dawned on Noah for the first time that Jeffrey's cordiality had had to do with the fact that he was a writer, that Jeffrey was wanting to gain prestige in the eyes of his friends by being on terms of intimacy with an author. It was, he sensed at once, pathetic, and for a moment he felt toward Jeffrey the same sort of sympathetic understanding that he had sometimes felt toward boys in the school where he had once taught.

But, remembering how meager his accomplishments as a writer were, knowing how little it took to call oneself a writer, he also saw it as absurd, ridiculously absurd. And the whole gesture had been so obvious, so like the speeded-up, exaggerated actions of a stage comedy, that he laughed in spite of himself—which, he realized, was all that Jeffrey needed to make the picture exactly as he wanted it.

2 ·

THE room was crowded, the air filled with the buzzing, shrilling clamor of a dozen laughing, chattering, shouting conversations.

Noah tried hard to concentrate on what these people standing in a semicircle around him were saying, and what the plump, overgroomed little man whose name he hadn't caught was saying was that his putter had gone back on him on the second nine. He didn't know what was the matter with him. He'd spent an hour every day this week on the practice green, and he'd putted fine on the first nine. "And then all of a sudden"—he waved his hands in a gesture of helplessness—"it's gone."

And the erect, hard-muscled woman with the weather-beaten skin whose name Noah couldn't remember either said with conviction, "You tightened up."

She looked awkward and out of character in a flowered green and white dress. She set her glass on the table and demonstrated with an imaginary putter. "You've got to remember to keep that left knee relaxed," she said earnestly, reaching down and patting her left knee.

"And keep your grip on the handle relaxed too. Then, when you're all ready to hit it, take a deep breath and let it all out again and then hit the ball. You'll find it'll make all the difference in the world."

The little man nodded, equally earnestly. "I'll try that," he said. "Thanks very much, Jeanne."

Noah remembered then that the name that went with Jeanne was Carter, so she would be the wife of the Sid Carter who was the first one he had met. Sid Carter was over by the door talking to a woman in a white dress. He was as lean and athletic looking and rough-skinned as his wife, and Noah thought that they were very well matched, like a pair of golf clubs.

Jeffrey was again at Noah's elbow, smiling at him with a possessive sort of approval. "The hell of it was, Noah," he said, "that Archie here was my partner." He clapped the plump little man on the back and laughed, and Noah had no idea what kind of a last name went with the name Archie.

"We were playing fifty dollars Nassau, and Archie here was my partner, the bum," he said in a tone that was intended to be bantering and good-sportsmanlike and that nevertheless had an edge of resentment in it. "We were going fine. Three up on the first nine. And then by God Archie here loses his eyesight and three-putts four of the next seven holes and chips over the green into the trap on the seventeenth." He opened his hands in a gesture of helplessness. "So instead of walking away with a hundred and fifty bucks, I'm out fifty. How do you like that?"

3.

For a moment, soon after the guests arrived, Noah found himself alone with Natalie by the door into the hall. "Which one is your sister?" he asked.

She smiled, a little distractedly. "They haven't come yet. I'm afraid Jeffrey was right about her. She *is* always late."

"What's her name, by the way—besides Betty?"

"Mrs. Howard MacGarry. They'll be along sometime. I'm glad you're going to meet them." Her eyes were moving restlessly around the room. "I was hoping my brother would be here this weekend too, but he couldn't make it."

Noah had forgotten that she had had a brother. He must have

looked bewildered, and she must have been watching him. "You'd forgotten that I had a brother, hadn't you?"

He stuttered, and she smiled in a way that told him that the fact that he had forgotten had some significance in her mind, and she went on over to her other guests, leaving him there alone.

But fifteen minutes later she brought a girl in a cherry-colored dress and a man as tall as Noah over to where he was standing in front of the fireplace, and she smiled at him very pleasantly and said, "This is Betty, Noah." She was watching his face, and he sensed that she was laughing at him.

Noah looked at Betty and remembered that he had said that he would believe she was lovelier than Natalie when he saw her, and he knew why Natalie was laughing—because Betty was, without a doubt, the most beautiful girl he had ever seen. She was blonder than Natalie, and only slightly, in the way her head sat on her neck, could he see a resemblance between them. Her features were smoothly rounded and flawless, her eyes a soft gray-blue, her skin, though somewhat tanned, as velvety and fresh as a sixteen-year-old girl's.

She smiled, and in her smile there *was* something that was like Natalie's. "I've been hearing about Noah Sibley ever since I was a little girl," she said, and Noah cocked his head in humorous surprise at Natalie and saw that she was blushing.

She motioned toward the tall man. "And this is Howard Mac-Garry," she said.

Howard was almost slender and almost handsome. "Glad to know you, Sibley," he said, shaking hands vigorously. "Natalie tells me you're something of a fisherman." He would have been slender, Noah was thinking, but for that bulging at the back of his neck and that little pendulous stomach that his double-breasted suit didn't quite hide, and he would have been handsome if his mouth and nose had been a little larger.

"I do quite a bit of fly fishing for trout," Noah said modestly, and he knew from Howard's expression that fly fishing for trout wouldn't do. Howard laughed. "Fly fishing is right," he said. "Flies in your hair, mosquitoes on your neck, gnats up your nose. Not for me. We're all salt-water people around here."

The cocktail hour lasted on and on and, constantly milling, people moved from group to group and conversation to conversation, to and from the drink-mixing table in one corner and the *canapé* table in the other and back again into new groupings that were always much like the old ones.

[30]

Confused by all the names and all the faces, lost in too much, too fast talk of things unfamiliar to him, Noah found himself planted in front of the fireplace, his glass in his hand, cut off from moving in any direction, feeling like the buoy in the tide rip that he had watched from the ferry that afternoon, the only stationary object in a maelstrom of movement. He was conscious of his size and his awkwardness among all these thoroughly at home, sure-of-themselves people. He wondered if the grin he kept determinedly on his face looked as glassy and forced as it felt.

He could remember some of the names, only a few of the many conversations he had been in. There had been one early, when Jeffrey had gathered people around him and he had realized that they had been forewarned that he was a writer and a celebrity.

"Tell me, Mr. Sibley," someone had asked, "have you been writing long?"

If Natalie had not been there in the group, watching him, her eyes a little amused and a little appraising, he might have let the misconception stand, but before her he couldn't. "Actually," he said, "you can hardly call it writing. It's more a matter of poring through a lot of old papers and books and fussing around libraries and then just writing out what you've found out. It doesn't call for any real skill in writing. Such as it is, I've only been working at it full time for three years. Before that, I worked at it summers and during my spare time when I was teaching school."

He was looking at Natalie's face, and the amused look disappeared quickly from her eyes. "Teaching school?" she asked, frowning. "Did you teach school?"

"For nine years," he said.

Her frown deepened, and Noah sensed that her mind was making some sort of readjustment to this bit of information. "I thought you worked as your father's secretary."

He smiled at her. "Just for one year. After that I—"

"Just for one year?" She seemed disturbed—and mystified.

"You heard him, Natalie," Jeffrey said, laughing. "You're not deaf."

Natalie paid no attention to him, nor to the other people standing there listening. "Was it—was it the school where you turned down the job the year you were at Columbia?"

"That's right, Milburn. My old school."

"And you taught there for nine years?"

"For Christ's sake, Natalie," Jeffrey said, laughing in exasperation, "how many times does he have to tell you things?"

Noah glanced at him, then turned back to Natalie, smiling. "Five years before the war," he said, "and four years after. Then I quit three years ago and started working full time on the history."

She was staring at him, her mind apparently still at work on the readjustment. Finally she smiled, the sad sort of smile with which people accept the inevitable. "And you worked as your father's secretary for just one year," and Noah had a feeling that here, in this stupid conversation, lay the answer to the things he had been wondering about for so long. He was annoyed with himself for not seeing it, but a man in a pink shirt and a white bow tie was telling him that he had some stories that would sure make *some* book if he could only get somebody to write them up for him. He had a very red face that didn't go very well with his pink shirt and he'd crossed the Atlantic under sail four times and he'd been in two hurricanes and a typhoon and every Bermuda race since some year or other and believe me he could tell you some stories that would make your hair curl and he'd been in a mutiny once too.

And Noah remembered a conversation about the children. He had found himself alone for a moment with Jeffrey, and in desperation for something to talk with him about, he had asked, "When am I going to see your children, Jeffrey?"

Jeffrey had suddenly looked serious and said, "Well, we'd better see about that," and, taking Noah by the coat-sleeve, pulled him across the room to where Natalie was talking with two of the guests. "Where are Pamela and Peter?" he asked, breaking in.

Noah saw the annoyance in Natalie's face. She excused herself from the guests and said evenly, "Pammy's on a beach picnic, and Peter's spending the night over at Jackie's."

Jeffrey looked helplessly at Noah, then nodded with exaggerated sweetness. "Always a pleasure," he said, "to find out where one's children are spending the night. I don't seem to remember Peter's asking my permission to spend the night at Jackie's."

Natalie's face was expressionless. "You weren't here," she said. "You were playing golf."

Again Jeffrey's glance at Noah was a comradely one. "In the modern American home, Noah, the father is the only one whose wishes are never consulted." He turned back to Natalie. "Did it occur to you that Noah might have enjoyed hearing Pammy play? All these people," he said, with a sweeping gesture around the room, "always enjoy hearing Pammy play." He turned to Noah. "Our daughter has an unusual talent as a pianist."

Noah nodded solemnly.

Natalie's face was still expressionless. "She couldn't play very well with the piano locked and the key hidden."

Noah had noticed that the cover was down over the keyboard.

"You know very well," Jeffrey said, making no effort now to cover with a humorous overtone the irritation in his voice, "that I'd have unlocked it for this occasion."

Natalie looked at him for a moment, then turned back to her guests.

4.

STILL the cocktail drinking went on and on, and Noah, who had been in the habit for many years now of stopping after the second cocktail, lost track of how many times Jeffrey refilled his glass.

The sweet-acrid smell of gin and whiskey and cigarette smoke and perfume and well-soaped bodies and tweedy jackets blended with the unabated noise into what seemed to him like a single element, an element that enveloped him, hazy, mildly pleasant, mildly disturbing. People appeared in front of him as if by magic. Voices seemed to come from a little distance, loud enough but somehow remote. Suddenly people who had been there would be gone and others would have taken their places.

There was a little woman named Rosemary Something-or-other who seemed to have appointed herself his guardian, with the special function of keeping him informed as to who people were and what they did. She would chatter away there in front of him, giving him thumbnail sketches of the different people. And he would lean over to get his ear nearer to her mouth and nod and smile vacantly, sometimes catching it and sometimes not catching it and sometimes forgetting to listen.

"Oh, Pete," she said of the red-faced man in the pink shirt, "he's a big bag of wind. The real sailor in this crowd is Sid—Sid Carter, you know. He's a real one. He can make a fifty-foot schooner stand up on its hind legs and beg for a wind, and he could lay a course for the South Pole and split the pole right down the middle. Of course his brain stops working as soon as he gets his feet on dry land. He's never earned a cent in his life, but he sure puts in the overtime at his sailing."

Everything she said had a sprightly twist to it, and when Noah remembered to listen he was always amused—and always annoyed with

[33]

himself for not having listened more. Sometimes he would find that he'd been listening to the conversation behind him. "We were twenty miles south of Block Island," a man's voice behind him would be saying, "and we had four lines out, two from the chairs and two from the outriggers."

About Howard MacGarry, who was always very much in the center of things, Noah had noticed, always surrounded by a group of laughing people, Rosemary said, "Isn't he a superlative egg? Such a party man—and I don't mean the Republican party either, though of course there aren't any of us here who wouldn't have liked to fry all the eggheads. I mean, seriously, that he's just about as much fun on a party as anybody I ever knew. And a three-fisted drinker if there ever was one. He's as much of a genius at entertaining as Jeffrey is at thinking. Between them, they keep MacGarry, Humeston Associates humming along like a souped-up motor."

Noah nodded thoughtfully while his mind caught up to what she was saying. "What," he finally asked, "is MacGarry, Humeston Associates?"

"Don't you even know that?"

He smiled. "I never met Jeffrey until just before you came in tonight."

"That's right," she said. "You're an old flame of Natalie's—or maybe she's an old flame of yours. I suppose it all depends on who burns the hottest. Anyway, she's all burned up about something. You can feel it, can't you? Someday she's going to burst a boiler, and then poor Jeffrey's the guy who's going to get burned."

"Really?" Noah asked.

"And how!"

"Well!" Noah said, and after a moment, "Where did she meet him, do you know?"

"Good God, don't you even know that? As I get the story, they were palsy-walsy way back in their high school days, out in Minneapolis or some one of those places out there in the wilderness. And she got her father to give him his start in business. That explains a lot, doesn't it?"

"Does it?"

"Of course. Nobody a gal loves like a guy she's helped. It does things for the grand old ego."

"Oh," Noah said. She was looking spryly around the room, and he asked again, "What is MacGarry, Humeston Associates?"

"Advertising," she said. "One of the smartest little advertising outfits in the city."

And a voice somewhere was saying, "I get it by the case. Comes from a little distillery down in Virginia. In my books nothing they turn out in Kentucky can touch it."

And a woman's voice was saying, "We thought at first we'd have it at the club, but the club is so crowded with teen-agers on Saturday nights—"

From time to time Noah caught glimpses of Natalie, but only a couple of times, and then for just a moment, was she there with him. From time to time he caught glimpses of Betty too, and sometimes their eyes would meet and she would smile at him. Of her Rosemary said, "Isn't she a knockout? Of course she should have been a model. A waste of talent, but of course Howard's share of the MacGarry, Humeston profits isn't peanuts, so I suppose she'll go right on wasting her fragrance on us jerks."

Rosemary's face had a bland, featureless quality that worried Noah. He couldn't decide where her nose stopped and her cheeks began, and there was also the question of her eyebrows—whether she didn't have any, or whether they were just so blond that he couldn't see them in this light.

And a voice behind him was saying, "We laid a course for Stonehorse Light, and she was really startin' to blow up by that time—"

And suddenly the red-faced man in the pink shirt was there in front of Noah saying, "If somebody wanted to write up that stuff I've got in my head, there'd be a fortune in it. Everybody'd buy the book. And I'd be willing to go fifty-fifty on the royalties—and that's pretty generous, if I do say so, when you figure all he'd have to do would be to sit down at his typewriter and write it up."

And the voices kept coming from all sides:

A man's voice, "He was short on Chrysler, and boy, was he wetting his pants—"

And a woman's voice, "And all the time she was supposed to be taking art lessons she was meeting him up in his apartment, and poor George didn't have an inkling—"

And another man's voice, "We were trolling for blues on our way back in and it got hot and we broke out the beer and Ken had been hitting the bottle every time he went below—"

And long after Noah had given up trying to keep track of time, some of the crowd seemed to have melted away. Rosemary explained that only some of them had been invited for dinner; the rest had been invited just for cocktails.

They went into the dining room and picked up plates and silverware. There were so many different dishes on the table that Noah stood looking at them helplessly until Rosemary said, "Jeffrey sure puts dynamite in his martinis, doesn't he?" She helped him decide what to take, pointing first to one dish and then to another. And when his plate was full she guided him back into the living room and settled him with his plate in the biggest chair in the room.

5.

IT was long after midnight when Noah wandered disconsolately out of the still crowded living room into the hall. Natalie had disappeared somewhere, and nobody had paid any attention to Noah, or seemed to notice him at all, for a long time.

He stood still in the hall, then went on through the dark dining room and peeked into the kitchen. Natalie was there with an apron on, wiping the dishes as the maid washed them. He watched them, standing well back in the dark. They were talking in what seemed to be a friendly, confidential sort of way. He felt that he would be intruding if he went out there, and after watching them for a long time he wandered back into the hall.

The people in the living room were still drinking—or at least had been when he left the room—and now they had begun to sing. They sang without the piano, which was still locked. He stood beside the stairs and listened. The songs they were singing were not the ones he and his family and friends tried to harmonize on around campfires at the Lake. These people were not trying to harmonize at all; they just sang the melody in chorus, very loud.

The songs were all new to him, long ballads with endless verses, and so startlingly blunt about sex and the various parts of the male and female body, so full of the four-letter words that he, who had never thought of himself as a prude, who had, after all, taught in a boys' school for nine years, was, he had to admit to himself, shocked, especially when he heard some of the women's voices joining gleefully in the choruses.

He suspected that he was blushing. In any case he knew that he couldn't take part in this particular singing, and he knew that he couldn't play convincingly the part of an amused audience. He couldn't go back in there. He looked around nervously, afraid that someone might come into the hall and find him standing there listening. They would think he was the sort of person whose susceptibilities were tickled by this sort of humor but was ashamed to show it. His susceptibilities were not tickled; he was bored and tired and depressed.

He thought of going on up to bed, but he couldn't do that without having said goodnight to Natalie, without having told her that he had enjoyed her party. He thought of going out onto the veranda, but the front door was in full view of the living room and somebody in there might see him on his way out.

Finally, stealthily, because he could think of no other place to go, he stole on tiptoe to the back door, at the other end of the hall, and stepped out, closing the screen door carefully behind him. The night was clear and balmy, with a newly risen moon shining through the pines.

He found a flagstone path running along the back of the living room. He walked down it softly, afraid that his footsteps might be heard inside. The raucous singing was loud through the open windows, and as he walked by he could see Howard MacGarry leading the singing with a forefinger for baton, smiling mischievously as he sang. His was the only head Noah could see.

The path went around the living room and joined the gravel path from the front door out to the edge of the bluff. He followed it out to a long flight of wooden steps and went on down across the beach to the water's edge. The air was filled with an iodine-like smell, very different from the soft, woody aroma that came up from the shores of a fresh-water lake at night. And although the wind was light and the Sound quiet, there was a restlessness in the water along the shore, a constant noisy movement, a loud sucking and sighing that wasn't anything like the faint whispered lapping of the water at the Lake.

He trudged on along the beach. It was very bright now in the moonlight. He kicked at piles of seaweed, picked up shells and examined them and dropped them again. The beach was springy with an underlay of seaweed. He had to admit that it was nice underfoot, a pleasant surface to walk on.

He came to a flat rock and sat down. The air was cooler down here by the water, and he was beginning to enjoy the smell of it. And his head, which for the last hour had felt full, as though it were an overstuffed cushion softening all his efforts to think, was beginning to feel clearer—not really clear yet, but clear enough for him to begin to wonder what was the matter with him.

Mostly what was the matter with him, he told himself disgustedly, was that he had been a fool and drunk more cocktails than he could handle. He'd learned that lesson two or three times before in his life, and why he should have picked this night of all nights to forget it—

He kicked his heels into the sand and scowled down at the toes of his shoes. He *had* forgotten it, and most of the evening he had been tongue-tied and stupid, a big smirking fool who couldn't keep his mind on what people were saying to him. These people had expected him to be brilliant because he was a writer, and for the first hour they had listened expectantly to everything he said. And for the last hour nobody except Natalie had known he was there, and he had sensed that she had been disappointed in him. He could see himself now, how foolish he must have looked, sitting there in the biggest chair in the room, grinning his silly vacant grin and saying nothing at all.

He watched the lights blinking at him across the water. It wasn't that he cared a damn what these people up there thought of him, he told himself. He didn't like any of them really, except Natalie and perhaps Betty. The rest of them were all too foreign to him, too unlike the people he knew around home, or the people he knew up at the Lake, or the people he'd known at Milburn, or the people he saw around the New York Public Library or the Columbia Library or the Princeton Library.

There was probably some word to describe them, but he didn't know what it was. They were yachtsmen mostly, he guessed. They sailed and they fished and they went to Florida in the winter and they played golf and Jeanne Carter had won the Something-or-other women's championship.

What all that made them Noah didn't know. They weren't the idle rich because Jeffrey and Howard MacGarry had this advertising business in New York and Archie had an office in Philadelphia and somebody had had a manufacturing business in Worcester. They weren't what you could call titans of industry, though—they weren't that big— and they weren't quite the bourgeoisie and they weren't quite the upper middle class. Maybe there wasn't any word for them.

Whatever they were, they were Natalie's life. Collectively, they were the milieu she lived in winters as well as summers, he had gathered from the conversations. They made up the life she had lived for fifteen years, the life that her marriage to Jeffrey or Fate or whatever you wanted to call it had thrown her into.

What he still didn't know, what he hadn't been able to make out, was how much she had become a part of it and it a part of her. Not, of course, he told himself quickly, that it really mattered to him one way or the other. He was here strictly out of curiosity—to see what Natalie had become.

He snorted and slid off the rock and walked down to the water's edge. And he stood there gazing out at the water, frowning, annoyed with himself because the thing he had been feeling was something more than curiosity.

Then he smiled. After all, she was the girl he had once loved. It was natural enough that he should care about what had happened to her. It was natural enough that he should care about what was happening to her now, that he should wonder about how much all this that went on up there in that house had become a part of her.

From chance expressions he had caught on her face, he felt sure that she was not entirely happy. But he had seen her at other moments when she *had* seemed a part of it, times when she had looked amused at what people had said, times when she had seemed to be on terms of intimacy with some of the women and others when she had looked at some of the men as though she liked them. And couldn't she, with her intelligence, with her force of personality, have made herself a different life if she had really wanted to?

He went back to the rock and lit a cigarette. Of course you could half like your life, he supposed, or two-thirds or three-quarters like it. But from everything he remembered of Natalie, from everything he had, over the years, thought her to be, it seemed incredible that she could be even halfway congenial with those people up there or, to put it bluntly, that she could be halfway happy with a man like Jeffrey. And she had looked happiest of all washing dishes with the maid out in the kitchen.

He sat hunched over, looking down at the sand, forgetting to puff the cigarette that he held in his fingers. Did she, in her secret moments, long for a different life? Did she ever regret that she had—

He got to his feet again and paced the beach, back and forth in front of the rock. He flicked his cigarette into the water and, without knowing that he was doing it, got out another one and lit it. It could be. It could have been—but for the something, the thing he had never guessed.

Her life with him would have been—what? The life of a master's wife in a boys' school. Would she have been happy in it—or half happy, or three-quarters happy? It was hard to imagine it of that woman up there in that yellow dress, but if she had started out with it—she might have been. She might have been nine-tenths happy, and that was about as high as it came, he guessed.

[39]

So what? So she had a husband and two children and a home here and a place in Florida and an apartment in New York. So sometime around midnight Sunday night he would be getting off the train at the station in Middlefield, New Jersey, and if it wasn't too hot it would be very nice in Middlefield. There would be nobody there but Mark, and Arlene coming in to make the beds and get dinners, and maybe Connie. It should be very restful there.

Well, anyway, that would be for only one week. A week from Monday night he would be driving in at the back of the cottage at the Lake, and there would be all the good old familiar things, the good old canoe, the good old picnics, the good old trout streams. He tried hard to rekindle in himself the excitement he had always felt at the thought of starting out for the Lake at the beginning of the summer, and he took a final long drag on his cigarette and tossed it into the water and started back toward the house, pushed into walking fast by a vague small sense of panic.

And he had walked just a short distance when he saw Natalie coming along the beach toward him. She had on a loose coat that came a little above her knees. It was creamy white in the moonlight. He couldn't see her face, but he knew from her walk that it was Natalie.

He hurried on, worried at the thought that she must have been worrying about him. And when they came together she said, "I'm sorry, Noah."

His mind was very clear now. "I'm the one who should be doing the apologizing—for running away like this. Were you worried about me?"

"Not very."

"How did you happen to find me?"

"I thought you might be down here, and then I saw you light a cigarette—from up at the top of the steps."

He peered into her face, and she seemed to be studying the middle button of his coat. "What were *you* apologizing for?" he asked. "What did you have to be sorry about?"

She was still staring at the button, and her expression did not change. "The evening."

"It was a very nice party."

She chuckled mirthlessly. "I had a silly idea that this one might be different."

Noah thought about that and decided that she was right. There was no point in going on with the polite pretense. "I wasn't exactly a help," he said.

She looked up at him curiously. "What do you mean?"

"I drank too many cocktails."

"Did you?"

"I'll say I did. And all evening after that I was stupid and tongue-tied."

"I didn't notice." Then she was laughing up at him. "I thought you looked very nice, sitting over there in the big chair smiling. All evening I kept looking at you and thinking how nice you looked, how much more of a person you looked than anybody else there. I—I kept thinking that anybody would know just by looking at you that you were worth all the rest of them put together." Her voice trailed off a little at the end, and she was gazing out at the water.

His glasses had become clouded, and he stared at her, blinking, seeing her face only as a blur. He took the glasses off and wiped the lenses with his handkerchief and put them back on again, and when he got them back on she turned abruptly and faced him, looking up into his face. Her voice was urgent and frightened. "You won't do it, will you, Noah. You won't go?"

"Go?"

"Go away on that boat Sunday night and say to yourself, 'Now I've seen that girl Natalie I used to be engaged to and she'd changed quite a lot and that's that.' And then never come back. You won't do that, will you, Noah?"

"Well," he said, "I guess—I'm afraid I'll have to go on the boat Sunday."

"But you'll come back?"

"Well, I suppose, if you'd like to have me—"

And suddenly, without his knowing at all how it had happened, his arms were around her and her head was against his shoulder and she was sobbing.

He held her, firmly but respectfully, and finally, still sobbing, she said, "I can't take it any more."

He went on holding her gently, and after a while she said, "I kept telling myself that I'd made my bed and now I could lie in it and for all those years I lay in it and tried to be a good sport and—and now I just can't take it any more. You will come back, won't you, Noah?"

And he said manfully, "Of course I will, Natalie." He waited a moment and then, hesitantly, wondering if he was making a mistake, wondering if the need she felt for him wasn't purely on an emotional, non-physical level, he put his hand under her chin and tilted her face up and kissed her.

[41]

She did not draw away, but his own sensation as he kissed her was not quite the sensation he remembered from the days when they had both been twenty-two. There was something a little more solid, a little more corporal about it, something less of the sense of ethereal oneness, of that brief elusive moment of rapport between lonesome spirits. And already, although he found this moment thrilling enough in its way, although much of his old affection for her was still there, he was able to wonder in some small crevice of his mind what, in the world of day-to-day living, this moment might be leading to.

6·

In one motion, Noah threw the sheet off and sat bolt upright in bed, staring around the room. He didn't know whether he had just waked up from a sound sleep or whether he had been lying half awake, re-membering slowly. All he knew was that the realization had come to him suddenly, and with it a hollow, breath-taking sense of dread.

He sat hunched over, breathing hard, frightened, afraid of what he might have said, afraid of this day that was just starting, afraid to think of all the things his mother and Barrett and Mark would say, instantly and whole-mindedly conscious of all the things they *had* said in the past about Warner Boiland and people like him.

He snatched his watch up from the bedside table and stared at it. It was ten minutes to eight. "Nobody," Natalie had said, "will be stir-ring around here before eleven, maybe twelve."

That gave him three hours. His mind snatched at those three hours as it might have snatched at a reprieve on his life. Fleetingly the thought came to him that there might be some way of getting into the village and onto a boat and away before the people in this house were even up. He shook his head, ashamed that he had had the thought at all. You couldn't do that to Natalie. It wasn't Natalie's fault. It was his own, his own rashness and indiscretion.

What he needed was time to think, to remember just what he had said and to think about it and—and evaluate it, time to find out what he really wanted—most of all, time to see how this frightening new thing could be fitted into the pattern of the Sibley family life and the Sibley family thinking.

He tiptoed into the bathroom. He had a bad taste in his mouth and a suggestion of a headache. He put a lot of toothpaste on the brush and brushed his teeth vigorously for a full minute, and in the medicine cabinet he found aspirin and took two of them and drank two glasses of water. Then he washed in cold water and threw it over his head and onto the back of his neck. He tried to tell himself that it all made him feel better, but he still had a suggestion of a headache and his eyes looked puffy and uncertain in the mirror.

It felt like a hot day, and he put on a sport shirt and cotton slacks and sneakers and opened the door into the hall. He heard snoring from some distant room, but no other voices and no footsteps. And successfully, without being spied by anyone, he got down the stairs and out of the door and across the lawn to the steps that went down to the beach.

He looked up and down, and there was no one on the beach. He spotted a wooded point a half mile away, and, glancing quickly back at the house, hurried on down the steps and along the beach, thinking only about getting those woods between him and the house.

Finally safely out of sight of the house, he found an old rowboat upturned on the beach and sat on it. And although he had always believed that one cigarette before breakfast was worse than three after, he lit one and puffed it thoughtfully. And he started determinedly, methodically, to think about this frightening, startling, life-disturbing situation that he had gotten himself into.

He had kissed Natalie. He had promised her, without setting any specific dates, that he would come back here again. And, most compromising of all, he had certainly implied that he would help her to free herself from this life that she had said she couldn't take any more.

None of that, he started to tell himself, really committed him to anything—and then he stopped himself abruptly, ashamed for the second time that such thoughts were occurring to him. You didn't quibble over what you'd promised and what you hadn't promised. You didn't walk up to her and say, "Now look, I didn't commit myself to a thing." Not when it was Natalie, you didn't.

What did you do? What after all did you want? Probably you wanted Natalie. Last night, when you walked back along the beach beside her and sat on the veranda with her, saying very little, and then when you said goodnight and went to your room and she went to hers, you wanted her more than you had ever wanted anything in your life. This morning you guessed that you still wanted her. You could still dream of a life with her, if you shut your mind to a lot of things.

And if you didn't shut your mind to all those things? He scowled out at the hazy gray expanse of water in front of him. A life with her meant, before you got it, some terrifyingly sordid business. It meant a divorce, and at the word "divorce" he winced. It meant saying to his mother and Barrett and Mark and Kate, "Remember that girl Natalie Parkes? Well, I've persuaded her to get a divorce and marry me after all. Yes, that's what I've done. Okay, call it stealing if you want to. Yes, there are children, a couple of them. A broken home? I suppose that's what you'd call it all right."

That was the gist of what he would have to say. Perhaps to some people that wouldn't seem like much. Perhaps in some families it wouldn't be much. But some families weren't the Sibley family. The Sibley family was different. You had to have been brought up in the Sibley family to understand how different. You had to remember all the things they had said about Warner and about Louise's divorce. You had to have lived through that whole business, to have been the cause of it all, to have been at fault in it, before you could understand.

The Sibleys were different. They were, he supposed, pretty old-fashioned. They were—well, for one thing that might seem irrelevant and inconsequential to other people, they were a family of quoters.

IV

1.

A FAMILY of quoters. Suppose, for instance, that Mrs. Sibley were to come in from her afternoon walk exuding her usual gentlewomanly glow, suggesting exercises in deep breathing simply by the manner of her entrance, and suppose that Mark were to call jocularly from his desk in the study behind the living room, "Been wandering the streets again, Mother?" Noah could almost know that she would, equally jocularly, have been wandering lonely as a cloud. And if Mark should then wonder if it was time for tea, which it always was when she came back from her walk, it might be tea for two and two for tea, even though there were always three of them and sometimes four, five, or six.

Since all the Sibleys except Noah and Kate had phenomenal memories, the impression they made on strangers, Noah had always realized with pride, was one of great erudition combined with great good sportsmanship, for the quotations were quite as likely to come out of popular and even vulgar songs and limericks as out of Bartlett. And if people did sometimes notice that the quotations weren't particularly apt, that quite often they were nothing more than automatic, associative responses to the stimulus of a word, a phrase, or a situation, it still made for a delightfully silly evening, an evening from which people went away feeling, he knew, that they had been in contact with culture at its unpretentious and jolliest best.

It was a family habit, this quoting business, that had had its beginnings long before Noah's memories began, back in the days when William Huntington Sibley had been in demand as a lecturer, the days when no lecture was considered a proper one without a dozen or more quotations. His, of course, had come from the poets, with an occasional Biblical one for those contrasting moments of religious

[45]

solemnity which he used with such telling effectiveness. Today their quotations came from anywhere—poems old or new, the Bible, saws and proverbs, songs and limericks, even from the dicta of William Huntington Sibley himself, dicta which, endlessly repeated, came to have all the authority of quotations in their own right.

One such—the one that had been in the back of Noah's mind ever since he woke up—was the quotation from William Huntington Sibley which someone was sure to bring forth whenever the subject of divorce and remarriage came up. It went, "There is nothing lower than a man who steals another man's wife."

This one was never said nowadays in a spirit of jollity. It was said in angry remembrance of a still rankling blow to the Sibley family pride, and in loyalty to poor Barrett. And always, if Noah was present, it was said with an accusing glance at him, for it was he who had brought Warner Boiland into the home.

The fact that Dr. Sibley had made this pronouncement long before Barrett's divorce added immeasurably to its meaningfulness for the family, proving as it did that no one had invented it to suit the occasion. All through his life Noah had absorbed from the family atmosphere a feeling that divorce in itself was shameful. And along with it had been the feeling that, in cases where the woman remarried, the fault invariably lay not with her—she was considered to be almost completely helpless in the matter—and not with the husband—his disposition was considered irrelevant—but with the second man.

It was one of three or four rather old-fashioned beliefs to which the liberal-thinking Sibleys still held, like their prejudices against gambling and against sex in literature and against women drinking in public places. It was not a major doctrine of their lives, of course, but it was still a real part of their thinking. It was something that Noah had absorbed as he grew up, much as he had absorbed the Golden Rule and the Sermon on the Mount, or the family belief that the cure for all the world's ills lay in more and higher education, or their belief that, with the extension of good will and arbitration, war would someday disappear from the face of the earth.

But on top of that, as though to force the truth of Dr. Sibley's dictum into their minds, to imbed it deep into Noah's consciousness, had come the wretched business of Barrett's divorce. If it was low to steal another man's wife under ordinary circumstances, how much lower it was to steal her while he was gallantly serving his country in North Africa!

2·

IT was, and always would be, completely impossible to understand how any of it could have happened, but to try to understand it, Noah supposed, you had to go back to that Sunday dinner in September of '42, when his mother made her very generous offer to Louise, and Louise acted so ungenerously and unaccountably churlish about it.

Barrett, that September, was back in Middlefield on leave after finishing his course at the Intelligence School at Harrisburg, looking gallant in his tropical worsted uniform. He was smilingly but determinedly tight-lipped about the orders he was about to get, but the knowledge that he would not be on this side of some ocean much longer was in the air.

By a lucky coincidence, they were all home that weekend—all, that is, except Kate's husband Spence, who had volunteered the day after Pearl Harbor and was already on the West Coast, where Kate and her two children were soon to join him. But otherwise all of Dr. and Mrs. Sibley's children were there: Kate, up from her country place in Pennsylvania with her two children, Noah and Connie, both waiting to go back to their teaching jobs, Mark, on a weekend leave from Quantico, and with him his wife Winifred who, after having spent the spring and summer in a private sanitarium, had come out, pronounced cured, just two weeks before. To make the party complete, Barrett and Louise had come over for dinner from their apartment on Elm Avenue. And the breath-catching thought that this might be the last time they would all be together was also very much in the air.

Mrs. Sibley waited until the dinner was over and they had moved into the living room for coffee. "Louise, dear," she said, smiling benignly as she poured her own cup and settled back, "your father-in-law and I have been talking things over and we have a little suggestion to make."

Louise, looking very pretty again now that she had recovered from the illness that had followed her miscarriage, smiled at her affectionately and said, "Yes, Mother?" She had a delightful manner with older people, and as the time for Barrett's departure drew nearer she had acquired a new and charming sobriety.

"Your father-in-law and I are having a hard time," Mrs. Sibley said, "facing the fact that we're about to lose our flock. Kate is leaving for

[47]

the West Coast, and Mark believes that he'll be following her out there before very long, and Winifred is going with him. The fledglings leave the nest. Of course Noah and Connie will be home for vacations, but they'll both be going back to their schools this week, and then when the captains and the kings have all departed, the two of us will be left all alone, rattling around in this great big house. It's going to be very lonesome for us."

She glanced around at the rest of the family, asking with her eyes for their approval of the way she was approaching the subject. They all smiled at her—all but Winifred, Noah noticed. Winifred, sitting on the couch beside Mark, holding his hand, was frowning at his mother, looking serious and perplexed.

His mother had not noticed her. "We thought we'd reorganize the arrangements a little," she said to Louise, "so that the green room would be free. In some ways I think it's the nicest room in the house. It has its own bath, and with one person all alone in it, and with the alcove, you could make it into a nice sitting bedroom, a little room of one's own."

Noah glanced at Louise's face, and he was surprised to see a look of rigid determination on it.

"You could have your desk over by the window, and the tea table and two or three nice chairs in the alcove, and you would have sunlight in there almost all day long." She turned the full force of her smile on Louise. "I suspect you know by this time what I'm driving at, dear. Father and I would so love to have you with us while Barrett is gone. It would mean so much to us to have one of our children around, and it does seem silly for you and Barrett to go on paying rent on that apartment when there's no telling how long he's going to be gone. You all alone by the telephone over there just three blocks away, and we all alone by the telephone over here."

Louise stared at her with a frightened expression in her eyes. She looked around quickly at the others and then, desperately, back at Mrs. Sibley. "You mean—you mean that I should give up my apartment?"

Mrs. Sibley continued to smile, but with slightly raised eyebrows. "It *is* rather an expensive apartment, my dear, and Army pay compared to what Barrett's been drawing as a junior partner"—she opened her hands out toward Louise in a gesture that asked if anything could be more obvious—"and of course, Louise, if you preferred you could move some of your own things into the green room. Wouldn't you feel just as much at home then?"

Louise shook her head slowly, still looking frightened. "But it's— it's our home. It's where we live. It's where we"—she looked around pleadingly, as though she hoped that someone would come to her defense—"it's where we came after our wedding trip. It's where Barrett and I have—it's where we've been happy together. It's where I couldn't have my baby."

Noah glanced at Barrett, and the expression on Barrett's handsome face was a pained one.

Mrs. Sibley had stopped smiling. Dr. Sibley stood up and walked across to Louise. He did not look down at her. He stood beside her chair, looking off into space, with a fatherly hand on her shoulder. "My dear girl," he said in the mellow voice that he could play on as though it were a musical instrument, "none of us is going to try to make you come if you don't want to."

"I can't," Louise said, staring down at the floor.

"But we love you very much, my dear, and we just hoped that you *would* want to."

"I don't," Louise said.

"Louise!" Barrett said sharply.

She turned and stared at him, wild-eyed.

"I think you owe Mother and Father an apology."

Louise began to cry, sobbing convulsively.

Barrett stepped gracefully across to the tea table and refilled his coffee cup, and suddenly Winifred spoke up in a voice that was, for her, surprisingly emphatic. "Don't make her," she said. "Don't make her if she doesn't want to."

Louise looked up, startled, and slowly every other head in the room turned toward Winifred, as astonished as if the cat had spoken. Mark withdrew the hand she had been holding and half turned toward her, scowling. Then, after a moment, he smiled at her and patted her knee in a gesture that was both affectionate and restraining. Winifred sat back, still frowning, her face very red.

"Perhaps," Barrett said, with a sad and tolerant smile, "we'd better drop the subject for now. I'll talk it over with Louise alone."

Now it was as though Winifred had not spoken at all. They were all smiling approvingly at Barrett, and for a brief moment the thought crossed Noah's mind that most of the approving smiles that the members of his family bestowed were bestowed upon each other. He put the thought quickly out of his mind.

His mother, taking her cue from Barrett's timely and proper suggestion, was talking about the morning sermon. "I was interested," she was saying, "in what Mr. James had to say about the Nazi mind and Christianity."

They talked on, about the sermon and about the inevitable superiority of free men over trained robots, no matter how well trained the robots might be. As they talked, Noah was surprised to see that Winifred was not looking ashamed or contrite about her sudden outburst, as he and the rest of the family would have expected her to be. She was looking determined, almost angry, and he remembered a letter that Louise had once written him about how there really was a determined strain in Winifred's meek little character, about how that childish little chin of hers could, on occasion, actually jut out, if you could imagine such a thing.

He looked from Winifred to Louise, and Louise was sitting very quietly, paying no attention to the conversation, her eyes guarded, her color, like Winifred's, unnaturally high.

And later, after Barrett and Louise had gone back to their apartment and everybody had retired to his own room for the Sunday afternoon quiet hour and Noah had settled into his big chair with a book, there was a knock on his door. He called, "Come in," and Winifred opened the door and stepped in and closed it behind her. "Noah," she said, standing with her back against the door, "don't let them make her come."

He looked up at her, puzzled. Then he stood up, smiling doubtfully. He was, he knew, the only one she would have dared to come to. He was her friend, her confidant, in a way that no one else in the family was. He had been her friend when, to the rest of the family, she had been little more than a piece of office furniture. "Don't you worry about that, Winifred," he said, smiling reassuringly, trying to hide the fact that he was remembering that she was only two weeks out of a mental institution, the fact that, like the rest of the family, he couldn't help but wonder a bit how complete her cure had been.

She was staring hard into his face, and he knew that she knew that he was remembering and wondering.

"I'm sure nobody will make her come if she doesn't want to," he said stoutly.

She looked up at him, worried, very youthful, and very appealing. Once, long ago, long before Mark had ever noticed her, Noah had kissed Winifred. He had never been quite able to forget it. But now suddenly she was looking determined again. "Are you, Noah? Are you sure?" There was insistence in her voice.

He studied her face thoughtfully, trying to see what was behind it.

All he could know was that this took courage, this persistence of hers when she knew that he was wondering. And courage, he knew, did not come easily to her. Timidity, unsureness of herself—they, he had always felt, were somewhere at the root of her trouble.

"Of course I'm sure," he said.

She still looked determined, and he raised his eyebrows and smiled and asked, "Don't you think it was rather nice of Mother and Dad to ask her to come?"

"It wouldn't be good, Noah."

"Good? What do you mean 'good'?"

"I don't believe—" she started haltingly. Then, suddenly sure of herself, "I believe I know Louise better than the rest of you. It would be better, far better for everybody, if they didn't make her come."

"Nobody," Noah repeated, a shade of annoyance in his voice, "is going to make her come if she doesn't want to."

She stood still for a long time, looking, her hand on the doorknob. Finally she said, "I hope you're right," and before he knew that the door was open, she was out in the hall and the door was closing softly behind her.

3.

NOAH never did know what Barrett said to Louise. He went back to his job at the Milburn School the following Wednesday, and Barrett went overseas in late October. Just before he left, Noah got a letter from his mother saying that Louise and her desk and her table and her phonograph and four of her chairs and three of her pictures had been settled in the green room.

When he came home for the Christmas vacation, Louise was there, standing between his father and his mother at the door to meet him. After he had taken his bags to his room and washed up, she was waiting in the upstairs hall for him. "It's half an hour to teatime," she said. "Come and see my room." She took his hand and guided him in. "Isn't it lovely?"

Her furniture and pictures went very well with the room. "Wonderful," Noah said. "Great improvement. Looks a lot better than the old stuff did in here."

"Oh, good," she said. "I thought so too, but I didn't dare say so."

"They wouldn't have minded," Noah said.

[51]

"Oh, but they would have."

Noah frowned. "I really don't think so," he said.

She smiled at him, shaking her head. She took his hand again and led him over to the alcove and put him into the largest of her chairs. "There," she said, "isn't that comfortable? Ashtray right where your hand naturally falls? Coaster for your drink right beside it? View out into the trees? There's a woodpecker. I think he lives in that tree."

He settled back into the chair and smiled at her. Summer after summer at the Lake, all through his boyhood, he had worshiped Louise Hill with that awed and sexless respect which a gawky growing boy pays to the girls his older brothers go around with. She had been, by universal consensus, the prettiest, the most vivacious, the most charmingly mannered girl among the summer residents of the Lake. She had had—and still had—a lovely complexion, a mop of curly golden hair, and what most of the summer residents called a delightful girlish carriage—Noah had come to realize since that the phrase meant almost exactly what the other masters at Milburn meant when they said "one hell of a nice build."

And in a big-sisterly sort of way, during all those summers, Louise had been sweet with Noah, including him in picnics and parties when Barrett and Mark might have forgotten him, always asking him to dance one record with her when they danced to the phonograph on the porch, sometimes, with a mischievous glance at Barrett, making dates with him for swimming or canoeing, dates from which Barrett was excluded.

And now, Noah was thinking, here was that same Louise Hill, a lady of the Lake, living here in this house in Middlefield.

"Look," she said, opening her record cabinet. There, beside the records, were cups and saucers, an electric coffee maker, and a can of coffee. "Do you like coffee in the afternoon better than tea?"

For years Noah had liked coffee in the afternoon better than tea. He nodded, smiling.

"So do I. Maybe some afternoon while you're here they'll be invited out to tea, and then you can have coffee up here with me."

"We could do it any time," Noah said, trying hard to sound sure of himself. "They wouldn't mind."

"Oh, but they would."

He looked up at her unhappily. "How about not having too many preconceptions about this thing?" he said. "You're not going to find them as set in their ways as you think you are."

"Tea's important," she said. "It's a ceremony."

"Sure it's a ceremony." His mind was filled with an uneasy sense of apprehension. "Sit down," he said. "Let's talk things over." Louise, he was in the habit of saying, was one of the best friends he had in the world. Ever since she and Barrett had come back from their honeymoon and settled into the new apartment house on Elm Avenue, he had seen a great deal of her whenever he was home from school. She dropped in at the house very often when he was there. She was always asking him over for dinner, and those dinners with just her and Barrett were among his happiest memories. And a few times each year, on nights when Barrett was away or tied up at the office, the two of them had gone into the city alone together for dinner and a concert or play, and those were happy memories too.

Louise sat down and folded her hands primly in her lap and waited for him to start talking things over.

"I know they've got a few old-fashioned ideas," he said, assuming the old confidential tone they used when they talked alone together, "like not allowing a Hemingway or an O'Hara or a Caldwell in the house, but those things don't count for too much, do they? After all, they're still in their fifties, and you don't get too set in your ways that early. Little things like tea in the afternoon—"

"It's important," Louise said.

He shook his head vehemently. "You've got them wrong," he said. "Actually, if you'll just keep an open mind on the subject, I'll bet you'll find them about as liberal-minded a couple for their age as—"

"They're wonderful," Louise said.

"And I can tell you this, Lou." Lou was a nickname they had used jokingly at the Lake years before. Nobody used it any more except as a reminder of the old days, as Noah was using it now. "I can tell you that they're absolutely determined to make you happy while you're here. They're ready to turn backward somersaults to make things the way you want them. You haven't any idea how willing they are to make adjustments—how *anxious* they are to do anything to make you happy."

"Oh, but I have. They're wonderful. And it's going to be a very hard time for them, with Barrett and Mark overseas and the rest of you away and all the things your father has worked for all his life crumbling before his eyes. I'm not to make things harder for them. I'm to make a few of the adjustments myself. I'm not to be difficult, 'and you know, Louise, sometimes you can be difficult.'"

Her tone told him that she was quoting. "Did Barrett say that?"

She smiled at him. "It's almost teatime," she said. "I think we should go downstairs."

4.

Many, many times, in the nine years since, Noah had gone over those incidents in his mind, asking himself if with greater forethought, with better understanding of the feminine mind, with a more determined effort to understand the meaning behind the strange things that Louise did, he might not have been able to prevent the final disaster. He would try to tell himself that it wasn't his fault that he didn't have a better understanding of the feminine mind. How could he have had? Then he would try to quiet his conscience by reminding himself that if a dozen little things had been different, none of it would have happened, that it was all luck. Suppose, for instance, he had gotten the kind of duty he had hoped to get. But for that one little thing, might Barrett and Louise not still be happily married, still living in the apartment in Middlefield?

It was certainly none of his doing that he got the kind of duty that he did. With Barrett in North Africa, with Mark out in the Pacific and Winifred waiting for him in a little apartment in San Francisco, with Kate waiting out Spence's tour of overseas duty and her third pregnancy in San Diego, with even Connie leading a platoon of the newly formed Woman Marines in parades at Cherry Point, it had seemed to Noah the irony of a fate that had always been his to have drawn the only unglamorous duty. He was wearing a Navy lieutenant's uniform, all right, but he was commuting to a desk job in New York like any advertising man or broker.

But then he would have to remember that, living right there in the house with Louise, he had had a perfectly good chance to learn all these things about her and her idiosyncrasies that he had never suspected before. Perhaps, instead of writing them off as feminine temperament, instead of being merely disturbed by them, he should have thought harder about them, tried harder to figure out what they meant.

The days when she never did get out of bed at all; the long silences that he was always careful to respect, believing that she was longing for Barrett, or at least worrying about him; the sudden moods of frantic gaiety and the other sudden moods of affection, when she would throw

[54]

her arms around her mother-in-law and tell her that she was really sweet; the evenings when, in the midst of family conversation, she would jump up and run out of the door and walk downtown to sit through a double bill at the movies—all this he found disturbing, but it wasn't until long afterward that it occurred to him that he might have found in it a warning of trouble ahead for Barrett and for the family. And it wasn't until long afterward that he remembered that he had had a warning, from Winifred, and it was only then that it occurred to him that he might have taken that warning as something more than an unreasonable whim.

When, later, Louise began at unpredictable times to come down to tea in costume, he did, to be sure, begin to worry about the possibility that she might be going out of her mind. But his worrying hardly went beyond the thought of a possible sojourn in a sanitarium, a sojourn which, like Winifred's, would have been unfortunate but scarcely a tragedy. What he did think about it at the time was that she was becoming unbalanced in her mind grieving for the absent Barrett—or, to put it in the more modern way, frustrated in a sex life that he had always thought must have been an ideally happy one; she had always been so radiant.

The first time she appeared in costume she came down in a trailing white evening gown, neither smiling nor blushing, saying nothing whatever about what she was wearing, acting exactly as she always acted at tea. The second time, a few weeks later, she appeared in a Mother Hubbard, with her curls peeking out from under a sunbonnet. The third time it was a bodiced, hoop-skirted dress, and this time she did comment about it. "Isn't it lovely?" she asked. "It belonged to my great-grandmother and she was a sea captain's wife and she lived in Salem and sometimes he was gone for two whole years."

"It is very lovely, dear," Noah's mother said. "A reminder of by-gone days. Those faithful wives—how dreary their lives must have been!" She looked at the dress again. "But it is small for you, isn't it, dear?"

"A little," Louise said, smiling.

Noah looked to see what his mother was talking about and saw that the tight-fitting bodice revealed the contours of Louise's breasts in startling completeness. He looked away again quickly.

In an embarrassed silence, they all attended to the business of the tea and the lemon and the sugar. Dr. Sibley took his cup to the chair by the window and sat pointedly looking out at the street. Noah found it very hard to keep his eyes from wandering back to the bodice.

[55]

Finally Mrs. Sibley said, "Louise, it is a very lovely dress, but on you it is quite immodest. Would you mind very much going up and getting into something else?"

Louise did not speak. She put her cup down and walked across the room to the hall door, her face a deep crimson. She went on upstairs, and she did not come down again until dinnertime. When she did come, she was wearing a drab gray dress, very loose above the waist and very unbecoming to her.

5.

EVEN if you couldn't have expected him to understand all the intricacies of Louise's psychology, shouldn't he have been smart enough to have seen the full meaning behind the things Warner had said that night on the train, the things that had seemed so casual at the time and so significant in the light of what took place later? Mightn't he then have managed to forestall the whole thing? With hindsight, it all seemed so unmistakably clear.

They were on their way back to the city after the first weekend Warner had spent with Noah out at the Sibleys' in Middlefield. It was a rainy night in January. They had caught the nine o'clock, on their way in to sleep in Warner's apartment in Brooklyn.

"What's your brother like?" Warner had asked abruptly.

"Barrett?"

"Whichever one is that girl's husband." A flicker of his eyes and around the corners of his mouth hinted, as he glanced at Noah, that he was amused. Like his body, his face was lean and muscular, with prominent cheekbones that were hard round knobs above his hollow cheeks. He had the knack, Noah had discovered, of appearing to be the epitome of whatever part he was dressed for. Tonight, in his officer's overcoat and cap, he was the epitome of the naval officer on a winter's night.

"That's Barrett," Noah said. "He's quite a guy."

"He'd better be."

Noah looked at him out of the corner of his eyes. "Better be?"

Warner turned and smiled at him, frankly and ingenuously. "If he wants to keep a girl like that. That girl's got it."

"Got what?"

"Everything." Louise had been in one of her unpredictable moods

[56]

that weekend, gay one moment, affectionate the next, thoughtful the next. And that morning, from the time Noah's father and mother had gone to church until dinnertime, she had played records for Noah and Warner up in her room. She and Warner had liked the same music.

"Imagination," Warner said. "Spirit. And a whole lot of that something-or-other that makes a woman different from a man."

Noah looked at him quickly, then sat staring glumly at his knees, making no effort to hide the fact that he was annoyed. Louise was Barrett's wife, and very much in love with Barrett. It was bad taste, to put it mildly, for Warner to speak of her as he had.

"Where did he ever find her, anyway?" Warner asked.

"Up at that lake in Vermont we go to summers," Noah said surlily. And after a moment he added, trying to change the subject, "I've told you about the Lake, haven't I?"

"Yes," Warner said dryly, "you've told me about the Lake."

Noah realized that he had probably told Warner a great deal about the Lake. He knew he shouldn't keep talking about it, but he was thinking about Barrett and Louise. "It's quite a place for romances," he said. "Canoes, moonlight—"

"It must be," Warner said. "Where did she come from?"

"Louise?"

"Yeah, that girl."

"She comes from outside of Boston. Her father was pastor of one of the largest Congregational churches in New England."

"Minister's daughter, eh?" He grinned sideways at Noah. Then he chuckled. "Minister's daughter," he repeated.

In spite of all that had happened later, in spite of some things he had never liked about him, Noah could never quite forget that, during those months when they had seen so much of each other, he had been very fond of Warner Boiland—and very grateful to him. Warner had taught him a great deal about a great many things. He had given him some of the sophistication that a life divided between Middlefield and the Lake and schools had failed to give him. For that Noah was still grateful to Warner.

It was undoubtedly true that the things he had gotten from the men in that Navy office—and from Warner far more than any other —had completed for him another cycle in the spiral of his increasing awareness. Whenever people told him, as Natalie had told him, that he had gained tremendously in self-assurance, he knew that he could thank Warner Boiland as much as anyone else he had known in the intervening years.

[57]

But he always remembered too that some of the things Warner said had seemed to him to be in thoroughly bad taste. He had been disgruntled with him that night on that stuffy train, when Warner had seemed to find some peculiarly humorous significance in the fact that Louise was a minister's daughter. He sat staring at the cushioned back of the seat ahead.

"Weren't there any other men around that lake beside you and your brother?" Again his tone told Noah that he was amused.

"Plenty of them," Noah said sulkily. And then, smiling a little, "And plenty who'd have liked to marry Louise, too."

"I can imagine," Warner said. "But your brother got the inside track, eh?"

Noah, proud of all that Barrett had been and was, nodded, smiling quickly to himself, sure in his knowledge of Barrett's all-around excellence.

Warner was persistent. "What did he have that she liked? Good looks?"

"Yes, along with a lot of other things: honor student at Princeton, officer of his class, Senior Council—"

"What'd he look like?"

Noah tried to bring back the picture of Barrett in those days. "About as tall as I am, only slender and dark. Kind of wavy brown hair." He grinned. "He looked like a million in his track suit. The girls went for that."

"On the track team, eh?"

"Yeah, he was quite a hurdler. One of the best they ever had at Princeton."

Warner screwed up his face, as though to remember. "Sibley," he said. "Oh, sure. Won the Eastern Intercollegiates two years in a row. High hurdles. Right?"

"That's right."

"So he was your brother. What do you know about that? Wasn't he the swimmer too?"

Noah turned and looked at him, shaking his head. "You know something about everything, don't you?" He was still trying to find a subject that Warner didn't know about. At their desks, side by side in the little cubicle in the offices on Pine Street, they talked about everything under the sun: about places they had been—and Warner seemed to have been everywhere in the world—and about politics and history—and Warner knew far more about history than most laymen—and about women and philosophy and summer vacations. And

[58]

Warner talked about cruising, about how he had been cruising out of the East River ever since he was five years old, about how he probably knew as much about the water approaches to New York City as anybody in the world, about how stupid somebody in Bupers down in Washington had been to stick him on this desk job when they had punks from Kansas who'd never seen a mud puddle before the war out there on patrol. And most of all he talked about his power cruiser, which he had had built to his own design a few years before. Noah wished that Warner would ask him sometime if he had ever told him about his cruiser, so that he could say dryly, "Yes, you've told me about your cruiser."

"I never knew," Noah said, a little enviously, "that you knew that much about intercollegiate sports."

Warner smiled at him warmly. "I was at Yale along about that time," and that was something else that Noah had never known.

And, reverting to Warner's question about Barrett's being a swimmer, Noah said, "Barrett was on the swimming team. So was I. We all three swam against your damned invincible Yale teams. But it's probably my other brother, Mark, that you're thinking of. He managed to take two firsts in the Yale meet his senior year."

Warner nodded. "I remember," he said.

"He ran the four-forty too," Noah said.

Warner turned and smiled at him affectionately. "Quite a family you've got, eh? How'd they ever let you into it?"

Noah laughed, his annoyance with Warner already half forgotten. "I've wondered about that sometimes."

Warner took off his cap and ran his hand over his black crew-cut hair. "What does Barrett do?" There was a difference in his tone now, no longer any cynical hint of an interest in Louise. He was merely asking about Noah's brother, and Noah was liking him again.

"He's in Army Air Intelligence. Lieutenant colonel. Last we heard he was in North Africa."

"What does he do when there isn't a war?"

"He's a lawyer. Junior partner in Middleton, Laird, and Budlong."

As Noah might have expected, Warner knew about Middleton, Laird, and Budlong. He looked impressed. "A junior partner already? He can't have been out of law school very long."

"He made it after four years," Noah said proudly.

"He's going ahead fast," Warner said. "He's got just about everything a guy could want, hasn't he?"

There it was, plenty of it, as clear in retrospect as the "Next Boat" sign in the Jersey City station: Barrett had better be quite a guy if he wants to keep a girl like that; a whole lot of that something-or-other that makes a woman different from a man; he's got just about *everything* a guy could want, hasn't he?

If he had put it all together, and added to it the Sibley belief that a girl was always helpless if a man wanted to steal her from her husband, he might, he supposed, have kept Warner away from Louise after that first visit. But the possibility simply hadn't occurred to him, and if it had, the thought that any girl could leave the incomparable Barrett for a man like Warner would have seemed patently ridiculous, so ridiculous that he still would have thought of it as no possibility at all.

6·

The second time Noah took Warner out to the house, on a Saturday night in late February, it was beginning to snow when they got off the train. Noah suggested a taxi, but Warner said he'd like to walk. It was eight blocks out and three over, and Noah chose to take him out Elm Avenue, past the repair garages and the big old-fashioned houses that were now doctors' and dentists' offices and hairdressers' establishments and boardinghouses.

With big feathery snowflakes settling on their shoulders and flicking their eyelashes, they walked along together, their small canvas bags in their left hands, grinning at each other and at the world that was gradually turning white around them. Noah felt strangely delighted with the world and with Warner, exhilarated by the camaraderie of this small shared experience. Warner had been remarkably pleasant these last few weeks, and the occasional annoyances that Noah had previously felt with him and his manners were almost forgotten.

They passed the old brownstone church and beyond it came to the one-block section of small, old-fashioned stores: the tobacco store where the Sibleys bought their Sunday *Times*, the unimposing little butcher shop where the wealthy people from the residential sections west of Elm Avenue still bought their meat, the dry cleaner's, the florist's.

At the florist's, Warner insisted on stopping and buying a bouquet of snapdragons for Mrs. Sibley and a dozen rosebuds for Louise.

They went on, and now they were getting into the new apartment house section of Elm Avenue, where only an occasional window failed to glow with orange or yellow or pink light. The hedges and the little lawns in front of the apartments were already white, and now the snow was beginning to gather on the wet sidewalks.

They turned onto West Avenue, shuffling cautiously on the slippery pavements, and Noah looked up and saw that there was a light in the window of the apartment that had once been Barrett's and Louise's. Now they were coming into the old residential section, where the massive, turreted mansions, each with its own labored originality of stained glass and porte-cocheres and second- and third-floor balconies, stood like dark and formidable barricades against the weather and the eyes of passers-by.

And on the corner of West and Concord, Noah pointed to the largest of them all, a huge mass of red brick and brown timber and mullioned windows. "That's where my Grandfather Barrett used to live," he said, grinning shamefacedly.

Warner looked at it, and back at Noah from the corner of his eye, and back at the house again. "Quite a cabin," he said. "What did he make it in?"

"Railroads and warehouses and New York City real estate."

Warner smiled at him. "Those things add up, don't they?"

Noah shrugged his shoulders. "You ought to know," he said, "about the New York City real estate, anyway."

Warner laughed. "It's nice," he said.

Warner came from Brooklyn, and gradually, from casual references, Noah had been learning that he owned property in just about every part of the borough: an apartment house here, a store building there, an office building somewhere else. These buildings, Noah gathered, were the main source of his income, and he was getting the impression that it was a large income. But Warner never talked about money.

Because he was with Warner, seeing things through his eyes and mind, and because the thick snowfall gave everything a fresh and unexpected look, Noah saw the avenues, the houses, the elms and the maples, as he had not seen them before in years. And when they walked along the side of the Sibley house, on the corner of West and Lexington, he saw that it was as massive, as ridiculous, as buttressed and turreted, as *fin de siècle*, and as safe and solid and inviting and comfortable looking as all the others they had been passing. The lights were on in the dining room and living room, casting a dim glow out

[61]

onto the snow-covered yews and junipers under the windows. Lights were on upstairs too, in his room and the guest room.

Noah wondered if he had ever before looked at the house in a snowstorm when it was lighted as it was tonight. He had certainly never seen it as he was seeing it now, never realized how much it spoke of old-fashioned elegance and a kind of comfort that had nothing to do with overstuffed lounging furniture but had to do instead with candlelit dinner tables and small fires in white tile fireplaces and demitasses and butlers—the Sibleys had never had a butler, but his Grandfather Barrett had.

And seeing it through Warner's eyes, he supposed it spoke too of smugness and stolidity and safe bonds and at least a few generations of comfortably entrenched wealth. He suspected that if he thought about it, he would probably have to disapprove of it, but it was home and tonight it looked wonderfully inviting.

7.

Louise met them at the door, looking lively and excited and very girlish in a pale, gray-blue dinner gown with short puffed sleeves. "Quick," she said, "get upstairs and get cleaned up and get down again if you want a drink before dinner. The dinner hour is seven-thirty, and God wrote that on a tablet. Here, I'll take your coats and caps out into the back hall."

Warner grinned at her and handed her the small box of roses. "Here's something for the musical end of that nice room of yours," he said, and, like a pair of schoolboys home on vacation, they ran up the stairs two at a time.

Louise, who, along with Father and Mother Sibley, usually took sherry when other people were having cocktails, let Noah make her an old fashioned tonight. She stood smiling at the two of them, holding her cocktail in both hands as though she were afraid it might jump out of her grasp. Mr. and Mrs. Sibley had not come down yet. "I suppose you think you left here on the 6:56 this morning, Noah," she said gaily. She raised her glass up in front of her face and studied it whimsically and Noah knew that she was looking to make sure that he had given her a cherry. "Well, you didn't. You've been gone for weeks and weeks, and now you've come home at last and brought with you your friend Lieutenant Boiland and this is the big homecoming and we're having a fatted calf—we really are, too," she said. "It's a veal roast. *My* coupons did it, too. If it hadn't been for my coupons, we'd have had to have one of those meat loafs made out of nuts."

She stopped smiling and looked with determination first at Noah, then at Warner. "We'll make this a big weekend," she said, as though she expected someone to contradict her. She held up her glass. "We'll have our own private little toast before they come. Father will have another toast—he always does—but we'll have another cocktail for that one. This one will be to your homecoming," and her smile included Warner in the homecoming.

Noah smiled at her, thinking of Barrett. "To all homecomings," he said.

And she smiled back into his eyes and said, "To all homecomings."

They downed their drinks quickly, and Noah had the second ones ready before Mrs. Sibley came down. She too was dressed as for a gala occasion, in a brown silk dress with long loose sleeves, and she beamed at Warner and kissed Noah fondly on the cheek and smiled at Louise. And as though performing an obvious and necessary duty before she went on to other things, she wondered where were the snows of yesteryear. "Father will be a little late," she said. "He worked overtime on his speech. He's speaking tomorrow afternoon to the United Church Group. I'm sorry he won't be here for our cozy little Sunday afternoon teatime."

"What's his subject?" Noah asked conversationally.

"I think he's calling it 'How Have the Mighty Fallen!' Louise, dear, will you pour me some sherry? Oh, you're having a cocktail!" She sat down on the couch.

Louise poured a glass of sherry for her and took it to her and looked at her questioningly. "Do you mind? Just for once? To celebrate the homecoming?"

"Of course not, my dear." She looked up at Louise with the amused expression of a person confronted with a child's whimsy. "Is there a homecoming?"

Louise no longer seemed happy with her quaint thought. She laughed shamefacedly. "It just seems like a homecoming," she said lamely.

And with her customary tact, Mrs. Sibley said, "It really does, doesn't it? I put on my party dress too."

Dr. Sibley came down wearing his mulberry smoking jacket with its silk facings and a soft white shirt and a mulberry bow tie. Noah was proud of the way he looked. He watched Warner's face. Dr. Sibley shook Warner's hand and said, "Welcome, sailor." And, turning to Noah, he said, "Home is the sailor, home from sea—after having been gone for almost twelve hours." He patted Noah on the shoulder. "Never you mind, my boy! You're serving just as much as the rest of them are." He took the glass of sherry that Louise held out to him and said, "Thank you, fair handmaiden."

Then, noticing that all their glasses were full, he said, "Oh, my goodness, you shouldn't have waited for me."

Neither Noah nor Louise bothered to mention that they had already had one cocktail, and Warner grinned delightedly.

"I'm sorry I'm late," Dr. Sibley said. "But duty called, and I had to say, 'I come.' I'm giving them a few little thoughts at the United Church Group tomorrow afternoon. I'm calling it 'How Have the Mighty Fallen!' and I'm using France as my example. A few thoughts on the spiritual decay that led to her present plight. France has been very much in my thoughts today—how your mother and I loved France, Noah! And so, for our toast tonight, I'm going to suggest, 'France, may she soon be freed, and may she then begin to regain her former spiritual greatness.'"

They all drank solemnly to France and her spiritual greatness, and Dr. Sibley asked, "Have you ever been to France, Lieutenant Boiland?"

Warner nodded and said, "Yes, I lived there for—"

"Perhaps then you know the little village of Dinard in Brittany?"

Warner smiled.

"Dinard has a very special place in our hearts, doesn't it, dear? On our wedding trip, in 1910, we were walking through Brittany. 'Afoot and light-hearted we took to the open road.' No idea where we were going. A little food and a few articles of clothing in our knapsacks. A little money in our pockets."

Louise settled into the corner, at the other end of the couch from Mrs. Sibley. She still held her cocktail in both hands. She sat very still; only her eyes, Noah noticed, were restless as his father told about the little restaurant in Dinard where they had had chicken that tasted as no chicken had ever tasted before or since.

All through the cocktail hour and the dinner and the evening, Warner listened courteously and attentively. Noah was sure that no one but he himself, who was getting to know Warner very well indeed by this time, suspected that that look in his eyes and around the corners of his mouth meant that he was amused. It annoyed him a little to know that Warner should be amused, but so long as Warner was being so very courteous, so long as Noah's father was obviously enjoying his company, so long as he was obviously thinking so highly of Warner's intelligence, the fact that Warner was a little amused did not cut very deeply into Noah's family pride.

He was far more upset over Louise. Already worried for several weeks now over her mental condition, he became more and more convinced, as the evening went along, that there was real cause for worry. From the time that Dr. Sibley had appeared, she had not spoken a single word. During the last part of the cocktail hour and the first two courses of dinner, her face had flushed to a very unnatural crimson and her eyes had been set in an unnatural stare. Two old fashioneds, of course, were far more than she was used to, and Noah told himself that it had been very foolish of Louise to have drunk so much.

But during dessert the flush had left her face and her eyes had ceased to stare. Instead, she had become very haughty, very regal, turning her head from side to side like a queen reviewing her guard, but the turnings had had no relation to the conversation. It was apparent to Noah that she was paying no attention whatsoever to what was being said. And after dinner she had settled into the corner of the couch again and sat without moving a finger for at least two hours. Sometimes, when he looked at her, her face would be composed, completely expressionless. A little later, her eyes would be moving wildly, as though she were trapped in the room and looking for a way to escape. Then she would be looking at Warner with an expression of worried curiosity, as though he were some strange animal she had never seen before; then, a moment later, sideways at her father-in-law or mother-in-law, her face expressionless again.

Noah decided that he had better speak to his father about her. It might be possible to find some excuse to have Dr. Cullen come and see her. Perhaps a week or two in the South, Charleston or Pinehurst or Florida, during these gloomy late-winter days would be all she would need, although Noah understood that it was impossible to get reservations on trains for weeks ahead. He wished mightily that Barrett would come home for a leave—or, better yet, come home for good, but he wished it only because he was worried about Louise's sanity.

[65]

8

AT ten-thirty, Mrs. Sibley got up and emptied all the ashtrays and put the screen in front of the fire, her preliminary signals that the hour for retiring was approaching.

Dr. Sibley was talking to Warner. "And I suppose, Lieutenant, that, like all the rest of us, you followed the conference at Munich with interest."

Warner nodded, smiling modestly. "I was there," he said.

Dr. Sibley looked startled. "You—what?"

"I was there," Warner said. "I was in Munich in September of '38."

Dr. Sibley stared at him. "What were you doing there?"

"Just poking around," Warner said, "asking questions and seeing what was going on. I did send a few little articles back to some papers and magazines here, but they didn't amount to anything. The press credentials were handy, though. Got me into a few places I couldn't have gotten into without them."

Noah knew enough about his father's work to realize what this was going to mean to him. He was as excited as Dr. Sibley was.

"Actually there!" Dr. Sibley said. "On the scene!" He was so agitated that he jumped to his feet and walked over to the fireplace and back again. "And you saw some of the proceedings?"

Warner laughed. "Well, they didn't let me into any of the secret conferences. Most of the time we just hung around and listened to rumors and picked up odd pieces of information. Nobody really knew what was going on except the three big boys and maybe some of their secretaries. But we saw them all, once in a while, and I was in on a few interviews."

"With the principals?"

"Chamberlain and Daladier."

"Good heavens." Again he strode over to the fireplace and back again. "Lieutenant, you have no idea what this means to me."

Noah knew very well what it meant to him. It meant a chance to strengthen the weakest point in his great *History of World Arbitration*, the one important conference since 1910 concerning which he had no on-the-scene, first-hand information. Every scrap of memory that Warner could recall would make the difference to him between on-the-scene coverage and second-hand research.

Mrs. Sibley stood up, and Dr. Sibley glanced at her and looked at his watch. "You're quite right, my dear," he said. "It's time to go to bed." He turned to Warner. "Lieutenant, would it make a very dull morning for you tomorrow if we were to closet ourselves, *tête-à-tête*, in my study and you were to tell me everything, absolutely everything, that you remember about that conference?"

Warner looked at Noah quizzically. Noah realized that it probably *would* be a dull morning for him—but he realized too how much it would mean to his father. He didn't know what to say. He looked at Warner and shrugged his shoulders.

His father was talking again, to his mother. "Since I am laboring in the Vineyard of the Lord tomorrow afternoon, my dear," he was saying, "I believe that Mr. James can shepherd his flock through the morning service without me, don't you?" He turned back to Warner. "Would you find it too hopelessly dull, Lieutenant?"

And with very good grace, Warner said, "I don't know how much help I can be to you, Doctor, but I'll be glad to try."

"I can't tell you how much I'll appreciate it."

And Louise, who had been sitting so silent and still for two hours, made a strange little noise, halfway between a sob and an exclamation of disgust, and without saying a word to anyone, without looking to right or left, she jumped to her feet and ran out into the hall and up the stairs. And a moment later the door of her room closed with a bang.

After Warner was in his room, Noah stopped his father in the hall. "Dad," he said, "I'm worried about Louise."

"We all are, Noah. Far more worried than you realize. But we must all have patience. We must all remember that distance makes the heart grow fonder, and that these days, with Barrett gone, are difficult days for her. Your mother and I are trying our level best to be as helpful and understanding as we possibly can."

9.

THE hour for the famous Sibley Sunday breakfast, with Arlene's omelets and waffles, was eight-thirty.

At eight-thirty they were all gathered in the living room except Louise. At 8:35 Mrs. Sibley went back upstairs and knocked at her door. She came back down. "She doesn't answer my knock," she said, "and her door is locked. I'm afraid," she added tragically, "that it's going to be another one of her days. The only thing we can do, I suppose, is to leave her alone and let her work herself out of it."

It had stopped snowing sometime in the night, and while they were eating breakfast the sun came out. The snow lay heavy on the world outside the windows, blanketing the evergreens, block-printing every branch and twig of the bare-branched trees in gleaming white. "Fairyland," Mrs. Sibley said, "positively fairyland."

After breakfast Dr. Sibley and Warner went into Dr. Sibley's office and closed the door. Mrs. Sibley stood at the window, exclaiming over the beauties of the day. "This is a day to walk to church, Noah. Who could think of driving on a day like this? Would'st walk to the kirk with me?"

Noah hesitated. "It would be a nice day to walk, all right, but if you don't mind, I—I guess I'll just stick around. Got a few things I want to do."

She set off for church at ten-thirty, and Noah had not a thing in the world he wanted to do. He went upstairs and looked at Louise's door. He could see that it was still locked, and she had pushed a rug or newspaper or something against the bottom of the door. Muffled and soft, he heard the sound of her phonograph playing a piano concerto.

He stood looking at the door uncertainly, then finally knocked gently. The music went on, but he heard no other sound from inside the room. He knocked again and waited, and then he called softly, "Louise, it's Noah."

Still no sounds but the music came from inside, and after a while he went back downstairs. He put on his overcoat and cap and gloves and went out the door. He started out Lexington Avenue. None of the sidewalks had been shoveled yet, and he walked carefully, with short steps, occasionally slipping a little on the glazed snow. It was cold, and after he had gone a few blocks the sun went behind a cloud.

It was still beautiful though, still a fairyland, and he went all the way out to the end of the street and on along the rutted lane that was an extension of Lexington Avenue. There were open fields on both sides, and he liked the spacious, clean feel of the countryside. But he had stepped into deep snow a few times, and now the snow was melting inside his shoes and his feet were wet and cold. He turned and went back to the house.

Before dinner, when Warner and Dr. Sibley came out of the study, Dr. Sibley was still looking happy and excited. He glanced across the room at Noah with a meaningful look and shook his head delightedly.

Noah grinned at him. "Pay dirt?" he asked.

His father grinned back. "The Comstock Lode."

"Good." Noah was very pleased, happy that he could have, even unwittingly, contributed something to his father's work. Warner was still looking amused.

Noah looked at him gratefully. "Did he pluck your brains out, Warner?"

Warner glanced at Dr. Sibley, and there was a real respect in the way he looked at him. "He swings a mean pick," he said. "Dug out stuff I didn't know was there. He knows what he's looking for, and he knows how to get it out of you. It's not the first time he's done this sort of thing, is it, Doctor?"

"Not quite the first," the doctor said modestly.

When dinner was ready, Noah's mother went up and knocked on Louise's door again. Still she got no answer.

10 ·

No incident in Noah's whole life had impressed him more deeply than the odd little performance that took place at teatime that afternoon. Nothing he had ever seen caused him to wonder so much. Nothing had made him realize how little he had learned about life— and about women and how they felt and acted. Nothing had caused him more confusion. And no picture was more vivid in his memory than the picture of Louise on the stairs.

His father had gone off to make his speech. His mother had not knocked again on Louise's door when teatime arrived, but she *had* left the wide sliding doors from the living room into the hall open. The doors were never closed until the last person arrived for tea.

She sat, as always, on the couch, with her tea table in front of her. The couch backed against the wall between the two rooms, so that she looked toward the fireplace and the triple-windowed bay at the opposite corner of the room and away from the hall.

A small fire of birch logs was burning briskly in the fireplace. It had begun to snow again outside, a fine wind-driven snow that made the fire and the room seem peculiarly comfortable and cozy.

Because it was snowing and because Warner was there, Noah and Warner were having Scotch and soda instead of tea—an innovation which he and Mark had instituted for special occasions several years before, one which his mother accepted with smiling, sad-eyed grace. He was sitting in the brown chair between the bay and the long front window. From there, by a mere shift of his eyes, he could see through the open double doors and across the hall almost the full length of the stairs.

Louise had not appeared at five after four, but still Mrs. Sibley did not ask Noah to close the doors. She poured her own tea and rather ostentatiously set Louise's empty cup at the corner of the tea table.

"I hope very much, Lieutenant Boiland," she said affably, "that you'll have a chance to meet the rest of our family someday. Barrett and Mark and Kate and Connie—especially Barrett. I'm sure you and he would find you had a great deal in common."

"I'm sure of it," Warner said dryly, and suddenly—and for the first time—Noah sensed that Warner did not like his mother. A quick anger rose inside him. He wanted to argue the point with Warner, to explain to him what an essentially kind and thoughtful and—and remarkable woman she really was.

Warner looked at him noncommittally, then smiled, as though at a secret joke of his own. He took a swallow of his drink and said, politely but still smiling, "Your family is a very unusual one, isn't it, Mrs. Sibley?" He was sitting in the gold-brocaded chair beside the fireplace. From it he could see into the hall too, but of the stairs only the lower landing and the two steps that came down from it to the floor.

A few minutes later, after Noah had given up all thought that Louise might come down, something made him look up at the stairway. And there, beside the stained-glass window that was yellow and mulberry and green but mostly yellow, admitting a pale but glowing yellow light, stood Louise in shiny black and red Chinese pajamas. She was not moving, just standing there looking at the window. She stood still there for a long time, and Noah sipped his drink and watched her, doing nothing to show that he knew she was there.

Slowly she raised her hand to her mouth, and he saw that her fingernails were stained a violent crimson. She opened her mouth wide and put the back of her hand in front of it, in a gesture that was almost like the gesture a girl might make to keep herself from screaming. But Noah knew that she was not keeping herself from screaming. It wasn't exactly like that. It, and her expression, were more as though she were looking at a horribly shocking sight, but she was looking only at the window, and she could see nothing through it. If she was seeing something shocking, she was seeing it only with her mind's eye.

The thought crossed his mind, stronger than ever, that something would have to be done about Louise's mental condition. Yet somehow he couldn't quite feel that it was really insanity, or at least that it was any ordinary kind of insanity. It was something a little like it. And somewhere deep inside him, in some inexplicable way, he felt a bond of sympathy with her.

And because of this sudden, unexpected feeling of understanding and compassion that he had for her, he looked at her again, with fresh eyes, and what he saw was a picture as exquisite as any Chinese painting: the slender girlish figure that seemed at the moment to have been made to wear pajamas, the birdlike pose, the jet black and the shiny red, so startling and yet somehow so right, the dainty hand in the odd pose that was both graceful and charmingly awkward, like a Chinese painting. And topping it all the incongruous childish mop of yellow curls.

He gave no sign that he had seen her. He sat, watching and at the same time smiling at his mother, nodding to what she was saying. He told himself afterward that he had given no sign because he had been hoping that she would go back upstairs and change into a dress before she came down, but he knew that in some other part of his mind he had been hoping that she wouldn't. He had wanted her to come on down and walk into the room in the black and red pajamas. Why, he didn't know.

She finally came, stealthily, watching each foot before she placed it daintily on the step below. She had on black sandals, and her toenails were the same violent crimson as her fingernails. And when she reached the landing and turned, so that she was now facing the room, she still did not look up. She stopped again, her head down, her hands clasped in front of her, in the traditional pose of a slave girl before her master. At no time had Noah seen her look up, and he still didn't know, to this day, whether she had known that Warner was sitting where he was, directly in front of her across the room.

With a self-possession that amazed and pleased him, Noah still gave no sign that he had seen her. He did glance at Warner, and Warner, looking lean and hard and, as he always did, very much the picture of the competent naval officer in his trim blues, was looking at her, steadily, unsmilingly, almost, it seemed to Noah, thoughtfully. Like Noah, he was giving no hint to Mrs. Sibley that she was there, but his eyes were not moving from the figure on the stairs.

[71]

Then suddenly, lightly, Louise came down the last two steps and across the hall and into the middle of the room. "I'm sorry I'm late, Mother," she said, blushing a little but otherwise quite poised.

Mrs. Sibley looked up at her. For the bare fraction of a moment her eyes seemed to open a little wider, her mouth to take on a slightly different set, and then, trained to her duties as no Navy Reservist was ever trained to his, she smiled. "My dear," she said, "what a striking costume!"

Louise turned and stood facing her across the tea table, her back to the two men, while Mrs. Sibley poured her tea. "I'm glad you like it, Mother."

And Mrs. Sibley, still smiling sweetly, handed her the cup and said, "I didn't say that."

Noah could not see Louise's face, but her voice was amiable and undisturbed. "No, of course you didn't." She turned around, holding her saucer with both hands, and took a couple of steps toward the straight chair in the corner opposite the fireplace. Then abruptly she turned and looked, almost sternly, down into Warner's face. "Do *you* like it, Lieutenant Boiland?"

Warner grinned up at her and nodded. Noah saw the hint of a smile, a triumphant sort of smile, on her face as she walked on over to the straight chair and sat down, with her ankles daintily crossed.

Perhaps Mrs. Sibley had not seen Warner's nod. "I'm afraid, Louise," she said, "that your question puts Lieutenant Boiland in an awkward position."

Louise's eyes seemed to Noah unnaturally bright and the color in her cheeks unnaturally high. She glanced at Mrs. Sibley's face, then at Warner's with raised eyebrows. Warner was still grinning at her.

"Before you came in," Mrs. Sibley said, "we were talking about what a wonderful leader Mr. Churchill is turning out to be."

And as Louise sipped her tea, stealing surreptitious glances at Warner and Noah, making no pretense of listening to Mrs. Sibley, Mrs. Sibley went on talking about what a wonderful leader Mr. Churchill was turning out to be.

To Noah it was all acutely embarrassing. He was happy when the tea was over and Louise went back up to her room. She came down to supper, dressed sensibly enough now, to be sure, but still acting, to his mind, very strangely. What Warner could be thinking he couldn't imagine. It was with a tremendous sense of relief that, at nine-thirty, he kissed his mother goodbye and, with Warner, started out for the station.

I⊤ was odd that Connie, of all people, should have been the one who was there at the final episode, although she had no idea that it was going on.

It was a month and a half later, sometime in early April, when she called Noah at the Naval Offices.

"Where are you?" he asked.

"I'm right here in New York." There was always a humorous overtone in Connie's voice, as though she found everything she was saying mildly and secretly amusing.

"Where?"

"At Hunter College, of all places."

"How long are you going to be there?"

"Three weeks."

"Three weeks! Will you be living at home?"

"No, I have to live here. Detached duty."

"Well!" Noah snorted in amazement. "What are you going to do? Teach Waves how to drill?"

"No, I don't do very much drilling, actually. Just Saturday mornings—at Cherry Point, I mean. I won't be doing any drilling here. I'll be learning about photo interpretation."

"What's that for?"

"So I can interpret photos, ninny."

"Well!" Noah exclaimed again, smiling at the phone, happy to be talking to Connie. She was the one he never had to try to put on an act with. "Won't we be seeing you at all?"

"Maybe I can get out weekends. I don't know yet. But I can get off evenings. How about taking me out on the town? Everybody writes me that you're turning into a terrific night-club habitué."

Noah grinned into the phone. "Sure," he said. "When?"

"Tonight?"

Noah thought a moment. "Why not?" he said. "What time?"

"Six-thirtyish."

"Where do you want to meet me? Under the clock at the Biltmore?"

Connie laughed softly. "Once a Princeton man always a Princeton man. That would be all right."

"Fine. I'll see you there."

She waited. Finally she said, "Ah—I could bring another girl. Very nice too. Graduate of the University of Wisconsin. How about bringing your friend Lieutenant Boiland along? Everybody, from Dad down, writes that he's quite a something. I want to meet him."

"Sorry," Noah said. "He's in Washington."

"Oh." She waited again. "For good?"

"No, for forty-eight hours. The Commander gave him a forty-eight and permission to go down and see if he could pull some wires to get a transfer."

"Transfer?"

"Sea duty. Patrol duty. He's an authority on the water approaches to New York City."

"I thought he was an authority on Munich."

"He's an authority on everything. Never saw such a guy for knowing things."

"I want to meet him."

"We'll arrange it sometime."

"But not tonight," she said, accepting the inevitable. "Okay, I'll leave Wisconsin home. And you can squire me about."

"Right," he said. "Six-thirty at the Biltmore."

He hung up and felt in his pocket to see if he had the key to Warner's apartment. He did. He wouldn't have to take a late train back out. He called the house and told his mother the news. He would see her and tell her all about Connie tomorrow night. Louise, she told him, had left at three o'clock, to visit a friend in Greenwich for a few days.

Connie was late getting to the Biltmore, and when she finally came in the Forty-third Street entrance, he watched her coming up the steps and thought that her Marine greens did a little more for her figure than the clothes she usually wore did. Sometimes he wondered if he was the only man in the world who had ever noticed that Connie really had a very decent little figure. Not the kind they took pictures of for pin-ups, but a nice, slim, subtly feminine figure, neither tall nor short, with narrowish hips that swayed only a little bit when she walked and only slightly high shoulders and small but by no means nonexistent breasts.

The area under the clock was crowded, and as she got to the top of the steps, a group of officers and girls, all talking and laughing at once, moved into her way. She had seen Noah, and she wiggled a couple of fingers at him, very unobtrusively, and stood waiting, smiling just a little, making no effort to push her way through. None of them noticed that she was there.

It was so typical of her that Noah laughed, shaking his head. The thing was, he thought, that Connie just didn't like to be noticed. It was a funny psychological quirk—especially for a Sibley. The Sibleys, even including Noah, he admitted to himself, didn't like to go unnoticed. Connie did. That, he had always half known, was why she chose the kind of clothes she did, and why she did her hair the way she did, and why she always wore that mousy, secretive, amused expression on her face.

At last a small gap opened, and Connie stepped neatly and unnoticed through it. She kissed him briefly but firmly and enthusiastically on the lips. Then she stood back and studied his face. "You look wonderful," she said. But still there was the amused tone in her voice and the secretive smile on her lips. It always gave him the impression that she was thinking a lot of extra things that she wasn't saying. "The Navy's doing you good. But I wish you didn't have to live at home."

She sat down and patted the seat beside her, and Noah sat on it and said, "I *don't* have to. I like to, and it saves money."

"Well," she said. "You look wonderful and I'm glad to see you. I'm glad to see you without all the rest of them. It's more fun this way."

"Why?"

"Don't you know, ninny? You're the only one I give a damn about. The rest of them get me down."

Noah did know. People often said that Connie didn't seem to belong in the family at all. She didn't look like any of the rest of them, and she didn't seem to have the same way of thinking about things. Maybe it came from being the last one to come along, three years after Kate. Noah sometimes felt that he didn't quite belong in the family either, but at least he did have the same coloring as Kate, and people were always telling him that they saw a resemblance to his mother in his eyes and mouth.

"Let's not get mooning around about the family," Connie said. "Where are you going to take me? I have quite a lot of money if you need it."

He laughed. "I guess I can swing this one. What do you want? Noise, dancing, exotic food—"

"Exotic men," she said. "Men who wear their hair long and don't like to play slot machines and don't talk about 'The Slot' and have never seen the inside of an airplane."

"I guess there are plenty like that around New York," he said, "but they wouldn't be interested in you."

"Oh, you know about that, do you? I wasn't sure you knew about that. You're really getting quite sophisticated, aren't you?"

He grinned at her. "I didn't know *you* knew about that."

"Oh, I know all kinds of horrible things."

"Well, now let's see," he said. "Practically everything uptown will be full of uniforms. It's uniforms you want to get away from. Right?"

"Preferably," she said.

"Practically everything downtown will be full of uniforms too," he said, "only they'll be enlisted uniforms."

"That would be better."

"Would it? Some of them get pretty drunk."

"I see plenty of drunks in officers' uniforms too. Try thinking some more."

"I know where we're going," Noah said, as though he had just thought of it. He had known all along where they were going, but he had wanted to make Connie think that she was helping him to decide. "Practically Warner's and my favorite place. Good French food without a lot of French nonsense. Run by second-generation French. Light enough to see your food and room enough to move your elbows without bumping into anybody. Always a lot of foreigners there. If you see any uniforms they're likely to be foreign ones."

Connie was smiling at him. "I love you being sophisticated," she said, "but it sounds good."

"And people don't get very drunk there," he finished triumphantly, "and they have a nice string trio."

"Sounds elegant," she said. "Expensive?"

He grinned at her. "Fairly."

"I'll pay my own."

"Oh, no you won't."

The restaurant was an old brownstone in the East Fifties, and they took the bus and walked over, with Noah feeling big and big brotherly and quite pleased with himself beside the trim and unobtrusive figure in the green uniform and the little green hat. They climbed the steps and opened the heavy door, and Roland, the proprietor, came down the hall to meet them. Through the wide doors to the right Noah could see that already more than half the tables were filled.

"Lieutenant Sibley," Roland said with enthusiasm. "Your usual table?"

Connie squeezed Noah's arm. "The old habitué," she whispered.

[76]

Roland led them over to the table in the corner beside the wide doorway that opened into the smaller back room. Here Warner always chose to sit because, as he said, he could look at the women as they came in. Roland held the opposite chair for Connie, and Noah moved around to the place where Warner usually sat. "Lieutenant Boiland is not with you tonight," Roland said.

"He's in Washington."

"Such a rapid war," Roland said, shaking his head. "One night they're here, the next they're in Washington, the next night they're in Pearl Harbor or the Solomon Islands, the next they're back here again."

"That's right, Roland," Noah said.

"Almost," Connie said under her breath.

She let Noah order for her, and he did it with great assurance, knowing that she was laughing at him but feeling sure that he knew what she would like. She was gratifyingly delighted with the room, the linen, the *canapés*, the wine, the soup, and the people. There *were* a few foreign uniforms—and a number of men who wore their hair longer than Marine aviators did.

Over the main course she said, "Tell me about Lieutenant Boiland."

"He's impossible to describe," Noah said. "Not like anyone else you ever saw."

"Handsome?"

"N—no," Noah said doubtfully. "You might call him distinguished looking. He hath a lean and hungry look."

Connie shook her head energetically. "Don't do it, Noah."

"Don't do what?"

"Let yourself get into the foul Sibley habit of spouting quotations. I'm working hard to break it myself. Go on, what does he look like?"

"Well, he's dark, with very hollow cheeks and very prominent cheekbones. Close-cropped crew haircut—you wouldn't like that, would you?"

"You can't tell. I might."

"He's one of those guys who look different different times. You know? Sometimes up in his apartment he puts on kind of a brown bathrobe and I think he looks like a monk, an ascetic, you know? Or maybe like one of those old ducks in an El Greco. Then you see him in a place like this, in his blues, and he can look worldly as all hell."

"Confusing," Connie said. "How often have you had him out to the house?"

"Three times. It's kind of embarrassing, since Louise put on one of her acts the second time I took him out. Did anybody write you about that?"

"No. What did she do?"

"She locked herself in her room all day Sunday, and then when she did come down, at teatime, she was wearing red and black Chinese pajamas."

Connie took a forkful of salad and ate it before she spoke. "So what?"

"So—well, Warner must have got kind of a funny idea of what goes on around the place."

"Because she wore pajamas to tea? What's wrong with wearing pajamas to tea? I bet she looked nice in them. Did she?"

"Well—"

"I'll bet she did."

"I suppose she did," Noah admitted. "Seriously, though, Connie, I've been worried about her. I'm not sure she isn't going off the beam."

"You could hardly blame her, could you? Living there in that place—"

"Now wait a minute, Connie. That's not fair. I'm right there every day and I know. They're being simply swell. They're taking all these things she does like a pair of troupers."

"And how's she taking all the things they do?"

"Oh, come off it, Connie."

"All right," she said. "We won't squabble about them. They're remarkable people. This is delicious, Noah. I'm not sure it isn't the best food I ever ate. But in spite of the pajamas you did take him out there again?"

"Yes. Dad wanted to talk with him again, and he kept kind of hinting that he'd like to come."

"How did it go?"

"All right," Noah said, surprise in his voice. "Louise acted very well. Everything went off beautifully. She even took Warner out for a walk Sunday afternoon—to show him the town. And you know how she hates to walk."

"Nice for him," Connie said, "and I imagine very, very nice for her. Oh, dear, I wasn't going to say things like that, was I?"

Noah looked up at the door and there, standing in the hall talking with Roland, were Louise and Warner. He stared, his mouth open, unable to comprehend what he was seeing. They couldn't either of them be here. Warner was in Washington. Louise—Louise had gone to Greenwich. His mother had told him so just a few hours ago.

But it was Louise's profile, Louise's golden hair. And he had seen the scarlet, low-necked dress before. Warner's back was toward him, but there was no mistaking those angular shoulders either, or that close-cropped head of black hair.

His first thought was that they must be looking for him, that something bad might have happened to one of the family. But he looked again and saw that they were not looking for anyone. They were laughing, talking with Roland. He stared, frowning. And suddenly he felt, without knowing why, that it was vitally important that they should not know that he had seen them—and vitally important that Connie should not know that they were there.

He turned to her and tried to smile and said, "Now tell me this," racking his brain for something to ask her. "Tell me—tell me about this photo interpretation business."

She was smiling curiously at him, a puzzled expression in her eyes, and he realized that he hadn't done a very good job of acting. But she didn't turn her head. "Actually," she said, "I don't know much about it yet. We got a little of it in Officers' Training, and now I'm going to get a sort of graduate course. You look at aerial photographs and see things that most people wouldn't see. And it gets all tied up with a lot of map-reading stuff, and that's awful."

Noah was listening intently, nodding at everything she said, and she was watching him and still looking puzzled. And finally, when he couldn't stand the strain of curiosity any longer, he glanced toward the hall again. They were gone.

12·

Noah remembered that hour, the hour he spent walking the streets of New York after he had taken Connie to her subway station, as one of the soul-searing hours of his life, comparable to the hour when he got the letter from Natalie back in the spring of '38, the hour of his father's death, or the minutes that had seemed like an hour he had spent walking up and down in front of the Headmaster's House at Milburn, trying to get up his courage to go in.

Briefly, as he walked west on Fiftieth through the darkened city, he tried to tell himself that Warner and Louise could be innocent, that Warner undoubtedly *had* been to Washington and accomplished his mission and come back again, that they could have run into each other by some accident. But only briefly. It took too much stretching of obvious facts. Louise had told his mother that she was going to Greenwich, and you would have to try to believe that she could have gone to Greenwich, gotten into her scarlet evening gown, come back into the city without the friend she was visiting, and by some strange coincidence run into Warner. That was stretching with a vengeance.

And always there was the fact that they had come into the restaurant, talked to Roland, looked around, and gone away again. There were empty tables, and even if there hadn't been, Roland would have seen to it that there was one for Warner. There was no possible explantation except that they had seen him and Connie and, being guilty, hurried away in the hope that they had not been seen.

Because he wanted more time to think, he decided to walk down to Times Square, and because Madison looked dark and uninhabited, he turned south on it. The chill of an April night had settled on the city, but to Noah the air seemed heavy, difficult to breathe. And the darkness of the avenue did not give him the sense of peace, the chance to think without distraction, that he had hoped for. There was no peace in his mind, and he had the feeling that there was no peace in the city.

The impersonal darkened store windows, the taxis that crept past him and around the corners, noticing nothing, indifferent to any human plight, the pedestrians hunched in their collars, glancing hostilely at his Navy uniform, as though a man in uniform was already convicted of lechery and drunkenness in the mind of the city—he turned west again quickly, hounded by an oppressive sense of hostility and apprehension, hoping to escape into the crowds nearer Broadway.

Being guilty, Warner and Louise had hurried away. And their guilt, he felt, was also his guilt, in one way or another his fault. The thought made him panicky. He hurried on, walking faster and faster. His breathing was the breathing of a man caught in the most horrible of all fears, the fear of a self-caused impending disaster. He was almost running, feeling that if he could somehow get somewhere faster, he could still prevent it from happening. He lost all thought of where he was or where he was going.

Then, abruptly, in the middle of the block, he stopped. Could he get somewhere? Right now, at this moment, they were somewhere, somewhere in some one of the thousands or millions of buildings in this city. Warner's apartment? His mind refused to accept the thought

[80]

that they might be in Warner's apartment, the apartment that he knew so well, where the couch stood right here, the big chair right there, the twin beds, the bureaus, the bathroom—all exactly as he knew them. Stupendous things, disastrous things didn't happen in such familiar surroundings. Because he could visualize the room so clearly, he found it impossible to visualize Louise in it.

Somewhere, they were together. He hurried on again, still driven by a sense of fear and guilt. They were in some room together—his imagination grasped at the thought, shied away from it, returned to it again and again, try as he would to keep it on something less revolting.

And the logical part of his mind kept telling him that, whether he could visualize it or not, they were in Warner's apartment. Why should Warner, who knew all the angles, bother with the awkward business of a false registry, bother to try to find a hotel room when every hotel in town was overcrowded, bother to pay for a room when he had an apartment in which his privacy was complete and secure, a beautiful apartment with a view of the river, an apartment with his own expensive furniture, his own good pictures, his own excellent phonograph records? Noah remembered with a shudder that he himself had sometimes thought, in much the same way that he might have thought of a trip to China, that if he himself ever *did* have an assignation with a woman, he would like to borrow Warner's apartment for it.

And as he found himself approaching Seventh Avenue, his logical mind, by some unconscious process, worked the thought that they were in Warner's apartment into his consciousness, and at last he felt certain that that was where they were.

A dozen times, in that apartment, he had seen Warner step out of his shower and stand, with the bathroom door open, rubbing himself with his big turkish towel. It was a muscular body, but it was a lean and angular one too, and a hairy one, with heavy black hair covering most of his chest and stomach and tufts of black hair on his shoulders. And Noah's mind, horrified, repulsed, trying to back away, was held by the thought of Louise there in that apartment as helplessly as a small animal is held by the stare of a snake. And the Louise he was seeing was not the Louise of this last winter but the Louise of two years ago, three years ago, Barrett's sweet and loving wife, with her lovely complexion and her gay smile and her charming manner with older people.

The thought around which his mind skittered, repulsed and held, of *that* Louise surrendering her body to the hairy Warner was so repulsive to him that he felt nauseated. He was afraid he might be sick right there on Seventh Avenue, and he swallowed hard and, feeling miserable and ill, stumbled along the street to a drugstore.

He went in and sat on the stool and ordered an alka-seltzer, and the girl behind the counter smiled at him knowingly and asked, "Liberty?"

He nodded, unable to speak.

"Getting chilly out, isn't it?" she asked.

He swallowed and said, "Yes," and was mute again.

He drank the alka-seltzer and turned on the stool and looked around the store, and it was all ordinary and matter-of-fact and exactly like any drugstore, with its magazines and its counter of cosmetics and its glass cage in the back and the girl in her blue uniform. And suddenly he found it difficult to believe that there could be any tragedy, any disaster. That thing was all outside in the city, in the darkened streets. In here it couldn't exist. The thought of stepping out of the door filled him with fright.

He looked hopefully around the counter, searching for an excuse to stay, and there were sandwiches and pies and doughnuts under glass domes. His stomach felt better but still squeamish, and he wondered what of all he saw would be least likely to upset it again. He decided on a cheese sandwich and a glass of milk, and he ate very slowly, turning on the stool again and again to draw comfort from the prosaic ordinariness of the store.

And gradually he began to wonder if there really was a disaster, if he hadn't jumped to conclusions too fast, if his imagination hadn't run away with him. Louise had lied to his mother. They had not wanted him and Connie to see them. But those two things—did they necessarily put them into bed together? He began to construct other explanations in his mind, to reconstruct possible conversations that Warner and Louise might have had.

Warner, that last time he had been out in Middlefield, might have asked Louise to have dinner with him in New York some night. Perhaps Louise *was* finding life out there a little dull, perhaps the idea of a dinner with Warner in New York *did* appeal to her. Mightn't she have said that she'd like to but she didn't think that Noah's mother —or Noah himself perhaps—would approve? Mightn't she then have gotten the invitation from Greenwich and asked her friend if she might come but also if she might come back into town for a dinner with a friend the first night? Mightn't she have dropped Warner a note to that effect? And wouldn't he have hurried back from Washington to take her out to dinner at his favorite restaurant?

Noah looked at his watch. It was ten minutes to eleven. Louise could be over at the Grand Central, getting onto a train for Greenwich now. Warner would be seeing her to her train. He, Noah, could take the shuttle over there, find out when trains left for Greenwich, watch and see if she got on one. They would hardly break off their evening much earlier than this, and Louise would not be likely to start back to her friend's house later than midnight. If there was a train about now, it would be the one she would be taking. That, if he saw them, would settle everything, leave no rankling doubts in his mind.

He paid his check and went out and started walking briskly down toward Times Square. But out in the night again doubts began to batter his mind. The chances of his actually seeing her get on a train in the Grand Central were no more than one in a hundred. And if *they* were to see *him*, what would he say? And if he didn't see them, what then? Should he go to the apartment with his key and see if they were there?

What would Barrett want him to do? It was Barrett's wife, Barrett's life. What would Barrett's life be without Louise? Wouldn't it be better to take the late ferry back out to Middlefield, go to bed, and say nothing to anyone? Even if it was a—a dishonorable assignation, wouldn't that be better? He was the only one in the world who knew, and they did not know that he had seen them. Louise, after her disgraceful escapade—if it was a disgraceful escapade—would come back again, contrite, disillusioned, conscience-stricken. She would have learned her lesson.

Barrett would come home someday and start living with her again, never knowing that she had been unfaithful to him, happy in his ignorance. Was that what he would have wanted? And the answer that came to Noah as positively as truth itself was, "No." Barrett would want to know, painful as it might be. If he were ever to learn that Noah knew and had not told him, if he were ever to learn that Noah had reason to suspect and had said nothing, he would never forgive him, not in a thousand years.

Broadway was crowded—soldiers, sailors, marines, in twos and threes and fours, soldiers, sailors, and marines with girls and without girls. Here a marine with three girls. Here a trio of men with ten-gallon hats and cigars. Here a tall blonde with a little man in a striped suit. Here a pair of boyish college students out in the street trying to

[83]

find a taxi, while their even younger-looking girls stood back on the curb, pretty and fresh and excited.

Noah slowed down to the sauntering pace of the crowd. Barrett would want him to find out if he could. And there was one simple, obvious way to find out. He was absolutely sure now that, if they were going to spend the night together, it would be in the apartment. Warner would never be able to find another place so private, so free from intrusion, or, for that matter, so comfortable, so completely convenient for the purpose.

If they were there—they had no reason to know that he suspected anything. They did not know that he had seen them. And he would know. For Barrett's sake he would know. And Barrett would know, and that was what Barrett would want. It all seemed clear and obvious and—and inevitable, the only possible thing he could do, although he dreaded the moment when he stepped into that apartment more than he had ever dreaded anything in his life.

He took the subway to Brooklyn, came up and walked the two and a half blocks to the apartment house. And he got out of the elevator at the sixth floor and walked down the corridor and around the corner and on down to the second door on the left. He took the key from his pocket and inserted it into the lock, reminding himself to do it exactly as he would have any other time when he was sleeping there. He turned the key and opened the door.

The room was dark. He stood staring in, and the temptation to stand still, listening, was almost more than he could resist. But no; it was vital that he should act as he had always acted, that he should do nothing to let them know that he suspected anything. He snapped the light switch beside him and stepped on into the living room. The room was empty, in good order, and the door into the bedroom was open.

Already, from the living room, he could see that the beds were undisturbed, but to satisfy himself beyond doubt he went in and turned on the lights and, although it was obvious enough that no one was there, he opened both closet doors and looked in behind Warner's clothes.

He went back into the living room and there it was, just as it had always been. Its concrete familiarity was even more reassuring than the ordinariness of the drugstore had been. Everything was there, in its place. Nothing was wrong. Nothing could be wrong. And in the masculinity of Warner's possessions there was still more reassurance, seeming as they did to exclude Louise from any intimate part of his life, placing her in nice comfortable perspective as just another one of the safely large company of girls whom Warner had dates with.

He could feel the muscles in his stomach letting go, as though someone had loosened the ends of a knot. He took off his coat and tie and tossed them onto the couch, and he undid the button of his collar and sank into a chair. With the release of his tensions had come a limpness and a drowsiness. Slowly, a move at a time, he reached down and untied his shoelaces and kicked his shoes off. His eyelids were droopy, his hands and arms heavy and clumsy.

It was an effort to take a cigarette from the box on the table and light it, and even more of an effort to reach down and pull off his socks. But it was worth the effort. He sat there, his eyes half closed, dragging deeply on the cigarette and wiggling his toes and, with vast relief, puffing the smoke up at the ceiling in clouds.

He thought about how good it felt to have his shoes and socks off. That was all he had to think about. Thinking, worrying, was over. Everything was all right.

He finished the cigarette and pulled himself to his feet and stumbled into the bedroom, his drowsiness so overpowering now that he was slightly dizzy. He took off his trousers and shirt and without bothering to wash or brush his teeth, without bothering even to get out of his underwear, he pulled back the covers and got into bed.

13·

WHEN he woke up it was broad daylight. Warner was not there. His bed was undisturbed. Noah looked at his watch. He had twenty minutes to get to the office, and he shaved and dressed and hurried down to the restaurant on the corner for a quick breakfast.

Warner was not at his desk during the morning. After lunch Noah went to the CO and asked him if he knew where he was. Warner had got an emergency leave, the CO told him, and he understood that he was going to get orders to sea duty and that the orders would be coming through before the leave was over.

Noah went back to his desk, troubled in his mind but certainly without even the faintest suspicion that that moment when he had caught a glimpse of Warner and Louise in the hallway of the restaurant would turn out to be the last time he was ever to see either one of them.

It wasn't until the next day that the Sibleys discovered two trunks and a suitcase, all packed and locked, in the middle of the green room. The closets and drawers were empty. And the day after that two men appeared with a truck and said that their instructions were to get the trunks and the suitcase that would be in the green room upstairs. Mrs. Sibley led them upstairs without saying a word, pointed to the trunks, and went into her own room and closed the door.

They all found it devastatingly, heartbreakingly, unbelievably sudden. There must have been, they supposed, some correspondence that Louise had managed to hide. They racked their brains and figured out two possible occasions since Warner's last visit when Warner and Louise might possibly have met clandestinely.

That was all they knew, except that the next letter Barrett got from Louise came from Reno.

V

1 ·

SITTING in the morning sunlight on the upturned boat on the beach, Noah followed each disturbing thought all the way to its conclusion, going through in his mind every detail of those unexplainable incidents, recalling the weeping, incredulous bitterness of the things his mother had said, the stern rectitude of his father's remarks, the open, unqualified accusations of stupidity that Mark had hurled at him later when he came back from the Pacific, above all the things Barrett had said and, what was perhaps worse, the things Barrett had left unsaid.

It wasn't until the planks that his hands rested on began to feel uncomfortably hot from the sun that he started to wonder how long he had been there. He looked around, up and down. He had left his watch under the pillow, but the height of the sun in the sky, the force of its heat, made him think that it must be at least eleven. If it was, people would be stirring in the Humeston cottage.

He got to his feet, but having found no answer, still as unready to face the ordeal of what was waiting at the cottage as he had been when he came down, he walked in the other direction, down along the beach. The suggestion of a headache that he had had earlier was still with him, and to it was now added a lightheadedness, a feeling of remoteness, as though his mind were floating off a little way away from him. Perhaps a little too much sun, he thought distractedly. Or perhaps just a too empty stomach. Most of all, a terrific thirst. His throat was parched, the inside of his mouth cottony.

He walked idly, uncertainly, for only a few hundred feet before he stopped. He couldn't do any kind of thinking so long as he was this thirsty. And there was no place he could see or think of where he might quench his thirst except the Humeston cottage. He started back, his desire for a pitcher of cold water greater now than his fear of facing Natalie and Jeffrey and the questions they posed.

He came to the steps and, stopping once for breath halfway up, hurried on to the top and up the path to the front door. As he got near, he sensed that the people in the house were up and that something was happening inside. He didn't know what it was that he had seen or heard, but he knew that they were there. And as he reached the veranda steps, he heard Jeffrey's voice shouting, "Nonsense. If you can swim in four feet of water, you can swim just as well in twenty."

Noah stopped on the steps. Then, realizing that sooner or later someone would look out and see him, he walked across the veranda and opened the screen door and stepped in.

They were in the dining room and, engrossed in what they were saying, they had not seen him come in. They did not see him now as he stood there. Jeffrey, at the head of the table, had his head half turned, glaring at a thin, waif-like boy who stood with his back to the sideboard, his hands behind him. The boy was wearing tan shorts and a flimsy white pullover shirt that was too big for him. Beneath a mop of dark, uncombed hair, the face was delicately featured, tense, and nervous. Knowing boys as he did, Noah's mind immediately fitted this boy into a category, a category for which he had no name but one he knew well, with its complex pattern of fears and reticences and sensitivities.

Jeffrey still had not seen him. "I'm not going to have a little sissy of a coward for a son," he said loudly, accusingly, and the boy moved his arms with a jerky motion and glanced quickly at Jeffrey and then stood still, looking down at the floor again.

Natalie sat at the foot of the table, with her back to Noah, her hands in her lap, her back rigid. And between them, on the opposite side of the table from the boy, sat a young girl.

Jeffrey turned and saw Noah, glared at him for a moment, then, as his face turned a deep crimson, nodded his head quickly up and down in an effort to recompose his face into a smile. "Good morning, Noah," he said, his voice still too loud. And, lowering it, he said awkwardly, "We thought you were still asleep."

Natalie turned and looked at Noah, and her face was white. Her eyes blinked a quick recognition at him, but she did not smile.

"Oh, no," Noah said heartily, "I've had myself a good long walk on the beach."

The girl looked up at him. She had a pretty face, not so pretty as Natalie's sister Betty's but more like it than like Natalie's own. Only

[88]

in the strong line of the mouth could he find a resemblance to Natalie, and only in the sharply chiseled nose a resemblance to Jeffrey.

Natalie stood up, and the girl got up too and stood facing him. "This is Pamela," Natalie said, "and this is Mr. Sibley, Pammy."

Pamela smiled, and her smile, Noah thought with dismay, was too glittering, the smile of a girl too conscious of her beauty, too conscious, for her age, of the fact that she was a girl and he a man. She was fourteen, Natalie had said yesterday, but from her manner, from the blouse and slacks she was wearing, he might have taken her for a college girl. He realized that he was staring at her solemnly, and belatedly he forced his face into a grin.

"And this is Peter," Natalie said.

With Peter, Noah was on familiar ground. "Hello, Peter," he said. "Say, I'm just about dying of thirst. Do you suppose you could find me a glass and a pitcher of water? I feel as though I could down a whole pitcher in one swallow."

His manner obviously took Peter by surprise, and for a moment a look of suspicion crossed his face. Then, looking sideways from under his brow with a glance that contained the barest hint of a smile, he said, "Sure," and went out to the kitchen.

Natalie seemed to take a deep breath, and the expression with which she looked at Noah was one of gratitude, and he was momentarily pleased to have helped her. But Jeffrey's face told him that he had done nothing more than to postpone the crisis he had interrupted.

"I'll bet you're hungry too," Natalie said. "Do bacon and eggs and blueberry muffins sound good?"

He smiled at her. "I think they will after I've had that pitcher of water."

Peter came back in with a tall glass and a very large pitcher. He put them down in front of Noah and stood back, watching. Noah realized that he was being taken up on his statement that he could drink a whole pitcher. He grinned at Peter and drank two and a half of the tall glasses and puffed out a great sigh. He laughed. "Your pitchers run too big, Peter," he said, and Pamela chuckled and Peter was looking sideways again from under his brow with the same elusive hint of a smile.

The place was set for Noah across from Pamela, and he sat down and sipped the orange juice that the maid brought him, with Pamela smiling politely at him across the table and Peter watching him from a curled-up position on the window seat behind her. Natalie poured a second cup of coffee for Jeffrey and passed it down to him.

"I think it's going to be a hot day," Noah said to Jeffrey, feeling that he should bring him into the conversation.

Jeffrey smiled at him with complacent determination. "That's right," he said, looking at Natalie. "A good day for a swim. We're all going for a swim a little later."

"All of us who want to," Natalie corrected him.

"All of us," Jeffrey said, then added as an afterthought, "of course you don't have to if you don't want to, Noah. But the rest of us are going to. It won't take long."

Peter jumped up and ran out of the room and up the stairs.

"Jeffrey," Natalie said with despair in her voice.

"Natalie," Jeffrey said sternly, "that boy is eleven years old. He's been swimming for four years now. He can swim just as well as a boy needs to. It's just a silly piece of nonsense he's got into his head that he can't swim where it's over his head. He's got to get over it, and this is as good a time to do it as any."

It was a familiar problem to Noah. He looked down at the glass in front of him, purposely keeping his face expressionless.

"Once he's done it," Jeffrey said, "he'll be over it for good."

It was not the way Noah believed this sort of thing should be handled. It was, he had to admit, the way at least half of the other masters at Milburn would have handled it. His dislike for Jeffrey's personality made him want desperately to side with Natalie, to tell Jeffrey that it was not the way to do it. But the hell of it was, he told himself, that there was a very good chance indeed that once Peter had done it, he *would* be over it for good. And, after all, Peter was Jeffrey's son. Noah continued to sit still, staring down into his glass.

Jeffrey looked at his watch. "We'll leave for the cove at twelve o'clock," he said. "Glad to have you come with us if you'd like to, Noah."

And as the maid brought Noah's plate of bacon and eggs, he left the table. At the door he turned and smiled at Natalie. "I'll be up in my study until time to go," he said, "and I'm not to be disturbed." He turned to Pamela. "Pammy, I hope you've learned your lesson about playing that cheap stuff. Just one note of that cheap stuff—" He held up a single warning finger, and turned and went upstairs. Through the hall, Noah could see that the keyboard of the piano was open.

Pammy stared after him, turned and looked at her mother, then stood up. "Excuse me, please," she said to Noah, and when Natalie nodded to her, smiling a little, she left the room.

Natalie's face was still white. "I'm sorry, Noah," she said. She sat staring straight ahead. Then impulsively she got to her feet. "You don't mind if I don't sit here and watch you eat, do you?"

"Of course not," Noah said, trying to sound hearty and sympathetic and reassuring all at the same time. She turned and walked out quickly, and he heard her footsteps on the stairs.

He was smoking on the veranda when she came down. "I have an errand in town," she said. Her voice was calm and natural again. "Would you like to ride in with me?"

Noah said, "Love to," realizing as he said it that this was the moment, that in a few minutes he would have to be saying something to her, that he had no more idea what he was going to say than he had had when he stole down to the beach at eight o'clock this morning. Somewhere in the back of his mind, he guessed, he had been hoping that the crisis over Peter's swimming would make Natalie forget the crisis in their lives.

He followed her through the house and down the steps toward the garage. She was wearing a peach-colored dress that was very low in the back, and looking at her as she walked ahead of him with her characteristic, taut-muscled walk, he thought that it could have been the back of a twenty-year-old girl. A very beautiful back. A very feminine back, but firm-muscled, with none of the flabbiness that he associated with middle-aged women in bathing suits. The thought passed through his mind that his hands might someday clasp that beautifully shaped back, and the thought still seemed a little improbable and remote to him, but not so improbable and remote as it once had.

She led him to the station wagon and he got in beside her. She backed out and swung into the road and drove for a hundred yards or more before she spoke. "Did you sleep well, Noah?"

"Like a log," he said, "until eight o'clock. I woke up at eight o'clock and couldn't go to sleep again."

"You weren't worried?"

"Worried?"

She didn't answer, and the expression on her face didn't change. Finally she glanced at him and said, "Noah, you understand that you didn't commit yourself to anything, don't you?"

"Commit myself?" Noah asked, as though the words were unfamiliar to him.

"All women have their weak moments," she said. "You just happened to catch me in one of mine."

Noah looked at her, and her face was strong and self-possessed. It was hard to imagine her ever giving way to weakness. He tried to remember how her face had looked down on the beach in the night, in what she had just called her moment of weakness.

"What I said was not true," she said. "I *can* take it. I can go right on taking it as long as I have to take it."

Noah looked at her cautiously, feeling uncomfortably breathless.

"In other words?" he asked.

"In other words you're not committed to anything."

He stared down at his feet, feeling depressed and deflated. There was none of the feeling of relief he might have expected himself to feel. An hour ago he had been worrying about his family, thinking about Warner and Louise, fearing that he might have committed himself. And now he was being offered a chance to forget all that, and instead of relief he was feeling injured and vaguely insulted. "And suppose I wanted to be committed?" he found himself asking.

She smiled, a little sadly but still full of self-possession. "I don't believe you do, Noah."

He turned and looked at her, scowling.

"I don't believe your family would approve of your running off with a wife and mother. And I don't believe you could be happy without your family's approval."

He clenched his hands in his lap. Stated so baldly, it seemed like an insult to his family, and an insult to his own manliness.

"It annoys you to have me say that, doesn't it?" she asked. And when he didn't answer she said, "But it does happen to be true too, doesn't it?"

"I think if they could be made to understand all the circumstances," he said lamely, "they—"

She interrupted him with a quick, impatient, disgusted turn of her head. He stopped and frowned, feeling like a not too bright schoolboy who, trying to lie his way out of trouble, finds himself helpless before the mature understanding of an adult. Natalie knew nothing about the family feeling about divorce; she knew nothing about Warner Boiland, but somehow she had managed to read the thoughts he had been having since early this morning. He felt helpless and abused.

He was suddenly aware that she was driving very fast. He looked at the speedometer and it read sixty. These were narrow roads, and winding. She was gripping the wheel, the sinews in her forearm standing out taut and hard.

He braced his hands against the seat and watched the road, stealing

[92]

quick glances at her face. Her expression was set, angry looking. They were coming into the village, and she didn't slow up until they were almost there. Then she set her brakes, screeching them on the macadam, and came to a quick stop across the street from the grocery store. She opened the door beside her. "You wait here," she said, her voice husky, and without glancing at him she ran across the street and into the store. Something about her shoulders as she went through the door made Noah wonder if she could be crying.

She was gone for ten minutes, and when she finally came back, he looked at her eyes and wasn't sure whether they looked as though she had been crying or not. All the way back to the cottage she talked about Pammy and her music and the question of finding the right school for a child with an unusual talent like hers.

2.

For a moment, climbing into the station wagon in the new swimming trunks that he had bought for this trip, Noah felt self-conscious about the bulky whiteness of his body. All four of these people were so slender and so smoothly tanned. But then, sitting beside Peter in the middle seat, he began to wish that he could somehow transfer a little of his own flesh onto those skinny arms and legs. In spite of the heat of the day, Peter looked cold. The muscles of his arms and narrow chest were taut, twitching intermittently.

From under his mop of hair he was staring at the back of his father's head, his eyes sullen and frightened. He gave no sign that he knew Noah was there.

Forgetting, after that first moment, all about himself and how he looked, Noah wished mightily that he could have fifteen minutes alone with the boy before he had to go through with the ordeal. He didn't know what he would say, but he felt that somehow he could think of something—something to ease his tension, to relax those taut muscles, something, perhaps, to make him laugh. Tension was the enemy of good swimming. But with Jeffrey right there in front of them, his ears only a few inches from their lips, there was nothing he could say to him.

They swayed down a short steep slope to an open spot beside a boathouse and stopped. Before them lay the cove, a neatly rounded, pondlike body, not much more than two hundred yards in diameter,

Noah guessed, with a wide creek running out from it to the open Sound. Out in the middle was a raft, and in front of the boathouse a small dock with three skiffs tied to it. In the still air, the surface of the pond was unruffled, and Noah had to admit that it made a fair and uncomplicated place for a swimming test.

"All right, Pete," Jeffrey said in a let's-have-no-nonsense tone of voice, "let's go."

He went into the boathouse, and Peter walked slowly, hunched around his chest, toward the head of the dock. Pamela got out and followed him. Now, in her trim, blue bathing suit, stepping sure-footedly over the rough ground, she no longer seemed older than her fourteen years. And as she stood beside Peter, patting him gently on the rump, Noah had a different feeling about her, a feeling that beneath the self-conscious, too mature manner he had seen at the breakfast table, there might be a different person. He could hear her saying, in a schoolgirl voice, "Take it easy, Peter. You can do it all right. You can do it all right if you just take it easy."

Natalie did not follow them down. She stood in her skirted brown and white bathing suit with her back against the fender of the car, leaning back a little, her hands flat against the top of the fender, her arms straight, bracing her weight. Her face was impassive, expressionless. She turned once and smiled at Noah, but otherwise her eyes did not leave the thin, stooped figure of the boy.

Jeffrey came out of the boathouse with oars and oarlocks. His deeply tanned legs and torso were thin and wiry, like a larger, better-fed version of Peter.

Noah hesitated, not sure whether he should stay there with Natalie or go on down to the dock. Without taking her eyes off Peter, Natalie said, "I guess it doesn't matter where you stand, Noah. There isn't much you can do to help, is there?"

Noah nodded and stood still beside her, and after a moment she said, "You have no idea how Jeffrey hates this."

He looked at her sharply.

She nodded. "He loves them both—more than anything else in the world, but he takes his duties as a father very seriously."

Jeffrey had gotten into the rower's seat of one of the skiffs and motioned Peter into the stern.

"He wants them to be everything he hasn't been," she said. "But of course he's not very sure of himself—not very certain that he knows"—she took a deep breath and smiled briefly at Noah—"that explains a lot though, doesn't it?"

He wet his lips and watched Jeffrey as he put in the oarlocks and pushed off from the dock. Finally he asked, "Are you sure he doesn't do some of it to hurt you?"

She waited, her eyes still on the boat. "No, I'm not sure," she said at last.

"Why?" Noah asked. "Why does he keep trying to hurt you?"

She shrugged. "I suppose his life hasn't been what he wanted it to be, and a good deal of it is because of me, I guess."

"Good God, Natalie."

She nodded and said nothing more, as though she felt that she had said all that need be said.

They were now out on the raft. Jeffrey held it alongside while Peter got out. Then he pushed off and rowed back toward the dock, leaving Peter, a lonely, skinny scarecrow of a figure, alone in the middle of the raft.

When Jeffrey got a little more than halfway in, he stopped and took one oar out of the lock and pushed it straight down until the end of the blade hit bottom. "There, Pete," he called, marking the depth of the water with his hand on the upturned oar, "when you get this far in you can stand up." And he rowed on in to the dock and tied the painter and got out and stood on the end of the dock, waiting.

Peter, still in the middle of the raft, stood looking at him mutely. He did not move.

"Come on," Jeffrey called, angry impatience in his voice.

Still Peter did not move.

Jeffrey stood watching him for what might have been a half a minute. Noah tried to imagine what thoughts, what sort of feelings, could be passing through his mind as he stood there, and it occurred to him that, whatever Jeffrey might have done if he had been alone with his family, his, Noah's presence, now made it impossible for him to relent. He wished he had stayed at the cottage.

"All right, Pete," Jeffrey called angrily, "I'm giving you one more minute. After that we're going back to the cottage, and you can swim in any time you feel like it, without anybody here to watch you."

The boy's body seemed to stiffen, and Noah sensed a new tension in Natalie as she stood there beside him. Pamela, standing back at the foot of the dock, put her hand to her mouth. She turned and looked at her mother, and Noah saw that there were tears in her eyes. He began to wonder if he might not perhaps like Pamela very much.

Peter took two quick steps forward, his legs moving jerkily, disjointedly, and Noah, watching him, suddenly knew that, if he did go in, he would not make it. Nobody could swim with muscles as taut as that.

Suddenly, making no effort either to dive or to jump, Peter ran off the edge of the raft and into the water. There was very little splash, but he was hardly in before his arms were flailing wildly. His head was back, his body curved backward in his effort to keep his face out of water. Noah could see that his feet were sinking fast, his body becoming more and more vertical. With no freedom now for his arms to work, his flailing became feebler, and steadily his head sank lower and lower, with the water coming closer to his tight-clamped mouth by the second. He did manage once to kick himself up out of the water a bit, and then immediately, as though in an inevitable sequence, his head went under.

Noah looked at Jeffrey, expecting to see him dive in. What he saw was a body taut with paralyzing fear, in a pose identical to the pose in which Peter had stood on the raft. Noah knew instantly that the man, at this moment, could no more swim than the boy could.

Before Natalie had time to say, "Hurry, Noah," Noah had started, running down across the little beach. He ran out into the water and swam out toward the raft. As he got close he saw that Peter had kicked himself to the surface again, still only a few feet from the raft, and again he was flailing the water helplessly with his arms.

Remembering his Red Cross training, Noah guessed that Peter would grasp at him as he got nearer. He swam up cautiously, and Peter did as he had guessed he would, trying to throw his arms around Noah's neck. Noah dodged him, moving deftly in the water, and as the convulsive grasp missed its target Peter sank again.

Noah backed away, dived quickly from the surface, and caught the boy's body from behind. With a big kick, he pushed his head and shoulders out of water and toward the raft, and Peter, still conscious, still in a panic, grasped at the raft as frantically as he had grasped at Noah.

Noah left him holding on there and swam around to the steps and climbed up. Peter had got his elbows up over the edge, and he hung there, coughing, his eyes staring. Noah pulled him up and onto his feet and pounded him hard on the back. "Okay, Peter," he said. "You're all right now."

Peter winced away from the blows and looked up at him sulkily. He stood staring down at the boards of the raft. Noah put his arm around his shoulder and turned to wave to Jeffrey to bring the boat out.

But Jeffrey was no longer on the dock. It was Pamela who was climbing into the boat. Jeffrey was on his way back to the car, walking fast, his head down as though he were bucking a strong wind. And as Peter squirmed out from under Noah's arm and went over to the other side of the raft and stood looking down into the water, Jeffrey and Natalie got into the car and drove back up the hill and out of sight.

Noah stared after them, puzzled and disturbed, disturbed for Natalie's sake, for the children's sake—disturbed also, oddly enough, for Jeffrey's sake. Dimly, along with the exasperation, he felt sorry for Jeffrey. Given those tensions that were so obviously a part of his nature, those fears and drives—was he sure that he himself, if the boy had been his own son, wouldn't have frozen on the dock? Would he, right now, be running away? That was something he would never know. He hoped not. He thought not. He'd been luckier, probably; his tensions were lesser tensions. Was it Jeffrey's fault that he had those tensions? Where did they come from? He shook his head. Where *did* these things come from? Way back, the psychologists said, somewhere way back.

The one thing he was sure of was that he would never have made that threat, the threat to leave Peter alone there on the raft. That was something he could never have done. Would Jeffrey have carried it out if Peter had refused to jump in? That was something else he would never know, something that Jeffrey himself would probably never know.

3.

PAMMY came rowing out to the raft, and as she coasted in alongside, she glanced up at Noah with a quick, understanding look. She looked away again at once and busied herself with taking out the oarlocks and holding the boat to the raft. "Come on, Peter," she said, "get in and we'll go ashore."

Peter looked at her sullenly, then turned his back on her and stood rigid again, staring down at the water.

"Come on, Peter," she said. "Get in and we'll row around the cove a little and then we'll go in and—and play around up there in the woods until Mommy comes back."

Peter turned and stared at her angrily. Without looking up at him,

[97]

he jerked his head toward Noah. "I won't ride with *him*," he said. He turned back again and stared down into the water.

This too was something about boys that Noah understood: the resentment that followed a fright, compounded with the resentment that came from having been seen in a failure. The thing, for now at least, was to leave him alone. "I guess I'll take a bit of a swim, Pammy," he said, and he dived in and swam lazily out in the opposite direction from the boathouse. He turned over on his back and rested, swam a few strokes and rested again, trying to act like a man enjoying a wallow in the water, deliberately refraining from swimming well.

He floated and rolled and swam and floated again for fifteen minutes, avoiding looking toward the raft or the dock. When he finally decided that it was safe to look, the skiff was back at the dock, Peter was not in sight, and Pammy was swimming out toward the raft. He swam over too, and he and Pammy sat side by side, dangling their feet in the water.

"He ran as soon as I got him in to shore," she said. "I guess he'll walk home."

"Sure," Noah said.

"He's a funny kid," she said matter-of-factly. And after a moment she asked, "Do you think he's a coward?"

Noah swung his feet up out of the water and studied his big toes as he wiggled them up and down. "I guess we're all cowards sometimes. I'm not scared of the water, but there are some things I'm scared to death of."

She giggled. "What are you scared of, snakes?" She giggled again, and now she didn't seem a day over her fourteen years.

"Yes, snakes, for one thing," he said. He hunched his shoulders and pursed his lips. "What I'm scared of mostly, I guess," he said thoughtfully, "is trouble."

"Trouble?"

"Yeah, you know. When people get mad at you and call—"

"Peter's not really mad at you," she said.

"Oh, I know. I wasn't thinking of him. I mean when you don't know whether you're doing the right thing or not and people blame you for what you do do and there's a lot of unpleasantness and—"

"I know," she interrupted. She was looking uncomfortable. "I hate all that stuff too." She got to her feet. "Come on. Let's have another swim." She stood ready to dive. "You're a very good swimmer, aren't you?"

"Pretty good."

"You saved Peter from drowning," she said.

Noah nodded.

Suddenly she stepped back from the edge of the raft and looked down at him in amazement. "You're the man who saved the little girl from drowning. I'd forgotten. You just go around saving people from drowning."

"Little girl?"

"Two little girls tipped out of their canoe and you swam right over there and caught the one that was drowning and brought her in and carried her over to the dock and—"

"Did your mother tell you about that?"

"It was my favorite story," she said. "I used to make her tell it to me every night before I went to sleep."

Noah looked up at her out of the corner of his eye. Then he looked beyond her at the wooded shore of the cove. Considering all the circumstances, it seemed a strange sort of story for Natalie to have put her babies to sleep with. He got to his feet too. "Okay," he said. "Let's have a bit of a swim."

They had finished their swim and were drying off on the dock when Natalie came back. Noah hoped, as he stood up, that she wouldn't go into a lot of business of thanking him for having pulled Peter out of the water.

She didn't. She called in a cheerful, natural voice as she got out of the car, "Have you both had enough swimming?"

They both said that they had, and she waited beside the car door, holding it open. There were to be no post-mortems at all, Noah decided, and that was all to the good. He relaxed and swung his towel playfully at Pammy as they came up the path together. When they got there, he put one hand on the hood and wiped the dirt off his feet with his wet towel, and while he was doing it he turned and smiled at Natalie, acting as nearly as he knew how as though none of it had happened.

She was looking at him hard, and the expression was so pregnant, so obviously and openly an outpouring of some deep and intense feeling, that he stared stupidly, the smile fading from his lips. And, with her eyes still looking hard into his, holding his gaze as though this thing she had to say had to be said with her eyes alone, she moved her head slowly back and forth in an overtly meaningful gesture.

Noah looked back into her eyes thoughtfully, concentrating, as he might have looked if her lips had been moving and he had been trying to read what they said. They seemed to say something more than

[99]

thanks for a simple physical rescue, but his mind, conditioned by the things she had said only an hour ago, by the thing she had done to him sixteen years ago, by a lifetime of never having been taken seriously by anyone, refused to believe that they said all that they seemed to say. It was, he insisted on telling himself, her rather overdramatic, overdone way of thanking him for what he had done. He smiled at her again, shaking his head, trying to say by his manner that the whole thing wasn't to be taken that seriously.

She looked puzzled for a moment, frowning. Then, when he continued to smile and shake his head, her gaze moved past him and she stared out over the creek to the Sound. And, all within a fraction of a minute, she looked back at him again and shrugged her shoulders and nodded, smiling a disappointed, cynical smile of acceptance.

Jeffrey was not at the house when they got back. "He's on the golf course," Natalie said. "He was on the phone when I left, trying to get up a golf match." She started up the stairs. "I ordered a two o'clock lunch," she said, "because breakfast was so late. But come down any time you like. Pammy and I will be around here somewhere." Her manner seemed distant and impersonal.

"Where will Peter be?" Noah asked.

"Heaven knows," she said. Then, starting up the stairs again, "He'll be all right. He's always all right—if people would just leave him alone. He gets along fine by himself." And from the upstairs hall she called, "He'll pop up when he gets hungry."

When Noah came down, Pammy was reading a magazine in the living room. She was dressed in black Bermuda shorts, very carefully pressed, and black wool stockings almost to her knees and a pink blouse, and her hair was set flawlessly, without a single hair out of place. Again Noah had the feeling he had had at breakfast, the feeling that she was too old for her age, and again her smile, as she looked up at him, was glittering and sophisticated.

He looked at her doubtfully, looked at his watch and saw that it was twenty minutes after one, looked at her again. She was watching him, smiling a knowing, enigmatic smile which he felt sure that she had practiced. He heard Natalie's step in the dining room, and he got up his courage and said, "I'd like to hear you play sometime, Pammy."

The mask fell away. She looked doubtful. "Oh," she said, "I'm not very good."

"The way I heard it, you're very good indeed."

"I haven't had a chance to practice in four days," she said sulkily, the young girl again.

Natalie came in from the dining room and stood in the doorway. Apparently she had heard the conversation, but she said nothing.

Pammy looked up at her and said, "Mr. Sibley wants me to play for him," and Noah sensed that she wanted to play for him and at the same time was, for some reason, afraid to.

"Just if you want to, Pammy," he said.

Natalie nodded, started to speak, stopped herself. Finally she said, "If you do feel like it, dear, this would be a good time. It's a half hour to lunch."

Pammy walked over to the piano stool and opened it and took out a handful of sheet music. Still sulky, she pawed through it, picking out three pieces and putting them on the piano. Then, without looking at either Noah or her mother, she sat down, arranged one of the pieces on the rack, and scowled at the keyboard.

She began to play, a quiet *étude* which she obviously knew so well that she did not need the notes in front of her. She played well. Noah suspected that she might be playing extremely well. Having never studied the piano himself, having only the sort of knowledge of music that one gets from occasional concerts and recitals and a moderate amount of listening to recordings, he didn't feel sure about that. What he was sure of was that she loved it, that she had a real feeling for it.

She finished the *étude* and Noah said, "That was very beautiful, Pammy."

Without looking at him, she opened up another composition and sat with her hands in her lap, glaring fiercely at the notes in front of her. Finally, tensely, she raised her hands to the keys, glared at the music for a moment more, then began to play. This was something much more difficult, more complicated, and it seemed to Noah that she was playing it well. But suddenly, without his having heard anything wrong, she slammed both fists down on the piano and jumped to her feet and said accusingly to Natalie, "You can't play if you can't practice." And she ran out of the room and up the stairs.

Natalie sat back in the chair with her eyes closed. She looked weary. "It's pretty complicated, Noah," she said, and she waited so long that Noah wondered if she was going to say anything more. "Her music means a lot to her. But she's getting to the age where popularity with the other youngsters means a lot to her too. And she can play popular stuff wonderfully well—I don't know where she learned to—so well that the leader of the orchestra over at the club always asks her to play a piece or two with them at the dances, and the boys and girls all gather around and listen to her."

Her voice was listless and emotionless, as though she was too tired to feel strongly about what she was saying. "Jeffrey's determined that she's not to play popular music at all. He's afraid it will spoil her playing, and I suppose he's right about that." She smiled wanly. "He has a tremendous respect for culture, you know. It's almost an obsession with him, and he's determined that, whatever it is, Pamela and Peter are going to have it." She paused again, gazing out of the window. "Whenever he catches her playing popular music, he punishes her by locking the piano and hiding the key."

She stood up and looked down at Noah pityingly, as though she were sorry for him that he had to be in on all this. "What seems logical to one person doesn't always seem logical to another, does it?" she asked.

4.

AT lunch, Pammy was sullen to the point of boorishness, and Noah realized that she was feeling some of the same sort of resentment toward him that Peter had felt after the incident on the raft. Natalie's manner was still distant and impersonal. Peter had not appeared, and Noah imagined that she was more worried about him than she had admitted. And it was only natural that she should be worrying about what would happen when Jeffrey came home from the golf course, about what he would say to Noah, about how he would act during the evening.

Noah was beginning to feel a little sullen himself, especially as Natalie seemed to be making little effort to keep a conversation going. The situation, he thought, was hardly what you could call a happy one. With Peter and Pamela both resenting his presence, with Jeffrey undoubtedly resenting it far more than either of them, with Natalie acting so—well, not unfriendly perhaps, but certainly a good deal less than cordial—

Anyway, whatever she was feeling toward him, it was certainly a peculiarly embarrassing time for her to be having a house guest.

After lunch she drove Pamela over to the club for her golf lesson. Noah went upstairs and changed his clothes and packed his bags. When she came back he was waiting for her in the living room. He stood up, and she stopped halfway into the room.

"Listen, Natalie," he said, "wouldn't it be a lot less embarrassing for you if I were to take that afternoon boat today instead of tomorrow? If I were to be gone when Jeffrey got back from his golf?"

It seemed to him that she looked startled, almost dismayed. Then quickly she composed her face and looked up at him politely. "Why, yes, Noah," she said, and her manner was even more distant. "Yes, I think that *would* be better. The boat leaves at four-thirty." She looked at her wrist watch. "It's three—" she didn't finish the sentence. She turned quickly and walked over to the window and stood looking out, her back squarely to Noah.

He stared at her, perplexed. And as he looked, he saw the same small movement of her shoulders that he had seen when she had disappeared into the grocery store that morning.

He strode across the room and took her by the shoulders and turned her around. She was crying, very quietly, her eyes filled with tears, her shoulders moving slightly with her sobbing. She closed her eyes and bowed her head, but when he tried to draw her closer to him, she braced herself, refusing to be drawn.

"Natalie," he said, "I didn't mean—I just thought it would be easier for you—I—"

She sobbed harder, her head still bowed.

He stared down at the top of her head, distressed and strangely happy. "I just didn't think I meant that much to you. But I do, don't I? I do mean something to you. You wouldn't be crying if I didn't."

Her sobbing stopped abruptly, but her head was bowed and he could not see her face.

"Suppose I were to tell you that those were lies I told you yesterday," he said urgently. "Suppose I were to tell you that you *are* the reason I've never married anybody else. Suppose—I love you, Natalie. I didn't know it yesterday, but I know it now. And I have a feeling that you love me. Do you?"

She did not answer.

"You do, don't you?"

Suddenly she stepped back, out of his grasp, and looked up at him defiantly. "No," she said angrily. "No, I don't love you." She was staring hard into his eyes, and gradually her expression changed from one of anger to one of disdain. She spoke more slowly, and there was contempt in her voice. "I love what you almost are. I love what you could have been. I love what I know now that you never will be. But I don't love what you are and I never will."

She pushed past him and walked with her taut, firm-muscled walk out into the hall, as though it took an effort for her to keep from running. He followed her into the hall, and at the bottom of the stairs she turned. Now again her manner was polite and impersonal. "The maid will drive you to the boat," she said. "She'll be down at the garage at four o'clock. I hope you have a nice trip back." And still walking as though she were trying to keep from running, she went on up the stairs.

Noah waited until he heard the door of her room close before he trudged on up, and in the guest room he sat on the bed, smoking and looking out of the window, until his watch told him that it was time to close up his bags and go down to the garage.

He felt sullen and helpless, overwhelmed with a sense of his own inadequacy, a sense of incompleteness. Why was it that he could never be quite his whole self, never quite say the things he should say, the wholehearted things that were there inside him but somehow never came out? What was it that held him back, that defeated him again and again?

When that door down the hall there had closed, had it closed forever on Natalie? Was this something else that you took sitting down— the way, it seemed to him, he had taken everything in his whole life? Did you let everything that was valuable, everything that had meaning in your life, everything that had helped you, go without a struggle.

Or, he asked himself, getting to his feet and pacing over to the window, if you were a man did you keep on trying, trying to find the key to this inadequacy of yours, this habit of letting yourself be defeated? If you kept on trying, someday you'd have to find it. And if you found it, you *could* come back, back to this cottage, back to Natalie. The things she had just said had sounded final, but they didn't have to be final, not if you found it.

To find it, you had to understand something you didn't understand now. And to understand that thing you probably had to think harder; you had to think more directly and more honestly. Perhaps what you did was to think about the other times you had felt defeated. There had been other times when he had felt just this way, times when he had known that he was defeated and unable to know why. There was, for instance, that morning three years ago, when he had walked the campus at Milburn in the early morning hours, knowing that he was defeated, feeling defeated, and wondering why.

VI

1.

WEATHERWISE, that spring of 1950 had been a peculiarly propitious one in the hill country that surrounded the Milburn School. Starting with the shadbush and the fugitive apple trees that were scattered among the second-growth maples and birches and oaks on the hillsides, following along with dogwood and mountain laurel and rhododendron in an overlapping succession that no gardener's planning could have equaled, the hills had blossomed forth in a profusion of bloom and fragrance. For thirteen springs, four as a boy and nine as a man, Noah Sibley had tramped those hillsides, and he had never seen them so beautiful before.

In every way that spring had been a peculiarly fortunate and happy one for him. Never had four finer classes of boys been at the school at once. The teams—baseball, track, and tennis—were all winning more than their share, and the spirit among the boys was confident and exuberant. By a fortuitous happenstance, the only two masters he had ever found it hard to get along with had both left the previous June. And fond as he had been of old Dr. Edmonds, he had to admit that Roger Reinhart was somehow managing to infuse a new enthusiasm, a new spirit of hope and liveliness into the faculty—in fact, into the whole school.

And, almost as important to him, he had, after years of trying, finally persuaded them to drop the outmoded old course in civics which he had always hated. Next year he would be teaching nothing but history. To that he looked forward with relish.

The feeling he had had ever since his return from the Navy, the feeling that he was no longer a young master on trial, but a real, though by no means important, part of the school, had grown year by year, until he now felt confident and at home in the job. And in his contacts with the boys, his touch, he felt, had grown surer. They still came to him for help and advice, perhaps a little more than to most of the other masters, but more for advice and less for help than they used to. He liked to think that he wasn't the soft touch for a phony request that he had been before the war.

Yes, by the spring of 1950 his way of living was finally beginning to seem a thoroughly desirable one, and he was looking forward with real pleasure to a life that would be full of the kinds of accomplishments and satisfactions that had gradually come to mean the most to him. All through that peculiarly fortunate spring his happiness, his delight in his work, his anticipation of this seemingly assured future had grown until it sometimes seemed to him that they must be building up to some kind of climax. But when the painful climax came, on the Saturday night before Baccalaureate Sunday, in the midst of all the routine happenings of the ritualized Commencement Weekend, he was as unprepared for it as if the thought of a climax had never occurred to him at all.

2.

FROM the Headmaster's Tea on that Saturday afternoon he had made his usual clumsy and confused exit, bumping into tables and doors, smiling hopefully, trying to wave a farewell to everyone at once and trying at the same time to be unobtrusive and not to draw attention away from the other masters.

On the front porch he had stood still for a moment, collecting his thoughts. He had taken a deep breath, once again disappointed in himself. Try as he would, he could never think of anything to tell parents but the truth. He had no skill with subtleties.

Finally he had gone on down the steps and along the walk toward the campus. Of course it hadn't been as bad this year as it might have been because the boys in this graduating class had been an exceptionally fine bunch of boys. The truths that he had found himself telling were, he guessed, truths that in most cases the parents might have found reasonably gratifying.

It was a cloudy afternoon, with a hint of rain in the air, and a strong wind blew across the campus. He walked on, picking up speed as he went along, while his white trousers clung to his knees in front and flapped out in back like pennants. He crossed the main quadrangle, frowning into the wind. When he met boys, he was quick to replace the frown with a smile, and when he caught the glimmer of friendship in their eyes, he felt a warm and comforting sense of accomplishment. Little by little he began to forget his annoyance with himself.

He came to the arch and went through it and down the long flight of steps to the lower quadrangle, then cut diagonally across to the last entry in old Seward. There, in the ground-floor suite in the corner, he had lived for nine years. It was a good suite, with a study and a bedroom and bath, and it was his own as his room in the house in Middlefield had never been.

He looked at his watch. He had an appointment at the Inn with a Mrs. Morris whom he had never met. He wasn't looking forward to that much, although he did take a certain pride in the fact that he alone, of all the masters, had managed to get somewhere with her problem boy. And after that he was having drinks and dinner with Walt Radmaker, his old friend from Princeton days, and his wife Mary. Their twin boys were third-formers, a fine pair of boys. Drinks and dinner with them would be fun, but what with the tea, the ballgame, the track meet, and the dozens of conferences and chats with boys and their parents since early morning, it added up to a long, tiring day.

The room looked inviting, and the bed, when he glanced into the bedroom, even more so. He was already late for his appointment with Mrs. Morris, but he loosened the knot in his tie, unbuttoned his collar, and took off his shoes. He settled into the big chair with his feet up on the straight one and lighted a cigarette. He smoked it slowly, with his eyes closed.

Then, with a sigh, he crushed the cigarette into the ashtray and put on his shoes and rearranged his tie. Drops of rain were beginning to appear on the window. He put on his raincoat and buttoned it up around his neck, got out his old rainhat and put it squarely on his head and turned the brim down. And as the rain began to fall harder, he trudged off down the road toward the village.

3.

At ten o'clock, his day finally finished, he climbed the steps to the entryway. There were lights in his living room. He frowned, wondering how he could have failed to turn them off when he left. He couldn't even remember that he had had them on at all.

He took out his key and, grasping the knob, discovered that the door was unlocked. He knew that it had been locked when he left. Suspecting a final weekend prank from the boys, he waited a moment, gathering his senses, alerting himself to whatever bucket of water or piece of cord might be awaiting him inside the door. Finally prepared, he opened the door cautiously.

There, comfortably ensconced with books in their laps, sat Barrett and Mark and his mother, smiling up at him delightedly. Tired from the long day, drowsy from the aftereffects of the drinks and his relaxing conversation with the Radmakers, Noah made a tremendous effort to appear glad to see them. He would, he thought disloyally, have been considerably gladder to see them the next morning.

"Well," Mark said, "we thought you were never coming back."

"I was having dinner at the Inn with Walt and Mary Radmaker."

And Mark, who had been two classes ahead of Noah and Walt at Princeton, said, "What you see in that dumb Walt Radmaker is something I could never understand."

Noah smiled at him, wearily but cheerfully. "I like him," he said. "I like both him and his wife very much."

Time, the years since that evening when Natalie and Margy Hendricks had come to dinner at the Sibley cottage, had brought unpredictable changes in Mark. The man who then had looked so much like pictures of his handsome father at that age, who had given such promise of developing into the same arresting figure that his father had been throughout his life, had, by some caprice of heredity, failed to fulfill the promise. In those thirteen short years the lithe body of the famous swimmer and quarter-miler had, under the too sudden shift to a sedentary life, taken on unexpected heaviness around the shoulders and under the belt. The head of curly hair, which in his father had remained one of the most imposing marks of distinction up to his dying day, had thinned and receded until now, at thirty-seven, the top of his head was almost entirely bald—the result, he insisted a little petulantly, of his two years in the tropics during the war. And while the classic features were still there, the face around them had, like his body, filled out, and the quick charm of his smile, so captivating in those earlier days, had been replaced by an expression which was, Noah had to admit to himself, sometimes sulky and often censorious.

"How did you get in?" Noah asked, and they all looked tolerantly bored with him.

"We got the janitor to let us in, stupid," Mark said.

"Old Michael?" Noah asked enthusiastically. "Did he remember you?" Old Michael's memory for old boys was legendary.

"Of course he remembered us—all three of us." His tone made the statement a tribute not to Michael's memory but to the prestige of the Sibley family.

Whenever Noah caught a fresh and freshly disappointing image of Mark, as he did now as he dropped into a chair and looked uncertainly around at the three of them, he told himself, with his habitual loyalty, that he tended in his own mind to exaggerate the unfortunate changes in him, that other people would undoubtedly still find him an attractive person. And he told himself too that, even if there were some unfortunate changes, they were understandable enough when you considered the tragedy of Mark's marriage. His wife, Winifred, had been in a sanitarium for most of their married life. She had gone in for the last time four years ago, and all the family were wondering now if she ever would be capable of living out in the world of reality again. It was enough to explain a great deal about Mark, and you could add to it the fact that, through no fault of his own, his career had not been what he had hoped it to be. That he had risen above it all, that he was already achieving fame in a new direction, proved to Noah that there was still real stuff in this brother whom he had worshiped so wholeheartedly in his earlier days.

"Where are you staying?" Noah asked, and again they all looked bored with him. They had no idea, he thought, how tired he was, what an effort it was for him to try to make conversation.

"We're driving back home tonight," Barrett said. "There wouldn't be any chance of getting rooms at the Inn this weekend."

Noah sat up, startled. It was a two-and-a-half-hour drive from Middlefield. This was something more than a friendly visit. "You just drove down," he asked, "and you're going to drive back tonight?"

His mother smiled at him. "We have a surprise for you, Noah."

"What kind of a surprise?" Noah asked, still worried.

"The happiest surprise in the world."

They were all three smiling at him.

"Well!" he said. And as they still sat smiling, he asked, "What is it?"

Barrett and Mark both looked at their mother. Smiling importantly, she picked up her handbag and took out her glasses and a piece of paper.

4.

"WELL, Noah," she said, "all the legal complications have finally been straightened out and the William Huntington Sibley Memorial Foundation is officially in existence—one year and one month to the day from the date of your father's death. Barrett says that considering everything it could have taken a great deal longer, and I'm sure it would have if he hadn't been so unstinting in the amount of time he's given to it. And of course he isn't charging the Foundation a cent for all his work."

Noah smiled approvingly at Barrett, who was holding his heavy black horn-rimmed glasses a few inches out in front of his face, waving them slightly as he listened. Except for a certain increase in the gravity of his mien and for this little set of legal-profession mannerisms with the horn-rimmed glasses which had become so much a part of his manner, Barrett had changed very little. The years which had changed Mark so unpredictably from a slender, gay-mannered youth into a heavy-set, balding, irritable-looking man had served only to accentuate in Barrett the qualities that had always been there. He still had the tall trim figure, the full head of wavy brown hair, the sternly handsome features, the gravely courteous, always reasonable manner. And his air of a man who was on his way to achieving distinction in the world and unerringly sure of the road ahead, which he had had ever since his college days, had, since his first stay in Washington, become more and more pronounced.

Much of the difference, Noah thought, could be laid to the fact that his second marriage had proved eminently successful. Joan, the daughter of a State Department official, had turned out to be just right for him. They had had four happy and successful years together. If Mark could only have had the same sort of break, he might have—

"We had the first meeting of the trustees this morning, Noah," his mother said, "and we took steps to get the work of the Foundation under way." She put the glasses on and opened the paper. "Its purpose, as Barrett stated it so well in the papers he drew up, is"—she read—"'to further study and research on, and to stimulate public interest in, the various agencies devoted to co-operation and arbitration among nations, with especial emphasis on those agencies which have come into being since the First Hague Conference in 1899.' "

Noah felt sure that if his mind weren't so weary he would have seen that there was something especially wonderful about the way Barrett had stated it. As it was, it was going to take a little while for it to sink in. He had known, of course, that his mother had started on the idea of a Memorial Foundation only a few weeks after his father's death. And in a general way he had assumed that it would have something to do with his father's life work, with world peace. But Barrett had been the natural one to work with her on it, and nobody had bothered to tell Noah any of the details of the plan. "That's wonderful," he said. "Would you mind reading it again?"

With a sigh she put her glasses back on. " 'To further study and research on, and to stimulate public interest in, the various agencies devoted to co-operation and arbitration among nations, with especial emphasis on those agencies which have come into being since the First Hague Conference in 1899.' "

Slowly, significantly, underlining by her manner the momentous nature of the things she was about to say, she put the paper and her glasses back into her handbag. "Of course, Noah, the ultimate goal of the Foundation is to establish peace among nations, but, as your father so often said, 'The springboard from which progress leaps is knowledge.' Before we can go on to bigger things, there is a tremendous amount of spadework that has to be done, and, as you can see from what I just read, all that spadework is in the nature of historical research."

She paused, as though to let the importance of what she was saying sink in. She had always been a great one for working up to what she had to say, building it up to a dramatic climax. Noah wished that she would get to the point.

"Fortunately," she finally went on, "your father developed the habit early in his career of keeping copies of everything he wrote, and of keeping all the letters that he received if they seemed to have any importance at all. Those files in his study—there are twenty-four drawers of them—are crammed with first-hand source materials that aren't duplicated anywhere else in the world. For a young historian, they're a gold mine. There's correspondence with Elihu Root, Nicholas Murray Butler, Lansing, even some with Taft and Wilson and Harding and Coolidge themselves. You just can't begin to name them all."

Having worked as his father's secretary for one full year, and for all the time he could spare from his school work since then, Noah suspected that he knew more about what was there than his mother did. He wished she would say what she had to say and let him go to bed. "I know," he said.

"Yes, of course you know," she said disapprovingly, "but I wanted to outline the whole situation so that you would have it clearly in mind. I doubt," she went on with the momentous manner, "if there is a young historian in the country who, if he knew about those files, wouldn't give almost anything for the privilege of getting into them. Whoever does get at them will hardly be able to escape becoming famous. But for your father's sake and for the family's sake and for the Foundation's sake, it's extremely important that whoever does should have a sympathetic understanding of your father's work and of his aims in life."

Wearily stupid though his mind was, Noah could see the direction his mother's speech was taking. It was, he saw, swinging around toward him. He sat slowly nodding his head up and down, his eyes closed. Then he opened them and looked up at her. "Of course I'll be anxious to co-operate all I can," he said, "but you all know that I don't have either the time or the ability to do the important part of the work."

All three of them, frowning, sat staring at him.

Finally Mark said, "I find that rather an uncalled-for statement, Noah."

And his mother said, "I can't imagine where we could find anyone else nearly so *well* qualified, Noah. After all, you *have* worked as his secretary. If there's anyone who does understand his work and his aims, it certainly should be you. You are an historian and—"

"Teaching history in a boys' school doesn't make you an historian," Noah interrupted.

Again they all stared at him. And again it was Mark who finally broke the silence. "I seem to remember," he said, "that you had a course at Columbia in the techniques or methodology or whatever they called it of historical research. Wasn't that so?"

It was so. That winter—the winter when he had been commuting into the city—when his mind had been so full of dreams of his future life with Natalie that he had never understood how he had managed to pass any examinations at all! And, thinking then that he was going to devote his life to secondary school teaching, he had paid less attention to the course in the techniques of historical research than to any other. All that was left today of that course were a few old lecture notes and a couple of textbooks.

"As for your not having the time," Barrett said, his tone somewhat more conciliatory than Mark's, "that is something that we've pretty well taken care of. You'll have all the time there is."

"What do you mean?"

Suddenly they were all smiling again delightedly, as people smile when a birthday cake is brought in.

"At the meeting of the trustees this morning," Barrett said, "you were elected secretary of the Foundation at an annual salary of ten thousand a year. That, I believe, is a little more than twice what you're getting now from the Milburn School. There will also be an expense account to cover your clerical and travel expenses."

Noah sat bolt upright. "You—you don't mean that I should give up my job here?"

"For heaven's sake, Noah," Mark said impatiently.

Barrett was looking at him sadly. "You could hardly expect to draw a ten-thousand-dollar salary from the Foundation and go on working here, could you?"

Slowly Noah rose to his feet. "I can't do it," he said, gazing apprehensively around at the three of them. "I—my job is here. This is where I've put in all my best years. I'm getting to know this job. I can't leave it now."

"Good God, Noah," Mark said.

Barrett was beginning to look as though even *his* patience was wearing thin. "How many masters are there at Milburn, Noah?"

"Thirty-six," Noah said. "Thirty-seven, if you count Roger Reinhart."

"One out of thirty-six," Barrett said, "and very little chance, I should say, to become pre-eminent even among them. What kind of distinction in life is that, to spend your life aiming for? Working for the Foundation, you can't help becoming famous. You'll have access to materials that—"

"It's not what I want," Noah shouted, suddenly angry. "The rest of you can have your damned distinction. I want to work at the kind of work I like, the kind of work I'm good at."

"You've always written very well indeed, Noah," his mother said. "Your thesis, all your written work in college—you never got anything but First Groups. Remember? Even Mark, whose business is writing, said just the other day that he sometimes envied you your facility with the written word. I think you have just the abilities that the job calls for."

"Far better suited for it, I'd say," Mark put in, "than for trying to teach a bunch of school-age boys. You're the studious type, Noah, not at all the kind that full-blooded schoolboys go for. I've never felt that this was what you were ideally suited for."

"It's not what I want," Noah said forlornly, apprehensively conscious of the fact that he was losing ground in the argument. "I love it here. It's where I've been happiest. I love—" He stopped himself, suddenly realizing that he had a real point. He stood up straighter and looked around at them confidently. "In any case, it's out of the question for this year. It's too late." He smiled at them, triumphant in the knowledge that he was about to throw the blame back onto them. "If you'd had this in mind, you should have let me know back in February, when the school was filling vacancies in the faculty for the fall term. Now it's far too late to fill them. To give them notice at this late date would be inexcusable, absolutely unfair to the school and to Roger Reinhart."

For a moment they did look taken aback, and, trying to cover his feeling of triumph with an expression of reasonableness, Noah went back to his chair and sat looking around at them. "That gives us some time to think it over," he said.

They all three sat quietly, looking down at the floor.

"What," Mark finally asked, "would they have done if you'd been killed by an automobile on your way back from the Inn tonight? Disband the school?"

"Well"—Noah hesitated—"well, I suppose—I suppose they'd have to fill in somehow—maybe other teachers would have to double up— or maybe they could pick up somebody somewhere—"

"It would seem," Barrett said, "that there must be at least one young history student getting out of some graduate school in the country this June who would welcome a teaching job at Milburn. Wouldn't you think so, Noah? Don't you honestly believe they could find one if they had to?"

"I don't know," Noah said defensively. "I certainly don't know that they could." He realized that it was not a brilliant answer, and he felt, as Barrett and Mark had always made him feel, like a stubborn child who refuses to concede any points in an argument, arguing for the sake of arguing. Never in his life had he won an argument with either of them. He tried to think of a more reasonable reply. "In any case," he said, "it would certainly make it very awkward for them."

"Don't you think," Mark said, "that it's going to make it a little awkward for the Foundation to try to get along for a year without its executive secretary?"

Again Noah jumped to his feet. "That's not fair," he shouted. "I'm not the executive secretary. I haven't accepted the job of executive secretary. You go ahead and elect me executive secretary without even asking me if I want it, and then you try to make me feel like a heel because I don't want it, and I'm damned if I'm going to take it. You can go find yourselves another executive secretary." He stared around at their shocked, unresponsive faces. He knew that he was shouting too loud, that he was red in the face, that he was making a scene. The Sibley family disliked scenes. He didn't care. "And the next time you decide to plan my life for me, you can tell me about it ahead of time."

Their faces were impassive. None of them spoke.

Finally his mother sighed a great, soulful sigh and picked up her handbag. She looked up at him. "I never thought, Noah," she said in a very subdued voice, "that the time would come when I would be ashamed of one of my boys." She stood up, and Barrett and Mark, taking their cue from her, stood up too. "And I certainly never thought that, just a year and a month after his death, one of my boys would renounce his obligation to his father, refusing to carry on where he left off, leaving the fruits of his whole life's work to rot away and be forgotten. I believe," she said, as the tears welled up in her eyes, "that this is a sadder moment for me than—than even his death was."

Quietly, soberly, as he might have done it if she were leaving her husband's deathbed, Barrett opened the door for her. Without looking at Noah again, she walked out, her head bowed.

But outside she stopped, and as Mark walked on past her she turned and came back in, smiling through her tears. "Kiss me, Noah," she said.

Noah kissed her, and now there were tears in his eyes too.

"Your room will be waiting for you, my boy," she said, and quickly she turned and walked out. Barrett followed her out and closed the door quietly behind him.

NOAH woke up at six o'clock, feeling limp and depressed and harried. The rain had stopped during the night, and he got up and dressed and walked softly down the entryway and out into the quadrangle. No one was stirring.

The campus, newly trimmed and mowed for Commencement and freshly washed by the night's rain, was, he thought, more beautiful in this early morning light than he had ever seen it before. The sun was already up above the dormitories, glistening in the tall elms, casting long shadows across the lawns. Wherever its rays reached the ground, a delicate hint of mist rose a few inches off the grass. The air was soft and warm and pungent with the smell of wet earth and wet leaves. Quietly and reverently he walked out across the quadrangle and on up the steps and through the arch and on, and in front of old Wainwright where, in the southeast corner room, he had held every class he had ever held, he stopped. The room had been assigned to him by old Dr. Edmonds the day he had arrived in September of '38, and neither he nor anyone else had seen any reason for changing it since. He liked the room. He had always hoped that nobody would ever change it, and one sentimental evening just a few weeks ago he had gotten to wondering if someday, twenty-five or thirty years hence, he would be holding a final class there, the last class for old Mr. Sibley. He thought of it again now and smiled. It had been a silly thought, but in a way an appealing one too.

He went on across the campus, and he stopped again when he got beyond the gymnasium, where he could look out over the playing fields to the hills beyond. He stood there for a long time gazing at the hills, and for the first time since his mother and Barrett and Mark had left the night before, he found himself thinking about his father, for whom hills and mountains had had some extravagant sort of meaning. It was his father's unreasoning, overwhelming love for hills that had sent the family back to Vermont summer after summer, no matter what other plans might have been discussed during the winter.

Noah was thinking now about how his father would sit and look at hills, longingly, hour after hour, and how, right up to the last year of his life, he would climb them with a greedy, insane zest, pushing ahead with his arms swinging and his head thrust forward, his eyes gleaming, shouting exhortations to the rest of the family to keep up with him. "Excelsior," he would shout, turning without slackening his gait to wave them on, "Excelsior,"—a ludicrous, excited though always handsome figure in a blue flannel shirt and laced khaki breeches and high black basketball shoes. And as he reached the top he would shout, "Eureka," and then, staring ecstatically at the view which held nothing but more hills with perhaps an occasional glimpse of a lake nestled between them, he would shout, "Ship ahoy, ship ahoy," again and again, a performance which the whole family found excruciatingly embarrassing even when there were no outsiders with them.

It, this odd performance, had been so incongruous, so entirely out of character with the suave gentleman of the dinner table and the lecture platform whom they and the world had known! It had been, Noah suspected now, his outlet, his one escape from the restrictions of the courtly, restrained manner which, self-imposed, had become a part of his stock in trade early in his career and from which he could never afford any more public deviation. Whether the crazy performance had had any deeper psychological meaning, whether it had symbolized in some way the inner urgings of his father's nature, Noah had often wondered. But mostly he, along with the rest of the family, had wished that he would stop doing it, and as the years went by they had tried more and more to avoid going with him when he climbed hills—and especially to see to it that strangers did not get a chance to see the weird performance.

Slowly, Noah started back across the campus toward the arch. Those quoted exhortations, "Excelsior" and "Eureka" and a half dozen others like them! They *had* been a part of his normal manner, but he had always said them half humorously, and because he had said them half humorously they had not seemed incongruous. They *had* had, Noah felt sure, some sort of meaning for him—his own peculiar way, perhaps, of spurring himself and his family on to greater endeavor.

After his midmorning cup of chocolate, as he stood up to go back to his study: "Play up," he would say, smiling a little shamefacedly, "play up, play up, and play the game." Or sometimes, "Fight the good fight," or, "Fight on, fight ever."

During the last thirty-six hours of his life, as he lay staring at the ceiling in his bed in the front room, exhortations of this sort had been the only things he had said that came out clearly. The stroke had affected his speech centers, and although he had talked a good deal, it had been so thick and so jumbled that Noah had understood very little of it. But twice, clearly, he had heard him say, "Play up, play up, and play the game." And twice he had heard him say, "Carry on, Lieutenant." Just what all the others had been he couldn't remember now, but he was sure there had been some "Fight on's" and at least one "Excelsior."

And once very clearly, as clearly as he had ever spoken, he had said, "God damn it, Charlie." Charlie was his brother, older by a year, who had stayed in the small town in northern New Jersey where they had been brought up and had achieved, with some of the same histrionic ability that William Huntington had, a considerable local fame as a trial lawyer.

6·

Noah had told himself that he had to think the thing out. But before he got down the steps into the lower quadrangle he was, with a fearful sense of emptiness, trying to fight off the realization that this walk had been a sentimental journey, a farewell. He tried to tell himself that the emptiness was simply hunger, that what he needed was a good breakfast. But when he thought of breakfast at the Unmarried Masters' table in Commons, he knew that he could not face it.

Instead he went back to his quarters and washed his face and hands and brushed his hair and put on a clean white shirt and a summerweight suit. The day was already giving promise of being a hot one. He walked down to the village and got a breakfast at the Snack Bar and went back to his room and bolted the door and told himself that he was going to think the thing through. He sat in his big chair and lighted a cigarette.

But before he had finished his second cigarette, he knew that he was not thinking anything through. He was sitting there panting, with sweat breaking out on his forehead and on his body, staring in horror first at one, then at the other of two inconceivable, dreadful alternatives, trying to tell himself that he did not have to choose between them.

He stumbled over to the desk and sat with his hands over his eyes, his elbows leaning heavily on the desk, sighing with each breath and whispering to himself between breaths. How long he sat like that he had no idea. Once he got up and stood in the middle of the room, staring fiercely around at the walls. He went back and sat at the desk again, his chin in his cupped hands.

Thoughts of his mother kept coursing through his mind, of her and of her feeling about her husband and her family. Last summer at the Lake, not many weeks after his father's death, she had talked to him about it one late afternoon when they were walking home from the village together—the first time, it had seemed to him then, that she had ever talked to him as one adult to another.

"Your father was a very great man, Noah," she had said that afternoon. "Few people know how great. The world accorded him some recognition, but not nearly all that he deserved. That will come later —some, undoubtedly, when his book is published, but not in full measure until arbitration is finally established as the normal way for nations to settle their differences. Then they will realize how vital his part in it was."

She had walked on along the rutted road, her eyes thoughtful, her face serene, before she had gone on to talk about her children. "All five of you children," she had said, "have inherited some of his unusual abilities—in varying degrees, of course. I am very proud to have been the vehicle through which some of his exceptional qualities have been carried on into another generation, just as I was proud to be his helpmate during his lifetime. It's been a great privilege. But it's also been a responsibility, Noah, a very great responsibility. I've felt that those abilities that he had and that he passed on in some degree to you children are—well, I've felt that they are a sacred trust in my hands."

Noah had sensed that she was a little embarrassed to have used that phrase, but he had known too that it described her feeling accurately.

"Ever since I married your father, I've devoted all my energies to trying to make it possible for him to realize his potentialities to the fullest. I've devoted the income I inherited to it too, and was very happy to do so. And when you children came along and began to show such unusual promise, I gave myself to that too, trying to see that you took full advantage of the splendid educational opportunities we were able to give you, trying to see to it that you realized all the potentialities that were in *you*. I've worked hard at it and—"

She hesitated, and, glancing sideways at her face, Noah saw, for one of the few times in his life, doubt and uncertainty there.

"Perhaps sometimes I've tried too hard," she finally said. "I know that sometimes people would have liked me better if I hadn't been so determined, if I hadn't always demanded so much of him, and of you, and of others." She paused. "I know that some people have felt that I demanded too much of poor little Winifred, for instance. I liked Winifred, Noah. She's always been a well-meaning child, a sweet child in many ways. But, Noah, I *just can't have* flighty girls like Winifred Bunce and Louise Hill"—there was bitterness in her voice when she pronounced Louise's name—"I can't have flighty girls like them upsetting the careers of men like Mark and Barrett. You can see that, can't you? I can't let anything interfere with their doing the things they were put here to do. I can't let *anything* get in the way of their realizing all of their potentialities. It's been my duty, Noah, and whatever else I may have been, I think I can say for myself that I have never shirked it."

Sitting there at his desk with his chin in his hands, Noah seemed to hear the quality of her voice as she spoke. He could see the expression in her eyes. Slowly he got to his feet and dragged himself into the bedroom. He fell face down on the bed and lay there, not caring that his coat was hunched awkwardly up around his shoulders, knowing now that, dreading the talk with Roger Reinhart more than he had ever dreaded anything in his life, he dreaded even more walking into the house in Middlefield and facing his mother, living all summer at the Lake with her accusing eyes.

He sat up on the edge of the bed, his shoulders humped, looking down at his shoes. He could write a letter to Roger from Middlefield. It would reach him on his vacation, bring him scurrying back to Milburn, send him, perhaps, on a few trips around the country. It might cost Roger a week or two of his vacation.

Today, this afternoon maybe, before all the universities had had their commencements, Roger would be able to get on the phone. He might find someone in a day or two. By writing a letter you would save yourself a little embarrassment, a painful quarter hour. You might be weak. You suspected that you were being weak now. But you didn't have to be a coward too.

He walked over to the bureau and looked into the mirror at a face that told him nothing, a face that was impassive and surly and stupid. And feeling completely detached from what he was doing, watching himself as he might have watched someone else, he brushed his hair again and put on his glasses and straightened his tie and tried to pull the wrinkles out of his coat.

Doggedly, at a steady, even pace, he walked through the sitting room and down the entryway and across the quadrangle and up the steps and on diagonally across the campus. But when he got to the walk in front of the Headmaster's House, he walked on past it, looking at it fearfully out of the corner of his eye, feeling like a criminal who, having decided to give himself up, can't quite get up the courage to do it.

He stood still, looking back at the house, then walked back very fast and climbed the steps and rang the bell. At least it would be Roger Reinhart and not old Dr. Edmonds. If it had been Dr. Edmonds, he couldn't have done it. There had been too strong a tie of understanding between them, the young master and the old headmaster.

It wouldn't be quite so bad with Roger. Noah had no such feelings about him. Roger had been a class behind him in school, which made them, of course, old schoolmates. If they had met for the first time since school days, they would have fallen into each other's arms. But actually Noah had no very strong feelings about him either way. What he thought about him mostly was that he was making a good headmaster—an all-around man in school and college, an athlete and debater, a graceful, sincere speaker, the perfect choice for a young headmaster. He was good for the school, and for that Noah liked him very much.

Roger would say the right thing. He would be genuinely perturbed. But he would be more perturbed by the necessity of finding somebody else before school opened in the fall than by any feeling that Noah's leaving was a great loss to the school. Noah had never felt that Roger believed that he, Noah, was very vital to the school's success.

It was Roger himself who came to the door, in a dressing gown over dark trousers and a white shirt, half dressed for the Baccalaureate service in the chapel. He was freshly shaved and thoroughly scrubbed, but his eyes were tired, as a headmaster's eyes had a right to be on this weekend. "Noah," he said, grinning cordially.

Noah smiled back at him weakly. "Sorry to bother you at a time like this, Roger, but it's something important."

"Not a bit, not a bit, Noah. Come in."

Noah followed him into the study that looked out over the back lawn. He opened the French doors that gave out onto the back porch. "It's a lovely morning," he said. "Let's sit out here."

They sat with their feet on the window boxes.

Noah began, haltingly, with a brief outline of his father's career. He knew that he was not stating the case well, that he was trying too hard to make it brief and trying too hard to make it convincing. He was afraid that he was talking too much about his father's fame, that it sounded as though he was bragging. He stopped talking about his father and shifted too abruptly to a discussion of world peace.

Soon after he started, the friendly smile faded from Roger's face. As Noah talked on, he sat staring across the lawn, his eyes seemingly riveted on one particular bush in the border that edged the yard, his mouth grim and tired. Never once did he turn to look at Noah's face, and when Noah looked at his there was no response, only the grim and implacable stare.

Confused and hurt, Noah went on more and more haltingly, more and more confusedly, stumbling over words, jumbling his sentences. He apologized lamely for not letting Roger know sooner and explained at too great length why it had been impossible for him to do so. He finally stopped. "I—I just can't see how I can do anything else, Roger."

Roger continued to stare at the bush, unmoving.

"I hate to put you in this situation, Roger," Noah said helplessly. "I know how hard it's going to be to find somebody to take my course at this late—"

"Oh, that," Roger said disparagingly. "We can always pick up a youngster or two from the graduate schools." He glanced once at Noah, then sat back with his hands clasped behind his head and looked up at the sky. "You left the Headmaster's Tea early yesterday, Noah," he said.

Noah looked at him. It seemed a trivial thing to be bringing up at a time like this. "I'm sorry," he said with dignity. "I had an appointment with Morris's mother."

Roger smiled at the sky. "For just a history teacher, with no other official position in the school, you have quite a few conferences with parents, don't you?"

"I can't very well refuse to talk with them if they ask me to," Noah said defensively.

"And quite a few of the boys bring their problems to you too, don't they?"

"Their problems," Noah said glumly, "and their phony requests— I've been the worst sucker on the whole faculty."

Roger smiled again, and it seemed to Noah that it was a cynical sort of smile. "How long have you been with the school, Noah?"

"Nine years. Twelve years with three out during the war."

"Kind of unusual, wouldn't you say, the way the parents and the boys bring their problems to you, when you joined the faculty only twelve years ago?" Now he took his hands from the back of his head and sat forward. "Look, Noah, after you left the tea yesterday, were your ears burning?"

Noah's mind was not at its most alert. He looked at Roger, scowling.

"What would you say, Noah, if I were to tell you that there are probably twenty boys in this school right now who wouldn't be here if it weren't for you?"

Noah scowled at him. "I—why, Roger, of course that couldn't be—"

"You probably don't know it, Noah, but I know that this school could get along better without me than it could without you. A lot better."

Noah stared round-eyed through his glasses. He took out his handkerchief and wiped the sweat from his forehead. "You're talking nonsense, Roger."

Roger grinned at him, the same friendly grin with which he had greeted him at the door. "I'm the fair-haired lad around here," he said. "I have a beautiful head of hair, haven't I?" He bowed his head so that Noah could see. "I make lovely speeches. In college, I made the run that beat Harvard. All the parents know about that run. They think I look just dandy in a gown. They think it's wonderful that the school should have me for a headmaster.

"But you're the guy they love, Noah," he said, and there was a suggestion of envy in his voice. "They send their boys here because they want them to have the experience of knowing you—at least some of them do, and I could name you some of them too. The ones who know anything about education have the feeling that no boy who has taken history under you will ever be completely provincial and narrow-minded again. You don't know it, Noah, but your history courses are masterpieces. Everybody else knows it."

Noah knew that he was blushing, and he was afraid there were tears in his eyes. He took off his glasses. "Goodness, Roger," he said, "I didn't come here to—"

Roger got to his feet. "For those reasons, Noah, I think this is probably the most serious crisis I've had to face since they made me headmaster." He walked over to the end of the porch and sat on the railing, facing Noah. The lines of fatigue in his face were very strong. "Is there anything I could say that would make you change your mind?"

Noah looked at him stupidly, too full of emotion to speak.

Roger waited, and when Noah still said nothing he said, "Your loyalty to your father is a pretty strong thing, isn't it?"

"I think he was a great man," Noah said huskily, "and he was working on the most important thing in the world—more important right now than it ever was. Don't you think so, Roger? If getting all the things he had collected and the things he had to say about peace published will help to bring about peace—well, you can see, Roger."

Roger sighed. "Yes, I can see," he said, but his tone made Noah feel that he was not seeing in quite the way Noah had tried to make him see.

"Is there any chance that you could finish editing the papers in a year?"

Noah shook his head.

"Two years?"

"It might be ten years, Roger. It might be a lifetime too."

Roger sighed again. Finally he said, "Well, perhaps you'd do this much for me, Noah. Would you let me keep your name on the roster and call it a leave of absence? I suppose it would have to be without pay? And not say too much about how long you think it might be?"

Noah looked up at him quickly, and Roger smiled dismally. "I know," he said. "It's not a very honorable suggestion, is it? I suppose you'd have to call it a deception."

"I wasn't thinking that," Noah said. "I'd like very much to have you keep my name on the roster. I'd—I'd love it."

"Good. And maybe you could take time off from your editing once in a while to put in an appearance around here. Commencement, some of the football weekends? It's not too long a drive from your home, is it?"

"Sure, Roger, I could do that all right," Noah said hopefully. "I'd like doing that. I'd probably be doing it anyway."

"Good." Roger looked at his watch. "Good God, I've got ten minutes to get dressed and get over to the chapel." He ran into the house. "How about coming down for opening day in the fall, Noah?" he called from his study. "And if you do, plan on having dinner here with us."

He disappeared, leaving Noah to find his own way to the front door. He walked slowly on out and again stood on the front porch of the Headmaster's House, trying to collect his thoughts. Finally he ambled down the steps and on toward the quadrangle, walking like a man in his sleep, his glasses in one hand and his handkerchief in the other.

VII

1.

THE road came to an end in the middle of an open pasture. The top of the hill was still a quarter of a mile away, off to the west. They got out of the car, and Noah took the two thermos bottles and the binoculars and Connie the brown paper bag, and, without bothering to say anything to each other, they started slowly toward the top, looking around at the hills and sniffing the air.

It was the kind of day that came to Noah's mind whenever one of the family asked, "What is so rare as a day in June?" although it was now late July—a spectacularly beautiful day, with a bright sun and sparklingly fresh air. The climb was an easy, gradual one, through a field dotted with cedars and wild raspberry bushes. The raspberries were dead ripe and warm in the sun, and they zigzagged along from bush to bush, picking only the ones that had turned deep crimson and popping them into their mouths.

As they approached the top, the Green Mountains gradually came into view ahead of them. They were sharply outlined, deep blue and very near today, and beyond them, through an occasional gap, they could make out the dim, cloudlike outlines of Adirondack peaks.

And being here with Connie, here in this clean air on this fantastically lovely day, Noah began to feel alive for the first time in a month. It was a month in which he had learned that there is no more poignant experience in a man's life than the experience of having nothing happen at all, this month that had passed since the afternoon when Natalie's maid had driven him to the Island ferry.

Still stopping now and then to eat berries, they went on over the crest and down a little way on the other side, and they sat on a low ledge of rock and opened the lunch.

"It's been a long time since I've seen you," Noah said. He had driven in from Middlefield after midnight the night before, and Connie had had the lunch all put up before he had finished his breakfast at ten o'clock. She had not asked him if he wanted to go on a picnic, she had told him that she had put up a lunch, and that it would be a lovely day on Randolph's Hill. And later he had heard her telling their mother and Mark that they were going on a picnic, and Noah had wondered if their feelings had been hurt that she hadn't included them.

He poured milk from one of the thermos bottles into paper cups, and Connie gave him a sandwich and a deviled egg. "It has been a long time," she said, hunching her shoulders in her peculiar, secretive way as she sipped her milk. "I was home one weekend, but you were away. Visiting somebody on some island, Mark said. Was that the Radmakers at Nantucket?"

"No."

"Who was it?"

Noah was munching away on his sandwich. He finished chewing a mouthful. "Some people I know named Humeston."

"Humeston," she said. The lake, below them there at the foot of the long slope, was very blue today against the black-green of the conifers that rimmed it. Outside the rim, the newly mowed hayfields were tawny in the sunlight. Connie ate a half of a deviled egg in three mouthfuls. The mixture in the middle was soft and gooey, and she licked her fingers thoughtfully and wiped her mouth with a paper napkin. "Humeston," she repeated. "That was the name of the man who married that girl you used to be in love with."

Noah looked at her sideways, reminding himself that it was nothing unusual for Connie to pull a name she hadn't heard in fifteen years out of her memory.

"Natalie Parkes," she said. "Is that who you were visiting?"

"Yes."

"Are you still in love with her?"

Noah took another big mouthful of sandwich and munched it slowly, trying hard to keep his expression an amused one. "I came back a day earlier than I'd planned to. Does that answer your question?"

"I think so. You still are."

It seemed to Noah that he had never succeeded in keeping anybody from guessing anything, least of all Connie. He was just not born an actor.

"What's her husband like?"

"I didn't care much for him."

"Does she care much for him?"

"I don't know."

"Of course you know. You were there for a weekend."

"Well"—he thought of telling her that he'd rather not talk about it, but then he realized that he wanted to talk about it and there was no one in the world he *could* talk to about it except Connie—"well, I got the impression that she found some things about him pretty hard to take."

Connie poured herself another cup of milk. "What sort of things?"

"Well, he was disagreeable with her in front of me—you know, picking on her for little things, finding fault."

She nodded. "Go on."

"And he put on kind of a silly act with me in front of all their friends, trying to act as though we were old cronies." He grinned at her sideways. "I guess he was impressed with the fact that I'm what he called an author."

She smiled back at him. "After all you are. Go on."

"I don't believe the friends he chooses are exactly the ones she would choose if she had her own way about it."

Connie nodded again, the amused expression in her eyes. "Anything more?"

Noah looked into the paper bag and found a cookie. He took it out and examined it, as though it had some point of peculiar interest about it. Connie was amused. But after all Connie was always amused. He did not feel that there was anything unsympathetic in her amusement. "Well, his attitude toward the children was a bit on the dictatorial side," he said.

"So there are children," Connie said. "Are they problem children?"

He looked at her sharply. "What makes you ask that?"

"The dictatorial father. And the mother who doesn't love him."

"I didn't say she didn't love him. I said there were some things about him she found pretty hard to take." He took a bite of his cookie and chewed it fiercely.

"I don't believe she loves him," Connie said. And after a while she added, "She might even still be in love with you."

Noah shook his head, staring glumly down at the lake.

"How do you know she isn't?" Connie asked.

"For one thing," he found himself saying, "she told me so." He wished as soon as he'd said it that he hadn't.

"So it got that far, did it? It must have been quite a story, the one that unfolded that weekend on that island. Would you care to tell me all about it?"

He thought. It wasn't, after all, the sort of story you could tell. "No," he said, "I don't believe I would."

She laughed. "Suffice it to say that you left a day earlier than you had planned."

Noah had a feeling that she had probably already pieced the whole story together in her mind. Connie was never wonderful, like the others, but the things she could do with her mind were far more wonderful than anything any of the others could do.

She took a plum from the bag and ate it, holding her paper napkin under her chin. Then she wiped her hands and took a package of cigarettes from the pocket of her blouse. "Are they problem children?"

"Sort of. The girl wasn't bad."

"I always liked Natalie," Connie said.

"She liked you too. She wondered if you'd like to have dinner with her in her apartment in New York sometime this fall."

"Very much. There's also a boy or two?"

"One. He seemed a bit tied up in knots."

"Because of the dictatorial manner?"

"Yes, because of the dictatorial manner."

Connie lighted a cigarette and, curling her feet up under her, sat puffing the cigarette and gazing off at the mountains, looking suddenly like a little girl too young to smoke. "You know," she said, "in spite of what she said, I'll bet she's still in love with you. She was really crazy about you that summer. You could never quite make yourself believe that, though, could you?" She shook her head, smiling at him appreciatively. "Noah the Humble." Now she was studying his face. Then, cocking her head to one side, she asked, "Why don't you see if you can't get her to divorce him and marry you?"

Noah laughed, too abruptly and too loud. He toned it down.

"Don't laugh," she said. "I'm not being funny. Why don't you?" And when he shook his head with great determination she eyed him suspiciously and asked with contempt in her voice, "Because there's nothing lower than a man who steals another man's wife?"

"Well," he asked, "is there?"

She turned away from him with a gesture of disgust, then sat staring down at the lake. Finally she turned and looked at him again. "Aren't you ever going to wake up, Noah?"

"Wake up to what?"

"Oh, Lord," she said helplessly. Then, dully, looking angry, as if they had been having a bitter argument, she said, "Let's have some coffee."

Noah picked up the thermos and poured two cups.

"There's a little bottle of cream in there somewhere," she said, "and an envelope of sugar."

Noah found them and put them into his coffee. She drank hers black.

"I don't think there's anything very admirable about divorce, if that's what you mean," he said defensively. "I think it's a messy, nasty business."

"Of course it's a messy, nasty business."

"At least half of the boys we had trouble with at Milburn came from broken homes."

She nodded, still looking angry. "And the other half came from homes where they wished they were divorced but weren't. A lot of people can't," she said thoughtfully, as though she was figuring out what she thought as she went along, "because they're Catholics. That's all right if you happen to be a Catholic. And I suppose some others can't because they can't arrange it financially. Maybe that's all right too. But then there are the ones who think they can't because of the children. They're the ones I wonder about. Suppose Mother and Dad had hated each other every day of their lives, right up to the time he died. Suppose we'd felt it in the air all the time we were growing up, overhearing fights and all that. Don't you think we might have been problems when we got away at school?"

Noah smiled, a little hesitantly. "I can't imagine it," he said.

"Of course you can't. I can't either. But maybe that's why we shouldn't be too ready with the pat answers about broken homes and stealing wives." Now she was grinning at him. "You know the picture I always see when they start spouting that one about nothing lower than a man who steals another man's wife. I see a burglar with a black mask over his eyes tucking a nice limp wife into his black bag and dropping her out of the window."

Noah laughed. He sipped his coffee and set the cup down on the ledge and lighted a cigarette. "You've got a point there all right," he said, feeling happier than he had felt in some time and having no idea why he should feel happier. "You can't quite class a wife with the silverware, can you?"

"Our father," Connie said, "had a wonderful knack for making non-sense sound impressive."

Noah looked at her out of the corner of his eye, no longer amused.

With his lips clamped tight, he poured himself another cup of coffee and elaborately, avoiding her eyes, put in the cream and sugar.

Connie seemed unconscious of his annoyance. "They say people don't change much from generation to generation," she said, "but it does seem to me that people today don't go for silly platitudes like that one the way they used to back in his day. Maybe that's why his fame hasn't lasted very well. You didn't get anywhere with the man you hoped was going to publish the book, did you?"

In the Sibley family, "the book" was never Noah's book, in which two university presses had already expressed an interest, nor either of the two books Mark had had published, but the massive *History of World Arbitration*, which Dr. Sibley had finished two years before he died. "No, I didn't," Noah said shortly.

"You sweltered away down there in Middlefield for a whole month," Connie said, "waiting to talk with him about it, and all you got for your trouble was another rejection. Right?"

"Yes," he said grumpily.

"On what grounds did he turn it down?"

Noah frowned at her. Then, feeling helpless before her keen mind, knowing that if she didn't know the answer already she would guess it, he sighed and told her the truth. "What he called 'too much editorial comment.'"

She nodded, as though she *had* known all along that that was it. She seemed to be waiting for him to go on.

"He said that if it ever were to be published it couldn't be called a history. It would have to be called *Essays on the History of Arbitration* or *William Huntington Sibley's Views on World Arbitration*."

She nodded. "That's what they've all said."

"What makes you think so?"

"I know so," she said. "You've never found his correspondence with the publishers, have you?"

"No."

"You never will. He burned it."

"How do you know he burned it?"

"Because I knew him. They all turned it down for those reasons you just said, and all this stuff about their wanting him to popularize it and his refusing to do so was pure baloney."

Noah jumped to his feet and stamped out into the field and stood looking off at the mountains. The sun was hot on his face, and the drone of bees was in the air. He went back and sat down again and lit another cigarette and puffed it hard. "Why did you hate him, Connie?"

She was picking up the paper cups and the plum pits and the scraps of food and putting them all back into the paper bag. "I didn't hate him," she said. "I loved him. I loved him very much." She folded the top of the bag over carefully and held it in her lap. "I think I loved him more than any of the rest of you did, because I loved him for what he was and not for what he kidded the world into thinking he was. What he was," she added, "was one of the greatest actors of the century." She smiled up at Noah. "And a very pathetic, well-meaning guy. I think he died because he couldn't stand being a charlatan any longer."

2 ·

WHEN, in midafternoon, Noah and Connie came back from their picnic on Randolph's Hill, Mark was lying in one of the low porch chairs with a book on his stomach. The day had grown warmer, and he was dressed in bathing trunks and a plaid shirt. "You have a letter," he said to Connie, "from the Sunburst Sport Shirt Company of Los Angeles."

"Really?" she asked, and her tone made Noah turn and look at her face. She was looking at Mark with an expression that seemed to contain both amusement and annoyance, and she turned quickly and went through the screen door into the living room.

Mark put a placemark into his book and dropped the book on the floor. He swung his legs out of the chair and followed her in. In spite of the extra weight which had accumulated over his shoulders and around his waist, his legs were still firmly rounded and well muscled, and his barefoot walk still had some of the grace of the former track man.

Mrs. Sibley, aroused by their footsteps, was on her way down the stairs when Noah came in. "Everybody ready for tea?" she asked cheerily.

"I'd like mine iced," Noah said.

"So would I," Connie said.

"Horrible custom!" Mark said. He had acquired definite ideas about tea during his year at Oxford.

"*Chacun à son goût,*" Connie said. "Oh hell, there I go again."

Over the years, Mrs. Sibley had learned to take mild profanity without wincing. "What do you mean, dear, there you go again?"

"*De gustibus*," Connie said disgustedly, "*non est disputandum*. Mark wants his hot."

The letter, a large envelope with the company imprint in the corner, lay conspicuously on the table. Mark was eying it and Connie.

"I'm afraid I side with Mark," Mrs. Sibley said amiably. "You can't teach an old dog new tricks. That will be two hot and two cold." She went into the kitchen.

Mark was still eying the letter. "I hope," he said to Connie in a tone that was more paternal than fraternal, "that you're not speculating in unlisted securities."

"I'm not," she said. She sank into a chair and sat with her hands in her lap, looking thoughtfully at the floor.

Mark settled into the big chair beside the fireplace and stared up at the ceiling, and Mrs. Sibley came in from the kitchen and sat in the Windsor chair beside the kitchen door. "A watched pot never boils," she said.

For a while nobody said anything, as they waited for the unwatched pot to boil. The things Connie had said about their father hovered in the back of Noah's mind, as they had ever since she had said them, filling him with a withering sense of apprehension.

Connie walked over to the table and picked up the letter. "If Mark were to burst," she said, "we'd have an awful lot of bloody flesh to clean up."

With a weary sigh, Mark put on an expression of bored indifference. Connie opened the letter and read it. Noah watched her, observing how well she had learned to keep changes in her thoughts from showing in her face. What changes of expression there were were minute, but it seemed to him that, as she read, he could still see the struggle there between annoyance and amusement and, along with them, a hint of pleased embarrassment. He wasn't sure she wasn't blushing just a little.

She folded the letter and laid it primly in her lap. Then she stared thoughtfully at the floor again, and slowly she began to smile, an impish little smile. "It's about a date, Mark," she said. Increasingly, these last few years, she had seemed to take delight in baiting Mark.

"A date? What kind of a date?"

"For dinner and whatever I'd like to do afterward."

She smiled at him, and he looked at her disdainfully. "You're having a lot of fun, aren't you?"

"Yes."

"I suppose you want me to ask you if it's a date with a man from the Sunburst Sport Shirt Company."

"You don't have to ask me. It is."

"Do you know him?"

She chuckled. "After all, he couldn't very well have gotten my name out of Who's Who. I'm one Sibley who isn't in it."

Mrs. Sibley sighed and went out to the kitchen. Connie smiled after her. It occurred to Noah that Connie enjoyed baiting her mother almost as much as she enjoyed baiting Mark. With a final disgusted glance at Connie, Mark picked up a magazine and turned the pages slowly. Restless and distracted, Noah went to the window and looked out at the lake, his hands in his pockets, still resentful in one part of his mind of the things Connie had said about their father, in some other part feeling more appreciative of her than he had ever felt before, a feeling that somehow she was his only ally. He was half interested in learning more of this man who wanted a date with her, half annoyed to have the thing intruding on his attention on this particular afternoon.

"The tray is ready, Noah," his mother said from the door of the kitchen. "Will you bring it in?" She cleared a space on the table and sat in front of it, waiting for him to bring the tray. "Where did you meet this man, Connie?" she asked.

"At a sidewalk café in Greenwich Village."

There was a significant silence.

"When was this?" Mrs. Sibley asked.

"Last June—during those two weeks when Grace and I borrowed an apartment in the Village."

They all busied themselves with their tea, Mark sipping his while still turning the pages of the magazine, Noah taking his glass back over to the window.

"Of course it's your own business, Connie," Mrs. Sibley said, "but I must say that I don't see why you always have to be so secretive and enigmatic about everything. We're all interested in what you're doing, just as much as we are in what Kate and Barrett and Mark are doing, but every time we show an interest you act as though we were trying to pry into your secrets."

Connie glanced at her out of the corner of her eye, then sat gazing into space, her face impassive. She took a breath before she spoke, and she spoke rapidly, in a monotone. "Grace and I were having cocktails last June in a sidewalk café in Greenwich Village and there were two men at the table next to ours and after a while they came over and asked if they could join us and we said, 'Yes.'"

"In other words," Mark said, without looking up from his magazine, "you let them pick you up."

"In other words, we let them pick us up," she said in the same rapid monotone, "and afterward they took us to dinner and after that we went dancing."

"At a night club?"

"At three night clubs, one after another. And the next day he took me over to Brooklyn to see the Dodgers play the Cardinals and that night he took me to dinner and—"

"He, I gather," Mark said, finally laying his magazine down and sitting forward, smiling delightedly, adopting the manner of an older brother teasing his little sister, "is the man from the Sunburst Sport Shirt Company."

Connie stared back into his face, a little bored and a little scornful. "Yes," she said. "His name is Jones."

"Jones," Mark said, bowing with exaggerated courtesy. "And how many night clubs did he take you to that night?"

"That night we went to a concert at Carnegie Hall."

"This is fascinating," Mark said. "As Mother pointed out, we're all very much interested to hear about what you've been doing. Tell us more."

"The next day we spent the whole day out at the Bronx Zoo." She finished her glass of iced tea and set it down on the table.

"How touching!" Mark exclaimed. "Tell me, what did you call him all this time? Mr. Jones?"

Noah thought he detected the flicker of a smile on Connie's face, and when she spoke there was a quaver of amusement in her voice. "No," she said, "I called him Jonesy."

"Jonesy?"

"Yes, his first name is Rentwood, but he doesn't like the name and prefers to be called Jonesy."

Mark grinned delightedly. "So you call him Jonesy."

"Yes."

"Go on."

She resumed her monotone. "The next morning we took the boat trip around Manhattan Island and in the afternoon we went out to Yankee Stadium and saw the Yankees play the Red Sox and—"

"Jonesy is a ball fan," Mark interrupted.

"Yes, he's a ball fan."

Mark lighted a cigarette and settled back in his chair and blew smoke at the ceiling. Noah watched him, sharing with him some of his condescending pleasure at having Connie at something of a disadvantage, at the same time sharing with Connie her half-humorous annoyance. He looked at his mother and was proud to see that she was looking far more amused than shocked. She had, he thought to himself, a great adaptability, a great resiliency of spirit.

"Somewhere along the way," Mark said, "we seem to have lost Grace and the other man."

"The other man," Connie said, "lived out on Long Island. He just stayed in town that first evening to entertain Jonesy."

"A married man, no doubt," Mark suggested.

"That's right. A married man with four children."

"Is Jonesy a married man with children?"

"He's a widower."

"Are you sure?"

"Yes."

"How do you know?"

"He told me so."

Mark shook his head at her naïveté.

"He has two children," Connie said, "a boy in the Army and a girl who is eighteen and going to get married next month."

Mark grinned. "Does he carry snapshots of them in his wallet?"

She nodded, smiling.

"And did he show them to you that first evening?"

She nodded again, still smiling.

Mrs. Sibley took the teapot over to Mark's chair and refilled his cup. He squashed his cigarette into the ashtray. "Now tell me this," he said. "What was he doing in New York?"

Again the flicker of a smile and the amused quaver in her voice. "He was what is known in New York as a visiting buyer."

Noah laughed and Mark looked up at him and winked. "What was he buying?"

"Things like rayons and prints and—well, fabrics of one sort or another. I don't remember the words they use very well."

"Purchasing agent of the Sunburst Sport Shirt Company, is that it?"

"He's the president of the company."

"President? And he does the buying himself?"

Connie looked pensively out of the window. "Half of the battle in sport shirts is buying right, so he does all the important buying himself."

Mark sat back and scratched his head. "I suppose there *have* been purchasing agents," he said, "who have told girls they picked up at sidewalk cafés that they were president of the company when they were really just the purchasing agent."

Connie nodded solemnly. "I suppose there have been." She pointed to the envelope in her lap. "His name is on the letterhead as president."

"Not a very big company, I suspect."

"Not a very big company," she agreed.

"What," Noah asked from his position by the window, "is the other half of the battle in sport shirts?"

She turned and looked at him, and in her glance was a suggestion of disappointment, as though she felt that he was letting her down. "Imagination," she said. "Keeping one step ahead of the competition all the time."

Mark chortled.

Connie sat back and closed her eyes. "Any other questions?"

"Yes," Mark said. "Is he handsome?"

"No."

"What does he look like?"

"He's short and stocky and—and he has a cowlick." She was staring straight ahead, her face impassive again.

"A cowlick?" Mark asked.

"Yes. A lock of hair that keeps falling down over his forehead, like Huey Long."

"Does he look like Huey Long?"

"No."

"What does he look like?"

She looked at him calmly.

"Can't you think of anybody we know he does look like?"

She picked up her glass, which had nothing but ice and a little ice water in it, and studied it. Then she held it to her lips and, tilting her head back, drained the ice water. "Yes," she said, still staring up at the ceiling.

"Who?"

She waited a moment longer. Then, closing her eyes again, she said, "He bears a strong resemblance to Yogi Berra, if you know what he looks like."

Mark and Noah both shouted.

"To whom?" Mrs. Sibley asked.

[136]

Mark was laughing delightedly. "Yogi Berra. He's a baseball player, Mother."

"He's the catcher for the New York Yankees," Connie said, "and one of the best in the business."

"But not exactly an Adonis," Mark said, still chuckling.

Connie stood up and put her glass on the tray. "I told you he wasn't handsome." She picked up a book from the table and went over to the window seat in the corner and curled up against the cushions with her feet under her.

Mrs. Sibley started putting the rest of the tea things back onto the tray. "A very amusing episode, Connie dear," she said. "Such things are all a part of our education, aren't they? All a part of growing up." Noah realized that she was being a little self-conscious about her broad-mindedness. "And," she added, "I suppose no real harm done."

"I suppose not," Mark said.

Connie opened her book. "No real harm at all," she said. "As a matter of fact," she added, starting to read, "he didn't even *suggest* that I might sleep with him."

3 ·

No more mention was made of Connie's letter. Noah assumed, and undoubtedly Mark and his mother did too, that she had written Mr. Jones that she was in Vermont and would not be able to see him. Everybody's mind, in the meantime, was filled with other things.

"It looks," Mrs. Sibley put it, "as though everything was going to happen at once during the first two weeks of August."

Barrett and Joan and their two children would be arriving on the first day of the month. Sometime later that night—or, more likely, sometime in the early hours of the next morning—Kate and Spence and their six children and their three handsome retrievers and their two dilapidated station wagons, having started at daybreak from their farm in Pennsylvania, would be driving in to the old Severance cottage, where they were to spend the month. And the next day Aunt Constance Applegate, who was not an aunt at all but a friend of Mrs. Sibley's from school days and the headmistress of Connie's school, was beginning a two-week stay at the Inn.

Noah kept telling himself that he would be glad to see Barrett and Joan and their two boys, Barry and Billy, of whom he was fond. He would also be glad to see Kate and Spence and their whole brood, of whom he was even fonder. He would even be glad, after a fashion, to see Aunt Constance.

But when he thought of all the confusions, all the demands on his time, he found that he was dreading the coming of the first day of August much as he had, when at Milburn, dreaded the coming of the final exam period. The two children, Barry and Billy, would have to sleep in his study. That meant that, if he was to get any work done at all, the cots would have to be set up every night and taken down every morning. (The Lion's Lair, the cabin study in the woods behind the cottage, had been assigned to Mark when Dr. Sibley died, the thought having been that he, with his weekly and monthly deadlines on his book reviews, needed absolute quiet more than Noah did. Kate's old bedroom, Mrs. Sibley had felt, would make a satisfactory study for Noah, although of course it did have to be used as a second guest room on occasions.)

Aunt Constance was coming by train, and it had already been arranged that Noah was to make the thirty-mile drive to the Junction to meet her. And during her two-week stay at the Inn, she would need a certain amount of chauffeuring about. Spence would want Noah to go fishing with him. The children, both families of them, would want him to go swimming with them, and to take them out in the canoe, and to take them perch fishing in the rowboat, and to go on picnics with them, and in the evenings to play hearts or rummy with them.

This summer, of all the summers in his life, he needed solitude. He needed to be left alone. He needed time to learn to live with the bitter truth that he could no longer push down into a deep recess of his mind and leave there to smother. Although thoughts of Natalie and the things she had said were frequently in his mind, it was not they that were bothering him most.

Day after day, since the picnic on Randolph's Hill, he had gone to his study and locked himself in, and hour after hour he had pored through his father's papers, rereading here, penciling here, rearranging them in sequences that had meaning only for him, an article or a lecture dated 1913 with one dated 1921 and another dated 1928; an article dated 1937 with a chapter of the book written in 1947.

It was a devastating exercise in the acceptance of disillusionment. So long as it had never been said, he had been able, faced with new evidence every month, to close his mind to it, subconsciously to excuse it with the excuses with which his father himself had half consciously excused it. "It's a question of effective presentation, Noah," he had said time and again. "You can never succeed in putting anything across to an audience or to the reading public if you antagonize them first. First you have to get them with you, win their sympathy with statements they want to hear, give them generalizations you know they'll agree with. Then, when you've got them with you, you can go on and give them the truths they ought to hear."

So long as it had never been said, you could close your mind to it. But Connie had said it, sitting with a paper bag in her lap on top of Randolph's Hill, and now you could no longer close your mind to it. Now you were driven by some cruel, compelling honesty to gather the evidence in neat little piles and clip them together with paper clips and write out on slips of paper the names of these things you had, all through this last spring, been calling to yourself inconsistencies —"Disarmament, Hague 1907," "Geneva Protocol," "Kellogg-Briand," "Munich"—and to slide the little slips under the paper clips, giving, with sickening finality, name and validity to these things that you could no longer call inconsistencies.

And day after day, when his spirits couldn't take any more, he would get up and stumble to the door and lumber downstairs and on out to the dock. And he would get into the heavy, clumsy old rowboat and row around and around the lake, until the blisters on his hands stung and his arms ached and his legs were cramped from pushing against the slats. Finally he would coast back in toward the dock and sit there, with the sweat dripping off his face and running down his back, feeling a little better, a little purged, but knowing little more than he had known before, knowing only, perhaps, that he could probably never lie again as he had lied the night after their picnic on the hill, when, just before they went to bed, his mother had accused him of thoughtlessness.

"Noah," she had said, "you arrived at midnight last night, and right after breakfast this morning you went on a picnic with Connie, and ever since, except for a few minutes at teatime when we were busy talking about Connie's little escapade, you've been out enjoying yourself, swimming, rowing around the lake in the boat, going out to see your friends and accepting their invitation to stay for dinner and staying all evening long. Hasn't it occurred to you at all, Noah, that we were waiting anxiously to hear what you have to report on a matter that is very close to all our hearts?"

And Noah, feeling squashed and weak, as criticism from other members of the family always made him feel, had said, "I'm sorry, Mother.

I supposed you'd know that if I had anything good to report, I'd have told you right away."

"But what we don't know, dear, is whether there is still any hope."

Noah shook his head unhappily. "Not so far as they're concerned."

"They're definitely not going to publish it?"

He nodded. "That's their decision."

She sighed a sigh of great patience and long-suffering. "And as usual," she asked wearily, "their reasons were entirely mercenary?"

And Noah had lied. "Entirely mercenary," he said. "They just couldn't see a profit in it, with production costs what they are today and it such a big book and—"

Mrs. Sibley sighed again. "Where are the high-minded men who used to be in the publishing business? Did they have the decency to admit that it was a vastly important book, that it should be in every library in the country?"

This time he had managed to get by with a half lie. "They called it monumental," he had said.

"And did you point out to them, Noah, that there are eleven thousand libraries in the country, and that practically every one of them would have to have it on its shelves? That that in itself would make quite an initial sale?"

Noah had not felt called upon to argue with them after their minds had been made up. "I'm afraid their minds were already made up, Mother."

"You didn't point it out to them then?"

"It wouldn't have made any difference."

"You didn't, in other words." She and Mark exchanged significant glances. "I'm very much disappointed, Noah," she had said, and with that she had gone up to bed.

4.

In the dark hours of the morning of the second day of August, Noah woke up to the flash of lightning and the roar of thunder. He heard windows slamming down in other parts of the cottage, and he jumped out of bed and ran in his bare feet to his own window.

He was not sure whether the loud rustle in the trees was wind or rain, and he stooped in front of the window, his hands pushing down against his bent knees, looking out. For a while he could see only blackness. The echoes of the last clap of thunder, swelling and falling off and swelling again, still reverberated through the hills. It was wind and not rain that he had heard in the trees, but he could hear the sound of rain in the distance, coming closer.

Now he began to make out the masses of the spruces outside the window, then the swinging tips of the branches, penciled black against the gray of the maples out by the Lion's Lair. He leaned farther forward and looked up. There was a faint luminance in part of the sky, enough to make the cloud overhead stand out dark and menacing.

The rain came nearer and nearer, and just as the heavy patter of spattering drops began on the trees and on the window ledge, a sharp, white-lighted flash of lightning burst through the trees, bringing every needle and twig out in individual outline, cracking as only a bolt that has hit nearby can. And in the second that intervened between the crack of the lightning and the rolling, enveloping roar of the thunder, he heard a scream from behind him inside the cottage.

He slammed the window down and fumbled along the wall to the light switch. And in his pajamas, not bothering with his dressing gown or slippers, blinking in the sudden light, he stepped out into the hall. Except for the glow from his own door, he could see no lights anywhere. He snapped on the hall light and looked at the line of doors. They were all firmly closed. No one of them gave a hint of any movement behind it. The thunder was still echoing in the hills, but he was sure that he would have heard if there had been anyone stirring.

He stood still, listening, looking at one door after another—that of his mother's room beside the top of the stairs; of Barrett's, where Barrett and Joan, who had arrived that afternoon, were sleeping; of his study, where the cots had been set up for the children; of Mark's, beside his; of Connie's, down at the end of the hall.

The scream had been a woman's scream, and after a moment of hesitation he went down the hall and knocked at Connie's door. Immediately light appeared around the crack of the door. "Who is it?" she called.

"It's Noah."

"That last one was a beaut, wasn't it?" she said. "It's all right. I closed my window some time ago."

"Did you hear a scream?"

She didn't answer. After a moment she opened the door. She had put on a baggy white quilted robe over her pajamas. Her hair was pulled away from her forehead and held in back with an elastic band. "A scream?"

"Yes. I heard a woman scream."

"I didn't hear anything." She looked up at him curiously.

There was another crack of lightning, almost as loud as the last one, and one of the children in the study started to cry. Other lights began to appear under doors. The thunder was roaring again.

Barrett came out of his room in a silk dressing gown. His hair was as unruffled as if he had just combed it. He looked at them in good-humored surprise. "Well," he said, "all kinds of people moving about. Quite a storm we're having!" He opened the door into the study, and the crying turned into a loud wailing.

"Noah thought he heard a woman scream," Connie said. "It wasn't Joan?"

Barrett glanced at Noah, and Noah knew that he was thinking that he had been imagining things. "No, it wasn't Joan," he said smiling.

"Connie," Noah said, "you take a look in Mother's room and see if she's all right."

Connie stepped down the hall and opened the door. She looked in at the bed, then turned quickly and switched on the light. "She's not here," she said.

Barrett, suddenly sober, moved with authority to the head of the stairs and turned on the stair light. He started down. "Good God!"

Noah was two steps behind him as he reached the landing. He looked down and saw a crumpled, disordered heap in the green bathrobe that was his mother's lying at the foot of the stairs.

Barrett went down the stairs two at a time. He knelt beside her and lifted her wrist. But before he had time to find the pulse he said, "She's breathing."

Leaning against the post at the bottom of the stairs, Noah could see her shoulder rising and falling. Her breathing was heavy and regular. Gently, Barrett straightened out her body. There was blood on the floor, blood oozing slowly through her hair. Barrett turned and called up the stairs, "Joan," and Noah remembered that Joan had had nurse's aide training during the war. Connie stepped quietly past him and around Barrett and on out into the kitchen.

It was not Joan but Mark, looking puffy-eyed and angry, who appeared on the landing. "Good God!" he said, and like Barrett he came down the stairs two at a time and knelt beside his mother, on the other side from Barrett.

"Somebody had better get dressed," Barrett said, glancing up at Noah. "We're going to have to find a doctor."

Noah said, "Yes," and turned up the stairs. And there above him on the landing was Joan in a long black silk dressing gown with a Japanese flowered design on it, and he thought at once of Louise in her black Chinese pajamas on the landing of the stairs in Middlefield—and was quickly ashamed of himself for having thought of anything but his mother at a time like this.

"Heavens!" she said, and came quickly on down and brushed past Noah and, pushing Mark aside, bent over the limp figure on the floor. She seemed very self-possessed and efficient. Noah went on up and hurried into his clothes.

When he came out of his room, the two boys were standing in the hall in their pajamas, looking frightened. Billy was sobbing. "It's all right, boys," he said, realizing for the first time when he heard the quaver in his own voice how frightened he was himself. "Your mommie will be upstairs again pretty soon. You can go into my room there, and look, boys, I'll tell you what you can do. You can get into my bed *together!*"

They looked puzzled for a moment, but the thought of getting in Noah's bed together was obviously enticing. Billy's sobbing turned into a whimper and stopped.

At the foot of the stairs, all four of them were kneeling around his mother. Barrett was holding her head up off the floor while Connie, with a pan of water and a towel, was washing the blood out of her hair. Noah caught his first glimpse of his mother's face. She was pale and her eyes were closed and she seemed to be frowning. He felt sure that she was still unconscious.

He stepped around them. Joan was probing cautiously along his mother's leg, watching her face as her fingers moved along. He hurried on out through the kitchen to the back closet and put on his slicker and sou'wester. The pounding of rain was loud through the kitchen door, and thunder still rumbled in the distance.

5·

The rain beat a tattoo on the brim of the sou'wester as he hurried across the muddy yard to his car. He drove out the lane, the car splashing in the puddles, and when he got onto the road he turned east toward Ledwick. It was twelve miles to Ledwick. He scowled at the road ahead. With all the curves and the wet roads, you couldn't do better than forty. He tried to figure it, saying over and over to himself as he jounced along, "Twelve miles at forty miles an hour." He concentrated harder. "Twelve into forty is—twelve into forty is three and a fraction—three and four-twelfths—three and a third."

What do you do with three and a third? He gripped the wheel, staring at the road ahead. Nowhere in his mind could he find what to do with the figure three and a third. If it had been ten miles, that would have been a quarter of forty. That would make it what? Twenty minutes?

But then he remembered that they had always had to count on a half hour to get to Ledwick. Call it a half hour, then, a half hour over and a half hour back and some length of time to—

He took his foot off the accelerator. Dr. Mooney! Old Dr. Mooney in his cottage over behind the point. He drew off to the side of the road and stopped. Dr. Mooney had been retired for God knows how many years now—ten—fifteen. He must be nearly eighty. A good bit of an old fool, fancying himself as a wit, making bad jokes around the store and the post office. But he'd been a surgeon once, a famous surgeon of the old school, rough and ready. Noah's mother had never liked him.

But he could be at Dr. Mooney's cottage in five minutes. Ten minutes round trip versus an hour round trip. Fifty minutes' difference. She could die in those fifty minutes.

In the headlights he could see a farmhouse ahead beside the road, and he started up and drove to the farmhouse and turned around in the barnyard, with a dog barking somewhere inside. He went back through the village, took the left fork, passed the church and the big meadow. He slowed down as he came to the woods, watching for the driveway that he remembered as being half hidden by trees.

As he slowed down he thought, "What if Dr. Mooney won't come?" He was an old man, retired for some godawful number of years now. It was a bad night, a stormy night. It was—he had no idea what time of night it was—his watch was back on the table beside his bed. If Dr. Mooney wouldn't come, all this was time wasted. He'd have to turn around again—and still have to go to Ledwick. Well, all you could do was try.

He found the driveway and drove in and turned the car so that the headlights were on the back door. And, leaving the motor running, he sloshed through the puddles to the back door and knocked.

He waited and knocked again.

A voice, Dr. Mooney's voice, grating and gruff, called from over his head, "Who is it?"

Noah went back out from under the porch roof and stood in the light of the headlights, with the rain falling in vertical lines of light around him. "It's Noah Sibley. My mother fell downstairs and hit her head."

"Christ's sake," Dr. Mooney said.

"Her head is bleeding and—and she's unconscious."

"Knocked herself out, eh?"

Suddenly Noah felt a little less frantic. People got knocked out. It occurred to him that she might not be dying.

She might be too. He waited, expecting to hear the doctor say, "I'm not practicing," or, "I can't go out on a night like this."

"Well, God damn it," the doctor said. He coughed. "You just wait a minute, son," he said, and he slammed the window.

6 ·

They had gotten her onto the couch. Joan stood beside her, holding a wad of gauze to her head. Connie was sitting at the table, her chin in her cupped hands. There was only one dim light in the room. Barrett and Mark stood at the foot of the couch, and they both looked up sharply at Dr. Mooney, then glanced at each other and stood still, staring at him.

Dr. Mooney grunted and stepped over beside the couch, puffing. He had the gaunt look of a man once heavy and full-blooded who had shrunk with age. His skin was mottled with brown spots, and he needed a shave and a haircut.

Mrs. Sibley opened her eyes and looked at him sideways and closed them again quickly, screwing up her face as though the effort of looking had hurt her.

"Got to have some light here," the doctor said.

"The light hurts her eyes," Mark said.

"Too bad." He pointed to the standard lamp and spoke to Noah. "Here, son, turn that light on and point it over this way."

Mark went over to a chair in the corner and sat down, and Barrett paced restlessly out into the middle of the room. Noah turned the light on and aimed it at her. She made another face. The doctor already had his fingers on her pulse. He nodded and turned around and picked up his bag from the floor. Noah's eyes followed his movements. As he looked down at the floor, he saw the doctor's pajama legs sticking out from under his gray flannel trousers. He had on rubbers over an old pair of carpet-cloth slippers, and his bony ankles were bare.

He took out his stethoscope and looked up at Joan. "How long before she came to?"

Joan was looking down at him coldly. "It was about ten minutes, I think, from the time we found her lying there on the floor."

He opened her bathrobe and nightgown, making no effort to protect her modesty, and moved the stethoscope around her chest. He nodded and, still puffing, took her blood pressure. Then, putting the instruments back into the bag, he lifted Joan's hand away from her head and looked at the cut, fingering it as he looked. He grunted again.

"Here, son," he said to Noah, waving Joan aside, "you get your arm around her here and lift her up a bit."

Noah worked his arm in behind her and pulled. He was surprised at how easily she came up with the pressure of his arm. He had his other hand ready to put behind her head, but her head did not loll back.

The doctor started to pull her eyelids back with his thumb, but she fought him, shaking her head. He grasped her jaw in his left hand and held her head steady while he forced the lid back. Then he moved to the other eye. He turned and grinned at Noah. "She's got one hell of a headache," he said. He waved his hand, and Noah let her gently back down onto the cushion.

The doctor stood up and looked at the cut on her scalp again. "Guess I'd better take a couple of stitches in this thing. Go get me your razor, son."

When Noah came down with the razor, he took it and asked, "Been doing any trout fishing this summer?"

"I haven't had time for much," Noah said shortly, scowling, feeling Barrett's and Mark's eyes on the back of his head.

The old doctor chortled. "Shouldn't ever let your work interfere with your fishing." He worked quickly, with apparent carelessness, talking about fishing as he worked and humming when he wasn't talking.

He finished and put his instruments back into the bag. "There you are, son," he said and headed for the door.

"Just a minute, Doctor," Barrett said, and Noah was conscious of the disapproval in his voice. "What's your diagnosis?"

"Mild concussion. She'll have a headache for a couple of days. Better keep her in bed. Might as well leave her here for tonight."

"You don't think we'd better have X-rays?"

The doctor looked at him with a humorous glint in his eye, obviously conscious of his disapproval. "Have 'em if you want to," he said. "They won't show anything."

"How about food, Doctor?" Joan asked.

"Feed her when she gets hungry." He looked around at all of them, then grinned slowly and winked at Noah. "Come on, son," he said. "Take me home."

7·

When Noah came back, Barrett and Joan were alone in the living room with his mother. They had drawn chairs up into positions from which they could watch her. The lights had been dimmed again, and to Noah there was something unreal about them as they sat there—so handsome, so unruffled, so self-righteously patient. They were like actors on a stage, in stage dressing gowns. In life people roused in the middle of the night didn't come out so smooth and flawless.

"Mark and Connie gone up to bed?" Noah whispered. His mother appeared to be asleep.

Barrett did not turn his head. "Mark," he said, "has gone up to the Inn."

"What for?"

"To telephone to Ledwick." He stood up and faced Noah. "For a doctor." His voice and his manner, Noah suddenly saw with surprise, were full of exasperation—a rare thing for Barrett who, unlike Mark, was almost never openly censorious, almost never lost his temper, almost always made his point with sweet reasonableness, was always beginning his arguments with such phrases as, "Do you honestly believe, Noah . . ."

But now, for once, he was making no effort to hide his exasperation. "Aren't you ever going to get any sense into your head, Noah?" he asked. "For heaven's sake, we ask you to get a doctor, in a moment of great crisis, with your mother's life at stake, and you come back with a cackling old imbecile in his dotage. Frankly, Noah, I just don't know what to think of you."

Noah swallowed, feeling weak and trembly. He looked at Barrett sullenly. "It saved almost an hour."

"Did it?"

"Yes, it did." He spoke louder, arguing defensively. "It would have taken me a good half hour to get over to Ledwick and—"

"Couldn't you have done what Mark did? Gone to the Inn and tele-phoned?"

Noah sagged, inexpressibly tired. Of course he could have gone to the Inn and telephoned. He ran his tongue around his dry lips, gazing down at the floor. Then he looked up at Barrett sullenly. "It still would have taken a lot longer than it took to get Dr. Mooney."

At the mention of the name, Barrett shook his head. "Tell me very honestly, Noah," he said in a tone of patient reasonableness, "do you really feel deep down in your heart that you want to entrust your mother's life to Dr. Mooney?"

"I don't know why not," Noah said doggedly, feeling as he always felt when he tried to argue with Barrett. "It looked to me as though he knew what he was doing."

Joan laughed. "Did you observe his sterile technique when he sutured the wound?"

Noah hated to argue with Joan, but he said, "He washed it out with a disinfectant."

"He washed it out," Joan said, amused, "with something out of a dirty old bottle."

A sound came from Mrs. Sibley. They all turned and looked at her. Her eyes were half open, and they moved slowly from one to another of them. She smiled a wanly beautiful smile and closed her eyes again.

Noah tiptoed up to his room. Joan, he found, had gotten the boys back into their own room. He turned out the light and lay down on the bed in his clothes. The rain had stopped before he had taken the doctor home, and now the pale gray of dawn was beginning to appear in the sky behind the spruces. Soon he saw Mark's headlights swinging into the little area beside the Lion's Lair where he kept his car. Noah went to the top of the stairs and listened. He heard Mark's step in the kitchen, then voices, and he heard Mark say, "He's been out since midnight on a delivery case, but his wife will tell him as soon as he comes in."

Noah went back to his room, feeling justified and vaguely triumphant. But he knew better than to go down and point out to Mark and Barrett that if he had done as they thought he should, they would still be waiting for a doctor. They would think of things to say that he would never have thought of. Never in his life had he been able to win an argument with either of them.

He lay down again, still in his clothes, and smoked a cigarette. After that he dozed, and when he woke up the sun was bright on the trees outside the window. There were brisk footsteps moving about the house. He looked at his watch. It was ten minutes after seven, and he ran into the bathroom and threw water on his face and head and brushed his hair and hurried downstairs.

He stopped by the table, looking across the room toward the couch. His mother opened her eyes and looked at him. She raised her hand an inch and beckoned to him with one finger. He stepped over beside her. "I'm sorry I caused so much trouble in the night," she said weakly.

"Don't you worry about that." Noah tried to sound hearty and reassuring. "How did it happen, anyway?"

Her eyes were closed again. "I don't remember anything."

"There was a thunderstorm," he said.

She moved her head in a suggestion of a nod. "I suppose I was coming down to see if it was raining in anywhere."

"That's what I thought," Noah said. "And you must have tripped on the stairs and hit your head on the newel post."

She seemed to nod again.

"You should have turned on the lights," he said.

She waited quite a long time before she spoke, and when she did her voice was still weaker. "I suppose I didn't want to disturb people."

He looked down at her, shaking his head. It was so like her—wandering around the house in the dark in a thunderstorm because she didn't want to disturb people.

She opened her eyes again and looked at him. "You haven't forgotten that you have to leave for the Junction at eight-thirty to meet Aunt Constance?"

Noah had forgotten.

"You haven't shaved," she said. "Perhaps you'd better go up now and shave and change your clothes."

8 ·

WHEN he came down again, dressed in a clean white shirt and a blue tie and a pair of gray trousers, Mark was pacing up and down on the veranda, still waiting for the doctor from Ledwick. Barry and Billy were shouting to each other down by the beach, and Mark called to them to tone it down.

Noah looked at his mother, and this time he was sure that she was asleep. Barrett and Joan were talking in subdued tones in the kitchen, moving about quietly, and the smells of coffee and bacon were in the air. Apparently Connie hadn't come down yet.

Barrett came into the living room with an apron around his waist and smiled at Noah, as though to suggest that their altercation was to be forgotten. "Breakfast in about five minutes," he whispered, "only I can't find the egg turner. Do you know where she keeps it?"

Noah smiled back at him and nodded and followed him into the kitchen. He found the egg turner and gave it to Barrett. Joan, calm and competent, was turning the bacon. She had changed into a simple cotton dress, and her yellow-brown hair, skillfully and unobtrusively waved, was remarkably neat and fresh looking. Noah watched her, making no effort to help, feeling, perhaps as an aftermath of all the excitement, strangely detached, strangely unself-conscious.

Joan, he was thinking as he watched her, was still very much a stranger to him, although she and Barrett had been married for seven years now. Because he had had a special, personal relationship with Louise, he had found it impossible to have any kind of relationship at all with Joan. His mind told him that she was an admirable person and, within limits, an attractive one, too girlish to be called matronly, a little too matronly to be called girlish. She was everything that Louise had not been: sensible, adjusted, level-headed, competent as a housekeeper and mother and hostess and all the other things that Barrett's career called for her to be, and Noah's mind told him that that was a very good thing. But it was all in his mind.

"Noah," she said, "you could fill a pitcher with cream for the coffee and another one with milk for the boys' cereal."

"Righto," Noah said. He moved over to the refrigerator.

Mark came in from the porch and stood watching, his eyes sullen, his mouth a grim line. Noah, still feeling detached, looked at him and smiled, knowing that every minute the doctor from Ledwick delayed in arriving would add something to his annoyance, since every minute made Noah's mistake in getting Dr. Mooney a little less of a mistake.

Noah heard a light but brisk step in the living room, and Connie came through the door with a suitcase in one hand and a small handbag in the other. They all turned and looked at her, and without looking up she walked quickly across the kitchen and on out the back door. She put the bags into her car and came back in. She had on a navy-blue silk suit and a white blouse with a primly neat collar.

"What's all this about, Connie?" Mark asked, and there was an ominous quality in his voice.

"I'm going to New York," she said, "to keep an appointment."

Mark picked up a pot-holder and threw it down at the floor with all his might. "This damned family will drive me nuts." He glared at her. "Don't you have any sense at all?"

"I think I have," she said serenely.

"With your mother lying in there at death's door—"

"With my mother lying in there with a scalp wound and a mild concussion—"

"Are you willing," he asked with exaggerated incredulity, "to take the word of that old—that old poop?"

She smiled. "Yes, I'm willing to take the word of that old poop."

Mark was standing flat-footed, his hands on his hips, glowering at her. "Connie," he said in the stern tone of a prosecutor with a witness, "are you going to New York to keep a date with that clown, that ball fan—"

"If that's what you want to call him," she said, no longer smiling, "yes, I am."

He shook his head. "With Aunt Constance arriving today—"

"Aunt Constance," she said, "sees me every day, Sundays included, for almost nine months out of the year."

"Oh, God." He threw out his arms in a gesture of helplessness. "So," he said bitterly, "with everything happening around here at once, with Mother laid up and Aunt Constance arriving and Kate and Spence and the kids in the offing, you're going to take off. You're going to leave Joan here with the whole burden of this household."

"The whole burden?" Connie asked. "I certainly hope I'm not. Noah's a far better cook than I am, and you and Barrett can pitch right in on the dishwashing and bedmaking and house cleaning."

Mark snorted and stamped into the dining room and sat at his place, drumming on the table with his fingers.

As he had before when Connie and Mark had crossed swords, Noah found himself sympathizing with both of them. It was easy for him to sympathize with Connie, to find Mark's censoriousness irritating, but this time he felt that Mark did have a point, that it *was* thoughtless of Connie to go running off at a time like this.

The breakfast was a silent one, with even the boys subdued by the tensions in the air. As they were finishing, a car drove in at the back. Mark jumped up and went to the window. "It's Spence," he said, disappointed.

"With how many kids?" Barrett asked.

"Three or four." He came back and sat down and went on with his breakfast. "Noah," he said, "why don't you go out and head them off.

Tell Spence he'd better keep the kids away from here all day today. Tell him we'll let them know how things are going tomorrow."

Dutifully, Noah laid his napkin down and got to his feet.

"Tell him," Mark said, "that Mother might like to see Kate sometime this afternoon."

As Noah appeared at the back door, he was greeted with whoops by the children. He waved them down with his right hand, holding his left forefinger to his lips. The whoops subsided into excited talking, all four of them talking at once. Noah walked on out, still holding his fingers to his lips.

Spence, ruddy and tanned, stood beside the car smiling, the picture, with his clipped mustache and firm chin and merry blue eyes, of the outdoorsman—right out of an advertisement for shotgun shells, as Connie had put it. The children, the four oldest, two boys and two girls, were neatly paired, two of them the picture of Spence, the other two the picture of Kate, although the blood lines did not follow the sexes—all, as Connie again had put it, unbiologically handsome; it just doesn't happen in one family, she said; it was enough to make Mendel turn over in his grave.

Spence was looking at all the cars. "What is this," he asked, "an auto show—or is there a football game around here somewhere?"

Noah told him about his mother's accident, and he was properly—and very genuinely, Noah knew—solicitous. He quieted the children down and hurried them back into the car. "Absolutely, Noah," he said. "You won't see hide nor hair of them until you give us the word. And if there's anything, anything at all, we can do, don't hesitate to call on us. Absolutely."

Nobody Noah had ever known had quite the unfailing, gentlemanly charm that Spence had. Or, as Barrett had once said, nobody had ever wasted his life quite so gracefully.

"You bet I will, Noah," he said. "I'll tell Kate to drop around this afternoon. About three o'clock be good?"

"Fine," Noah said. "How is Kate?"

Spence's eyes became big and round. "She's enormous, Noah."

"Oh, of course," Noah said, remembering. He had not seen Kate since Christmas, and at that particular moment of her career she had not been noticeably pregnant. "When's the baby due?"

"October."

"I suppose she's had to give up her sculpture."

"Almost," Spence said. "She can't get up on the scaffold any more."

"Is she working on something big again?"

[152]

Spence smiled at him, a charming, resigned smile. "Did you ever know her to work on anything little?"

9.

NOAH followed Connie out to her car. "Look, Connie," he said, catching her before she got in, "couldn't you send him a telegram?"

"No."

"Things really are going to be pretty thick around here."

"With me gone," she said, "you can set up one of the cots in my room and put the other boy's sheets on my bed and have your study all to yourself. Doesn't that thought have appeal?"

"Yes, but honestly, Connie, it does seem—"

"For one thing," she interrupted, "his train doesn't get in until six tonight. I'm meeting him at the Grand Central. I wouldn't know how to send him a telegram. For another, I don't think he had any very good business reason for having to come to New York right now."

"What do you mean?"

"I mean that I think that business was more an excuse than a reason."

"You mean that he's coming all the way across the continent to see you."

"I mean that I think that might be the case."

Noah stared at her, his mind trying to encompass the thought. "He's really taking you seriously?"

"I think he might be."

He stared at her again. "Do you think you're being quite fair with *him?*"

"I think perhaps I am."

"To let him come all the way across the country to see you when—" He stopped and stared blankly, his lips parted. Then he studied her face, cocking his head to one side. "You don't mean that you're taking him seriously?"

"I like him," she said.

"Like him, yes. But you know very well you're not going to marry a shirt manufacturer from Los Angeles."

She laughed. "Somebody has to make shirts. You've got a Sunburst Sport Shirt hanging up in your closet right now. I peeked the other day, just to see." She got into her car and turned on the ignition.

"For heaven's sake, Connie," Noah said, "don't go jumping into something before we've had a chance to—"

She laughed again. "You mean, 'Promise not to marry him until I've had another chance to argue you out of it.' This sounds like an old-fashioned novel. Okay, Noah, I promise. I won't marry him until I've talked with you again." She stepped on the starter and raced the motor. Then she looked up the lane. "Oh, Lord," she said, "here comes another car."

Noah looked and saw the black sedan coming in.

"Who is it?" Connie asked.

"I suspect it's the doctor."

"Doctor? What doctor?"

He remembered that she had been upstairs in her room during the arguments of the early morning hours.

"The doctor from Ledwick."

"What's he doing here?"

"Mark called him, hours ago. He and Barrett didn't feel they could trust Dr. Mooney's diagnosis."

She slammed her fist down onto the wheel. Noah looked up at her, startled, and she was looking angrier than he had ever seen her look. "Noah," she said, her voice shaking, "aren't you ever going to get up the courage to tell those two self-righteous bastards to go to hell?" And as the doctor came nearer, she leaned out of the window and called to him, "Put your car way over there by that tree, will you, please? I've got to get out of this damned place."

10 ·

THE doctor was a gaunt, loose-jointed man, taller than Noah by a couple of inches. Like Dr. Mooney, he needed a shave, and on the way into the cottage he apologized to Noah, saying that he had just come in from a case and hadn't had time to shave.

In the kitchen Noah explained the circumstances of the accident as briefly as he could. And by some instinct, whether of discretion or of perverted loyalty to Barrett and Mark he didn't know, he avoided any mention of Dr. Mooney. The doctor walked into the living room and nodded to Mark and Barrett, who laid down the books they were reading as he came in, and to Joan, who stood respectfully beside the couch as she had learned to do in her nurse's aide course.

Noah drew up a chair for him, and the doctor sat down and looked at Mrs. Sibley. She opened her eyes and smiled at him. But because, Noah supposed, Noah had been the one who had ushered him in and explained the circumstances of the accident to him, he addressed all his remarks to him. "Somebody," he said approvingly, pointing to the bandage on her head, "knew how to do a neat job of bandaging."

"A neighbor," Noah said.

The doctor's examination was skillful, concentrated, and far more thorough than Dr. Mooney's had been. Barrett and Mark came nearer, watching and smiling. When he finished, he smiled up at Noah. Then, leaning forward toward the bandage, he said, "Now I'd better take a look at this thing."

He took off the bandage and looked. He stared at it for what must have been a full minute. Finally, in a voice that was several tones lower, he said, "You've already had a doctor on this case."

"A neighbor," Noah said hurriedly. "A very, very old man, almost eighty. He hasn't been practicing for many, many years now."

"But a doctor," the doctor said, without looking up.

Barrett stepped over to the foot of the couch. "A doctor a very long time ago," he said. "We really didn't feel, Doctor, that we dared trust his diagnosis."

The doctor cast one sideways glance at him. Then, his mouth grim, his eyes half closed, he rebandaged the wound. "What was his diagnosis?" he asked, without looking up.

"A mild concussion."

When he had finished with the bandage, the doctor stood up and walked over to Noah. He towered over him, looking down into his eyes. His mouth was still grim, his voice still low, half weary, half angry. "Young man," he said, "the nearest doctor to Ledwick on the south is thirteen miles, and the nearest one on the north is twenty-two. I'm the nearest doctor for eight villages, almost twenty-five hundred people, not counting summer people. I've got two other emergency calls waiting for me right now, and when I get home from them there'll be some more, and by one o'clock my waiting room will be full and there'll be people waiting outside in their cars."

He picked up his bag, then turned back to Noah. "That will be twenty-five dollars," he said, "and I don't mind telling you that it's several times as much as I'd ordinarily charge for this call."

Noah's hands trembled as he took his billfold out of his hip pocket and counted out the bills. He handed them to him, staring beyond his shoulder, not daring to look up into his face. Nor did he feel that he could, at the moment, look at any of the members of his family.

The doctor took the money and strode toward the door.

"Just a minute, Doctor," Mark said icily. "If we're paying you that much, we have a right to know what your diagnosis is."

"A mild concussion," he said. "She'll be all right tomorrow."

"You don't think we should have X-rays?"

"Have 'em if you want to. You'll be throwing some more of your good money away." He slammed the kitchen door as he went out.

Noah stood still in the middle of the room, staring off into space. Joan said something about finding the boys and went out the front door and down the steps. Barrett and Mark moved aimlessly around the room, picking things up and laying them down again, starting toward the stairs and coming back again. Mark finally picked up a book and started to read it, standing by the table. Barrett sank into the big chair and took his heavy, black, horn-rimmed glasses out of their case. He sat back, holding them thoughtfully a few inches from his face. "Of course, Noah," he said, very calm and reasonable, "we'll reimburse you for that."

Noah turned around and looked at him.

"Noah," his mother said, her voice surprisingly strong.

Now Noah turned and looked at her, a little breathless, a little wild-eyed.

"If you don't hurry, Noah," she said, "you're going to be late for Aunt Constance's train at the Junction."

He took a deep breath. He ran his hand through the thin fuzz on the top of his head. "Yes, of course, Mother," he said. "I'll get going right away." He hurried out through the kitchen, but when he got outside the back door he stopped and lighted a cigarette. And he stood still there, puffing it, before he finally went on out to the car.

11 ·

THUS began for Noah—and, he supposed, for the rest of the family too—the nightmare week.

First there were Barry and Billy, usually decent enough youngsters, who managed to become, for a whole week, unbearably brattish, Billy constantly whining and complaining, Barry bumptious and self-assertive. Every hour of every day, it seemed to Noah, they were a trial to his patience.

[156]

There were Spence and Kate and their tribe of children, all exuberant, uninhibited, extroverted, incapable of believing that anyone could not want to do all the wonderful things they wanted to do, even more incapable of understanding subtleties of mood or of believing that anyone could ever want solitude. There was Aunt Constance. There was Connie's absence, a tougher thing for Noah to take than he would ever have believed it could be. There was his mother, refusing to take the rest he knew she should be having. There was, before the week was over, the depressingly familiar revelation of Spence's financial troubles.

And as though all that were not enough, it seemed to Noah that at least every other mail, when he picked it up before lunch at the post office, contained something disturbing. One day it was a letter from Roger Reinhart. He was beginning to wonder, Roger said, how much longer they dared go on with the deception of carrying Noah's name on the roster of the faculty. He hated to say it, but it was beginning to look to him as though Noah never would be coming back. There was no great hurry; the catalogue didn't go to press until March, but he wanted to give Noah a fall and winter to think it over. If, by March, there didn't seem to be any chance that Noah could arrange his affairs so as to rejoin the faculty by a year from September, he was afraid, much as he regretted to say it, that they had better drop his name.

It was a letter that Noah had known that he would be getting someday. He had anticipated it, come to agreement with it in his mind, learned to accept it as inevitable. But for the rest of that day he went about his chores and obligations in a mood of deep despondency.

Another day it was a letter for Mark from the director of the sanitarium saying that he felt that Winifred was now ready to try living out in the world again. Along with it came a note from Winifred herself, asking Mark what he wanted her to do. It was, everyone hastened to assure everyone else, good news, wonderful news, but that it added a new complication to a family life that was already far too complicated nobody could deny. It presented problems, Mrs. Sibley and Barrett agreed, that called for a great deal of thought.

That Mark himself had seemed more confused than jubilant at first was, Noah supposed, understandable in a way. He had certainly been faithful enough in his visits to the sanitarium during Winifred's first two sojourns there, and he was still faithful, Noah believed, with his fortnightly letters. But it had been seven years now since she had gone in for the last time, and hopes of her ever coming out again had grown dimmer and dimmer. In the meantime, with the demands of his career constantly increasing, Mark had remade his life in a new pattern.

Maybe it was natural, Noah thought, that concern over the readjustments he would have to make in his life would somewhat dampen his joy over getting his wife back.

Or maybe there were things going on in the depths of his emotions that Noah knew nothing about, things that he was making a deliberate effort to hide. Mark moved around the cottage as though in a trance, and he mentioned Winifred and the two letters only to his mother, making it clear to the rest of them that he would rather not discuss them. Perhaps he was thinking of Winifred far more than Noah suspected. Noah found that he himself was thinking of her often in those next few hectic days.

The one letter that did not come was the one Noah looked for in every mail, the one he knew would never be coming but that he still kept imagining—the letter from Natalie, saying that she had changed her mind and wanted to see him again. What he would want to do, what he was prepared to do if she did want to see him again, he didn't know. He only knew that he kept looking for a letter in that distinctive handwriting, postmarked at the Island. The consciousness that there was a Natalie was, he realized, always there somewhere in the back of his mind.

But in spite of all the distractions and complications of those next few days, it was, most of all, thoughts of Winifred that kept popping into his mind, memories of her as he had first seen her, memories of those nights when he had driven her home, memories of Mark as he had been then, memories, strangely enough, of Thérèse Robinson.

VIII

1·

Noah supposed that it was true, as he knew that the rest of the family believed, that Mark's one great love had been his love for Thérèse Robinson. Noah resented the thought—he had been genuinely fond of Winifred—but in all honesty he had to admit to himself that the family was probably right.

Thérèse was the daughter of the head of the French department in a small college in northern New York State.

"Is everybody who comes to this lake either a college professor or a minister?" Natalie had asked Noah one day during that summer, sixteen years before.

And Noah, proud of the distinguished company that gathered there, had laughed and said, "Very nearly. A few writers and editors."

Thérèse's mother was French, the daughter of a Parisian manufacturer whose son had been studying at the Sorbonne at the same time that Dr. Robinson had. Mrs. Robinson, or "Madame," as everyone at the Lake called her, had a certain fondness for the Lake and its summer residents, but she found the New York State climate and her husband's colleagues and their wives all equally bleak, and on one excuse or another she had managed to spend almost half of her married life in France.

Thérèse herself was as much at home in France as in America. Her English was not what one could call accented, but it was slightly tinged with an essence of foreignness. She was a slender girl, not so dark as Americans are inclined to expect French girls to be. Nor, taking her feature by feature, was she so beautiful as Noah thought of French girls as being. Her charm lay in the suppleness of her slender body, in her voice, and in the contradictions of a manner which seemed at one moment foreign and exotic and at the next so extremely down-to-earth and practical and American that everybody, including Noah as well as Mark, felt that here, in one girl, might be combined the glamor of a French mistress with the companionship and comfort of an American wife.

Noah could remember at least fifteen romances which had flowered at the Lake, plus a number of others which, begun elsewhere, had received there the added impetus they needed. "These mamas don't have to be matchmakers," Dr. Mooney was reported to have said. "They just furnish the canoes and leave the rest up to the moonlight."

But of all the romances that had flourished at the Lake, Noah had to admit now when he recalled how he had felt then, none had ever been surrounded in his mind with such an aura of glamor as had Mark's love affair with Thérèse. For one thing, the Robinson cottage was at the other end of the lake, so that Thérèse was seldom if ever among the crowd of young people who loafed together around the beaches in various unbecoming costumes. He had no memory at all of what she looked like in jeans or slacks, but very clear memories of a number of chic and appealing dresses. For another thing, she and Mark tended to keep to themselves more than the other young couples, adding an element of the mysterious and unknown. And Mark, still graceful and slender and curly-haired at that time, was as romantic-appearing a young man as Noah had ever seen, and in addition a budding novelist. All this, added to the exotic foreign strain in Thérèse's nature, made it impossible for Noah to imagine anything more glamorous.

And when, two years after Mark got out of college, his letters from Oxford spoke of frequent trips to Paris, the thing took on in Noah's mind an international flavor, with visions of Mark and Thérèse riding through the streets of Paris in fiacres and of Mark pacing the decks of Channel steamers on windy nights, the collar of his greatcoat turned up and his mind filled with thoughts of Thérèse.

But when Mark came back in June, he was unaccountably silent about Thérèse. It wasn't until sometime later that Noah got, largely from Barrett, the story of disagreements concerning where and how they were to live after they were married. Thérèse had not been able to see why, since a novelist can do his work anywhere, they couldn't afford to live in Paris just as well as in Middlefield, especially with the rate of exchange at the time so favorable. Nor could she understand why the stipend they were to live on until the money started coming in from Mark's novels should have to be so small, since everyone at the Lake knew that the fortune Mrs. Sibley had inherited from Mark's Grandfather Barrett had been a very large one.

Thus the love affair that had begun in such an atmosphere of high romance had ended in squabbles over money and places to live. The Sibleys learned from Dr. Robinson a year later that Thérèse had married a businessman from a small city in south-central France, a city which none of them had ever heard of. Noah looked it up in the encyclopedia and found that it had almost exactly the same population as Middlefield, and he had wondered ever since if her life there had been any more exciting than a life with Mark in Middlefield would have been.

2.

MARK had finished his first novel and gotten it off to Dr. Sibley's publisher before he left for Oxford. There had been considerable discussion before he left, Noah remembered, concerning what he was to do about reading the proofs, and it had been decided that, if necessary, he could make a hurried trip home during the Christmas Vac.

The action of the novel was placed in Vermont. "They say you should write about what you know," Mark had said, "and if there's anything in the world I do know, it's Vermont."

All of the action took place on a dreary, run-down farm far back in the hills, and it all took place during one winter. It concerned a widower father and his two sons, all three of whom cast a lascivious eye on the hired girl who arrived one week before Christmas to keep house for them. "Whatever else you may say for it," Mark said modestly, "I do feel that the thing has a certain power."

When, to everybody's amazement, the publisher turned it down, he did as much as admit that Mark was right on that point. "It is reminiscent," he wrote Dr. Sibley, "of some of the more powerful plays of Eugene O'Neill."

On his own initiative, Dr. Sibley took the manuscript into New York to another publisher he knew personally, but when the second publisher turned it down, it was put aside to wait for Mark's return. All this had taken place during the year when Noah was studying at Columbia, the year when his mind had been so full of thoughts of his future life with Natalie, and Noah had often thought that the collapse of Mark's romance with Thérèse must have coincided rather closely in time with the collapse of his own romance with Natalie.

Anyway, what with the failure of his love affair and the rejection of his novel, that next summer and fall had been difficult ones for Mark. Noah remembered how he had wandered around the cottage, and later around the house in Middlefield, where Noah was now working as his father's secretary, and how very much at loose ends he had seemed to be. But late in October he reread the novel and, armed with the additional knowledge of literature that he had acquired at Oxford, admitted that there was considerable immaturity in the writing. "Someday," he told Noah, "I shall rewrite it. I still feel that it has a certain power, but for the present I think I'll leave it to season. The idea for a new novel is beginning to germinate in my mind."

The idea did germinate, and that winter, while Noah was working with his father down in the study, Mark was up in his room writing his new novel. In this one the action moved from New York to London and Paris. He was interested this time, he said, in trying to portray the differences in the psychology of Americans, British, and French.

3.

When, part way through that winter, Dr. Edmonds made his second attempt to get Noah to come and teach at Milburn, Dr. Sibley was beginning to realize that what he needed for a secretary was not an historian but a stenographer. So Noah accepted Dr. Edmonds' offer to start teaching the following September, and Dr. Sibley made inquiries about a stenographer.

The girl the agency sent was Winifred Bunce. She came one afternoon when Mrs. Sibley and Mark were out and Noah and his father were working together in the study. At that time of day the maid was usually up in her third-floor room, so Noah went to the door. Winifred stood there looking at him with frightened eyes, and she swallowed before she spoke. "Mr. Sibley?"

"One of many Mr. Sibleys," Noah said good-naturedly. "Which one did you want?"

Her voice was thin. "Dr. William Huntington Sibley."

"That's my father," he said reassuringly, "but he's here. What name shall I tell him?"

"Winifred Bunce."

[162]

"Oh, yes. You're the girl the agency called about. Come in." He ushered her into the living room and went back into the study and told his father that the girl the agency recommended was there.

"You'd better be in on this too, Noah," his father said. "Ask her to come in here."

At the threshold of the large, high-ceilinged study, dark on this winter day except for the low-hanging light which flooded the top of Dr. Sibley's enormous mahogany desk and the table lamp on Noah's smaller one, she stopped. Noah, behind her, heard a small sharp intake of breath, and as she finally moved on in, unsteadily, he sensed that she was trembling.

Dr. Sibley, handsome and distinguished as always in his black work jacket, his forehead catching highlights from the light above him, sat reading a paper on the desk in front of him. For a few moments he kept on reading. Then, as though he had come to the end of a paragraph, he pushed the paper aside and stood up, smiling. "So you're Miss Bunce."

"Yes, sir." Her voice was so weak that it barely reached him, and he inclined his head sideways, as though listening for anything more she might have to say.

She said nothing, and Dr. Sibley said, "Here, Noah, you take Miss Bunce's coat—and pull that chair up here a little closer, so that I can see her face."

She had on a little black hat, and underneath the coat a simple, immaculately clean black dress, with starched white collar and cuffs. A very correct outfit for a stenographer, Noah thought, and he noticed that her fingernails, though short, were carefully manicured and —fortunately for her if she wanted to win his father's approval—their natural color.

She sat in the chair that Noah placed for her, and Noah went back to the swivel chair at his desk.

"How old are you, Miss Bunce?"

"I'm twenty-one, sir." She was a thin, wanly pretty girl with appealing blue eyes and trembly, very feminine mouth and chin. Her skin was soft and delicately tinted, like a child's.

"Couldn't you speak a little louder?" Dr. Sibley asked, not unkindly.

She flushed. "Yes, sir," she said, much louder, and when her voice came out so much louder, she laughed nervously.

"And you're a graduate of a secretarial school?"

"Yes, sir." The voice was thin again.

[163]

"And where have you been working since you got out of secretarial school?"

"In New York, sir, in a publisher's office."

Dr. Sibley raised his eyebrows. "Well," he said, "that ought to be handy. What publisher?"

She named it, and it was not a name that was familiar to Noah.

"Never heard of them," Dr. Sibley said.

She visibly gathered her courage and said, "It's a small house, sir. Once in a while they do a trade book, one or two a year, but mostly they handle technical and special category books."

"I see. And why did you leave them?"

She looked frightened. "I haven't left them, sir. I—I just took the afternoon off to come out here and see you. I get pretty tired, going back and forth by train. I have to leave the house before seven-thirty to get to the office by nine, and lots of nights I don't get out in time to catch the six o'clock ferry, and if I don't I don't get home until quarter of eight."

"Well, that does make a day of it, doesn't it?" Dr. Sibley said sympathetically.

"Yes, sir. I thought if I could find a job right here in Middlefield—"

"So you live here in Middlefield."

"Yes, sir."

"Where?"

"On Proctor Street."

The name of the street told Noah a good deal about the kind of home the girl came from. Proctor Street was, literally, on the other side of the tracks, a good mile and a half away. But there was nothing wrong with Proctor Street at all—a pleasant, maple-lined street of decent frame houses, most of them one-family and almost all of them with front porches.

"You wouldn't happen to be related to the Bunce of Bunce's Clothing Store, would you?" his father asked.

The correct name, Noah thought, smiling to himself, was Bunce, Ltd.

"Yes, sir. He's my father."

"Well, I know your father then," Dr. Sibley said. "I've bought haberdashery from him for years."

"Yes, sir. He said you had." She smiled cautiously at Noah. "And he said all three of your boys bought their things from him."

Noah nodded, returning her smile. Bunce's was where they all went

[164]

for underwear and handkerchiefs; none of them, of course, had ever thought of buying a suit there.

"And he said that old Mr. Barrett used to buy all his shirts from him—a dozen at a time." She stopped abruptly and clenched her hands in her lap, and Noah knew that she was afraid she had said too much. He looked at her curiously. It always came as a surprise to him to find that these people in Middlefield whom he had never seen and of whom he had never heard knew all about himself and his family, even to the point of knowing that his mother was a Barrett.

Dr. Sibley was gazing off into space, not smiling, and it occurred to Noah that perhaps the girl *had* said too much.

"Well, I guess that's about all we need to know," Dr. Sibley said. "You have a phone?"

"Yes, sir." She gave him the number and he wrote it down.

"We'll think it over and give you a call," he said.

Noah took her to the door, and before they got there he sensed that she was trembling again and almost crying. There was something about her that he had found very likable, and on an impulse he held out his hand and shook hands with her. "I hope it works out," he said.

She smiled up at him, her lip quivering, and said, "Thank you," and turned and hurried out to the street.

He went back into the study.

"I don't know, Noah," his father said. "I'm afraid she's too sickly —and too painfully shy."

Noah seldom argued with his father's decisions, but this time he got up the courage to say, "I think the shyness was mostly fear of you. She's probably been hearing about your reputation all her life, and she's probably never met a famous man before." He avoided mentioning the fact that she had probably also been hearing about the Barrett fortune all her life. "I have a hunch that when she finds out that you're really a pretty human sort of guy, she'll get over it."

Dr. Sibley looked mollified. "Well," he said, "we'll have to see."

"The agency says that she's very conscientious and accurate," Noah said, "and a whiz at shorthand and typing."

"Do they?" his father asked, impressed. He thought a moment. "Well, perhaps we could give her a try." He smiled at Noah. "She's really kind of an appealing little thing, isn't she?"

[165]

4.

Within a month Dr. Sibley was calling Winifred the find of the century. The agency had not been exaggerating when they called her a whiz; he had never known that dictation could go so fast or so smoothly. She had begun a cross-index of all the papers in the files, and already, by the end of the first month, she was able to lay her hands on almost any paper he wanted in a matter of minutes, whereas formerly he and Noah had often searched together for a half hour.

She was quiet and unobtrusive. She never took advantage of small kindnesses, always insisted on eating her lunches by herself in the study. She was immaculate and dainty in her person. She was bashful, to be sure, but appealingly so, a very feminine sort of person, with her funny little chin that was like a child's. She adored Dr. Sibley—and the rest of the family along with him. There was nothing she wouldn't do to gain his approval, no hour too late for her to stay to finish up the work he wanted finished up.

When she did stay late and miss her bus, or when she came back in the evening for an extra hour or two of work, it fell to Noah to drive her home. And although her bashfulness with the rest of the family was still painful, with him she got over it surprisingly fast. Soon she was acting completely at ease with him, and he was feeling as much at ease with her as with any girl he had ever known. She was so undemanding and so entirely uncritical. The thought of a possible romance between them didn't occur to him, and because it didn't, and because of her obvious conviction that any Sibley was, by innate right, wonderful, he was able to relax and talk with her much as he had once talked with his closest friends on the Milburn faculty, never once feeling that he had to watch his words, never once wondering if what he was saying might sound stupid.

More and more, as the spring went along, he got into the habit of sitting in the car with her for a half hour or so out in front of the house on Proctor Street. She took a surprisingly intelligent interest in the work, and more often than not it was the work they talked about. She had even gone to the library and gotten some books on international relations, so that she would have a better understanding of what the work was all about.

But sometimes the conversation would drift and they would talk about their childhoods and about what an odd sort of city Middlefield really was, or Noah would tell her about the Lake or about his school days at Milburn and Princeton. And as the May nights grew warmer and the night air, after an evening in the study, began to smell wonderfully fragrant and balmy, Noah took to driving out into the country a bit before swinging around to Proctor Street. Sometimes they would stop in at a drugstore for a coke or a glass of orangeade or an ice-cream cone.

Noah found these little evening excursions, these half hours that often stretched into hours, wonderfully relaxing, and he began to develop toward Winifred a feeling that was something between gratitude for the comfort her presence gave him and a brotherly affection not unlike the feeling he had for Connie. He found himself, as they sat together licking their cones or sipping their cokes, taking delight in her piquant little face, in her piquant little way of saying things, in the soft, delicate, childlike quality of her skin.

And one night in June, just a few nights before the time for the family to move up to the Lake, he began to wonder, as they sat across from each other at the table in a little drugstore outside of Middlefield, if that skin would feel as soft and tender to the touch as it looked. The thought made him very nervous, and all the way back to Middlefield he kept trying to force himself to think about something else.

He stopped in front of the house on Proctor Street and turned off the ignition and the lights. It was late, and, aside from the street lights that seemed to flicker up among the heavily leafed maples, the porch light on the Bunces' house was the only one on the whole street. The air, which had been hot all day, had become fresh, as cooling to the skin as a lotion.

He glanced sideways at Winifred. She was sitting quietly, her hands in her lap, but he sensed a tension in her, a little pulling in of the shoulders and a gripping of one hand with the other. He knew that she knew that he was going to put his arm around her. She probably did not know that what he wanted to do then was to put his fingers on that amazingly soft-looking, thinly veined spot on her neck just beside her throat. What she probably thought was that he was going to kiss her.

Awkwardly, trying too hard to be casual about it, he did put his arm around her and let his hand fall onto her shoulder. The shoulder gave a little under the weight of his hand and, suddenly confident, he did put the three fingers of his left hand on the spot beside her throat.

It was just as soft and tender as he had imagined it would be, and far more alive and more vibrant. This, he thought, was all he had wanted, and even now, as he moved his hand up to her chin and turned her head toward him and tilted it back, he was thinking in the back of his mind, "This is a mistake. This isn't what I want to do."

But he did kiss her, and her lips were soft and surprisingly sweet and refreshing, and it was much more delightful than he had imagined it would be. He held her tighter and tighter, pressing his lips harder and harder against hers, and it was much more thrilling than he had thought it would be. And suddenly, with surprising strength, she pulled her face aside and pushed him away. She wiggled free of his arm and slid into the corner of the seat, as far away from him as she could get. He looked at her face, and she did not look angry. She looked, it seemed to him, contrite.

She waited to get her breath, looking down at her hands. Finally she said, "That spoiled things, didn't it, Noah?"

He stared at her, puzzled by the intensity of the excitement he had been feeling. He made an effort to regain his self-possession, and finally he smiled at her and said gallantly, "I thought it was very nice."

She shook her head. "I've enjoyed these little rides so much, Noah." She smiled, a little pensively. "And the ice-cream cones." She opened the door beside her. "Well, you'll be going to Vermont Monday, won't you?"

She got out, and Noah, almost himself again now, knowing that she was right, that it had spoiled things, said, "I'm sorry."

She smiled at him sadly. He felt suddenly that she was very wise, very worldly-wise, a girl who in twenty-one years had learned a lot about the world, a lot about acceptance, a lot more than he himself had learned in twenty-four years. "You don't have to be," she said.

Dr. Sibley paid her a retaining fee for the summer, so that she would be there waiting for him when he got back in the fall. He couldn't imagine, he said, working without her.

In September, Noah, beginning his career as a teacher, had to go to Milburn early, and he spent just one day in Middlefield repacking his clothes. The letters he got from home during the fall mentioned Winifred only enough to let him know that she was still there.

They were full of news of Mark's novel. He had twenty-five chapters finished and five to go. He had twenty-eight finished and two to go. He had finished the first draft and was starting in on revisions. And as the Christmas vacation approached, he was working fast on revisions, and as soon as he had a chapter whipped into shape he was turning it over to Winifred for typing. She was coming back nights to do them for him; he was anxious to get the manuscript off to the publisher as soon as possible after the first of the year.

5.

CHRISTMAS vacations in the Sibley household, back in those days, were always hectic, always crowded with activities and festivities. But that Christmas vacation, the Christmas of 1938, had been bedlam.

Connie arrived from college the same day that Noah arrived from Milburn, and she brought with her a friend who couldn't afford the carfare to her home in Pasadena. Kate, at the height of her popularity then, was scrambling out of bed at ten in the morning, rushing through a breakfast, begging Noah to drive her to the 10:45 so that she wouldn't be late to her afternoon sculpture classes at the Art Students' League in New York; then, arriving back in Middlefield on the 6:38, she would have to be met again. She would rush through a bath and a change and be off to her party or date, and, almost as often as not, the date involved putting up a young man or two in the extra guest room on the third floor.

Barrett and Louise, finishing their first six months of married life, seemed to be around the house as much as they were in their apartment on Elm Street, and they were both full of exuberance and the Christmas spirit. Dr. Sibley had given up all thought of trying to work until the tumult subsided. Mrs. Sibley was at her best, the leader, the hostess, the planner, and the caterer all in one.

Poor Mark was trying to work in all the confusion; the lust to finish, as his father expressed it, had him in its grip. He took to getting up at five-thirty and getting in a couple of hours of work before anyone else in the household was stirring. He stuffed newspapers under his door to keep the noise out. He had his lunches brought up to his room, so that the table conversation wouldn't start distracting trains of thought. And when he did appear at dinner, he looked tired and pale and handsome, very much the picture of the young writer in the throes of creation. The girl from Pasadena became self-conscious as soon as he came in, and for an hour after he left she would sit starry-eyed, often failing to answer when spoken to.

And at ten-thirty or eleven or eleven-thirty at night, whenever Winifred finished typing the chapters Mark had turned over to her when she came in after dinner, Mark would drive her home to her house on Proctor Street.

6 ·

"He's driving her home all right," Barrett said, laughing, "but not always by the most direct route."

It was an evening sometime between Christmas and New Year's, and Noah was having dinner with Barrett and Louise alone in their apartment—a quiet interlude in the week of commotion. And they had a *soufflé*, Noah remembered; Louise had thought that something light would be a relief after all the turkey.

Barrett took a mouthful of the *soufflé*. "As I get it," he said, "it started with their stopping in at the lunchroom for a sandwich and a cup of coffee. Then they began to go for a bit of a ride and then they began to stop in at one of those roadhouses out on the highway for a beer or a drink or something. And of course they dance in most of those places."

"Sounds fun," Louise said gaily.

"Ever been in one of those joints, honey?" He shook his head in answer to his own question. "I'm afraid you'd find it pretty depressing." He ate a few more mouthfuls of the *soufflé*. "Delicious, dear." He laid his fork down and sat back. "Joking aside, though, Noah, I don't really like it."

Noah, busy with his *soufflé*, looked up at him with raised eyebrows. "She's a pretty decent kid," he said. "I know. I worked with her and Dad last spring."

"Absolutely," Barrett agreed. "A very decent kid. And a very appealing kid—maybe a little too appealing." He ran his two hands back over his head, looking up at the ceiling. "The thing we don't realize, Noah, is how those people who live over there in that part of town look at those of us who live over here in this part. We're creatures out of another world. Look at Winifred there. She has to swallow twice before she can get up the courage to say hello."

"She certainly is bashful," Noah said.

"Well, maybe you could call it that, but how bashful do you suppose she is with the boys who live over there on Proctor Street? I'll bet she can kid them along just as well as any other stenographer can."

"*Soufflés* are made to be eaten hot, dearest," Louise said.

Barrett smiled at her. "You're absolutely right, honey. Not another word out of any of us until the *soufflé* is consumed."

They all ate in silence, laughing at each other with their eyes.

When they had finished, Louise said, "You were saying that Winifred could kid the boys along, dear."

Barrett took a cigarette from the little glass container in front of him. "What I was trying to say was this: those people who live over there, the people who run the little stores down on Main Street and work in the factory offices around this area and so on, all their lives they've been hearing about the Clarks and the Stevensons and the Devereauxs and, if I may say so, the Barretts and the Sibleys. All their lives they've been looking at these damned big houses we live in. Maybe to our eyes they're atrocities, but to them they're the Elysian Fields. They're forbidden ground. They've got invisible signs up, 'Do Not Enter.' All they know about what the insides look like is what they can learn from our maids and delivery boys."

He opened his hands out in a gesture that seemed to concede a point that Noah or Louise might make. "It's silly," he said. "I don't deny it. It's undemocratic. It's an indictment of us, if you want, for being so damned exclusive. But there it is."

Louise gathered up the plates, and Barrett waited for her to come back in from the kitchen with the desserts.

"We'd all agree," he went on, after they had gotten started on the desserts, "that there's nothing wrong with Mark's taking Winifred for a ride and stopping in at a roadhouse for a drink. It's a nice thing for him to do, when she's going to all the trouble she is to help him with his book.

"But here's the thing, Noah. Here's Mark, a Sibley and the grandson of a Barrett, and on top of that the son of probably the most famous man who ever lived in Middlefield, a man the whole city never misses a chance to brag about. On top of that, he's a promising young novelist, and on top of that he's a damned attractive boy, even if he is our brother. And here's Winifred, a very decent kid, as you say. Probably a little more rigid in her moral code than most of the girls we knew and went around with. But she lives on Proctor Street and her father's a haberdasher. She had probably never been in one of these houses until she got this job with Dad. Do you honestly think, Noah, that if the occasion ever arose, she would have the *courage* to say no to Mark?"

Noah smiled to himself. For once he knew more of what they were talking about than Barrett did. Winifred could push with surprising strength; he knew that. But of course, he thought, sobering, he wasn't Mark. Lots of people who took him, Noah, for just another guy found Mark impressive. Winifred would probably be afraid of Mark in a way she hadn't been afraid of him. In any case, you didn't let on that you knew any more about it than Barrett and Louise did. He laughed. "I doubt if she could even find the voice to say it," he said.

"Absolutely," Barrett agreed approvingly.

"So," Noah said, smiling at Louise, "maybe all we can do is put our trust in Mark's nobility."

"Or his fatigue," Louise said.

Barrett looked as though he had not heard her. "I'd be happy if I thought we could," he said to Noah, "but human nature is human nature. He's still on the rebound from Thérèse. He's lonesome. He's probably got a need to reassure himself as regards his masculine charms. And a couple of drinks at the end of the day, when you're working the way he's working, can do strange things to you. Winifred is a very appealing little girl, with the sort of skin you love to touch, and if they're parked somewhere at one o'clock in the morning and she's looking up at him with those adoring eyes of hers—well, maybe I'm making a mountain out of a molehill, but all I'm hoping is that, on the spur of a chance impulse some night, Mark isn't going to get himself hooked into something that could ruin his whole life."

Noah was smiling to himself again, amused at the thought that even Barrett, so happily married to Louise, must at some time or other have had an impulse to touch that skin of Winifred's. It made him feel closer to Barrett, just as his father's eye for a pretty girl had always made him feel closer to him.

7.

DURING the week that he had been home, Noah had seen very little of Winifred. When he had seen her, there had always been other people there except for once when they had met in the hall and talked for a few minutes. Both of them had succeeded very well in acting as though the episode in front of the Bunce house had not happened. Noah had found himself thinking of her with much the same amused, brotherly liking that he had felt for her during the spring, although of course he couldn't forget that kiss entirely.

The evening after his dinner at Barrett's, he happened to be the one who let her in when she came at eight o'clock. With the things Barrett had said in mind, he couldn't help but look at her with fresh curiosity. That Mark might well find her appealing seemed quite probable; that she could say no to him—well, he just couldn't tell about that. Maybe she couldn't.

He led her into the study and stood watching her and smiling as she took off her coat and hat and sat down and removed the cover from the typewriter. She looked up at him expectantly, half smiling, waiting for what he had to say. He had nothing in particular to say, and for a confused moment he stared, then asked hurriedly, "How's everything going?"

"It's going along very fast," she said, and Noah knew that she was talking about the novel. She looked up at him with a rapt expression on her face. "It's the most wonderful story I ever read. It's so exciting, it's—I can hardly wait for evening to come so I can come and get the next chapter. I think it's going to make your brother a very famous writer."

"Well," Noah said, a little ashamed that he had been wondering about roadside adventures when she was so high-mindedly thinking about literature, "well, that's wonderful. I can't wait to read it either. I haven't heard a word of it, you know."

"You shouldn't," she said earnestly, "not until it's all done."

It was done the day after New Year's, and Noah had a chance to read it in manuscript before he went back to school. After all the build-up, he found himself vaguely disappointed in it. He couldn't say why. It was full of beautiful writing, with some wonderful descriptions of Paris in its various moods, and there was some very clever dialogue.

For two months after he got back to school he heard nothing whatever about the novel. Then, in early March, he got an amusing letter from Louise.

"A new side of little Winifred's character is coming to light," she wrote, "the pugnacious side. She is so mad at the two publishers who turned the book down that I honestly think she would tear their eyes out with her fingernails if she could get at them. And she read the old novel and got mad all over again because they had had the nerve to turn it down.

"A few days ago she got Mark to let her take both manuscripts in to the little publishing house where she used to work. She says they sometimes publish what she calls 'trade books'—I gather that means ordinary books rather than school books or some other kind of books. Anyway, I happened to be there when she left for the city, and there was fire in her eye and that little chin of hers was almost jutting out —if you can imagine such a thing. I don't know what kind of coercion she was planning to use on them—for all I know, she might have had a pistol in her handbag."

And three weeks later, a week before Milburn's Easter vacation was to start, Noah got a letter from his mother saying that Mark and Winifred were engaged to be married. His first reaction to the news, as he sat reading his mail in the room in old Seward, was concern. He had no feeling of either approval or disapproval, merely concern that somehow it might prove a mistake for Mark and for Winifred.

He reread the letter, and as he finished it the second time he was thinking affectionately that his mother was certainly taking it like the old trouper that she was.

"We could all wish," she had written, "that she could be a little more at home among the kind of people with whom she will now be thrown. Perhaps that will come with time. I'm sure we'll all agree that she is a sweet girl and that there is nothing objectionable about her at all. I doubt if Mark could have found a girl who would worship him quite as she does. Her devotion is really beautiful to see. That and her great faith in his writing and her great anxiety to help him with it are all big items on the credit side of the ledger."

It wasn't until later that Noah remembered the things Barrett had said that night at dinner and how plausible they had sounded. He hoped, for Winifred's sake more than Mark's, that it hadn't worked out as Barrett had feared, but he went home half expecting to find Mark and Winifred already married and about to leave for Europe or the West Coast or some other faraway place, to be gone for a year or whatever length of time was deemed necessary to blur dates. But when he got there he discovered that they seemed to be in no hurry at all; they were talking about a June wedding.

Again Connie arrived on the same day that Noah did. That night Mark had a dinner engagement in New York, and Dr. Sibley had had a last-minute request to speak at a dinner in Plainfield. Mrs. Sibley was going with him, so Barrett and Louise came over to eat their share of the roast.

"I hereby publicly eat my words," Barrett said jocularly. "Everything seems to be completely under control. Either she did know how to say no, or else Mark was sufficiently noble."

"Or tired," Noah said, smiling at Louise.

[174]

"The only painful thing," Barrett said, "was when Mr. and Mrs. Bunce came to call. They'd already started making plans for a wedding in that little Methodist church over there and a reception for two or three hundred people at the Middlefield Arms. I suspect the poor guy was figuring on mortgaging his store and his house and everything else he owned. Can you imagine anything more embarrassing than that reception at the Middlefield Arms?"

"Did somebody manage to kill the idea?" Noah asked.

"Mother, of course," Louise said. "Who else would have thought, in the twinkling of an eye, of asking them if they didn't think that a wedding in the little church at the Lake and a small reception at the cottage would be wonderfully romantic?"

"Nobody else," Noah agreed, pleased.

"What is it you lawyers call it, Barrett?" Connie asked. "A change of venue by reason of prejudice?"

They all laughed. "That's very clever, Connie," Barrett said, "and you can call it prejudice if you want to, but I'll have to admit I'm awfully darned glad I'm not going to have to go through the ordeal of that reception at the Middlefield Arms. Aren't you?"

Connie smiled. "I'd be happy if I never had to go through the ordeal of any kind of a reception ever."

"And I'll have to admit," Barrett said, "that I don't envy Mother her job of being joint mother-in-law with Mrs. Bunce year after year either."

They all stopped, thinking about the problem Mrs. Sibley was going to have. Finally Noah said, "She'll handle it."

"Of course she will," Barrett said, "but it won't be fun."

"And *I'll* have to admit," Louise said, "that I don't exactly envy poor little Winifred either."

Barrett sat up and looked at her. "Why, honey," he said, "that's not a very nice thing to say."

"Oh, I'm sorry, dearest," she said quickly, flushing. "I didn't mean it the way it sounded. Anybody who marries Mark will be a lucky girl. All I meant was that she's such a bashful little thing and we're all such strangers to her really and—well, I suspect that to somebody like her we do seem kind of a formidable family."

She smiled doubtfully at Barrett, apparently still afraid that she had hurt his feelings. "It was different with me," she said. "I'd known you all my life—and we'd all had the Lake in common and—and we're all pretty much the same breed of cats anyway. I'm already beginning to feel as much a Sibley as a Hill." She smiled at him again, with radiant affection. To Noah's eyes she had never been so sparkingly pretty as she had been during that year, her first year of married life. She had seemed, when she smiled like that, to radiate some sort of light. "And I have a feeling," she said, "that I'll get to be more and more of a Sibley every year."

IX

1·

AND now, during the nightmare week at the Lake, as though there weren't complications enough already, there came the letter from the director of the sanitarium and the note from Winifred.

Noah had noticed the return address on the director's letter when he brought it back from the post office, but he had left it on the mantelpiece with the rest of the mail and had heard nothing more about it until the next morning. Then, after breakfast, Mark had gone out to the Lion's Lair to work as usual, and Mrs. Sibley had told Barrett and Joan and Noah that she wanted to have a chat with them out on the veranda. The bandage on her head had been replaced by a smaller one which she was able to hide almost entirely with her hair, and her step and her voice and her manner were as strong and self-assured as they had always been.

Sensing something important in the wind, Joan had sent the boys over to Kate's to play with her children, sending a message by them that Mother Sibley was not to be disturbed this morning.

The four of them, there on the veranda, were having a second cup of coffee. Mrs. Sibley waited until they were all settled, saucers in hand. Then she said, "What I have to tell you is that Mark has had very wonderful news. At least, I hope it's as good as it sounds. The director of the sanitarium has written him that he feels that poor Winifred is ready to try normal living out in the world again."

"Well," Barrett said heartily, "isn't that splendid?"

"How wonderful!" Joan said. "I've always been so anxious to meet her."

Winifred had gone back in for the last time the day before Barrett and Joan's wedding.

"What's more," Mrs. Sibley said, "he says that she herself is ready to try it. I've forgotten the exact wording, but it was something to the effect that she was facing the prospect with full courage."

"Splendid!" Barrett said.

"And Mark had a short note from Winifred asking him where he wanted her to go," Mrs. Sibley added, her tone hinting at the difficulty of the question.

Noah stared at her sleepily, uncomprehendingly. His mind, during these last five days, had been doing strange things, disturbing things which he couldn't understand at all. It had been as though he had had two minds at once. They were like two trains running along side by side into a station. With his ordinary mind he had been going about his business as usual, answering the questions the children asked him, agreeing to plans, figuring out ways and means of doing all the things he had to get done. And all the time, along with it but on the other track, this other mind went gliding along, full of weird, disturbing thoughts, thoughts that were as foreign to everything he had ever thought before as nightmares are from reality.

And now, as he stared at his mother, the other mind was thinking things that were almost the exact opposite of what his ordinary, business-of-the-day mind was thinking. He frowned, trying by an effort of will to shut off the current that kept the other mind moving along on its track.

His mother was gazing out at the lake, her expression placid and motherly. "Of course," she said, "we all have to remember that this is the third time in ten years that they've pronounced her cured, and both other times she's had to go back in again."

The other mind would not be stopped, and what it persisted in knowing was that his mother was annoyed with Winifred for getting well again. He looked at her, frightened, then jumped up and paced a half-dozen steps away down the veranda. He came back and stood looking at the three of them, and now for a moment the other mind was his only mind: they were actors on a stage, so poised, so calm, feeling nothing of what they were saying, unreal, untrue to life, just as they had been that early morning five days ago when he had come back from taking the doctor home and found them sitting so theatrically perfect there in the living room.

His mother looked up at him quizzically. "Why, Noah, you don't look very happy about Mark's good news."

He nodded and stood still, glaring down at them. Behind his back, his left hand was squeezing his right wrist, and the fingers of his right hand were working, kneading the palm.

His mother looked up at him again, her expression puzzled and disapproving, then turned deliberately back to Barrett and Joan. "I'm sure that Mark is really very happy at the news," she said, "but I think we can all understand that it comes as quite a shock to him too. It means a complete readjustment in all his thinking—and possibly in his whole manner of living. He seems almost stunned by it. I think for the present the best thing we can do is to say nothing to him about it at all. All in good time, he will bring the subject up himself. They also serve, you know, who only stand and wait. I'm sure that is the way we can help him most."

Noah had only half heard the last part of what she said. "It comes as quite a shock to him," his ordinary mind was saying. "It means a readjustment." And in his other mind he was thinking of Winifred, of Winifred hiding under the desk in the study, peeking out at him through the lattice of her fingers while all the polite voices droned on in the dining room; of Winifred running away, always running away; running away from Doris Stevenson's wedding with her coat over her head, after Mark had spoken to her about being too shrilly gay on two glasses of champagne; running away from the front door of the Sibleys' house as she and Mark were about to come in, and running all the way back to her apartment to change her dress for the fourth time in an hour; of Winifred curled up in the corner of her bedroom, fully dressed, with her bathrobe over her head.

"It's a matter," Barrett was saying, "that's going to take a lot of thought, not only for Mark, I imagine, but for all of us."

And Noah's other mind was thinking of Winifred that last summer, seven years ago, the only summer she had ever spent at the Lake, and of how different, after her two stays in the sanitarium, her voice had been; how calmly she had talked and listened; how readily she had smiled, with what a quick eye for the amusing and the incongruous; of the hours she had sat right here on this veranda, looking out at the lake, absorbing, he had sensed, strength and peace from its beauty; of how sure he had felt then that she had won her fight, that she had conquered at last whatever it had been that had possessed her; of how he had gone right on thinking so into the fall, as she settled into her life in Middlefield, avoiding social engagements but otherwise her old self—or, rather, a more assured, more humorous, more likable self—until, three days before the wedding, she had disappeared. And in his other mind he was remembering how frantically his mother had called the police, ordering them to find her, and how exasperated the whole family had been with Winifred for injecting this discordant note into the happy wedding preparations.

And now, while his mother was agreeing with Barrett that it was a matter that they would all have to give a great deal of thought to, Noah's other mind was thinking about how the police had found her, on the day before the wedding, in a small uptown hotel in New York, where she had registered under her own name. And how they had reported that when they walked in, she had been sitting beside the window with a book in her lap and two other books and a few magazines scattered on the bed. She had admitted her identity readily enough, they had said, and had offered no resistance. And when, at Noah's prompting, Mrs. Sibley had asked them on the phone if she had seemed frightened, they had said no—no, they wouldn't say she had acted frightened exactly. All she had told them was that she didn't think she ought to go to the wedding.

"Of course all the final decisions will be Mark's to make," Mrs. Sibley was saying, "but my thought at the moment is that the cares of an apartment of her own might be too much for her at first."

Noah was still only half listening, because now, out of the deep wells of his subconscious memories, there was coming a vague recalling that was hardly a memory at all, a vague recalling of something he had felt on that day. What he had felt, half consciously, putting the feeling aside then as he had ever since, was that the decision to have the police take Winifred straight from the hotel back to the sanitarium had been a too hasty one, that regardless of how busy the household was, regardless of how much she might have upset the wedding, they should have waited and talked with her at least once before they sent her away again.

It wouldn't have mattered, his ordinary mind told him. After all, the doctors had kept her there seven years; that proved that it was necessary for her to go back, didn't it, that it wouldn't have mattered? And his other mind persisted in knowing that in some kind of way it did matter, that whether the doctors had kept her there seven years or not, it did matter—and the reason it mattered was that they, his own family, these people sitting here, had been relieved to have an excuse to send her away again. And, his other mind insisted, getting more and more unruly by the minute, they had been relieved to have an excuse to keep her where she was during all those seven years.

His mind seemed to stare at the thought, repulsed, trying to reject it, but the thought would not be stilled.

He thought of what his mother had once said to him about Winifred, that she, as Mark's mother, couldn't allow a flighty little girl like Winifred to upset Mark's career. Was it Mark's career they had all been thinking of that day?

And even if it was? Even if you gave them the benefit of that doubt? Suddenly, through all the confusion of his two minds, he sensed that he was very close to the core of the whole matter. Couldn't it be that attitude of his mother's, the thought she had bred into her children so assiduously, that was at the core of the whole matter? Was it, in Mark, this very preoccupation with himself, with his own career, which his mother had fostered with such determination, that had made him what he was now, today? And could it be that it was not Winifred's weakness that had kept her there these seven years, but rather Mark's weakness, some failure of his, a failure in this, the most personal of all relationships? Had he failed because he was what his mother had willed him to be, and had the failure helped to make him what he was?

"I'm also wondering if, having been alone for so long," Mrs. Sibley was saying, "Winifred might not be happier in a room of her own. My thought would be that they might come and stay with us this fall, and we could turn over the green room to her and let Mark stay in his own room—just to start with, of course, until we see how things are going to work out."

And Noah's other mind was thinking that his mother knew as well as he did that what she was suggesting was the one surest way in the world to send Winifred back to the sanitarium once more. The green room—it was the green room Louise had been in that winter. He blinked and shook his head vehemently, then stared at his mother, not knowing whether to be horrified at her or himself. He didn't know—he only knew that he had to get away from this veranda. He spoke slowly, enunciating each word carefully, like a drunkard trying too hard to sound sober. "If that's all you want of me," he said, "I think I'll—I think I'll go out in the rowboat."

And before his mother had time to say whether she did or did not want anything more of him, he was down the steps and on his way out to the dock.

2·

AT one o'clock, Noah had an engagement to take Kate's two older boys over to East Ledwick to watch the bulldozers work on the site for the new creamery. He had to be back by four to pick up Aunt Constance at the Inn and bring her down to the cottage for tea. And he had agreed to take Barry and Billy perch fishing during the tea hour, because his mother was anxious to have Aunt Constance and Joan get to know each other, and of course it would be nicer if Barrett could be there with Joan.

"You do love children, don't you, Noah?" Joan said at lunch. "And you're so good with them. I've never seen one who wasn't crazy about you. You really should have some of your own." She smiled at him, and he thought sulkily that it was a patronizing sort of smile. "It's still not too late, you know. How old are you? Thirty-eight. There are lots of nice girls around who'd like to marry a thirty-eight-year-old man like you."

Noah looked at her. And his other mind, which had been dormant for a couple of hours now, started running again, and what it was thinking was that the girl she was visualizing for him, the girl who would like to marry a man like him, was very nice and very plain. It was some girl approaching spinsterhood and welcoming a chance to marry a clumsy, unprepossessing, well-meaning man. He found himself wishing that Joan could see Natalie, the modeling of her face, the expression with which she looked at people, the way she held herself and the way she walked, the distinction she had that was so much greater than any distinction that Joan herself would ever have.

He went on eating, his eyes on his plate, and after a while his mother said, "Noah, you're bolting your food like a hired hand."

At one o'clock Spence brought the boys over. "Awfully good of you, Noah," he said. "A bulldozer working is to them what fire engines were to us, you know. And I don't mind admitting that it's quite a relief to have 'em off our hands for a few hours—much as we love 'em. It's the boys who keep things stirred up. The girls are little angels when they're away." He grinned at the two boys. "Well, have a good time, fellas." He turned back to Noah. "Barrett in the house?"

"He's in there somewhere."

Spence smiled at him, a little sadly. "I've got to have a little sing-song with him," he said.

3.

At five-thirty, Noah drove Aunt Constance up to the Inn. When he got back to the cottage, Connie's car was in the yard. Joan was in the kitchen, getting the boys' supper, and the boys were sitting at the places that had already been laid for them at the kitchen table. Billy was banging the edge of the table with the blade of his knife, methodically and with concentration. Barry sang out, "Uncle Noah only caught two perch and I caught six."

Noah grinned at him, then turned to Joan. "Where's Connie?"

"I don't know," Joan said shortly, tight-lipped.

He went into the living room. Barrett and Mark were both reading. "Where's Connie?" he asked.

They went on reading.

"I think she went upstairs," Mark said, without looking up from his book.

"Where's Mother?"

"She's resting out on the veranda."

He went upstairs. Connie was coming down the hall with an armful of clothes. "Hi," she said, smiling at him. She looked very well indeed, pink-cheeked and gay and, compared to the rest of the household, unharried. "We'll leave the boys in my room," she said, "and I'll set up the cot for myself in your study. And I'll have it and myself completely out by eight o'clock in the morning—you'll never know I've been there. I never use perfume, you know." She smiled at him again.

"Oh, you don't have to do that," Noah said. "You should have your own room."

She shook her head and went into the study. "Much easier this way."

He followed her in, and she hung her clothes in the closet that had once been Kate's and went over and closed the door. She offered him a cigarette. "I'm not very popular around here, am I?"

He took the cigarette and sank into his big chair. "It's been pretty hectic."

She sat in the swivel chair at the desk. "And not having anyone but themselves to blame," she said cheerfully, "they're blaming me."

"It's really been pretty bad," Noah said.

She hunched her shoulders and smiled at him ruefully. "Worse than one might have expected?"

[183]

"Much worse," he said, shaking his head at the memory. "And of course now the Winifred business has added—"

"What Winifred business?"

"Didn't they tell you?"

"Their only conversation," she said, "was a very surly set of greetings."

"Mark's had a letter from the director saying that she was considered cured. She can come out and start living in the world again."

"Well!" She sat still, looking down at the floor, thinking. Then she frowned. "When did he get it? Today?"

"Yesterday. And a note from Winifred asking him what he wanted her to do."

"Yesterday?" she asked incredulously.

He nodded.

"Winifred's note? In the mail? Before lunch?"

"Of course."

She dropped her cigarette into the ashtray and stared at him as though she couldn't believe what he was saying. Then she took a deep breath and puffed it out in a sigh and covered her face with her hands. "I try so damn hard, Noah," she said. She got to her feet and paced across the room, and he knew from her face that she was really distressed. She went back and sat down and after a moment said distractedly, "I make such good resolutions, Noah—every time I'm about to come back here or to Middlefield—" She took her hands away and looked at him, her expression bleak. "Has he wired her, Noah?"

"I don't believe so."

She sat still, looking at his face. "He could have been down there by last night," she said. And after a while she asked, "Can you imagine that poor kid, sitting down there in that sanitarium, waiting." And suddenly her voice was vindictive. "And he sits here on his fat bottom reading a book." She clasped her head with her two hands, leaning back and staring up at the ceiling. Then, with a sweeping gesture of both hands, she seemed to toss the whole question off into space.

She sat forward again, limply. "Have you got any work done, Noah?"

He shook his head. "Not this week."

She swiveled around in her chair and looked at the piles of papers on the desk, each with its little labeling slip of paper. She did not seem particularly interested in them, but finally she said dully, "This isn't your stuff, Noah. It's Dad's. You're not thinking of trying to revise the book, are you?"

"No."

The tone in which he said it made her look up at him questioningly. He stared angrily back into her eyes.

"Well?" she asked.

He continued to stare at her, breathing audibly. Then he went over to the door and locked it. "*I'll* show you what those are," he said accusingly. He picked one up at random, took off the clip, and shoved it in front of her. "See," he said, underlining the typing on the slip of paper with his forefinger. "Kellogg-Briand. Kellogg-Briand Pact renouncing war as an instrument of national policy. Nineteen twenty-eight." He opened the magazine that was on top. "Here's what he said about it that fall."

The article he handed her was entitled, "The Road Lies Clear," by William Huntington Sibley.

He watched Connie as she read, knowing line by line, almost word by word, what the phrases were that she was reading: "The culmination of thirty years of effort to establish arbitration as the normal, the natural, the accepted way of settling disputes . . . mothers can sleep nights, knowing that their boys will never . . . never again can a warlike nation, against the accumulated indignation of a world opinion now rallied on the side of peace . . . the greatest step forward . . ."

He let her read on as he thumbed through the pile. "Okay," he said. "You got that?"

She nodded and laid it down.

"Okay," he said grimly, still thumbing. "We'll skip a lot of this stuff. Let me pick out a good one. Here, this one." He picked up a pamphlet. "Foreign policy speech. Nineteen thirty-five. Seven years later. Here's what he said." He laid it on the desk in front of her and pointed to a paragraph with a penciled line beside it. Then, looking over her shoulder, he read it aloud to her as she herself read along. "Japan and Italy have merely underlined the humor of one of the saddest jokes in the history of arbitration; namely, the Pact of Paris, commonly known as the Kellogg-Briand Treaty. Those of us who had followed the course of international affairs through the years knew all too well at the time that no such treaty could survive the test of time. Without provisions for enforcement, without practical guarantees and sanctions, it was doomed from the beginning to be nothing more than a meaningless gesture, a jumble of high-sounding phrases."

He finished reading and stepped back, looking down at her sternly. "That's what he said in 1935," he said.

She nodded, her face expressionless.

[185]

"That's just one," he said, suddenly eager, pawing through the piles. "Versailles. That's another pippin. But wait—here's Munich." He tore the clip off and thumbed impatiently through the pages. "Here's what he said when it happened, in '38. Read that." He handed it to her, grinning gleefully, staring into her face.

"Noah," she said, scowling, "you're acting like a madman."

"Read it," he said. "Read this." He ran his fingers along the lines, picking out words and phrases. "Another triumph for arbitration . . . reasonable concessions . . . sensible men reaching sensible accords without recourse to violence"—he came to the last line—"may truly be a guarantee of peace in our time."

Gleefully, triumphantly, he picked up a page of typescript. "And here's what he says in the book, Part Two, Chapter Twenty-four. He wrote this in '47." He read, "'As many of us pointed out at the time'—many of us maybe," he interrupted himself, "but not William Huntington Sibley, so far as I can find anywhere"—he read on—"'such dishonorable concessions could never be the foundation for an enduring peace. To buy peace by agreeing to the subjugation of a whole freedom-loving nation was to—'"

"Stop it, Noah," Connie said sharply.

"There it is," he said, wild-eyed. "I didn't make it up. '—the subjugation of a whole freedom-loving nation was—'"

Connie jumped to her feet. "You go over there and sit down."

He stared into her face. Then, suddenly limp, he stumbled to the chair and sat slumped, looking up at her grumpily. She stood erect, her eyes calm but implacable, and for the first time in his life he was able to imagine her controlling a roomful of schoolgirls.

"That hurt, Noah," she said, "and you were enjoying it. I never dreamed before that you could be so masochistic."

He pointed to the table. "There it is," he said hoarsely.

She sat down again and lighted another cigarette. "That's right," she said, "there it is. And it hurts. It hurts me too."

"But you knew it all the time," he said, still grumpy.

"I never had the evidence thrust at me quite like that before." She sat back in her chair and puffed her cigarette. "Just because it hurts is no reason why you have to start acting like a madman."

He chuckled mirthlessly. "What do you start doing?"

She blew a long cloud of smoke up toward the ceiling. "I suppose you start thinking all over again." She thought a while. "You don't stop loving him just because you find you can't admire him as much as you did." She sat forward and looked into his face, and her eyes were sympathetic. "Look, Noah, I know it's worse for you than it is for me. He was my father, but he was your father and darned near the biggest thing in your life too. He's been your life work for these last few years. For all practical purposes, you *are* the Memorial Foundation."

He laughed. "Memorial to what?"

"Stop it, Noah. You're being childish. Now look here. Let's agree he wasn't all we were brought up to think he was. He liked applause. He liked to see his by-line in all the important reviews. He didn't go out of his way to admit he'd been wrong. He tried to make believe he hadn't been wrong. Call him dishonest if you want to."

"I don't want to," Noah said, "but there it is." He pointed at the desk again.

"Okay, there it is. But that dishonesty wasn't all there was to him, was it? He had something else. He wasn't lazy, for one thing. He worked hard all his life. And he didn't have to either. There was always enough money. And he wasn't silly enough to feel, the way some men do, that he had to prove his manliness by earning his own living. He used the fact that there was money enough to work for something else. What was it?"

Noah smiled. "You said it yourself a minute ago," he said. "Applause."

"Was that all, Noah? Don't you believe that he really loved peace, that he really wanted to see peace established on earth?"

He stared at her, grumpy again.

"Don't you think he really believed that arbitration was the answer, the only way we could ever get it? Don't you think he was really sincere in that?"

He sat still, thinking. Finally he said, "I don't know."

She shook her head, and the way she looked at him made Noah feel a little childish. "Okay, Noah, you don't know. But just bear the possibility in mind when you get around to thinking it over." She stood up. "What do you say we have a dip in the lake before dinner? Come on, get into your trunks. We'll have to hurry."

4 ·

At first, with the two boys up in bed, dinner that night seemed delightfully quiet. Everyone seemed occupied with his own thoughts. Conversation was desultory.

But finally, as Noah was beginning to feel the muscles in his stomach and the back of his neck relaxing under the soothing effect of his swim, an old fashioned, and the good food, Barrett looked around the table with a sad, patient smile and said, "Well, you'll all be delighted to know that dear Spence is about to be broke again."

Noah glanced at him sideways and went on eating, showing that he had heard only by a more vigorous champing on his meat. He felt the muscles in his stomach tightening again. Nothing about his family annoyed him so much as the supercilious, condescending way they had of talking about Spence. It had been so for years.

Noah had a deep affection for Spence. Spence had qualities that he admired: a warmth of friendliness, a code of courtesy and kindness from which he had never known him to digress, a wonderful knack for fatherly companionship with his children.

Mrs. Sibley sighed, and Mark said humorously, "Dear Spence!"

And no situation left Noah so exasperated and helpless as the one he found himself in on these occasions when Spence had to come to them for money. He wasn't able to deny that Spence was a little impractical about some things, a little impecunious. But it wasn't all Spence's fault either—not by a long shot. That he knew. And none of the family would ever admit that Kate had even less of a sense of the value of money than Spence had. Spence was always on the spot, and he had never once even hinted that Kate might have been partly at fault.

"Spence seems to think," Mark said, "that this family's funds are some sort of a bottomless well."

"Aren't they?" Connie asked.

"No, Connie," Barrett said, as though from an eminence, "they're not. Not by any means. And the sooner we all get the idea that they are out of our heads, the better off we'll be."

They all ate in silence.

"He says," Barrett said, "that new babies are an expensive luxury, and so are bronze castings."

"We all know they are," Noah said defensively.

"Of course," Mark said, "the thought that he might get out and earn the money for the expensive luxuries hasn't occurred to him."

Barrett laughed. "Oh, but it has. 'The experiment with raising Hungarian partridge would have paid off in a big way,'" he quoted, "'if it hadn't been for a weasel and a flash flood one night that flooded the area.' And breeding the retrievers is really going to turn into a big thing. Retrievers are getting more popular around the country every year. If the young bitch hadn't got loose at the wrong time last spring—" He threw up his hands in a gesture of helplessness.

"How much does he need this time?" Mark asked with a weary sigh.

"Seven thousand dollars," Barrett said, "to pay for the last casting and the new baby and to rebuild the flock of Hungarian partridge and to keep the family going until next summer, when he's going to make thousands of dollars selling partridges."

Mark snorted. "The same way he made thousands raising pheasants and Chinook salmon, I suppose."

Barrett laughed. "Hungarian partridge are different. They're a really promising proposition."

"He can't do all those things," Joan said, "and feed himself and Kate and seven children for a year on seven thousand dollars."

"He has an income of his own," Barrett said disgustedly, "but it's never enough. Every two years or so he's around touching us up for another five thousand, another seven thousand—"

"We might call them stud fees," Connie said quietly. "After all, he's doing more to keep the noble Sibley blood in circulation than all the rest of us put together."

Noah laughed, and so, incongruously, did Joan.

"Very funny, Connie," Barrett said, "but just remember that it's your money he's getting just as much as it's the rest of ours."

"I remember," she said.

Again they all ate in silence. Finally Mark said, "Well, we all know we're not going to let Kate and the children starve. But it does seem to me that it's about time somebody laid down the law to Spence. Somebody's got to tell him that this sort of thing can't go on forever. He's either got to learn to live within his income and stop these foolish schemes of his, or else he'd better find himself a salaried job and settle down to—"

"What kind of a salaried job do you suppose he could handle?" Barrett asked, laughing.

"I don't know," Mark said.

"I agree with you, Mark," Mrs. Sibley said. "Somebody's got to talk with him."

Mark looked at Noah. "Couldn't you do it, Noah? You're his old fishing crony, and you seem to get along with him better than the rest of us do."

"No," Noah said abruptly. "I couldn't."

"Why Noah!" his mother said.

"Barrett's the manager of the trust funds," Noah said grumpily.

"A fact," Mark said, "which is entirely beside the point. I think my reasons for suggesting that you were the one to talk to Spence were rather good ones."

Noah went on eating.

"Noah," his mother said, "I don't know where you acquired that revolting habit of bolting your food like that."

Without looking at her, Noah laid his knife and fork on his plate and sat up. After he had finished chewing his mouthful, he said, "Why doesn't somebody speak to Kate? Whether they're broke or not, she goes right on paying for expensive castings and buying big expensive pieces of granite or whatever it is she works on. Why can't she work in wood for a change? They've got lots of trees on their farm down there."

Barrett and Mark and Joan all laughed, and Mrs. Sibley looked shocked.

"Your ignorance of sculpture, Noah," Mark said, "is quite overpowering. Wouldn't you say so, Barrett?"

"I should say," Barrett answered, "that Noah's whole remark was not only stupid but entirely uncalled for. You don't seem to realize it, Noah, but Kate is a very important artist. I believe, and I think Mark will agree with me, that Kate has achieved more distinction in her field than any one of the rest of us—except of course Dad. Wouldn't you honestly feel," he asked Noah with exaggerated reasonableness, "that it would be better to give up the Hungarian partridge and the retrievers and let Kate continue to have the materials she needs for her art?"

Noah looked at him stupidly. He couldn't think of an answer. There wasn't any answer to that, he supposed. And yet in the back of his mind he knew that there was something someone could say for Spence, that there was something valuable that Spence had that Barrett and Mark and Kate did not have.

His stomach now was a tight knot. He realized that he was breathing out loud, like a man with asthma. He knew he should never have tried to argue with Barrett and Mark.

He got to his feet. "I'm sorry," he said weakly. They were all looking at him as they might have looked at an animal in a zoo. "I don't feel very well," he said, and he dragged himself upstairs and into his room. He closed the door behind him and lay down on the bed, and as the light in the window faded from twilight to dark, he lay there, breathing hard, afraid to ask himself the questions that hovered, ready to pounce if he let them, just outside the circle of his consciousness.

He forced himself instead to think about the Ledwick River, to follow it along in his mind from pool to pool, remembering the trout he had caught in this one, the strike he had missed under this over-hanging tree. He followed it all the way down through the maple grove and on out into the open pastures and finally down into the dark piny gorge beside which, one day sixteen years ago, he had spilled a panful of fried trout onto the ground and he and Natalie had dusted the dirt off and eaten them anyway.

There was a knock on the door.

"Who is it?" he called.

"It's Connie."

He didn't want to talk now, not even with Connie, but she was his one ally and he couldn't afford to offend her. "Come in," he called.

She walked in and turned the light on. "I brought you a highball," she said.

He shook his head, still lying flat on his back. "Thanks just the same," he said, "but I've got a stomach-ache."

She set it down on the table beside him. "Of course you have," she said. "Have you tried prunes?"

"Yes. They didn't help." He lay still, staring up at the ceiling. Then, without bothering to tell her that he'd changed his mind, he got up on one elbow and took a sizable swallow from the drink. "Thanks," he said, smiling at her as he settled back on the bed. "It tasted better than I thought it would."

She nodded and sat down. After a while she smiled at him. "'Appy 'oliday, wot?"

"God," he said. "Can you imagine any worse complications?"

"Yes," she said. "I can."

He got up on his elbow again and looked at her.

For a long time she didn't answer the question implied by his change of posture. She merely looked at him with the cozy, half-humorous,

[191]

half-worried expression that was so typical of her. Finally she said, "My friend Jonesy is at the Inn."

Noah swung his feet around and sat on the edge of the bed. "Good God, Connie, you shouldn't have brought him up here. Not at a time like this. Now, of all times!"

"I had to."

"Had to?"

"It was our first quarrel," she said. "He wanted to meet my family, and I told him I didn't want him to, and that hurt his feelings. He thought I was ashamed of him, and I had to explain that he wasn't the one I was ashamed of. It was my family."

Noah was sitting there shaking his head at her. "But you brought him up here anyway," he said unbelievingly.

She chuckled. "He said that that was very wrong of me. Nobody should be ashamed of her family, no matter how bad they are. What could I say to that?"

Noah was still shaking his head. Suddenly he stopped. "You could have told him"—he broke in on himself and squinted at her—"Connie, you're not—"

She nodded complacently. "Yes, I'm going to marry him."

"You're not!"

"Oh, yes I am," she said gleefully. "He's wonderful."

He stared at her blankly, shaking his head again. "Connie, this is—"

"This is a mess," she agreed. "But it's what I'm going to do—and sooner than you expect."

"When?"

"In New York State you have to wait three days after they take your blood for the serological test. Those three days are now in process of passing, hour by hour."

"No, Connie, you can't—not like that. Can you imagine—"

"I have imagined," she said, closing her eyes. "What a stew! But that's why I want to get it over with quickly."

Noah got to his feet and stumbled across the room to the bureau. He looked at himself in the mirror. His hair was mussed and his tie askew. He straightened the tie and picked up the brush and brushed his hair. Then he went back and sat on the bed again, feeling considerably more self-possessed. This problem was Connie's affair, not his. He took another swallow of the drink. "Are you sure," he asked, "that this is the thing you want to do with the rest of your life?"

"Absolutely sure."

"You'll be living—where?"

"Los Angeles, of course."

"That's a hell of a long way away."

"I'll miss *you*. Maybe you can come out and visit us."

"Most of the people I know with tastes like ours don't have much use for Los Angeles."

She smiled. "Wives usually take what they get as regards places to live, don't they?"

Noah shrugged his shoulders. "Well, I hope you're—I hope—"

She laughed. "I know, Noah. You hope he's not as bad as you're afraid he is. I don't mind," she added. "It's nice to have somebody worrying about my happiness. That's the one thing the rest of the family won't even think of."

There was a knock on the door.

Noah picked up the glass. He whispered, "Well, if you're sure it's what you want"—he raised the glass toward her—"here's to you." He took a sip.

She got up, suddenly misty-eyed, and stepped across to him and patted his hand and went back and sat down again.

He smiled at her and called, "Come in."

Mark opened the door. He had on his smoking jacket and his leather slippers, and he had a manuscript in his hand. "I've finished that article for the *Literary Supplement*," he said to Noah. "Would you have time to go over it for me—you know, the usual—punctuation and phrasings. I'd like to get it off to the typist tomorrow if I can."

Connie stood up, looking at Mark. "Isn't it nice," she asked, unsmiling, "that Noah's so good at punctuation?" She looked at Noah, and he knew that she was hoping he would tell Mark to go to hell. He looked up at Mark and opened his mouth and closed it again.

Connie took a deep breath. "You'll be wanting your study," she said to Noah, disappointment in her voice. "You're welcome to it. I won't be in until late."

5.

NOAH took the manuscript into his study and closed the door. His stomach felt better. That highball had been a wonderful idea. Connie always had the best—he stopped still in the middle of the room. Connie was going to marry a man named Jones and go to live in Los

Angeles. He shut his eyes and screwed up his face, trying to visualize it, trying to imagine life with Connie far away.

He was suddenly overwhelmed by the consciousness of how empty a summer here at the Lake would be without her, how tasteless and flat a winter in Middlefield without the knowledge that she would be coming soon for a vacation or a weekend. Connie, of all people—his funny, inconspicuous, unimpressive little sister.

He tossed the manuscript on the desk and sat down in the swivel chair. Then, on a quick impulse, he got up again and went out into the hall. Soft music came from downstairs. He tiptoed along the hall and listened, then went cautiously down.

His mother was sitting at the table, writing letters. Barrett was in the big chair beside the fireplace, reading, and Joan sat beside the phonograph. The record she was playing was some string trio or quartet—variations on a jingle, it sounded like to Noah. Her expression was dutifully attentive, and her eyes looked through him as though he were not there.

He tiptoed toward the kitchen door. His mother looked up from her writing. "Feeling better, Noah?"

"Much better, thanks."

He went into the kitchen and looked out of the back door. Connie's car was gone. The light was on in the Lion's Lair. Mark must have gone back out there after he came down.

Noah got a small bowl out of the cupboard and filled it with ice cubes from the refrigerator. Then he went across the kitchen to the pantry and opened the door of the liquor cabinet. He found a half-filled bottle of Scotch and took it out and wrapped it in a dishtowel.

With the bowl in one hand and the bottle in the other, he went back in and started for the stairs.

"What have you in the towel, Noah?" his mother asked.

He stopped but did not turn his head. "A bottle of whiskey," he said. He waited, and when she said nothing more, he said, "I'm going to have a highball."

"I thought Connie took you a highball."

He turned and looked at her, and she was looking hard into his face. "She did." His mother's attitude toward anything more spiritous than sherry and table wines had always been one of firm-lipped, disapproving acquiescence. "I'm going to have another," he said. "The first one made me feel much better."

He started for the stairs again.

"Why did you wrap the bottle in a towel?" she asked gently.

"So that you wouldn't see it," he said, and he hurried on up.

Back in the study, he put ice into the glass and poured himself a moderate portion of whiskey, finding a strange comfort in the simple act of mixing the drink. He went down the hall to the bathroom and filled the glass with water and, lacking a spoon, stirred it with the handle of his toothbrush.

Back in the study again, with the door locked behind him, he lit a cigarette and sat down in the big chair, the glass in one hand and the cigarette in the other. He found himself smiling at the wall. Something odd had happened inside him. Suddenly, in these last few minutes, he had become imbued with an unbelievably pleasant sense of release, almost of happiness. Most of all, he thought, mystified, a feeling of self-assurance.

It wasn't, he knew, that he had become drunk from one highball. He wasn't going to be drunk after this one either. Perhaps the drink had helped to release this something inside him, or perhaps it was just that it had relaxed him enough to allow the release to take place. Perhaps it was some little thing that Connie had said, some little thing like, "Wives usually take what they get as regards places to live, don't they?" An inconsequential little thing, but maybe what she had given him was a feeling that you took what you got. Was that something?

But most of all this odd sensation seemed to be a feeling of freedom from obligation. Phrases like "ought to" and "have to"—all his past life, it seemed to him, had been built on phrases like that. And now he was feeling that there wasn't anything at all he really had to do. He didn't have to talk to Spence about money if he didn't want to. He didn't have to act the part of a brother with Joan if he didn't feel like a brother to her. He didn't have to admire Mark for thinking of himself when he should have been thinking of Winifred. He didn't have to try to argue Connie out of marrying a man who was a visiting buyer and a ball fan. He didn't have to hide a bottle in a towel.

He didn't really have to worry at all about what he ought to do and what he ought not to do. He didn't have to worry about what kind of person he was being. He didn't—his mind went off on a tangent, and he smiled to himself—he didn't have to wonder about whether or not he was running away from experience. Experience came. It came when your sister let a man pick her up in a sidewalk café. It came when your mother got up in the night to put the windows down. It came, he thought, no longer smiling, when you read the works of your father with an unbiased mind.

Leaving the drink half finished, he walked, calm and assured, over to the desk. He took two pencils and his penknife out of the drawer, and he sharpened the pencils with great care. Then he took the clip off the manuscript, readjusted his glasses, and started through the article. He found that his mind was unusually clear, his judgment sure. He corrected punctuation, circled phrases and moved them, with a line and an arrow, to more propitious places in the sentences, crossed out unnecessary adverbs, penciled a few suggestions in the margins.

When he had finished, he put more ice into his drink and went back over to the big chair and finished it. Then he adjusted the standard lamp for reading in the chair and settled down with the manuscript. And he read it all the way through again, to see what Mark was saying. His concentration became more and more intense as he read, his mind working with remarkable alertness, plucking memories out of its recesses, collating them with the statements he was reading.

He finished it and, taking it with him, went downstairs, no longer bothering to tiptoe. He walked across the living room without glancing at the people sitting there and on out through the kitchen into the back yard and on along the path to the Lion's Lair. The shades were drawn over the windows, glowing a dim orange, discouraging intrusion.

He looked at them and smiled and, without hesitating, knocked.

"Who is it?" Mark's voice sounded muffled.

"It's Noah."

He heard steps and the dull plug of the bolt in the door. The door opened and Mark stood there blinking at him. Noah pushed on past him and tossed the manuscript onto the big table that filled the middle of the room. For a brief moment he was conscious of the old sensation he had felt since his earliest childhood when he entered the Lion's Lair, the sensation of intrusion, of violated sanctum. Then, after that brief moment, he began to see it, for the first time in his life, for what it was: overdramatized, the second decade's gloomy conception of what a writer's study should look like—corny, he thought to himself.

The only light was the one over the typewriter at the desk under the window. Noah pulled the two chains on the table lamp, turning on both bulbs. And he stepped over to the wall and turned on the light in the wall bracket.

"Gloomy in here," he said, and, without waiting for Mark's reaction, he said, nodding toward the manuscript, "I made a number of changes and suggestions, mostly small things."

Mark picked the manuscript up and took it over to the desk. Noah stood beside the table, watching him.

"Thanks a lot," Mark said, sitting down and pulling up his chair, and he asked, noncommittally, over his shoulder, "What did you think of it?"

"Very well done," Noah said. "Very impressive." He waited. Then he said, "You've changed your mind about some things."

Faithfully, from the day in the spring of '39 when Mark's first book review appeared in one of the New York papers, Noah had read every word that Mark had had published. When at home, he had corrected the manuscripts before Mark sent them in; when at Milburn, he had kept his own file, complete with every review and every article. Most of it he had reread at least once, some of it—that which had been included in the two books of essays—as much as three or four times. He had two copies of each of these books, the inscribed ones and the ones he kept for lending.

Mark sat looking at the pages. Then slowly he turned to look up at Noah. "Changed my mind?"

Noah pointed to the manuscript. It was a commissioned article, planned for a special edition, and its subject was, "Influences That Have Molded Present-Day American Fiction." "Some of the opinions you've expressed in there aren't the ones you used to have, if I'm remembering correctly."

"What opinions?" Mark was frowning at him.

Noah stood with his head down and his eyes closed, rubbing his cheek with his hand. "Well, for one," he said, opening his eyes and looking beyond Mark at the manuscript. "Henry James. Don't I remember a passage in that series of articles you did for the *Review* back before the war where you called him a fussy bore? Now you're calling him perhaps the most important influence in bringing American writing to maturity."

Mark sat looking at him, his face expressionless.

Noah smiled down at him, a little grimly. "There was something in there about Scott Fitzgerald," he said, motioning again toward the manuscript. "Something quite complimentary about opening the way to the examination of milieus which fiction writers had previously neglected. Remember that article you had published just before you went into the service—it's in your first book—about the writers of the twenties. You called him shallow, as I remember it, and said that in spite of his early death he had outlived his fame."

"Those two opinions," Mark said, his voice husky, "aren't necessarily contradictory."

"Maybe not," Noah said, "but some people reading them together might think they were. Then there's this 'good and evil' business. You use that phrase 'good and evil' four or five times in there. You've been using it pretty regularly for several years now. No novel seems to be worth a damn if it doesn't concern itself with the problem of good and evil. But that isn't what you've always thought, is it? Remember your article on 'The Fiction Writer's Obligations,' the famous one, the lead article in your first book? Remember how neatly you laid out the people who tried to claim that a novelist must have a moral purpose, what fun you made of them? And how conclusively you proved that a writer's only obligation was his obligation to truth?"

Mark seemed to have regained his self-possession. He was looking up at Noah, half smiling, half bored.

"And now," Noah said, "I gather from this thing"—he pointed once more to the manuscript—"that no novelist who doesn't wrestle with the problem of good and evil is worth reading."

Mark smiled. "Do you believe that there is such a thing as good and evil, Noah?"

"That's not what I'm talking about," Noah said, alert to the fact that he was getting himself into another of those arguments with Mark, the kind of argument he had never been able to win. "I'm talking about the fact that you seem to have changed your mind about some things."

"Okay," Mark said, self-assured, "I've changed my mind. We all change our minds, only some of us don't have the courage to admit it. When you lose the ability to change your mind, you might as well quit; you're through."

"I'd agree to that," Noah said, still alert but still unpanicked by the thought that he was in the midst of an argument with Mark. It was a matter of keeping your head, of thinking clearly before you spoke. "The coincidence is," he said, speaking slowly, thoughtfully, "that they're all the correct changes, all the popular ones. We've had a Henry James revival since you called him a fussy bore. Everybody's been writing books and articles about him—and bringing out new editions of his work. We've had a Fitzgerald revival too, with biographies and critical appreciations and new editions."

"Okay, Noah," Mark said, his voice a little shriller, a little more defensive, "I'll admit I've learned from other critics. I believe that a critic has to learn from other critics. When they point out excellences in a man like James that you hadn't seen yourself when you read him in college, you change your mind. You keep an open mind all the time, and if you—"

"You learned from other critics, I suppose then," Noah interrupted, "that a writer does have a moral obligation after all, that he does have to wrestle with the problem of good and evil."

Mark didn't answer. He stared at the lamp on the table beside Noah's hand. Finally he said, "Well, yes. I suppose I did."

"And ten years from now, if they all decide that a writer's obligation is to truth after all, and not to 'any outworn moral code'—I believe that's the way you put it in your famous article—they might persuade you to change your mind again. Is that right?"

Mark got to his feet and stood looking at him, his hands on his hips, his expression one of exasperation. "What's eating you anyway, Noah?" he asked. "What's happened to you lately? You're developing the damnedest disposition and the most unco-operative—" He stopped and picked up his pipe from the stand beside the desk. He filled it from the jar that stood beside it and pushed the tobacco in with his little finger; then he sat down again and lit it, concentrating his attention on the flame. "I don't mind telling you," he said between puffs, "that I don't like it—and, if you want to know, neither do Mother and Barrett."

For a moment Noah felt the old sensation of weakness, of being squashed, that came over him so unfailingly when he was criticized by other members of the family. Then, regaining his courage, he asked, "What sort of thing are you talking about?"

"Well, for one thing, your attitude about Spence at dinner tonight."

"What else?"

Mark looked up at him as though he thought the question was stupid. "You know damned well that you've gone out of your way all week to be unco-operative—going up to your study and locking yourself in whenever there was dishwashing or housecleaning to do, sneaking out without saying a word to anybody and rowing around the lake in the boat—it seems to me you should be getting old enough to stop worrying about your muscles; that stuff's all right for prep-school kids, but you're getting to be a pretty big boy now—going over and playing with Kate's kids all the time and leaving Barry and Billy on our hands. After all, Barrett and Joan only have two weeks' vacation, and it seems to me you might be giving a little thought to making it pleasanter for them. They're not complaining, but it's obvious to me that they're having a pretty thin time of it."

Noah nodded thoughtfully, his face impassive. "I see," he said levelly.

"There's something else too," Mark said enigmatically, "something a damned sight bigger than any of that, something that's been worrying us all for some time. But this isn't the time to go into that."

"What is it?"

"This isn't the time," Mark repeated slowly, "to go into that."

Noah stared at him. Then he smiled and nodded his agreement. He started toward the door, but when he got his hand on the knob he stopped and turned. "Have you written to Winifred yet, Mark?"

Mark looked startled. "That's what I'm doing right now."

"What are you telling her to do?"

Again Mark looked startled. He hesitated. Then, his voice husky, he said, "I'm telling her to go to the Bunces'—just until things get straightened out, of course."

Noah made an effort to keep any hint of approval or disapproval out of his voice. "You think she'll be happy going there?"

Mark's answer came quickly, his voice shrill and defensive again. "I can't have her up here in all this mess. It would be the worst thing in the world for her."

Noah nodded, still careful to keep any hint that he was sitting in judgment out of his manner and his voice. "Had you thought of going down to see her?"

"I couldn't do it, Noah." The voice was still shrill, and Noah suspected that he was probing a very sensitive spot. "I had to get this thing out." He motioned toward the manuscript. "You can't turn down a commission like that one—not if you're going to keep your place in your profession. If you're not in that *Supplement*, you're on your way out, and everybody in the literary world knows it. The money I get for the article has nothing to do with it."

Noah nodded, still careful to show nothing of what he was feeling. "You're getting it off tomorrow. Right?"

Mark pointed to a pile of proofs on the corner of his desk. "I've got a Friday deadline on three reviews," he said, "and I haven't even looked at one of them yet."

Again Noah nodded. "Will you be having her up here after Barrett and Joan and the boys leave?"

"The summer will be nearly over by then. I don't know. It might be better to wait until—I just don't know, Noah. We'll have to see how things work out."

Noah nodded once more, smiling, and he kept his voice pleasant and friendly. "I was just thinking," he said, "of how much she liked it up here. She was very happy here that summer, remember? And of course this was where you got married." He went out, closing the door quickly behind him.

6·

AFTER breakfast the next morning, Noah and Connie did the dishes together, grinning at each other, while Barrett and Joan and Mark sat in the living room, looking self-justified and, Noah thought with delight, a bit foolish. Barry and Billy were hammering something down on the beach. Mrs. Sibley was out looking at her garden. She came in through the kitchen and smiled at the two of them there and went on through.

When they had finished, Connie, with her apron still on, followed Noah into the living room, drying her hands on a towel. "Is everybody planning to be around here for a while?" she asked.

They all looked up at her curiously. Finally Barrett said, "My only plan is for a swim after it warms up a little. And we'll have to see what Barry and Billy want to do."

Connie's voice and manner seemed a little overcasual. "I have a friend staying up at the Inn," she said, "and I'd like to have you all meet him. I thought that if this would be a good time—" She finished with a rising inflection, waiting for their answers.

"As good as any, I imagine, my dear," Mrs. Sibley said, with inquiring caution.

Mark was looking at Connie, his head cocked to one side. "Who is this friend, Connie?" There was an ominous quality in his voice, a hint of the censoriousness that had come to be in it so much these last years.

Connie was taking off her apron, walking backward toward the kitchen door. "His name is Rentwood Jones." She turned quickly and disappeared, and a moment later the screen door at the back slammed.

Noah headed for the stairs. He had no desire to be in on the conversation that would be going on while Connie was gone. Besides, he hadn't shaved.

He went up and shaved and rebrushed his hair and changed into a clean shirt. Then he sat upstairs there, waiting, until he heard the car drive in. He got to the foot of the stairs just as Connie was leading

Jonesy through the kitchen. Noah couldn't think of him as Mr. Jones, he found; he could only think of him as Jonesy.

He looked as they came through the door and was shocked, not at Jonesy but at himself. He realized at once that the image he had formed in his mind was not of a man who looked like a combination of Yogi Berra and Huey Long, but of a man who was a combined caricature of the two of them.

"Mother," Connie said, "this is Mr. Jones."

Jonesy was smiling, waiting to see if Mrs. Sibley was going to hold out her hand. She did, and he stepped forward quickly and took it. He did have a cowlick, to be sure—there it was, waving down across his forehead, but it was a good head of reddish-brown hair, and otherwise there was no resemblance to Huey Long at all. There *was* a noticeable resemblance to pictures of Yogi Berra, but it was no caricature of him either. It was a good face, a likable face, as likable as Berra's own.

"And this is my sister-in-law, Joan Sibley," Connie said, and Joan smiled very graciously from across the room. Connie took Jonesy's arm and, rather conspicuously passing by Barrett and Mark, led him over to Noah. "And this," she said, "is my brother Noah."

Noah shook his hand and smiled at him and turned and smiled at Connie. He liked the way this man looked, and he wanted Connie to know it. Like the fool he was, he told himself, he had been expecting not only a caricature of a man, but also something loud and awful in the way of clothes—a bright blue sport shirt, he had been picturing, with a yellow sunburst on the front of it. This man had on a soft white shirt and a good-looking tie and an inconspicuous, well-cut jacket; no one could have chosen a better outfit for meeting one's prospective inlaws at nine-thirty on a summer morning.

"Connie has told me about you," Jonesy said, and his manner of speaking was all right too. Noah wasn't sure whether he had been expecting a cowboy twang or a Babbitt-like boom. "She tells me you're quite a fisherman."

"I like trout fishing," Noah said. "I'm not much good at any other kind."

Jonesy grinned, and suddenly he looked like a little boy, exuberant, boyish, infinitely good-humored. "I like all kinds," he said, "from smelt to sharks."

Connie guided him on over to Barrett and Mark. He was, to be sure, short and stocky, but not as squat as Noah had imagined, nor as short. He must have been three inches taller than Connie.

To Noah's relief, Barrett and Mark were friendly and cordial. Considering what he knew they must be thinking, they acted very decently indeed. So did his mother. And so did Joan. And suddenly all his old pride in his family, in their collective good looks, their manners, their charm, came back over him. Whatever else you could say for them, however well you might know that this was just one more case of their being unable to refrain from putting on their act before a stranger, you had to admit that they were impressive.

Jonesy sat in the Windsor chair by the kitchen door. They talked about California, and Mrs. Sibley told very entertainingly about the trip she and her husband had made out there just after the first World War. And they talked about Nebraska, which was where Jonesy had lived until he was twenty-three. Mark had spent four exasperating and amusing days in Omaha on his way to San Francisco during the war.

Noah, beaming, taking no part in the conversation, watched Jonesy. And to his surprise he saw the exuberant, gleefully confident smile fade from his face. In its stead he saw a gradually increasing look of perplexity. He watched him glance around the room at the fireplace, at the furniture, at the pictures—all original water colors and rather good ones—at Mrs. Sibley, smiling so graciously, at Barrett and Mark and Joan, finally at himself. And slowly the look of perplexity changed to one that Noah could only interpret as one of embarrassed unhappiness. A flush started in his neck and moved upward, suffusing his face. He was no longer smiling, and he was avoiding looking at Connie.

And abruptly, at least ten minutes before what Noah would have considered the normal time to do so, he got to his feet and said that he had to go.

As soon as he and Connie were safely out of earshot, Barrett turned to Noah. "Noah," he asked, "have you any idea what possessed Connie to bring him up here at a time like this?"

Noah laughed. "I imagine she must like him. That would be a good reason, wouldn't it? He seemed like a nice guy," he added.

"As sport shirt makers go," Mark said.

Noah smiled at him. "Somebody has to make shirts."

"All too true, Noah, dear." Mark's voice had a sharp edge of animosity, an animosity which Noah realized was carried over from last evening's conversation. "But I don't know of any commandment that says we have to make bosom companions of them, do you?"

"Of course not. And I don't know any reason why you shouldn't like a nice guy no matter what he happens to make, do you?"

"All right, all right," Mark said.

Mrs. Sibley was busying herself straightening out the magazines on the table. "I still don't know why she even considered bringing him up here," she said.

Noah felt a sudden impulse to tell them, to see what their faces would look like, to hear what they would say. He wondered if Connie would thank him if he did, if she would be glad to have him save her the difficult job of telling them herself. He decided that she would. "Would you like to know why?" he asked.

"I certainly would."

"Because she's going to marry him."

Nobody said anything. Mrs. Sibley moved the whole pile of magazines, one at a time, from one side of the table to the other. Noah looked around at the other three. They were all staring at him, their expressions not so much surprised as angry.

"When did she tell you this, Noah?" his mother finally asked, her voice low and restrained.

"Last night."

"Are you quite sure she wasn't joking?"

"Quite sure."

"Have they gone so far as to plan when they are going to get married?"

Noah thought about that and decided there was no reason why he shouldn't tell them. "They took their serological tests in New York the day before yesterday, and, as I understand it, they have to wait three days after that. I imagine they're figuring on getting married down there the day after tomorrow."

Mrs. Sibley still retained her remarkable self-control. "Barrett," she asked, "is there any legal way that we can stop this thing?"

"No. There isn't. But there might be some ways of applying financial pressure."

Noah chuckled. Knowing Connie, he knew how much effect all the financial pressure in the world would have. And, knowing her, he felt pretty sure that Jonesy had no idea that she had any more money than any other schoolteacher. Even if he did know, he didn't look to Noah like a man who would marry for money; he was more the kind who would take a self-made man's pride in earning every cent his wife spent. If Barrett were clever enough, he might try to force a hundred thousand dollars on him; that would almost surely, he thought, make trouble for Connie.

[204]

"We may have to come to that," Mrs. Sibley said. "First, we'll see if we can use persuasion."

Noah was still chuckling. How little they knew about Connie! He looked around at them, so serious, so self-important. "Why?" he asked, smiling. Any fear he had ever had of them had vanished, vanished forever, he suspected, last night, just after he took the bottle upstairs. "Why do you want to try to persuade her not to marry him?"

Together, as though at a signal, Barrett and Mark and his mother drew in their breath. They stared at him with expressions of exaggerated helplessness. He was, they were trying to convey, a great trial to their patience.

"Because, Noah," his mother said, "it's obvious that such a marriage couldn't possibly work out. They have nothing in common. She's not interested in shirts, and I doubt very much if he's had education enough to be interested in any of the things she is. She'll be three thousand miles away from everybody she knows, from all her friends, from all her family."

Noah smiled at the thought of how much she would miss her family. "*I'll miss you*," she had said last night, underlining the *you* with her voice.

"We all know—or at least we all *should* know"—she looked meaningfully at Noah—"that the thing couldn't possibly last a year. And in that year she would ruin her career, and I can tell all of you that it's a very promising career, more promising than any of you imagine."

Noah heard the sound of a car in the back yard. He stepped to the kitchen door and looked through to the back. It was Connie's car, and he watched her drive it in and get out, alone, slamming the door behind her.

She came running in, her head down, and he knew at once that she was crying. She ran past them and up the stairs, sobbing.

They all looked at each other, and slowly Barrett and Mark began to grin. "A hitch," Barrett said, "seems to have developed."

Noah looked hard at his mother's face. For a moment he thought her expression might be one of thoughtfulness; then, gradually, he caught the hint of a smile. He stared at her, wondering how many mothers would be smiling at a time like this. It was the first time in his life that such a disloyal thought had passed through his mind. He thought of Connie upstairs there, crying, and suddenly he hated them all. He hated Barrett and Joan. He hated Mark. He hated his mother.

He looked around at them once more, then turned and ran up after her. She was in his study, in the swivel chair, with her head down in her arms on the desk. He stood in the doorway. Her shoulders were not shaking, but as he stood there he heard her sniffle twice.

He stepped in and put his hand on her shoulder. She shook him off without turning to look. He waited, then put his hand back on her shoulder. Again she shook him off, and he stood back, watching her.

Suddenly she sat up and swiveled around in the chair and looked up at him. Her face was puffy, her eyes swollen, her mouth twisted, her hair hanging down in wisps beside her face. She had never been beautiful, but never in his life had he seen her so completely unattractive. "He's gone, Noah," she said.

"Gone?"

She looked up at him stupidly. "He thinks I lied to him."

Noah waited.

"He thinks *he must* have been the one I was ashamed of—when I didn't want him to come up here. He says he knows I wasn't ashamed of my family. He says nobody would be ashamed of a family like mine." She stared limply, then sobbed again, and he thought she was going to start crying again. But she didn't. "He says he won't be married to a girl who's ashamed of him. And I'm not ashamed of him," she wailed, suddenly louder. "I love him. I think he's wonderful. And he won't believe me."

She settled back, limp again.

Noah hesitated for a moment, his lips parted. Then he went out into the hall. He got to the head of the stairs and came back. She was still sitting there, still limp. "You look like hell," he said. "Get some water on your face and comb your hair. And put some powder on your nose."

He ran downstairs and toward the kitchen door.

"Where are you going, Noah?" Mark asked sharply.

"Up to the Inn—to see if I can catch that man."

Barrett stepped between him and the kitchen door. "Oh, no you're not."

Noah pushed him, hard, and strode on out into the kitchen.

"Noah," his mother called.

He stopped.

"Noah, I forbid you to go up there."

He stood stock-still. It had been many years since she had spoken to him like that. He stood for a moment longer, then smiled and hurried on out to his car.

DRIVING up to the Inn, Noah hurried, although he had a pretty strong suspicion that he didn't need to. Getting away from the Lake when you didn't have your own car wasn't that easy. One of its charms, the summer residents felt, lay in the fact that it had none of the appurtenances of city living: no quick lunches, no beauty shops, no gift shops and—what mattered at the moment—no taxi service.

The people at the Inn would probably think of a few villagers or farmers who, for a consideration, might be willing to drive Jonesy to the Junction, but he might well have to make three or four telephone calls before he found one who was free. And, since everybody knew that the afternoon train didn't leave the Junction until 4:15, anyone he did find would see no reason for hurrying. Why sit around the station at the Junction, they would want to know, when you could just as well spend those same hours at the Lake?

Noah parked his car in the area beside the Inn and went in. The door opened directly into the room which served as both a lobby and an office. As he had half expected, Jonesy was sitting at the desk with the telephone at his ear. Two large suitcases sat on the floor beside him. There was no one else in the lobby, which was usual except before and after meals. Jonesy was looking exasperated, and as Noah walked in he did not look up.

Noah went across the room to the wicker couch and sat down. Jonesy's back was toward the couch. He was waiting, and he waited for a long time. Finally Noah heard a voice on the phone.

"Yes," Jonesy said eagerly.

The voice said something.

"Are you sure he can't?" Jonesy asked with desperation in his voice. "Did you tell him that money didn't matter?"

The voice said something else, and Jonesy hung up. He turned and looked at Noah and turned back to the desk; then, suddenly conscious of who Noah was, turned and looked again, scowling.

"I'd like to talk with you," Noah said.

Jonesy shook his head and the cowlick waggled. "There's nothing you can say," he answered, his voice lifeless. The eyes that looked at Noah were the eyes of a man who has been hurt, a little like the look of an injured dog—or perhaps more, that of an unhappy youngster.

He seemed very young, very boyish. Noah wondered how old he was. About his age maybe, thirty-eight. No, he had a boy in the Army. Well, he could have been married at twenty, or even younger. Forty, maybe, or forty-two, but he certainly didn't look it.

"Excuse me," he said, turning back to the phone, "I've got to make another call."

"*I'll* drive you to the Junction," Noah said.

Jonesy turned again and looked at him.

"If you still want me to, after you've heard what I have to say."

"There's nothing you can say," Jonesy repeated.

"I think there is. At any rate, it won't hurt you to listen, will it? The next train out of the Junction is 4:15, and I'll see that you make it—if you decide you want to."

Jonesy looked as though he might cry. Then, suddenly angry, he said, "No. I just don't want to talk about it. I'll get somebody else to take me." He turned back to the phone.

Noah stretched his legs out in front of him and clasped his hands behind his head. "I'm going to pester you," he said, "until you do listen to me. If I have to, I'll take the 4:15 myself—and sit behind you on the train all the way to Springfield, talking into your ear."

Once again Jonesy turned and frowned at him, and Noah smiled. "It can't do you any harm to listen for a few minutes," he said.

It occurred to him that Aunt Constance was here at the Inn and might be walking through the room at any moment. The last person in the world he wanted to see just then was Aunt Constance. There was no telling what she, as Connie's headmistress, might have to say about Connie there in front of Jonesy. "Look," he said, "I'll tell you what I'll do. I'll drive you around the lake. It's nine miles. It's a beautiful lake—some people say it's one of the most beautiful in America. You ought to see it before you leave. If, after we've driven that nine miles, you still want to go, we'll stop in and pick up your bags and be on our way. And I won't try to argue with you on the way to the Junction."

He walked across to where Jonesy sat and, smiling at him, took his arm.

Jonesy held back. "What's all this to you, anyway?"

"It's my sister's happiness. Isn't that something?"

Reluctantly, Jonesy let himself be pulled to his feet. "She'll never be happy with a man she's ashamed of."

Noah still had his arm, and he guided him along to the door. He smiled at him, cheerful and unperturbed.

"I just have a hunch she might be happy with you," he said.

He said nothing more until they were settled in the car and he had driven out into the road. Then he looked down at the speedometer. "Twenty-five miles an hour," he said. "These roads weren't made for speeding. Does a good steady twenty-five miles an hour seem fair to you?"

Jonesy looked at him out of the corner of his eye and grinned sheepishly.

Noah drove on down toward the village. "These Sibleys," he said. "They're quite a family. That's what you've been thinking, isn't it?"

"Yes."

"You don't know the half of it," Noah said. "Our father was a famous man. Did Connie tell you that?"

"She said he was a writer and lecturer."

"Among certain classes of people," Noah said, "he was very famous in his day. A very distinguished-looking man, too. Handsome. Very charming, just like Barrett and Mark. Barrett's a good-looking guy, isn't he?"

Jonesy was looking perplexed. "He sure is," he said, his tone hinting that he resented Barrett's good looks.

"He's in government service, you know," Noah said. "Not politics, remember, government service. I don't suppose you could say that he's really famous yet, but they tell me that his name is beginning to mean something down around Washington. They're all saying that he's a man to watch. I don't doubt that you'll be hearing of him in the next ten years."

He had passed through the village and was now driving along, at a steady twenty-five miles an hour, past the open fields.

"Mark has had two books published," he said. "His fame, like Dad's, is confined to certain classes of people—mostly people with a special interest in literature—you know, the new books and so forth. But among them he's very nearly the tops. He used to be better looking than he is now—before he lost his hair and put on weight. But, as you saw this morning, he can still turn on the charm when he wants to."

He glanced at Jonesy, and Jonesy was staring straight ahead at the road, smiling a bitter and disillusioned smile.

"You haven't seen Kate yet, have you?" Noah asked.

"No."

"She happens to be very pregnant at the moment," Noah said, "but actually, Jonesy, I believe she's the most wonderful one of the whole bunch of us. You never saw such a striking woman in your life. I've never been anywhere with her that people didn't turn around and stare. She's really beautiful, or maybe you'd call it handsome. Thirty-six years old. And the amazing thing about her is that, along with her good looks and the fact that she's about to have her seventh child, she's one of the most talked-about sculptors in the country today."

Jonesy continued to watch the road ahead. They had gone into the woods, past the road into Dr. Mooney's, and were now on their way up the long hill.

"It's hard to talk about your own mother," Noah said. "I guess I'll leave her out. You could see for yourself that she's—well, a very gracious lady."

Jonesy nodded.

Noah waited a while, and finally, he said, "And then there's me. I'm not as clever as the rest of them. I'm the dumbest one in the whole family—and I'm not saying that just to sound modest either. Anybody who knows us would tell you the same thing. But even I am getting to be a bit famous, among a very small group of people, the people who happen to be interested in one particular phase of American history." He laughed. "If you're a Sibley, you almost *have to* try to be famous."

They reached the top of the hill, and the road curved, so that the lake lay diagonally ahead of them, down the long slope of fields and woods. "Take a look at that," Noah said. The sun was out behind a sky half filled with clouds, and the pattern of their shadows lay on the hills. The waters of the lake sparkled. "Do you see what they mean when they say it's one of the most beautiful lakes in America?"

Jonesy looked at it and nodded.

Noah glanced at the speedometer. "I shouldn't be slowing down like that," he said. "That's cheating." He drove on for a while without speaking. Then he said, "We're a very remarkable family, and Connie was silly not to tell you so. She told you that she was ashamed of us, and you came up here expecting—well, I don't know what you were expecting. Bad table manners, I suppose, and bad grammar, or bad dispositions—anyway, something disagreeable and obvious, something that would show up right away. And you didn't find anything obvious and you jumped to the conclusion that she was lying to you."

He drove on again for a while, and now, having taken the turn in the woods, they were running along the opposite end of the lake from the village. Between every patch of trees they caught new glimpses of the lake.

"The thing I've got to convince you of, Jonesy," Noah said, "is that she wasn't lying. The trouble is that the things she's ashamed of aren't obvious; they don't show up in the first half hour. Everybody says that Connie doesn't seem like one of the family, that she's different from all the rest of us, and they're right. She is. Of course she doesn't happen to look like any of the rest of us, but that's beside the point. The real difference is that she's completely honest."

Jonesy looked at him with a disgusted, incredulous smile.

"In all my life, Jonesy, I've never known her to tell a lie. Oh, I suppose she's said she had a nice time at a party when she didn't really have a very good time, but I mean a real lie, the kind of lie that could make a real difference to anybody or—what's more to the point—the kind that would put her in a better light, the kind that would make people think better of her. Never once. You're going to have to take my word for that. And, what's even more to the point, I've never known her to act a lie. I've never seen her try to put on an act. I've never seen her try to kid people into thinking she was something she wasn't. I know you're thinking that's a pretty big statement, but it's true."

He looked to see if Jonesy had anything to say to that. He was still staring straight ahead at the road, but he was no longer smiling the disillusioned smile. His face was stolid, expressionless.

"That's where she's different from the rest of us. The rest of us aren't honest—oh, I don't mean that we go around cheating people out of their money. We don't have to do that. We have quite a bit of money. I don't suppose she told you that either, did she?"

"Yes, she did."

Noah raised his eyebrows. "How did she happen to do that?"

"I asked her and she told me. She didn't tell me how much. She said she didn't know how much."

"That's right; she doesn't. None of us does except Barrett. He manages the trust funds. Well, we're getting off the subject. And we're getting around the lake here, too. Doesn't leave me too much time."

Noah knew what he was going to say. He knew that they were disloyal things, shockingly disloyal things, things that it would have been shocking to hear any man say about his own family. But he knew, this morning, that they were true and that he was going to have to say them. He knew that the knowledge that they were true had been building up in the back of his consciousness for months, maybe for years. And he knew that his loyalties and his family affections— natural enough family affections, he supposed—had been holding that knowledge back, there in the back of his consciousness, for all those months or years.

It wasn't until yesterday morning, when that strange other mind of his had run so insistently along on its track while they were talking on the porch, that the bare, disillusioned truth had begun to force itself into the forefront of his consciousness. It wasn't until last night, when he was alone up in his room, that the individual truths about his father and Mark and Barrett and Kate had begun to come clear to his mind. And it wasn't until a few minutes ago, when his mother had smiled, that the whole truth had seemed to jell into something complete, something so obvious that he knew he should have seen it long ago, knew that a better man would have seen it and faced it long ago.

Probably it was inexcusable, he thought, this long-continued refusal to see the truth, but perhaps it was understandable too. All the things he had been brought up to believe, all the things he had learned at the parental knees, all the things he had wanted to believe, all the things it had soothed his pride to believe—

Anyway, for Connie's sake, he was now going to break loose from a lifetime of family loyalty and say these shocking things to this man, this stranger. He faced the thought hesitantly at first, then curiously, smiling to himself. Maybe this was the way you paid for not having been a better man. Maybe, it came to him out of nowhere, it would also turn out to be your catharsis.

He glanced over his shoulder at the lake and said, "What I've got to convince you of, Jonesy, is that we're a bunch of fakes. We live on admiration, and there's almost nothing we won't do to get it. We just love it when people come in and we can put on our acts, showing off how modest we can be in spite of our fame and how friendly and entertaining and learned—we're always slipping quotations from Shakespeare or somebody into the conversation—I don't remember whether we pulled any on you this morning or not. Did we?"

Jonesy grinned. "Your mother said something about wandering on a foreign strand. Was that Shakespeare?"

"I guess that was Sir Walter Scott." Noah glanced over his shoulder at the lake again. They had rounded the far corner and were following the road where it wound in toward the back of the point.

"Okay," he said, hurrying a little, "that's the point I've got to get across to you, then, the point that we're fakes. We're charlatans. We love applause, and there's almost nothing we won't stoop to to get it. Offhand, you wouldn't say that having seven babies was a way of putting on an act, would you? But with Kate it is. There's a picture there, see? A beautiful woman with her six beautiful children—they are beautiful too—carrying her seventh and climbing up on a scaffold with a chisel in her hand. I suppose you're thinking there isn't anything really dishonest about that, and maybe there isn't. But sometimes, Jonesy, there are other things that ought to come ahead of the beautiful pictures—other people's happiness or other people's dignity and integrity—but Kate never lets anything interfere with the beautiful picture. Do you see what I mean? Do you see why Connie might not be so proud of her as you'd think she'd be?"

Jonesy pushed his cowlick back up off his forehead and glanced once at Noah, then stared at the road again.

"Of course you've got to have something to do these things," Noah said. "I don't deny that. If you're going to be what Kate is, you've got to be born beautiful, and you've got to be born with the ability to do good work in clay and stone. If you're going to be what Barrett and Mark are, you've got to have brains. Barrett's a smart lawyer—there's no doubt about it—and Mark's a very, very clever writer. You can't imagine how clever."

They had passed behind the cluster of cottages on the point and were now in the long sweeping curve that swung back into the village, running along close to the lake.

"I suppose you're wondering about me—talking this way about my own family. You may be wondering if this is an act *I'm* putting on." Noah turned and smiled at him. "It could be, of course, but it just happens that it isn't. I'm not quite so bad as the rest of them—for two reasons. One is that I can't get away with it; I'm not good looking enough or clever enough. If I were, I'd probably be just as bad as they are. I spent the first twenty years of my life trying to imitate my father and my two older brothers, and all I succeeded in doing was making a fool of myself. Gradually, I stopped trying. In other words, I'm honest because I can't get away with being anything else.

"The other reason is Connie. She's always liked me better than the rest of them, because I wasn't so much of a fake as they are. And because she liked me better she talked to me more, and she's the one who's helped me to see them for what they are. She's made me mad as hell doing it. I've always been pretty loyal to the rest of them, and every time she'd stick a pin into another of their balloons, I'd get mad at her. It wasn't until just this summer, when she pricked a couple of the biggest balloons of all, that I began to see them for what they really are."

He looked at Jonesy once more. He was smiling again, but it seemed to Noah that the smile might be a little more friendly, a little more receptive. The church spire in the village was in sight ahead of them.

"Well, Jonesy," he said, "there it is. I don't know how honest you are"—he held up his hand—"I don't mean that as an insult—I don't mean that I think you may have robbed any widows or orphans. My hunch would be that you're probably a good deal like Connie, that you'd be just as embarrassed as she would to find yourself putting on an act, or to find yourself trying to kid people into thinking you were something you weren't."

Jonesy said nothing.

"Whether you are or not, Jonesy," Noah said earnestly, "try putting yourself in her place. Imagine yourself as honest a person as she is, and then imagine being part of a family who will do damned near anything to gain the fame and the—the esteem that they thrive on. Can't you see now why she's ashamed of us? Why she wasn't lying when she said that she was?"

Still Jonesy said nothing. They were approaching the Inn, and Noah was suddenly frantic, afraid that he hadn't stated the case well enough. "It's not just putting on a perpetual act, Jonesy. Maybe that wouldn't be enough to make her ashamed. It's actual dishonesty. It's lying about what you said ten years ago, because what you said ten years ago has turned out to be wrong or foolish. It's trimming your sails to every wind in politics, so as not to get caught out on a limb if there's a change of administration. It's thinking—and writing—all the thoughts that happen to be popular at the time, whether they happen to be your own real convictions or not. Or maybe it's not having any real convictions—except for the one big conviction that the most important thing in the world is fame. Distinction. That's the word Barrett's always using—'distinction.'"

He drove into the area beside the Inn and stopped. He waited, and still Jonesy said nothing. Jonesy opened the door and got out and started for the porch. Noah followed him, hurrying, and caught up with him as he opened the door.

He stopped, and Noah looked over his shoulder into the lobby. Connie was sitting in there. She had moved a chair over to the two suitcases, and she sat with her legs extended over them, so that they couldn't be picked up without moving her legs. She looked up at them, her shoulders hunched in her characteristic pose, her expression half frightened, half determined, ready to fight. Aside from the expression, she looked surprisingly well.

[214]

Noah stared at her. Then, on a quick impulse, he pulled Jonesy back out onto the porch. "Will you talk to her, Jonesy?" he asked.

Jonesy swallowed. For a moment he looked thoughtful. Then he smiled, and again it was the exuberant smile of a little boy. "Yes, I'll talk to her," he said.

Noah turned around and ran down the porch and on out to his car.

8·

BARRY held his two hands over the platter of perch. "Billy can't have any," he said exuberantly. "He didn't catch any."

Firmly, Joan took hold of his wrists and moved his hands away. She put the platter on the other side of her and served two of the perch to Billy. "I don't want to hear you say anything like that ever again, Barry," she said. Sternly, but without anger, she explained to him about sharing.

It was like every other lunch: Barrett at one end of the table and his mother at the other, Joan across the table between the two boys, Mark there at Noah's right, the big casserole and the little casserole, the white birch bowl of salad, the green place mats with their cream-colored flowers and leaves, the dessert plates, each with a pear and a slice of cake and a fruit knife, already on the table because in the summer at the Lake you did everything the easy way.

It was like every other lunch because, with Barry and Billy there, no one had said anything about Connie. No one had mentioned the fact that she had not appeared for lunch. No one had upbraided Noah for his part in delaying Jonesy's departure.

It was like every other lunch except for the wall of exclusion. Noah found himself remembering other times when he had been conscious of this same sort of wall of exclusion, times when he had joined a group of boys at Milburn and known at once that they were all on one side of a wall and he on the other; times when he had walked into a room where some of the other masters were gathered and had sensed that, for some reason he hadn't been able to divine, he was not included in whatever it was they were thinking; twice—occasions he had never been able to forget—when, back before the war, he had walked into a room where Louise and Winifred were talking, and they had been polite and distant, wishing, he knew, that he had not intruded.

Now, for the first time he could remember, the wall was between him and his family. He was conscious of it; he viewed it from a distance, detached and curious, but he did not particularly resent it. Since his talk with Jonesy, since he had said all the things about his family that he had never dreamed he would be saying, he had felt kindly and tolerant toward his mother and Barrett and Mark, as though saying those things had washed away the bitterness and animosity.

He didn't resent any of it except Joan. He did resent the fact that she was on their side of the wall, one of them, while he was on the other.

He ate with a hearty appetite, glancing up at Joan, saying nothing. It was silly, he told himself—this resenting Joan. It wasn't her fault. She hadn't said or done anything unfriendly, anything she shouldn't. But you still resented it, unreasonably, because she didn't have the blood of the family in her and you did.

9.

JOAN had a list of things to buy in Ledwick, and she was taking the boys with her. Noah sensed that this had been planned, that it had been arranged for her to get herself and the boys out of the way. He found himself resenting her departure more than he had her presence.

They had cleared the table and moved into the living room, and Noah, sitting on the stool beside the fireplace, flicked the ashes from his cigarette across the hearth and watched Joan as she gathered up her things and herded the boys toward the door. He looked up and saw that the other three of them had, consciously or unconsciously, placed themselves opposite him, so that he sat facing them as though facing a tribunal. And, because he was on the stool, they were higher than he was.

He stood up and sauntered toward the front door.

"Where are you going, Noah?" Barrett asked.

"Out on the porch," he said, smiling to himself. If there was to be a battle, he was going to choose his own ground. "Any of you care to join me? It's too nice a day to sit inside there."

He opened the screen door and went on out.

"Maybe you're right," Barrett called, and awkwardly, conscious of the fact that their concerted movement from the room to the porch seemed forced and premeditated, the three of them followed him out.

There were four chairs in a line, facing the water. Chuckling, Noah dropped into one of the middle ones. There would be no way, without a deliberate and obvious effort, that they could turn this into a tribunal; and all the chairs were of the same height. He looked up and smiled pleasantly as Barrett and Mark filed past him. His mother sat in the chair between him and the door. They all smiled back at him, as though trying to hide the fact that they were about to hold court.

Then, suddenly serious, Barrett said, "There are some things we'd like to talk over with you, Noah."

"I thought there might be," Noah said.

"First, about Connie."

Noah waited, and for a while it seemed that no one of them wanted to start saying the things they had to say about Connie.

"I hope your conscience is clear about the thing you did this morning, Noah," his mother finally said.

Noah smiled. "It hasn't started bothering me yet."

"I don't think this is a time for being facetious," she said reprovingly.

Noah opened his mouth to say that he had not intended to be facetious, then decided to say nothing. He waited.

"The kindest thing I can say about it," she said, "is that you acted in ignorance. You chose to abet her in doing something that's not only sure to bring her unhappiness but also to ruin a very promising career. To make you understand how promising, I'm going to have to betray a confidence—something I don't believe I've ever done before in my life."

She paused, as though to give Noah time to realize how serious a thing it was. "When Aunt Constance was down here for tea the other day—not yesterday but the time before—she told me—in strictest confidence, of course—that she and Miss Cobb and Miss Gettings have all been much impressed these last four or five years with Connie's abilities, her teaching ability and her knowledge of a wide range of subjects and her general, all-around competence. Aunt Constance is my age, sixty-seven, which means that she will be retiring in three years."

She paused again, and when she spoke her diction was careful and impressive. "Unless," she said, "something untoward happens in those three years, they expect to recommend to the trustees of the school that Connie be appointed to take her place."

"Connie?" Noah asked unbelievingly.

"Connie," his mother said triumphantly.

"Well!" Noah exclaimed. He tried to imagine it: that imposing array of buildings on that beautiful hillside, those acres of lawn, the walks, the walks swarming with girls, the girls, three hundred and fifty of them—all under the supervision, the command, of his unobtrusive, limelight-hating little sister. He tried to imagine her on the dais in the chapel, facing that wide mosaic of upturned, pink-cheeked faces, the yellow-haired, black-haired, brown-haired, red-haired mosaic. He couldn't do it.

He laughed. "It's completely inconceivable, Mother," he said.

None of the rest of them laughed.

"Would your idea be, Noah," Mark asked, "that Aunt Constance made the story up, just to please Mother?"

Noah shook his head at them, still laughing. "Connie?" he asked incredulously. "Why, she'd shrivel up and die. She'd jump out of the bell tower before she'd take that job."

"You don't think she's capable of handling such a job?" Mark asked.

"I'm not talking about what she's capable of. I'm talking about what she would want."

"You mean, Noah," his mother said, "that she'd be frightened at the prospect. Of course she would. There are very few girls in the country who wouldn't be frightened at the prospect—at first. After all, it's one of the most famous girls' schools in the world. And that, of course, is just the point. It's a distinction that doesn't come to one girl in a million. Of all the positions open to women in this country today—"

"Distinction," Noah interrupted. "Yes, of course. That *is* the point, isn't it?"

"I'm glad you see it, Noah," she said quickly, obviously happy to have convinced him so easily. "I'm glad you're so ready to admit that you were wrong. Now," she went on, her tone still firm but a little more kindly, "it would seem that there is only one person who might be able to undo the harm that you did this morning. I don't know what you said to that man, but if you will search your heart I think you'll agree that the only manly and honorable thing for you to do is to go to him this afternoon and unsay whatever it was you said."

She stopped, and Noah knew that all three of them were watching his face. He kept his expression courteous and attentive, giving no hint of what he was thinking. Finally he said, "You said there were some *things* you wanted to talk over with me, Barrett. Is there something else you want to talk about before I go?"

They looked startled at the abruptness of his capitulation. It took them a few moments to gather their thoughts.

"Well, yes, there is, Noah," Barrett said, his tone friendly and conciliatory, "something Mother wanted me to talk with you about while I was here, and time is getting short." Noah sensed that, having been prepared for arguments and recriminations, he was finding it necessary to replan whatever it was he was going to say—to suit Noah's surprising attitude of humility and co-operativeness.

"I hope you'll take this—this suggestion in the spirit in which it's offered, Noah," Barrett said. "It's—it's about your work. It's—well, you might call it just a matter of emphasis. We've been talking it over, and we've agreed that it may be partly our own fault. It may be that when we talked to you about the job with the Foundation—you remember, that night in your room at Milburn?"

Noah nodded, still keeping his expression courteous and attentive. "I remember," he said.

"It may be that when we talked with you, we didn't give you quite the right impression as to what the Foundation would expect of you."

Noah turned and looked at him with raised eyebrows. "Really?" he asked.

"It's just this, Noah, and I do hope you'll take this in the spirit in which it's offered. The Foundation really has a twofold purpose. The one purpose is the one stated in the charter: to further the cause of peace, and to do so by bringing to the public consciousness all the facts relating to the history of world arbitration. That, of course, has meant digging out all the facts about it that are buried in Dad's files and elsewhere and getting as many of them published as possible. On that phase of the work we're all agreed that you've done very well. You've had some stuff published, and you're making good progress on your book. Your name is already known among historians, and I have no doubt that in another ten years it will be known by a large segment of the public."

Noah winced. That was approximately what he had said to Jonesy about Barrett.

"I think I can say," Barrett said, "that so far as that goes, we're all proud of you."

He inclined his head toward his mother, and smilingly she nodded her agreement.

Barrett took his cigarette case out of his pocket and offered one to Noah. He took it and lit Barrett's cigarette and his own. Mark got out his pipe and his tobacco pouch.

Barrett sat back and puffed his cigarette and looked out at the lake. The water was calm. The clouds that had been in the sky when Noah was driving Jonesy around the lake had disappeared. The afternoon sun was bright on the point and gleaming gold on the opposite shore.

"The other purpose of the Foundation, Noah, is the one that's implicit in its name: the William Huntington Sibley Memorial Foundation. The fund was set up to perpetuate the memory of Dad's name. Naturally, the two things tie in together. For a good many years, his name was synonymous with world arbitration in the minds of most educated people; when you perpetuate his name, you're reminding the public of the possibilities that still exist in world arbitration."

Noah nodded. "Very well expressed," he said.

"And it's right there, Noah, that we feel you're falling down a bit. You're working hard on your own book, you're building up your own reputation as an historian, but it seems to us that very little is being done to keep the memory of *his* name alive."

Noah started to speak, caught himself, and sat back again, rearranging his face into the same expression of courteous attentiveness.

"You've been on the job three years, and the book is still unpublished. Mark has suggested several publishers who might handle it, and all you've done is send it to them and wait for their answer, and when it's come back you've simply put the manuscript back in the drawer and gone on with your own work. We think that a little more aggressive salesmanship on it might have made a difference."

"I believe, Noah," Mark broke in, "that it might be possible for you to *create* a demand for the book. If you were to mention it in some of your articles, then the various historians who saw your reference to it would begin to wonder why it wasn't available to them. Or if you were to mention it—just casually, you know—to the various librarians you see—you have contact with quite a few of them, don't you?—and perhaps to some of the people in the history departments at Columbia and Princeton, then—well, perhaps in time you might get a few dozen letters, saying something to the effect that there was a real need for the book in the various colleges and libraries. If you could submit them along with the manuscript, it would make quite a difference in the way a publisher would look at it."

He stopped, and together the three of them turned and looked at Noah. He nodded soberly. "Very interesting idea," he said. "I'd never thought of it. Perhaps I should have."

He sat still, patiently.

Finally, when none of them said anything, he asked, "Was there anything else you wanted to talk to me about?"

"I don't think so, Noah," Barrett said.

Noah got to his feet. "I'll think about the things you've said." Without looking down at his mother, he went on into the house and upstairs to his study.

10·

HE locked the door and sat down at the desk. And, picking up the piles of papers which had been lying there since he had shown them to Connie, he began methodically to take the clips off. As he did so, he crumpled the little identifying slips of paper and threw them into the wastebasket. Then he opened the file and, taking care to get them into their proper places according to subject matter, put all the papers back in, thus obliterating the evidence he had gathered of his father's inconsistencies.

He went to the closet and took down from the high shelf the trunk-like, specially built, black leather suitcase which he and his father before him had used to carry papers and pamphlets and manuscripts back and forth between Middlefield and the Lake, and he packed the contents of the file and the drawers into the suitcase and closed it. Then, leaving it there in the middle of the room, he unlocked the door and went into his bedroom and changed his clothes and packed all his personal belongings into his two brown leather suitcases. And he took the two brown leather suitcases downstairs.

As he was hurrying through the living room with them, his mother asked, "Where are you going, Noah?"

"Wait a minute," he said. He hurried on through the kitchen, calling, "I'll be back."

He came running back in and said again, "Wait a minute. I'll be right down."

When he came down with the black suitcase, Barrett and Mark were both standing, watching him. His mother was sitting at the table.

The suitcase was heavy, and he put it down. "Right now," he said, panting, "I'm going to New York."

For a brief moment they looked perplexed. Then his mother said, "Why, Noah." She smiled at him with motherly, tolerant affection, as she had smiled at him in his childhood when he had done something she liked. "That's sweet of you," she said, "but we really didn't mean that you should try to do something about the book right away. I'm sure that when we get back in the fall will be time enough. What I want you to do right now is to find that man and—"

"I wasn't planning to do anything about the book," Noah said.

Her expression changed quickly.

"I probably won't be back up here again this summer," he said.

"Where are you going?"

"After New York," he said, "I'm going out to Middlefield for a while. I'll probably go down to Milburn for a day or two, but I'll probably be around Middlefield most of the time until the first of September."

"What are you going to do in New York?" Mark asked.

Noah looked out of the window at the lake, rubbing his chin with his hand. "If I'm invited," he said, without looking at them, "I might attend Connie's wedding."

He made a move toward the suitcase, then stopped and looked around at them. They were all scowling at him, and the thing that was between them now was more than an invisible wall. It was an estrangement, a disparity, a finality of disunion. For a second he flinched. Then, speaking soberly, with his hands clasped behind his back, he said, "There's one other thing I want to tell you. I hope you'll believe it's not just a peevish gesture. It's not something I've thought up in the last fifteen minutes. It's something I've been thinking about for a good many weeks now."

He looked at them one after another, thoughtfully. "I'm resigning as secretary of the Foundation as of September first. I'll be straightening things out in the office down there these next few weeks. I'll have all Dad's papers in their proper place in the files by the end of the month. It's the same filing system, Mark, that Winifred put in years ago. Perhaps she could help your new secretary find everything he needs."

Mark's face was very red. Noah looked at his mother, and there were tears in her eyes.

He picked up the black suitcase. "I'll probably be seeing you all in September," he said, and he went out through the kitchen to his car.

X

1·

NOAH was surprised at how little of any emotion at all he felt as he drove out of the lane and up to the Inn. The image of his last view of his mother's tearful face seemed to arouse no particular sensation, and at the same time he felt no animosity toward her whatsoever, or toward Mark or Barrett. Knowing that the bond which had cemented his whole life had been broken might, he thought, have left him either wildly excited at the thought of his new freedom or panicky with the sense of aloneness, but he felt neither panicky nor wildly excited. If he were to try to name the thing he was feeling, he would call it a sober sort of self-assurance.

He found Connie and Jonesy and arranged to meet them in New York late the next afternoon. They were getting up early and driving straight through in Connie's car. While he was still there, they put in a call to New York and reserved three single rooms. And with that arranged, he got into his car and headed south.

It was good to be alone, to be sensitive to the lift of the car beneath him as he stepped on the accelerator, to be able, uninterrupted, to experience the happy little surprises of beauty that came around every curve of these curving Vermont roads. It was good, as you settled down to the driving, to feel that you were driving better than you had ever driven before, surer in your judgment of distances, defter with your touch on the wheel. And it was good to find that you could think of the future calmly, with no sense of harassment, no feeling of being involved with other people's opinions, with only the sober self-assurance which you had felt ever since you left the cottage.

This time you were going to make your own decisions. He chuckled to himself. This time you were damned well going to have to make your own decisions, whether you wanted to or not. There were decisions to be made, all right—such small details as figuring out what you wanted to do with the rest of your life, such things as finding out whether this whole Natalie business was something you just dreamed about or something you went and did something about.

Well, you had plenty of time to do your figuring. You had a month if you needed it, a month before they closed up the cottage and moved back down to Middlefield. You'd better know what you wanted before that month was over, though. But a month was a lot of time. You could take up your problems—your life work, Natalie, money— one at a time and think them out.

Or could you? How could you figure out what kind of work you were going to do or where you were going to do it until you knew whether Natalie was going to be in the picture or out of the picture? And how could you go waltzing up to Natalie and say, "Hey, my love, come along with me," when you didn't know where you were going or what you were going to do when you got there?

Probably what you did first was to make darned sure that you knew what you wanted. God, how little you knew, when you came right down to it, about what you really did want! What a poor, pitiable, confused guy the Noah Sibley of the last three years had been! The Noah Sibley of two weeks ago, for that matter, dreaming his befuddled dreams of some different kind of life, of some kind of life that contained Natalie!

What you dreamed and what you wanted when it came down to solid, day-by-day, year-by-year living might be two very different things. It was hard to imagine living without the dream of Natalie; it was something else again to think about doing the things you would have to do to turn the dream into a reality. It was pretty hard, actually, to imagine the reality itself after you had it. Again, though, it was impossible to imagine going on along without at least trying to see if the dream *could* be turned into a reality. There was even a possibility that failing to try, now, would be unfair to Natalie.

The situation now wasn't what it had been that last afternoon at the Island, when she had told him that she loved what he might have been but couldn't love what he was. One difference was that he now knew what that was all about. Probably, in these last two days, he had become the man she had felt he might have been.

Another difference—or maybe it was all part of the same difference —was that he wouldn't be worrying about how his family felt about stealing another man's wife. He didn't care what they thought any more. But what did he feel about it himself? Naturally, he didn't like it. It made him squirm. He doubted if any man could set about it cold-bloodedly to take another man's wife away from him without a qualm or two.

Jeffrey? He didn't like Jeffrey. He owed Jeffrey nothing but one night's hospitality, but still you couldn't help having a qualm or two when you thought about taking his wife away from him.

Of course a man could deserve to lose his wife. It was fairly probable that Jeffrey deserved to lose Natalie; he had seemed to get his greatest pleasure out of making her unhappy, or at least uncomfortable. Maybe she shouldn't have to take the beating of living with him any more. She had said that night on the beach that she had tried for fifteen years to lie in the bed she had made for herself and that now she couldn't take it any more.

But if that was true, why hadn't she divorced him already, whether there was a Noah Sibley in the offing or not? That was a logical question, wasn't it? Or was it too logical? Was it, human nature being what it was, asking too much of her? Could you really blame a woman for giving up something bad for something better just because she hadn't exchanged the something bad for nothing at all?

It got complicated, didn't it? He grinned to himself, still feeling unharried, still confident that, left to himself, as he was going to be, he would find an answer or two sometime. The something better wouldn't be much better if it was a man without a job. And that brought you all the way back around the big circle, back to trying to figure out what you were going to do for a living. Milburn? The book? Some other kind of job altogether?

Well, you didn't have to figure everything out in one afternoon. You could crank the windows down and settle back and breathe the last of this cool Vermont air that you might be breathing for a very, very long time. Would he ever again, he wondered, be spending a summer at the Lake?

You didn't have to figure that one out either. You just relaxed and drove on down to Rutland and picked up U.S. 7 and headed south into the Berkshires. You didn't hurry. You weren't going to make New York tonight, and the nearer you got to it, the hotter the night would be. You might as well stop somewhere around Bennington or Williamstown and find yourself a good cabin and a restaurant where you could get a couple of drinks and a bang-up good dinner.

You had a whole month to figure things out, and you seemed already to have made a few decisions without knowing that you were making them. For one thing, you were going sometime soon to drive over to Milburn and walk around the place and see if you had the same feel for it you used to have—or if going back there now would give you a bit of a feeling of going backward. For another thing, he knew that he was going to try to see Natalie—preferably, if he could arrange it, somewhere away from the Island, away from Jeffrey and that cottage and her children.

2 ·

THE city was hot. Not frightfully hot, Connie insisted, just hot. Pretty soon, she said, after the sun had set, it would be nice and cool. She was in the chair beside the window, looking trim and schoolteacherish in a white blouse and blue skirt, turning now and then to gaze out at the tops of the buildings.

Jonesy, too exuberant to sit still anywhere for long, was up and down and around, from the chair beside the other window to the middle of the room to the straight chair in front of the desk to the bathroom for a drink of water and back to the chair beside the window again.

Noah, sitting on the bed with his hands dangling between his legs, watched him and grinned, first at Connie and then at him. "Nervous, Jonesy?"

Jonesy grinned back at him sheepishly and settled back in his chair, momentarily giving the appearance of a man relaxing. "This is a big night in my life," he said, and Connie smiled at him as she might have smiled at the exuberance of a small boy.

Suddenly Jonesy looked serious. "How're we going to find a minister?"

"How about a justice of the peace—or a judge or whoever does that sort of thing in a big city?" Connie asked.

"No, sir," Jonesy said, "not in New York. They put 'em through forty at a time—mass ceremony—and the first thing you know, you're married to the wrong girl. Anyway, it's not dignified."

"Does that matter?"

"You bet your life it does—when you're marrying a girl like you. Don't you think it's undignified, Noah?"

"Sordid," Noah said. "What denomination are you, Jonesy?"

"Baptist. But that doesn't matter. Any kind will do as far as I'm concerned. What are you?"

"We're Presbyterians."

"That would be all right."

"So would Baptist be all right," Connie said.

They all sat thinking about it.

"I know a Congregational minister in New York," Noah said. "Classmate of mine. Prays at all the reunions."

"That would be all right," Jonesy said.

"A compromise," Connie said. "Call him up."

Noah found the number in the phone book. "What time shall I say?"

"Early," Connie said, "I want to be out West by nighttime. I'm marrying a Westerner."

"Are you flying or going by train?" Noah asked.

"We're driving my car—all the way to Los Angeles. That's going to be our honeymoon."

Noah laughed at her. "You won't be out West by night."

She smiled. "We'll be farther west than we are here."

"What time shall I say? Eleven o'clock?"

"That reminds me," Connie said. "I haven't any road maps."

"You can pick them up at a gas station."

"All right," she said. "Tell him nine o'clock."

"He might not be up that early. Ministers lead a soft life."

"Ten o'clock then."

Noah called the number, but the man who answered was not his classmate. His classmate was away on vacation. The man was his assistant, and if there was anything he could do—

"Yes," Noah said. "Could you marry a couple at ten o'clock tomorrow morning?"

He could, and Noah made the appointment, the ceremony to take place in the study of the church. Yes, they had their license.

He hung up.

"Noah," Connie said, "will you go and see Winifred?"

"What?"

"When you get back to Middlefield, will you go over and see Winifred?"

"Yes," he said. "Yes, I will. One of the first things I'll do."

"Don't forget," she said.

"I won't."

Jonesy looked at his watch. "Where're we going to have dinner?"

"You choose, Jonesy," Connie said. "You're a visiting buyer. You know all the best night spots."

Jonesy thought about it. "I don't know any good enough for this night. They're all too big and noisy or too little and—and ordinary. For tonight we should have something elegant."

"But not too elegant," Connie said. "Can you think of something just a little bit elegant, Noah?"

Noah grinned at her. "Me? I know less about the night spots than anybody."

She looked at him thoughtfully. "Remember that place you took me to during the war, the French place with all the foreign uniforms? Do you suppose it's still going?"

"I haven't any idea."

"Look it up in the telephone book and see."

He sat still, looking at her.

"Go on," she said.

He went on sitting still, looking at her.

"What's the matter?"

"I'd hate like hell to run into Warner and Louise."

She chuckled. "We won't," she said. "We don't even know whether they're alive or dead. They may be in Timbuktu for all we know. And even if they are in New York—after you're married you don't go to restaurants. You eat pork chops at home. That's what *we're* going to do, isn't it, Jonesy? Go on, Noah, look it up."

He looked it up. It was still there, and he called and reserved a table for three.

3 ·

ROLAND the proprietor didn't remember Noah's name, but he did remember that he was somebody he had once known, and even that was pretty amazing. After Noah spoke of his reservation, giving his name, he was very cordial and he managed to call Noah "Mr. Sibley" four times in the next ten minutes. But he didn't say "Lieutenant" and he didn't mention the war.

Their table was not the one Noah and Warner had always had. It was out in the middle of the room, nearer the door, and this time it was Connie who sat facing the door and Noah who had his back to it.

Jonesy, between them, looked around and grinned. "This is all right, Noah," he said. "This is about as near as you could come to it."

Noah was stealing cautious glances around at the other tables.

Connie laughed at him. "They won't be here, Noah. And what if they are? What harm would it do?"

Noah was thinking about Warner and the knowing way he could grin at you, and about the close, brotherly friendship he had had with Louise. "You don't know," he said. "That's one thing I don't think I could take."

"Embarrassing, you mean?"

"Worse than embarrassing, a whole lot worse."

She shrugged. "I think it might be fun," she said. "I'd be curious to see how they look. Personally, I'd rather see Louise than Joan any day. And I never did see Warner."

Noah picked up the menu. "You go right on hoping we see them," he said, "and I'll go right on hoping we don't."

Roland hovered over their table, and after some discussion and some translating from the French by Connie they decided to let Roland plan the dinner and the wines. Jonesy was doubtful about the wines. He wanted this to be a big evening. Finally he agreed. "So long as there's plenty of it. Lots of wine," he said to Roland.

"In a little while," Connie explained to Roland, "we want to be feeling very gay."

Roland beamed, and there was lots of wine. For the first two courses they tried a little to be gay, and after that they didn't have to try.

Halfway through the main course, Noah heard a new set of voices in the hall behind him. Connie laid her fork down and sat still, staring into the hall. Noah put his knife and fork on his plate and gripped his hands together in his lap and shriveled up inside his shoulders. He shut his eyes. "Don't tell me," he said, his eyes still shut.

"Tell you what?"

"That you're looking at Warner and Louise."

"I'm not."

He opened them. She was still staring. "What *are* you staring at then?"

"At the most beautiful girl in the world."

"Who is she?"

"I haven't any idea. I never saw her before. But she's the most beautiful girl in the world. Isn't she, Jonesy?"

Jonesy could see by merely turning his head. He looked for a few seconds. Then, laughing and almost blushing, he said, "She's pretty good looking all right. I'll still take what I've got." He squeezed Connie's hand.

Noah opened out his hands in a gesture of helplessness, smiling rue-fully.

"I think you could turn and look," Connie said. "She must be used to being stared at."

He pushed his chair back and turned it sideways and crossed his legs as though he had finished the course, which he hadn't. He lit a cigarette and then, very casually, turned and looked at the door.

He found himself looking into the face of a man whose name came to him instantly, Sid Carter. Sid had seen him as he turned, and he threw his head back and smiled and waved. And as Noah waved to him, a girl's voice said clearly, so that it could be heard all over the room, "Why, that's Noah Sibley."

Connie chuckled with delight. "My brother!" she said.

Noah turned his head farther and looked at the girl. He said under his breath as he got to his feet, "It's Natalie's sister, and I'm damned if I can remember her last name."

She and her husband and Sid Carter and his wife who had won the Something-or-other Golf Championship were all coming over to the table. Betty was ahead of the others, looking surprisingly pleased to see him. "Remember me, Noah?" she asked, holding out her hand. "I'm Betty MacGarry."

"Of course I do, Betty," Noah said, thinking, "MacGarry, that's it. Howard MacGarry." And he said aloud, "How are you, Howard?"

"And Jeanne and Sid Carter?" Betty asked.

Noah shook all their hands and introduced them to Connie and Jonesy. "Well, this is quite a coincidence, isn't it?" he said to Howard. "That we should all happen to come to this particular little restaurant?"

"Not very," Howard said, knowing and sophisticated. "You run into everybody here sooner or later. This is one of those places that everybody this side of the Mississippi thinks he's the only one who knows about it. That's Roland's biggest asset. That's why he never advertises."

Jeanne and Sid Carter were grinning at him a little vacantly, both self-consciously erect, as though they had to advertise their athletic inclinations.

"We were so sorry you had to leave that weekend, Noah," Betty said. "It was—wasn't it illness in your family? I hope—"

"Yes," Noah said, thinking fast, "it was my—it was a fall my mother had. She's all recovered now."

"I'm glad." She smiled at him. Probably Connie was right. She probably was the most beautiful girl in the world. Or at least she'd do until a more beautiful one came along.

"We missed you that night," she said. "We went to the dance at the yacht club."

As she said it, Noah was glancing at the other three and thinking, "Yes, she's a beautiful girl, but these other people—this husband of hers with his weak face and that supercilious manner that goes with a weak face—these Carters with their vacant grins. They were—what? Stupid? Ordinary? Something like that anyway." It was something you sensed in them.

He said to Betty, "I was sorry I had to go."

"Well, nice to have seen you, Sibley," Howard said, waving to Roland with one arm and herding Betty and the Carters toward their table with the other.

Noah nodded to them all and sat down. What was it Natalie had said that night on the beach? Something about anybody knowing by looking at him that he was worth all the rest of the people at her party put together. Well, even if it was true it might not be much to be proud of, but somehow seeing them made you think of it. Natalie and Betty had something different in them, but the rest of these people! And that included Jeffrey. Jeffrey was one of them. Seeing them here, seeing what they were, made you feel even more now than you had at the Island that Natalie didn't belong among them, that there would be some sort of ultimate justice in getting her away from them. You didn't have to feel that you were any great prize yourself to feel that.

Connie was smiling at him. "Are you going to see Natalie sometime, Noah?"

He smiled back at her. "I think I might."

She nodded knowingly. Of course she was remembering everything he had told her about Jeffrey that day on Randolph's Hill. She never forgot anything. She held up her wineglass. "Well, here's to you," she said, and he knew that in her mind she had already divorced Natalie from Jeffrey and married her to him. It wouldn't be quite that simple, but Connie was never one to worry about details.

They had champagne and brandy, and afterward they took a ride in Central Park in a hansom cab. They made jokes that they all three thought were very funny. Noah knew that he was being at his best, that the evening was better for them because he was along. For Connie's sake, that pleased him. For Jonesy's sake too, for that matter. Somehow they got down on Broadway and shot .22 rifles at little clay birds moving along on a track. Finally they walked all the way back to the hotel arm in arm, and Jonesy said he'd had the best time he'd ever had. Life, he said, was a great thing, and Connie squeezed Noah's arm.

4.

AFTER breakfast Noah went out and bought Connie a corsage and a present of a matched pair of suitcases. The old ones she had carried back and forth to school all those years were scuffed and battered. He went back up to the room, and Jonesy had bought her a corsage too. Of course she had to wear Jonesy's. She repacked her clothes and gave the old suitcases to the maid who came in to clean the room.

They got her car out of the garage and drove uptown to the church. They were married in the little study by a boyish-looking young minister, with Noah and the minister's girlish-looking young wife for witnesses. Out in the street in front of the church Noah kissed Connie and shook Jonesy's hand and wished them all kinds of happiness.

And then they were gone.

He found a little restaurant, a very ordinary little restaurant, and sat at the counter and ordered a cup of coffee and a sweet roll. And after he had finished them he ordered another cup of coffee to go with a cigarette. He sat there sipping the coffee and puffing the cigarette and thinking that now, by all the gods on Olympus, he really was alone. For the first time in his life, he really was alone. When he had stood at the curb watching that car head downtown toward the Lincoln Tunnel, he had been watching the last intimacy he had left go out of his life.

Of course you could say that as long as Connie lived, as long as there was a Connie somewhere, he wouldn't ever be quite alone. But when you wanted somebody to talk things over with, somebody to take your hair down with, somebody you could sit with, not talking, and feel that you were not alone, a sister three thousand miles away wasn't exactly the prescription. And without her, there was nobody now, absolutely nobody.

He sat there examining the fact of his aloneness, and on the whole he found it more interesting than disturbing. There was even a sense of exhilaration in it. Of course the exhilaration would probably wear off sooner or later, but you didn't have to worry about that right now.

By the time it had worn off, there might be something else. You broke one pattern, and soon a new pattern began to form. The new pattern would begin to form for him in this next month.

He took a subway downtown and got his car out of the garage and drove through the tunnel and on out to Middlefield. The important thing, he decided on the way, was to get the new pattern laid out before the exhilaration had faded out entirely. If you didn't, you might be leaving yourself vulnerable. Loneliness, the feeling of too complete aloneness, could, if it went on long enough, drive you back, merely because in the end you had to have somebody besides yourself. You did if you were Noah Sibley, anyway.

If you ever went back now, you would be absolutely nothing. You had never been more than a half of something, but after you went back you'd be nothing. You'd be defeated. This sortie would have been your one pitiful little gesture. And the memory of it would always be there, in your own mind and in their minds, to underline the completeness of your defeat.

At the house he carried the heavy black leather bag down the hall to the door of the study and set it down. All the doors from the rooms off the hall were closed. The only light was the pale yellow one that came through the stained-glass window at the top of the stairs, yellow and mulberry and green but mostly yellow. The air was close, full of the hot smells of dust and floor wax.

He went back out to the car and got the two brown bags and took them upstairs. The doors up there were closed too, and he put the bags in his room and went around opening doors and raising shades and opening windows. The air that came in was hotter than the air inside, but it was fresher.

On his way back from his mother's room to his own, he found that he was tiptoeing. Why? He stamped the last few steps down the hall. The sound of his heels was sharp but somehow lifeless, like the air here in the hall. The house gave him an uncomfortable feeling, like a morgue, and it seemed oddly foreign to him. Only a few weeks ago he had been here for the better part of a month, just as much alone as he was now, and he had liked it—liked the house, anyway, liked being alone in it. It hadn't been a happy month, but the house had been the best part of it, a comfort to him, a sanctuary. Well, it would never be a sanctuary to him again. It would never be anything to him again, he hoped. If it was ever anything to him, it would be a prison.

He took off his shirt and busily, trying to fend off the mood of the house by bustling, he went into the bathroom and soaped and scrubbed his face and hands, remembering with a chuckle the jokes they used to make back in his college days about getting dressed up before you called up your girl. He opened a suitcase and got out his toilet kit and a comfortable sport shirt that he wouldn't have to tuck into his trousers and took his brush from the kit and brushed his hair.

He went down to the study and closed the door behind him and, leaving the shades down and the windows closed, turned on the light over the big desk. Then he placed the telephone directly in front of the desk chair, found an ashtray, and placed it beside it and laid his cigarettes and lighter beside the ashtray.

He sat down and lit a cigarette and put it on the edge of the tray. Then he pulled the telephone toward him and held it with his two hands, cocking his head at it humorously, as though it were some complicated piece of machinery that he had to figure out how to operate. Finally he lifted the receiver and put in a person-to-person call to the Island.

He did not hear the talk involved in putting through the call, but the operator must have said, "Middlefield, New Jersey, calling," because Natalie seemed to know who he was before he told her.

"This is a surprise, Noah," she said, not sounding surprised.

"I know," he said, "of course it is. How have you been?"

"Busy, mostly."

"Happy?"

She waited a while before she answered. "Is that what you called up to ask me?"

"Maybe," he said. "Maybe it is. No, seriously, listen. I've got to talk with you."

"I'm listening." Her voice sounded cautious, not as though there was anyone within earshot, but as though she was trying to figure out the reason for his call.

"No, I mean really talk to you. A lot of things have happened to me since I've seen you—and I want to tell you about them. You couldn't meet me in New York sometime in the next few days, could you?"

Again she was silent for a while. Finally she said, "Not possibly, Noah. What sort of things have been happening to you?"

He shook his head at the phone. "They're not the sort of thing you can explain over the phone. It will take hours to explain them."

"Well!" She waited. At last she said, "Of course I'm awfully interested to hear, but I just can't—why don't you come out here to the Island, Noah?"

"No," he said. "I want to talk to you away from all that. Couldn't you get away for just part of one day, for lunch and a couple of hours afterward? I could meet you anywhere."

"Not possibly, Noah. I was just looking at my engagement pad. This is a pretty tight schedule we follow, you know. We have engagements and Pammy has engagements and Peter has to be taken places and—I just can't ask my maid to do all the chauffeuring and shopping and other things I do on top of her regular work."

Noah was feeling an animosity toward her calendar pad. For a confounded little calendar to stand in the way of—

"I'd love to have you come out here though, Noah. So would Jeffrey. He was terribly disappointed that you had to leave that weekend. By the way, it was illness in your family that called you away. Don't forget that, will you? He liked you very much, Noah."

Now it was Noah who sat still, frowning at the bookcase in front of him. By the elementary rules of psychology, Jeffrey should have disliked him thoroughly—after that incident at the cove. Of course he could have lied to Natalie about how he felt. Or she could be lying to him right now. Perhaps she was being very clever indeed. Perhaps she had divined what the things were he had to say to her, and perhaps she was fending them off in advance.

"We have people staying with us now," she was saying, "but—wait a minute—"

He knew that she was looking at the calendar again.

"The guest room is free after Thursday night," she said. "Why don't you come on the afternoon boat Friday, Noah? Jeffrey and Howard are going to be away Saturday and part of Sunday, but Betty will be coming over here to stay with me anyway, so—we'd all be glad to see you, Noah, and I'm really awfully anxious to hear about what's been happening to you. Wouldn't that be a good plan?"

Noah closed his eyes. It wasn't the ideal setup, but with Jeffrey away for Saturday and part of Sunday it seemed a little less complicated. There should be chances to talk alone, and after all that was what he wanted. But Betty might be a complication, and the background of the Island and her cottage and her children and her maid would still be wrong. "Did Betty tell you that I saw her?"

"Betty? She's away."

"Yeah, I know. I thought she might have gotten back today. We just happened to run into each other in a restaurant last night. She and her husband and the Carters."

"How nice! Betty thought you were wonderful, Noah."

[235]

"Really?"

"Yes, really."

"Listen, Natalie, how long would it be before you could get away for a day? There must be some day when your damned little calendar pad doesn't say anything."

She laughed. "It's a very nice calendar, Noah. It has pictures of New England scenes on one side and the dates on the other. Not until after Labor Day, so far as I can see now. But I'm getting excited about your coming out here this weekend. I do wish you'd be on that boat Friday afternoon. Won't you?"

He thought about it. "Okay," he said, "I'll be on the boat Friday afternoon."

"That's wonderful." She sounded as though she meant it. "I'm so anxious to hear about you."

"I'll be there."

"Good. Thanks for calling, Noah."

He waited until he heard the click of her phone, then put his own down gently. He realized as he did so that his hand was shaking and that he was a little out of breath. He had been more excited during that conversation than he had known. And he was still excited. He was going to see Natalie. Now it was no longer something you dreamed about and didn't do. Now it was something he was going to do. It was no longer something you wondered whether you ought to do. Now he was going to do it. Now he was going to go to that Island and see if he could get her to leave her husband and marry him instead. You really had committed yourself this time. It was hard to believe, hard to imagine yourself in the role. But it was harder still to imagine yourself backing water on it now.

XI

I·

It was odd, Noah thought, that he and Connie, who no longer felt an obligation *toward* the family, should still feel an obligation *for* them and their actions. But he did, and because he did he drove over to Proctor Street to see Winifred.

Mrs. Bunce had never learned to keep from fluttering at the sight of a Sibley. She greeted Noah and fluttered and called upstairs to Winifred and seated him in a chair beside the window in the living room and said that she was fine except that she had some trouble with her feet and agreed that it was hot and excused herself, looking down at her dress.

Winifred came down and walked across to where Noah was standing and held out her hand. Her walk and her manner were natural and unaffected, and although she was not smiling her expression was pleasant. "It's nice to see you again, Noah."

His first thought, as he looked at her, was the same as his first thought had been when, six weeks ago, he had looked down from the deck of the ferry and seen Natalie on the dock. He was thinking, "Of course that's the way she looked. How could I have forgotten?"

"You're looking fine," he said, and he was thinking that she had changed remarkably little.

"Thanks," she said, and for the first time she smiled just a little. "So are you." But instead of asking him to sit down, she stood still, looking at him, her expression sober again. "Noah," she said, great self-possession in both her voice and her manner, "it was nice of you to come and see me but"—she paused—"when did you see Mark last?"

"The day before yesterday," he said. "I came down from the Lake the day before yesterday."

She seemed to think about that, as though the date of his departure

[237]

had some significance. Finally she said, "It was nice of you to come, Noah, but perhaps you won't want to stay after I tell you." She paused again. "I wrote Mark yesterday that I wanted a divorce."

Noah looked into her face and she looked into his, and he knew that they were both trying to hide their true feelings behind the masks of their faces. At last he said, "That doesn't make me want to go—unless you'd rather I would."

She continued to look at him, still hiding her feelings. Then she said, "I'm not going to change my mind, Noah."

He smiled. "That wasn't what I had in mind. I won't try to argue you out of it." He looked around at the chair he had been sitting in. "Do you mind if I sit down?"

She shook her head, and after he had settled into the chair she perched herself on the edge of the one opposite, facing him.

"The truth of the matter is, Winifred," Noah said, "that Mark and I aren't as close as we used to be."

She looked startled. "A falling out?"

"Well, almost," he said. "We're still on speaking terms—or at least I guess we are. It's mostly just that—well, just that I see him differently from the way I used to."

"See him?"

"To put it bluntly, Winifred, I don't admire him as much as I once did."

"I'm sorry," she said. She was looking down at her hands as they plucked at the fold of her dress. It was a nice dress, Noah was thinking, very becoming to her, pale green, very simple and cool and summery. He had been thinking that she didn't look any older than she had ever looked. Then he remembered, smiling at the memory, his last class reunion, where he had told everybody—and meant it—that he didn't look a day older than he had in college; and how he had come back afterward and looked at their graduation pictures and seen that they had looked a great deal older.

"That sounds strange, coming from you, Noah," she said. "The Sibleys were always such a close-knit family—all so loyal to each other."

"Yes, I know."

Of course she looked older. It was just that, as you grew older yourself, your idea of youthfulness changed. College girls looked like children to him now. Winifred had lines around her eyes that undoubtedly hadn't been there fifteen years ago, and a suggestion of little lines beside her mouth. And even the beginnings of gray in her hair. But her skin was still unusually soft and smooth, and her figure and pose and manner seemed remarkably—how old was she, anyway? Three or four years younger than he, as he remembered it. Thirty-four or thirty-five. Yes, they were remarkably youthful for thirty-five.

"Anyway," he said, "that's why I don't hold it against you that you want to divorce him. Would you mind if I asked you *why* you want to divorce him?"

She sat still for a very long time. When she did speak, she spoke so softly that Noah had to strain to hear her. "A woman wants to be wanted," she said.

He did hear her and he nodded knowingly. "And he didn't come hurrying down to see you," he said, "and he didn't even hurry to answer your note, and when he did answer it he wanted you to come here instead of joining him at the Lake."

She stared at him, and finally she smiled, a sad and understanding smile, a very appealing smile, he thought. "That's right, Noah. I wanted to go to the Lake. I love the Lake. I've—I've dreamed about the Lake—all these years."

He nodded again. Connie had seen it, all right.

She had been studying his face. Perhaps she had liked the expression she had seen there, because now she sat forward, suddenly alive and smiling. He sensed at once that the restraint between them had been broken. Now she was a girl talking to a friend she felt she could trust, and her voice was no longer soft. It was strong and natural. "I haven't been very crazy for a long time, Noah," she said. The emphasis on the word "crazy" was a humorous one.

Watching her, he now knew that, however little her appearance had changed, the girl inside had changed more than a little. She was still girlish, still surprisingly youthful, but in the youthfulness there was a mature quality he had never seen in her before.

"I've been working in the office at the sanitarium," she said, "and I did very well. Dr. Adams said I was the best secretary he ever had. He hated to have me leave." She settled back in her chair, smiling at him. "I never *was* very crazy, Noah, except for what Dr. Adams called my 'Big Fear.' If it hadn't been for my Big Fear, I could have come out almost any time—five years ago, if I'd wanted. Dr. Adams told me five years ago that he was leaving it up to me, that I could come out any time I felt sure in my own mind that I had conquered my Big Fear."

This, Noah realized, was something he had known about all along —without knowing that he was knowing it. He nodded, motioning with his thumb toward the southwest end of the city. "And your Big Fear," he said, "was the other end of Middlefield."

"That's right." She was looking at his face, her expression a curious blend of puzzlement and amusement and liking. "I'd never put it quite that way before, but that's it." She cocked her head a little to one side. "You're smart to know that, Noah. You're much smarter than the rest of the family give you credit for, aren't you? I remember I used to think that, way back in the old days. You're the only one who would understand that."

"Except Connie," Noah said.

"I never knew Connie very well. She was different from the rest of them too, wasn't she?"

"Yes. She got married this morning."

"This morning?" For a moment she looked amused, then quickly her eyes clouded. "At the Lake?"

"No. No, in New York. I was the only representative of the family. The rest of them didn't like the idea of her marrying a shirt manufacturer from Los Angeles. That was part of the—part of the climax. We've been having a bit of a set-to in the family, with Connie and me on one side and the rest of them on the other."

He waited, surprised to find himself talking such intimate things to somebody who was so nearly an outsider. It gave him a momentary qualm, but he went on, "Another part of it was Connie and me being disgusted with Mark for not hurrying away to the sanitarium as soon as he got your note."

She was looking down at her hand as it smoothed the cloth of her dress across her lap. "I wanted him to do that," she said, and her voice was low again, full of self-restraint, "to come to me quickly. And I wanted to go to the Lake, and after that I wanted to go away from Middlefield and have a place of our own"—she shrugged and smiled briefly—"any kind of a little place where he could write and I could cook and keep house and type for him. And then—well, I guess you know what he suggested in his letter."

Now Noah was sensing something more that was new in her, sensing that behind the restrained voice and the restrained words there was fire, some sort of inward fire. It had always been there, he was remembering; a few times, way back, she had shown a spunkiness, a capacity for courage, but so much of the time it had been hidden behind the timidity and the fear. "No," he said, "I don't know what he suggested in his letter."

"Don't you? He suggested that we should move in with you and your mother and—and that we should have separate rooms."

Noah stared at her. So that was what his mother had done. He felt the veins swelling in his temples. His mother had said after breakfast that morning that the best thing would be for them all to say nothing to Mark about it until he brought the subject up himself. And then, sometime between morning and the time that night when Mark had been out in the Lion's Lair writing his letter to Winifred, she had put her ideas across to him. He scowled across at Winifred, his jaws clamped, his eyes sullen.

"It isn't easy, Noah," she was saying, and the inward fire was still there. "It isn't easy fighting a fear like that one of mine. It's not fun. It's like making yourself walk when your leg hurts, only a hundred times worse. But I fought it because I thought Mark wanted me to. I made myself, every day. Every day I would sit there in my room—I did it regularly, like doing exercises—and I would say to myself, 'Now, Winifred, you are walking into one of those dining rooms—' You know those damned big dark dining rooms, Noah?"

She smiled at him out of the corner of her eye, an amused smile, then went on, " 'And now, Winifred,' I'd say, 'all the women have on dinner gowns or evening gowns and yours isn't like the rest of them, and you're just not going to think about it. You're going to act as though you knew yours was the only one that was right and all the rest were wrong, just the way they do. And at dinner you're going to find yourself sitting beside old Mr. Devereaux and you're going to say to him, "Isn't it splendid about the Princeton football team?" And he's going to look at you down that long nose of his and say, "What is it you find splendid about it, young lady?" ' and—and all at once, Noah, sitting there alone in my room with my eyes closed, I'd be trembling all over and I'd be perspiring and my heart would be thumping and—and I'd wish I could die. I'd have to hold on to the arms of the chair to keep myself from crawling under the bed and hiding there."

Noah was listening with parted lips, nodding, glimpsing for the first time a world of mental turmoil of which he had known nothing.

"That's a sort of torture, Noah, that most people don't know anything about. You get to dreading the trying to cure yourself more than you dread the thing itself. The easy way would have been to stay there at the sanitarium, where the fear could never reach me. That's what I wanted to do. Oh, how I wanted to do just that! But instead I fought it. I fought it day after day and month after month. I used every bit of will power I had. I wore myself out fighting it, until some-

[241]

times I hardly had the strength to walk down the hall to the stairs."

She sat forward, and now the fire was no longer an inward fire. It was there, on the surface. "I did it for *his* sake, Noah, for Mark's sake. I thought he was longing for his wife. I thought he was wanting all those things I'd dreamed of, the place of our own and somebody to cook for him and keep house for him and—and go to bed with him. And I knew he'd have to see his family and their friends sometimes, and I knew I couldn't be all the wife for him I should be until I could take that too. So I fought it, and finally I did it, Noah, for *his* sake. I could look Mr. Devereaux in the eye tomorrow and tell him what was splendid about the Princeton football team, just as easy as that."

She snapped her fingers, and her eyes as they looked into his were sparkling, sparkling with fire—sparkling too, he suddenly saw, with amusement. He stared, dumbfounded. In all of this, in spite of all of this, she was, he realized, seeing the humor, the irony, the tragic comedy in the incongruity between the things she had dreamed and the things Mark had said in his letter.

That, Noah knew, was more than he himself could ever have done. He could never have stepped outside of himself and looked at himself and laughed as she was doing right now. Somehow, out of her long years of loneliness, out of the long hard fight she had fought, this girl who had once been so childlike, so meek, so overwhelmed by a world that was too unfamiliar to her, had achieved this perspective, this sanity that was saner, he knew, than his own, or Connie's, or perhaps anyone else's he knew. He felt very humble as he looked across at her.

"I don't want to have separate rooms, Noah." Her eyes were still amused, the overtones of her voice humorous. "I don't even want to have twin beds. If I'm going to be married, I want to be—married. I suppose you think that's vulgar." She looked at him triumphantly. "The wonderful thing about it, Noah, is that I don't give a damn whether you or your mother or the whole west end of Middlefield think it's vulgar or not. You see?"

He laughed. "I see," he said. And after a moment, "I don't think it's vulgar. I think it's just the opposite of vulgar. I agree with you—absolutely."

"And I don't think they have a right to ask me to live in that house, or even in that part of town."

"Absolutely," he agreed again.

They sat still, looking at each other, and he knew that any animosity she might be feeling toward the rest of the family did not include him. It made him happy to know it. By listening, by feeling humble, he supposed, he had somehow put it across to her that he was on her side. "What are you going to do, Winifred?" he asked.

"I'm going to try to find a job—somewhere away from Middlefield. This place"—her gesture signified the house they were in—"isn't right for me either. And Middlefield isn't the place where I want to be, even though I do know I could take it if I had to."

She was calm again now, once more a girl chatting with a good friend about her plans. "I suppose it won't be easy. People will want to know where I've been. I'm sure Dr. Adams will give me a recommendation, and if I asked him to he might leave out about my having been an inmate. But I don't want it that way. I don't want to be afraid all the time that people will find out."

Noah nodded, then shook his head. "It wouldn't be good to be afraid about that all the time—that's sure—but it does make it tough, doesn't it? I'd be glad to give you a recommendation, if you think that would help any—about the work you did for Dad."

"Thanks, Noah. That might help, only—it was a long time ago—and Mr. Sibley recommending Mrs. Sibley! I think somebody might take a chance with me if Dr. Adams were to say that I was cured and that I never was violent or—or dangerous."

Noah gazed into space, hoping somebody would take a chance with her. Jobs this year weren't as plentiful as they had been, and, with other girls available, he wondered if any employer would—

If she could just get in somewhere, he thought, she'd be all right. She'd once been a whiz, and he had a suspicion that she still would be. He believed her when she said that Dr. Adams had found her the best stenographer he had ever had.

He had a feeling that she would be glad now to have him go. "I'll do anything I can to help you, Winifred," he said. He stood up, expecting her to do the same.

But she did not stand up. She sat still, looking at him. "You're a good man, Noah," she said, "an awfully good man. That's something everybody should know just by looking at you. I hope someday you find a girl who knows how good you are—and knows that it's enough for you to be good, without having to be great."

Noah looked back into her eyes, remembering Natalie, knowing that the thing Winifred had just said was the sort of thing Natalie might have said, knowing that it was something he needed to have said to him, surprised and confused that it should have been Winifred who had said it. He was touched, and he felt a bond of sympathy and understanding between them.

At last she did stand up and hold out her hand. He took it and smiled at her. "You're smarter than the family gave *you* credit for too, aren't you?" he asked. Then he laughed. "I don't mean about my being good. I mean about my not having to be great." He got to the door and stopped. "I'm going to be around here off and on for the next few weeks. If you'd like to have me, I'll drop in now and then and see how things are going."

"I'd like it very much, Noah," she said.

2.

Two days later, at nine o'clock in the morning, Noah called Winifred on the phone and asked her if she had found a job yet.

"I haven't started to look." Her voice sounded calm and cheerful. "But I've written Dr. Adams. I won't start looking until I hear from him."

"I've got a line on a possible job for you."

She waited a while before she said anything. Then she asked, her voice a little flat, "In Middlefield?"

"No. Do you remember that I used to teach at a place called the Milburn School?"

"Yes."

"I don't believe you were ever there, were you?"

"Mark took me to a track meet once. It was beautiful country."

"That's right. I remember now—that track meet. Well, I went over there yesterday—just wanted to walk around the place a little. I had no idea that the headmaster would be there, but he was. He's an old friend of mine. We were in school there together. He's there just for this week—had a few things to get straightened out about the fall term, and one of them was finding another girl to work in the administrative office. Do you think you'd be interested in something like that?"

This time there was no hesitation. "Of course I would. Did you tell him about me, Noah?"

"Yes. All that he needs to know. He wants to talk with you, of course, but he thinks that if you can get the sort of letter from Dr.

Adams that you spoke of, and if you seem qualified in other respects, there's no reason why they couldn't hire you."

Now her voice was very low, as it had been from time to time when they were talking at her house. "That was wonderful of you, Noah."

"He's a nice guy, Roger is," Noah said. "That's the headmaster's name, Roger Reinhart. You'd like working for him. I grow to like him better and better. A very understanding guy."

"I hope I can get it, Noah." There was a quaver in her voice. "It sounds—it sounds so much better than anything I'd imagined. I'd imagined a factory office in Newark or New York and a one-room apartment in a—where would I live, Noah?"

"You'd have to find a room in the village. I think we could find you one all right. The salary wouldn't be much—he didn't know just how much when I talked to him."

"Enough to live on?"

"Just about, I guess."

She waited, and he wondered if she was losing her enthusiasm. "That's all I'd care about," she said, "just so I wouldn't have to ask Daddy for money or run into debt."

"You wouldn't have to do that." He smiled at the phone, affectionately, thinking that there weren't many girls who wouldn't, at this juncture, be thinking in terms of alimony. But whatever else you might say about the Sibleys, this was the sort of situation where you could count on them to do the right thing. Winifred wouldn't have to worry about money.

"What do I have to do to get the job, Noah?"

"Well, that's what I'm calling about. Roger will only be there a few more days, and I have to go away Friday. I was wondering if you could ride over there with me this afternoon. We could get a couple of rooms at the Inn, and you could see him tomorrow morning and we could come back in the afternoon."

"What time, Noah?"

"About one o'clock."

"I'll be ready."

"That's the spirit," Noah said. "I'll pick you up at one o'clock."

As they climbed higher and higher into the hills, getting farther away from the cities and the railroads and the low flat valleys, the air grew cleaner and fresher. They seemed to notice a new difference every fifteen minutes. They spoke about it again and again.

During the first half hour, when they were driving away from Middlefield, Noah told her all about Connie's love affair. But after that it was hard to find another subject. Talk about the rest of the family would almost inevitably get around to Mark; he couldn't talk about Natalie, the only other subject that had been occupying his mind; it wasn't up to him to bring up questions about Winifred's sojourn in the sanitarium.

So more and more they had silences. Between silences they remarked about the views, or the freshness of the air, or the cattle in the pastures, or the cool dark streams that ran along beside the road for a while before they meandered away across the fields. Winifred remembered that he had liked trout fishing. "Would there be any trout in there, Noah?"

"Not unless the State has stocked it. Not this near the road," he said, and again they had a long silence.

Noah knew that the silences did not disturb her, that she was content to look at the hills and the trees and the brooks, to ride on along, settled back so quietly in the seat beside him there. And because she was content, he was enjoying the drive, feeling a unique sort of contentment of his own, a unique sense of peace and adequacy. He couldn't remember when he had been with anyone who demanded so little that he should be entertaining or clever or sophisticated or knowing or alert to appreciate the cleverness of others.

Natalie, many years ago, had tried to give him a sense of his own adequacy, and to some extent succeeded, but in the end she had found him inadequate—for reasons which, of course, he now understood. And again that weekend at the Island she had found him inadequate, and he understood that too. Connie? Connie gave him affection; she liked him for what he was, but she was always two jumps ahead of him, always reading his thoughts before they were formed in his own mind, always reminding him, without intending to, that he wasn't very bright.

Of course a feeling of adequacy wasn't everything. He probably needed somebody more demanding than Winifred to keep him stimulated and alert and on his toes. Well, not demanding maybe. Demanding wasn't the word. More what? More—he couldn't think of a word, and he smiled at himself—more like Natalie.

But for now, for this interim between that hectic last week at the Lake and the crucial weekend that was coming up at the Island, Winifred was all right, a soothing influence, just what the doctor ordered.

"I haven't heard anything about your book in a long time, Noah," she said. "How is it going?"

For a moment he was surprised that she knew about the book. But of course Mark had been writing to her, and he had still been making occasional visits to the sanitarium.

"I don't know," he said. "I'm not even sure there's going to be a book."

She looked up at him and said, "Why?" so simply that it made him feel that the problem itself was simple, that perhaps he'd been making it unnecessarily complicated in his own thinking.

"Well," he said, "I've resigned as secretary of the William Huntington Sibley Memorial Foundation. You knew about that job of mine, didn't you?"

"Yes. Do you have to be secretary in order to write the book?"

"I was using the material that was in Dad's files." Actually, he thought, he didn't have to have that material. There was plenty that was his own, the stuff he'd dug out of the libraries, other source materials he had access to. There was good stuff in those files, but he didn't have to have it. "No," he said, "I can go on with the book if I want to."

"Do you want to?"

"I don't know."

"What would you do if you don't?"

"I don't know that either. I might go back to Milburn. That's another thing I was talking to Roger about yesterday."

"Oh," she said, "that would be nice—for me, I mean, if I should be there. I'd see you once in a while."

They were climbing a hill, and Noah waited until he had reached the top, where he could see the road leveling off ahead, before he said, "If I were in your place, I'd be just as happy if I never saw a Sibley again."

She laughed. "I'd be happy to see *you* any time." And again there was the peculiar simplicity in the way she spoke. He wondered if there was something about going through what she had been through and coming out of it that made you see things more simply and therefore say them more simply.

He tried to imagine walking into the administrative office and seeing Winifred seated there at her typewriter, along with Miss Minton and that other girl whose name he couldn't remember. There was always something strange about seeing someone you had known in one environment in another that was equally familiar to you. He remembered thinking so in some other connection. Perhaps it was about Louise being in Middlefield, or maybe about Winifred herself at the Lake. "Do you like to walk?" he asked.

"Walk?"

"You know, take walks—out around the hills, in the fall and in the winter and in the spring." He grinned, a little ashamed of the clumsy way he had said it.

"Yes, I like to walk. I liked to walk around the grounds at the sanitarium."

She sat still for a moment. Then she laughed and said, "There was a fence between me and the hills."

She laughed easily, comfortably, and because there was no embarrassment in the way she spoke of it, Noah felt no embarrassment as he grinned down at her. "If I'm here," he said, "we'll take some walks in the hills sometimes."

"I'd like that."

He found himself thinking that if he did go back, he would like having Winifred there on the campus, there in the administrative office when he happened to go in there for something. He suspected that he might find himself making excuses to go into the office. He had always liked her, he remembered, with one of those natural likings you sometimes have for people, one of those feelings that have no connection with the whole complex of social relations in which you have reasons for liking or disliking people.

And now, since their talk the day before yesterday, he was finding that he could think of her as not only likable but admirable, admirable in a way he had never thought of her before, admirable for the courage he knew it had taken to accomplish this thing she had accomplished, for the self-control she had finally achieved—above all, he thought, for the sense of humor. That was the biggest accomplishment of all.

Yes, sir, she was a relative—or, he supposed you'd have to say now, an ex-relative—he could be glad to have there at the school, one, he felt absolutely sure, he would never have to worry about.

He sensed that she was looking at him. He turned, and she was smiling a speculative sort of smile. "Why have you never gotten married, Noah?"

The question startled him, because these days thoughts of Natalie were never far from the surface of his mind. He laughed, a conscious effort to be jocular and casual. "I just don't seem to be the kind of guy that girls go for."

She cocked her head and eyed him appraisingly, and Noah laughed again, this time without an effort. Most girls would have protested, in reply to a remark like that, that it wasn't true. She seemed to be considering it as very possibly true.

"Not all girls, no," she finally said. "But some girls—some girls could fall in love with a man who looks the way you do—especially the way you look sometimes when you don't know anybody's watching you."

4.

THEY had dinner in the dining room of the Inn. Tonight it seemed lonesome there, with only two other diners in the big room that had been planned for the weekend influxes of parents and alumni. Winifred looked around at all the empty tables and seemed quiet and subdued.

After dinner Noah got from the proprietress the addresses of three women in the village who took roomers and boarders. In the cool still twilight they walked around to the three of them and looked at the rooms they had to offer. Winifred still seemed subdued. She chose the one she would like best, a large corner room in a house a quarter of a mile from the Inn. They promised to let the landlady know after Winifred's conference with Roger in the morning.

By the time they had finished talking to her and started back to the Inn, it was dark. There was no moon, and the weak little bulbs of street lights were placed only at intersections. They groped their way along the left-hand side of the tree-shaded streets, with Winifred's hand in Noah's arm. There was little wind, and the only sounds were the distant hum of cars on the highway and the occasional muffled voices that came from the houses they were passing, houses that were back from the street and half hidden in trees and shrubs. When there were no voices, the stillness seemed a positive thing, forcing itself on their attention.

"Do you think you would be lonesome here, Winifred?" Noah asked.

"Yes, I think I would."

He wondered if she was feeling it so strongly that she would prefer to look for some other job, but she said, "I think I'll be lonesome wherever I am."

"That's right," he said, trying to sound reassuring, feeling a defensive proprietary desire to have her like Milburn, "and it won't be like this most of the time. There's nothing deader than a school town in vacation time, but as soon as they all start coming back there'll be all kinds of excitement."

"Of course," she said.

They walked on in silence, and then she said, "I've been lonesome a great deal, Noah."

"Of course you have. I suppose you're—sort of used to it."

Again they walked on, until finally she said, "You don't get used to it."

He could think of nothing to say to that. Then it occurred to him that this was the moment when he could bring up a question that had been worrying him. "Actually," he said, "there's quite a lot of social life around here when school's going. All very informal, of course— just a few of us getting together at one of the masters' houses for dinner and that sort of thing. And we see some of the townspeople—we just passed a house where I've been to dinner often. And once in a while we can work it to go on a picnic or something of that sort. And unattached girls are in great demand. Do you suppose you'd enjoy that?"

She did not answer for a moment. Then she said, "What you mean is, would I be afraid of it?" She was looking up at him, and her tone was reproachful. "I told you that I had that licked, Noah. You didn't believe me?"

He hurried to say, "Yes, I did believe you. I do believe you." He felt panicky at the thought that he had hurt her. The odd thing was that he *had* believed her. He *had* known that she really did have it licked. He didn't know why he had had to ask that question, why he had been so stupid.

"I suppose it's natural," she said, acceptance and a touch of weariness in her voice. "I suppose it will take everybody time to learn to believe it."

"It won't take me time," Noah said. "I believe it right now. I know it."

She acted as though she had not heard him. "After all," she said, "I did come out twice before. People can't help but remember that, can they?"

That was it, Noah thought. That must have been what was in the back of his mind when he asked her that question.

"No, Noah," she was saying, "I'd like it—those picnics and dinners and all. I'd like it very much. I never would have been afraid of it here in Milburn. I never was afraid of anybody unless they lived in Middlefield. I met some very wealthy people when I was working in Dr. Adams' office, some of them more prominent socially than anybody in Middlefield—you know, people you see on the society pages in New York and Philadelphia—and I wasn't afraid of them at all.

"That's funny, isn't it? Or at least it seems funny to me. Dr. Adams says it isn't funny at all. He says all these things go back to your childhood, and Middlefield is where I spent my childhood. He made me tell him all the little things I remembered, and the things he was interested in were things like Daddy's coming home from the store and bragging because one of the Sibleys or the Devereauxs or the Clarks or the Stevensons had bought something from his store, as though all of you were some kind of gods and different from other people. Or about how we'd take Sunday afternoon drives out through your part of town and he'd point out your houses and tell us who lived in which one, and how there was never anybody you could see around any of them, as though you were all closed up in your castles and ordinary people weren't supposed to see you. And how I never did see any of you really, because none of you went to public schools or high school, and all I knew about you was your names. But I knew your names better than I knew the names of the presidents."

Noah trudged on along, thinking about the way he and his family and their friends went on about their living, busy with their own affairs and their own friends, never once suspecting that there were people in the city who felt this way about them.

"I knew that it was just Middlefield," she was saying. "I knew that way back. I knew it that first time I came out, during the war. I probably shouldn't have tried to come out then, that time. I was just as much afraid of Middlefield then as I'd ever been. But Mark came up from Quantico and said that he could take me out to the West Coast with him, and because it wasn't Middlefield, I thought and Dr. Adams thought—"

[251]

She didn't bother to finish the sentence, but after a while she went on, "We were right, too. I was all right so long as I was out there. It wasn't until we got back, after the war—"

Again she let Noah finish the sentence for himself. And again she went on, "I suppose you could say that we should have looked ahead to that. But—it's hard to remember now how we felt then, isn't it? That first fall of the war? There wasn't any future, remember? For all we knew, the war might go on forever. And for all we knew, Mark might not be coming back from the Pacific. I could have gone crazy thinking about that too." Noah detected a different quality in her voice. "Sitting in that little apartment out there in San Francisco, sitting on a bench in that park, watching the pigeons—I loved him an awful lot back in those days, Noah. He could be—he could be very sweet."

Noah shook his head, thinking about Mark as he had been in those days. And he found himself saying, "He doesn't seem like the same guy now, does he?"

"Do you think so too, Noah?" They walked on, and when she spoke she sounded puzzled. "Sometimes these last few years when he has come to the sanitarium, I've looked at him and listened to his voice and—and I'd try to see that boy who used to come running up the stairs to the apartment in his green uniform, smiling and hugging me and laughing, and—and I just couldn't find him, Noah. He just wasn't there any more."

Noah was plowing his way along the road, his head forward, nodding and scowling. "I know," he said. "I've looked for him too. It's hard to figure where it could have gone, isn't it? That way he had of smiling? The friendly way he had?"

They had reached the main street, and here the lights came oftener and were brighter. He could see her face now, although still in half shadow, and the thought that came to him was that there was no longer anything childish in that face. It was the same face, the same oval, the same chin, still the face of the painfully bashful girl who had come to the door that afternoon, and still young looking. But the childish quality was gone The changes were subtle ones, but they were there, visible even in the half shadow.

"I didn't go crazy thinking about his never coming back, though," she was saying. "That's the kind of thing I can take. I always could take that kind of thing. It wasn't until we got back to Middlefield—"

Noah's mind went ahead to those years after the war, and now he was thinking about the vague memory that had come to him the other morning on the porch of the cottage, the memory of having felt that the decision to send Winifred back that second time had been a too hasty one. "You might have made it the second time, though, mightn't you?" he asked.

She thought a long time before she answered. Finally, as they were approaching the Inn, she said, "I thought if I could do it my own way, if I could stay away from the parties and the dinners and the wedding receptions—but they wouldn't let me do it my own way. I could see they weren't going to let me do it my own way. I saw it long before Barrett's wedding, but then when they didn't pay any attention to my note and sent—"

"Note? What note?"

"The note I left for your mother, before I went away to the hotel."

"You left a note?"

"Yes, didn't you know?"

"No," Noah said, overwhelmed by a sudden wave of weariness. "No, I didn't know."

"Well, anyway, when they sent the police after me, I knew. I knew I could never do it that way. I knew I'd have to learn to take it all before I could be all the wife to Mark I ought to be. That's why I stayed so long, Noah. That's why I stayed until I knew I really had it licked."

They sat on the porch of the Inn, looking out across the tree-studded lawn to the street beyond.

"When I said I'd be lonesome here," Winifred said, "I didn't mean I don't want to come. I do. I want to very much. I have a feeling that if I should get the job, this place will turn out to be right for me."

"That's the feeling I have too," Noah said.

"And I didn't mean that I'm not grateful to you for suggesting me to Mr. Reinhart. It means more to me than you realize."

They sat still. The tires of cars passing on the street out in front hummed softly on the macadam.

"But if I don't get the job, Noah," she said, "if Mr. Reinhart doesn't think I'd be right for it, you're not to worry about me."

"I will worry about you."

"No, you're not to." She waited, thinking, and then, with a smile that was both appreciative and sad, she said, "Yes, of course you will. You wouldn't be you if you didn't, would you?" She laughed. "I guess I'm not really very sorry, either. It'll make me feel less lonesome to know that somebody is worrying—"

She stopped, and when she went on she was serious again. "This wasn't a good time for you, was it, Noah? Just after your—what did you call it, a 'set-to'?—just after your set-to with your family. That's been on your mind, hasn't it? That took courage, for you to have a set-to with your mother and Mark and the rest of them. I think I know more than anybody else how much courage. And I think there's something else on your mind too. I don't know what and I don't want you to tell me, but I've been feeling it all afternoon, ever since you picked me up at the house."

Noah turned and looked at her, then turned back and gazed thoughtfully out across the lawn.

"It's good of you to be bothering about me when you have these other things on your mind. You're an awfully good man, Noah. I told you that the other day, didn't I?"

He smiled. "Yes, you did."

"Well, you are, and whatever all these things are, I hope they work out right for you."

And Noah, feeling inexpressibly sorry for Winifred, inexpressibly sorry about the things life had done to her, said, "Thanks, Winifred. I appreciate that very much."

5 ·

SHE went up to her room early, and he sat on the porch, smoking and thinking about all those years of Winifred's life, thinking about his own family and how unimpeachable all their actions still seemed to the world. His mind went on to thoughts of Mark, of the youth he had been and the man he was now, and he wondered what interrelation there might have been between the changes that had come over him and the changes that had come over Winifred. He wondered if there could be some sort of hare-and-tortoise business involved. He wondered what sort of future could lie ahead for Winifred, for this new Winifred who had come so far along the slow road, how this amazing new personality of hers would interact with the people and the events with which she came in contact in the future.

He hoped mightily that Roger would hire her tomorrow, that the thing would be settled and settled right. It would be, he felt sure, a good way for her to start toward that future, whatever it might be. He could visualize her here, fitting into the life of the school, liking it and the kind of things that went on, liking the people and being liked by them. And he had a feeling that after a while she would be less lonesome here than in any other place he could think of.

It was important, important to him, that she should find something that was right for her. Since their talk the day before yesterday he had been feeling very strongly that, as a Sibley, he had a responsibility toward her, that it was up to him to see that she found some sort of happiness, that the Sibleys had no right to allow her to know any more loneliness than the loneliness they had already forced upon her.

It was pure happenstance, of course, that Roger had mentioned yesterday that he was looking for a girl for the office. But if it worked out, he, a Sibley, would have been the intermediary. It would be a wonderfully expedient way to expiate the family sin. Too expedient, perhaps, too much by pure luck, to soothe his conscience entirely, to soothe his conscience for having been born a Sibley. But it was something, and in any case, wherever she was and wherever he was, he would keep in touch with her. He would see to it that she knew she could always call on him. To that extent, at least, she need never feel completely alone.

But right now the time element was important. It would be wonderful, he thought again, if it could all be straightened out by tomorrow noon. Because Friday he left for the Island. This weekend he would be seeing Natalie, talking to Natalie about their own future. His new pattern of living would be starting to unfold. And the new pattern would, he knew, take all of his attention. It would be much better if there were no tag ends of the old life left to be tucked in.

6 ·

At nine-thirty in the morning he took her into the administrative office and introduced her to Miss Minton. Miss Minton said that Roger was in his office and that Winifred was to go right in. Noah waited outside and talked to Miss Minton about the old days.

After twenty minutes Winifred came out and smiled at Noah and nodded and said that Mr. Reinhart would like to see him before they left. Noah went in and closed the door behind him.

Roger was laughing. "You might have prepared me a little better, Noah."

"Prepared you?"

"I was expecting some wild-eyed, fidgety creature with straight hair hanging down beside her face. And in walks this damned attractive little girl with a figure like a nymph and a skin like a cold-cream ad and all the poise in the world—God, it took me two minutes to remember what I was supposed to talk to her about."

Noah sat down, chuckling. "Did you hire her?"

"Of course I did. It'll save us the expense of redecorating the office."

Noah shook his head at him, still chuckling. "You'd better not let your wife hear you talking like that."

"Don't worry. Diplomacy's the one thing you do learn trying to run a place like this."

"Can't tell you how much I appreciate it, Roger. It'll be wonderful for her. And I think she'll work out in here. She's a really competent secretary."

"I'm taking your word for that, Noah. I'm damned sure she'll work out. She's going to have that doctor write me a letter—just so I'll have something in the file to cover myself. That's the way you get on this job, Noah—you're always figuring the angles."

Noah laughed. "You'd damned well better."

"I'm figuring an angle on you right now, Noah. What's this about a history?"

"History?"

"Your sister-in-law tells me you're writing a fine scholarly history. I knew you were doing something with your father's papers, but I didn't know you were doing anything for publication under your own name."

"I'm not sure I'm going to go on with it, Roger."

"Why the hell not?"

"You don't buy roast beef on the royalties from scholarly histories, and I like roast beef."

Roger sat forward and leaned his elbows on his desk. "Well, here's what I was thinking, Noah. Of course publication isn't important in a little gentleman factory like this the way it is in the universities, but it sure wouldn't do Milburn any harm to have a noted historian on its faculty. See how I figure the angles?"

Noah grinned at him.

"Have you got any money at all, Noah?"

"Some."

"A couple of thousand you could afford to invest in the future?"

"A little more than that."

"Okay. Then here's the proposition. A year from now you're back on active duty at your regular salary, but maybe with a lighter schedule than you used to carry. We can figure that out later. For this year the budget's all allocated, so we can't pay you a salary. But it wouldn't take much finagling to get you back your old quarters in Seward and your old place at the Unmarried Masters' table. Free room and board, in other words. Your duties would be a little indefinite. One of them would be to come over here and sit in this chair and try to look important when I'm away on speaking trips. Maybe a certain amount of counseling with boys and parents—that was always your forte, you know. Maybe fill in on a course or two when somebody's sick. Still plenty of time for working on the history. How long would it be before you'd have something ready for publication?"

"I'd been hoping to have the first volume, out of three or four, ready this winter—if I'd gone on working on it full time."

"And working on it part time the way I just outlined it? What would you guess?"

"Maybe next summer."

"And the other volumes?"

"I'd figure about a year and a half for each one."

"Well, you'd still have your summer vacations—and a light schedule. Suppose it was every two and a half years, or every three years. That wouldn't be too bad, would it? There are lots of years ahead. Would it?"

Noah thought about it. "No, it wouldn't."

"And in the meantime you'd be drawing a salary and doing a job you were always damned good at. What's wrong with that picture?"

"It's a wonderful picture, Roger. I can't tell you how much I appreciate it. Frankly, I think you overrate me a little, both as an historian and as a teacher."

"Okay. But so long as I'm doing the rating—"

"There are some complications."

"Such as?"

"Such as I can't tell you about."

"Oh." Roger looked a little hurt.

"I might know more next week," Noah said. "I don't mind telling you that it sounds damned attractive, Roger. It sounds wonderful. It kind of ties together everything I've wanted—could you give me a week or two to—to check into things, Roger?"

Roger looked doubtful. "It *is* going to take a certain amount of finagling. Do you think you could let me know next week?"

"I'll try," Noah said, thinking hard. Then he sat forward. "Yes, I'll let you know next week—Wednesday."

"Good." Roger wrote a phone number and the name of a Connecticut shore resort on a slip of paper. "Call me at that number Wednesday night."

Noah took the slip and stood up and put it into his pocket. Then he sat down again. "Just one question, Roger."

Roger looked up at him.

"I haven't any immediate plans in this direction but—well, I'm thirty-eight years old, Roger, and sooner or later—would all this work out the same if I were to pop up some year with a wife?"

Roger laughed. "You're the damnedest guy, Noah. One minute you're somebody, and the next you're Mr. Milquetoast. Hell, what do you think we're running here, a monastery? Of course you can get married—any damned time you please. It's time you did find yourself a wife. And when you do, I'll put your name at the top of the list for one of the Woolcott Road houses."

Noah stood up again and grinned at him. "Just wanted to be sure," he said.

XII

1.

NOAH sat in the sand with his arms wrapped around his knees, talking as much to the ocean out there in front of him as to Natalie, who lay on her beach robe beside him. She lay on her stomach, scooping up handfuls of sand and watching it thoughtfully as it trickled out from the side of her palm. Her tan, now toward the end of the summer, was far darker than it had been when he was here before, but still her skin seemed to have the golden quality he had always thought of as so distinctive of her. And still her shoulders and back had the youthful, firm-muscled smoothness that had surprised him when he saw her then.

The fog that had enclosed the cottage while they were eating breakfast had disappeared, although a rearguard of elusive wisps was still slinking about in the woods as they drove away from the cottage. And here on the beach a crystalline haze seemed to catch the sunlight, lending the atmosphere a sparkling and cooling freshness, giving the distant headlands the weird appearance of detached islands hanging in space, blurred and vaguely ethereal.

"It was like turning on a light in an unfamiliar room," Noah was saying. "All of a sudden the things that had looked so dim and—and unintelligible were as clear and understandable as chairs and tables and couches. I would never have believed it could happen like that, so suddenly. It was sort of a Paul-on-the-road-to-Damascus business. Suddenly I could see myself as you must have seen me, as practically everybody must have seen me all my life. All of a sudden I understood all the things I'd never been able to understand before, especially the things about you.

"Here I'd been wondering all my life how, that summer up at the Lake, you could have acted so wonderfully sometimes and then been so disagreeable other times. And suddenly last week I knew. I knew that the times you were something less than agreeable were the times when I kept insisting on our going on picnics with the family and parties with the family and—and doing all kinds of other things with the family."

He glanced down at her, to see if he could catch a confirmation in her face, but her head was turned and he saw only her hair.

He stared out at the twin white lines of surf. "That letter of yours— the one that knocked me out—that was in answer to the one I wrote you, wasn't it? The one in which I said I'd given up the idea of teaching at Milburn and was going to work as Dad's secretary instead? How could I have been dumb enough, for fifteen years, not to see that? And I even said that it would be nice if we could find an apartment within walking distance of the family's house, didn't I?"

She did not answer.

"And then this summer when I was here, and you said that you didn't think my family would approve of my running off with a wife and mother, I said something feeble to the effect that they might approve if they could be made to understand all the circumstances! And I didn't even know why you looked so—disappointed." He chuckled disgustedly. "My family has always had a prejudice against divorce, and of course that was exactly what I *was* thinking about."

She still did not turn her head, and still the sand trickled out from the side of her hand.

When they had come on to the beach they had noticed a group of children playing down by the water with a honey-colored spaniel. Now the spaniel came and crouched in front of them, barking, inviting them to play. Noah tried to order him away, but at every wave of his arm the dog barked more enthusiastically, bouncing into a lower crouch. Finally Noah got up and walked down to the water, snapping his fingers and talking to the dog, until the children saw what was going on and called the dog away. Noah came back up and sat down and went on talking.

"I find now," he said, "that I don't have any particular feeling about divorce one way or the other, except that superficially it's a rather disagreeable business. But I don't have the family's feeling about it, and I doubt if I ever did. I just took what they thought for granted. I took everything they believed for granted. If they thought it, it must be true. I've been trying to think of something I disagreed with them about, and I've thought of just one thing. I didn't agree with them about my brother-in-law, Kate's husband. But even there I always kept my opinion to myself. That's quite a record, wouldn't you say? One thing in a lifetime?"

He was looking down at her, and now her head was turned just enough for him to see that there were tears in her eyes. She sat up energetically and found the pocket of her beach robe and took out a handkerchief. She sat facing the water, wiping her eyes and nose. Because she was a little ahead of him, he could still see only a part of her face. "You don't have to beat yourself over the head, Noah," she said, her voice husky. "If you think that humility was your fault, it's time you started getting over it."

He stared at the back of her head. Then he smiled. "A point well taken," he said.

"Of course humility *was* your great weakness," she said, "but it was an awfully likable one." She turned and glanced at his face. Her nose was a little red, and she was smiling a desolate sort of smile. "How I hated it!" she said. "And how I loved you for it!"

She turned away again. He watched the small angle of her cheek that he could see, waiting minute after minute for her to say more. Finally, after a long time, she said, "I have to go over to the harbor and get Peter."

"Is that all you have to say?"

Again she sat still for a long time before she answered. "Right now it is, Noah. I have to have time to think." She got to her feet and took her beach robe a dozen steps down toward the water and shook it. And from somewhere the honey-colored spaniel came running again, taking the waving of the robe as a signal that they were ready to play. She turned and laughed up at Noah and bundled the robe in her arms, so that there were no edges for the dog to snatch. He danced around her, yipping. Then, like a halfback breaking suddenly into the clear, he swerved away at full speed, picked up one of her sandals without breaking his stride, and headed for the water.

Noah jumped up and ran after him. He ran well, his legs feeling firm beneath him. He herded the dog in the direction of its owners. They were calling to it, their voices thin and wailing. And near the water's edge, again without breaking his stride, the dog dropped the sandal and went scurrying away down the hard-packed sand.

Laughing, Noah brought it back up to her. "It doesn't seem to have been hurt any," he said.

She was smiling at him, her eyes a little misty. "You seem quite agile, Noah. Haven't you lost a little weight during the summer?"

"I suspect I might have." He smiled shamefacedly. "When things got hectic, I worked off steam by taking the boat out and rowing around the lake. Silly habit I have."

She nodded thoughtfully, and he wondered if she was agreeing that it was a silly habit. Then, her manner suddenly casual, as it might have been with any guest, she said, "Why don't you stay here and have a dip, Noah? The water's not nearly so cold this time of year as it was earlier in the summer. Have a dip and lie around here and relax, and I'll send somebody over for you in time for lunch." She was fumbling through her beach bag, looking for something. "I was thinking that we might have a picnic this evening, just you and me. There's a lovely spot way out at the end of the Island where nobody ever goes, and we could take a steak and some charcoal. Maybe by that time I'll know what I want to say."

She smiled up at him, the timid, pathetic smile that had always been so vivid in his memory. "If you don't mind, I'm going to let Betty entertain you this afternoon. I'll be hiding up in my room or somewhere. We'll start out for the picnic at five-thirty. Meet me in the living room. And wear something warm, because the nights get cold on the beach."

Her hand found the things she was searching for in the bag, a package of cigarettes and a lighter. Noah stood still, watching her light a cigarette. She tossed the package and lighter back into the bag.

But she did not leave. She stood there beside him, looking down at the sand. "Perhaps I can say this much now." She thought a moment, then said, "There have been times in the last fifteen years, Noah, when I've dreamed that you would come to me and say almost exactly what you said this morning. There were times when—when things weren't going very well for me, when I wasn't very happy—when that dream was what kept me going. It was what I lived on. You've seen enough, these weekends, to know that my life with Jeffrey hasn't been all it might have been. Twice I've gotten as far as talking to a lawyer about a divorce. And there have been times when if you *had* come to me and said the things you said this morning, I wouldn't have hesitated."

She was biting her lip, concentrating, he could see, on what more she was going to say.

"The trouble is that there were just as many times when I thought I knew absolutely surely that you never would come and say those things. Those were the times when I made myself learn to accept what I had, when I learned to adjust to it and—and live with it. After you've spent fifteen years adjusting to something, you don't readjust to something else in a half an hour. You see that, don't you? That's why I've got to have this afternoon to myself. I've got to think about Pammy and Peter—and Jeffrey—and about myself. One afternoon isn't going to be very long—to think about all that. It's a big decision you're asking me to make, you know."

"Of course it is," Noah said.

She smiled briefly, then frowned at him for a moment before she started up toward the dunes, walking as fast as she could in the loose sand.

2 ·

A SENSE of unreality pervaded Noah's thoughts all through the afternoon. It was a feeling that none of all this that was going on was actually happening to him, Noah Sibley, a feeling that he was an entirely different person from the Noah Sibley of other days and other years. This was a different man, this man who was marking time through this afternoon, waiting for five-thirty and the picnic on which he would learn something that he feared might seem equally unreal.

Of course the man who had driven away from the cottage at the Lake a week ago had been different from the old Noah Sibley too, but this man was different in a different sense. Where that man's eyes had been opened, this man's were slightly dazzled. Where that man had become, for the first time in his life, hardheaded, this man was a little lightheaded. And lingering in his mind along with the sense of unreality was an uncomfortable suspicion that, in presenting his case to Natalie, he had somehow fallen short, that he had been something less than totally convincing.

He had stated his case, but had he really pressed his claim? He had cited reasons. He had told her that he was now the man she had always hoped he would be. But had he shown any real ardor? Had he, in brief, told her that he loved her? He knew that he hadn't.

Of course she could assume that he loved her—from the mere fact that he was here, saying the things he had said, talking about his feeling about divorce. But that wasn't enough—wasn't, he knew, what a woman wanted. They wanted to be told.

Could he have come all this way, then, only to fail at the last moment because of some odd, subconscious reticence? The possibility

[263]

that he might have done just that worried him all through this afternoon of waiting.

He went on about the business of being entertained by Betty as though he were the same Noah Sibley he had always been, listening, laughing, answering questions, learning, as they talked, a lot of things about how Betty and Natalie and their husbands lived and thought and felt. And everything he learned reminded him of how little he actually knew about Natalie, adding a new dimension to his sense of unreality.

They had driven around the harbor and on out to a point from which they could watch the start of the Saturday afternoon sailing races. Betty, a delight to look at and, he was finding, pleasant and amusing company, chatted gaily as they sat there with the top down on her convertible and the breeze blowing through their hair. They were watching the shifting pattern of sails as the three classes of boats jockeyed for position around the starting line, and Noah was feeling bemused, detached from this breezy, blue and white world around him.

Pammy, she told him, would have been racing in the smallest class if she hadn't gone on the cruise. But of course she was the central figure on that cruise. They had gotten off at seven-thirty as planned, the man at the yacht club dock had told her, before she or Noah or Natalie was even up.

"In that fog?" Noah asked.

"They've got all the gadgets in the world on that boat," she said, "and I guess they knew from the forecast that it was going to burn off. And they know their way around the Sound better than I know my way around my kitchen." She laughed. "That's not saying much, of course. I'm even less domestic than Natalie is."

Noah had no idea how domestic Natalie was. He smiled. "What do you mean," he asked, "that Pammy is the central figure on this cruise?"

She laughed delightedly. "These Skinners they're taking on the cruise—they have a boy a year older than Pammy, and he seems to be quite taken with her. And Mr. Skinner is vice-president in charge of sales of a shoe company that does a certain amount of advertising. It wouldn't be a big account, but MacGarry, Humeston Associates wouldn't mind having it. So they invited Donald to go on a cruise with Pammy, and then they asked Mr. and Mrs. Skinner if they wouldn't like to go along. It made an excuse, you know—chaperonage, sort of."

Noah smiled thoughtfully. "And Natalie doesn't mind?"

"Mind?"

"Their, ah—their using her charms for business purposes?"

She pursed her lips, shrugging humorously. "I hadn't thought of that, exactly." Then she chuckled. "I doubt if Natalie had either. We get so used to—you can't be half-hearted about the advertising business, you know. The competition's terrific. You use all the tricks you've got in your bag—if you're going to get on top and stay there. And entertaining is at least half of it—more than half, these days, for Howard and Jeffrey. It's more important than the campaigns they plan or the copy they write. Somebody else in the office can do that."

Noah laughed. "There are a lot of things we bookworms don't get to know much about, aren't there?"

She smiled at him, and he sensed that she liked him. She proceeded with his education. "This cruise," she said, "combining business and pleasure—that's just typical. That's what all our weekends are. But this one is simple. Next week"—she shrugged again, shaking her head —"next week we think the Hittles will be dropping in here on their cruiser. Arnold Hittle, of Hittle and Weed—you know who they are."

"I'm afraid I don't."

"The candy bar people? You know Creamy and Nutty and Chewy."

He smiled. "I'm afraid I don't."

"The animated candy bars? On TV?"

He shook his head, still smiling.

"I thought everybody knew them," she said. "Anyway, they're awfully important little people—to us. They make the difference between being rich or poor almost—to us."

Could animated candy bars really dominate people's lives like that, Noah wondered.

"Well, anyway, Hittle and Weed is MacGarry, Humeston's biggest account. It's our one big account—our bread and butter. All the others are our cake—or the frosting on the cake. And of course when Arnold Hittle speaks, we jump. And that means Natalie and me as well as Howard and Jeffrey."

"Do you mind?" Noah asked.

"Oh, Arnold's all right—after you learn how to take him. Kind of childish, some ways. He likes to think he's surprising us—never lets us know they're coming. And of course we have to make darned sure we do know they're coming, and then make believe we're surprised. We have ways of keeping track of his cruiser—it's one of the fanciest cruisers anywhere in these waters—and right now we know they've just started out on a cruise. They always finish their cruises with a week-

[265]

end here, so we're practically sure they'll be here next weekend. And will we be ready for them!"

Noah nodded. "They'll be royally entertained."

She shook her head, chuckling. "That doesn't begin to describe what we'll do. We'll turn the place upside down for them."

Noah still wanted to know how Natalie felt about all this, how much the dissatisfaction she had felt with her life with Jeffrey had to do with turning the place upside down for his business associates. "And you and Natalie don't mind?" he asked. "All this entertaining?"

She pursed her lips, smiling, shrugging in a gesture that seemed to say it was all in a lifetime. "Oh, sometimes the people are bores, but most of the time it's fun. And I doubt if there are very many other kinds of jobs where you could write off so much fun on your income tax."

"And do you think that Natalie thinks it fun too?"

She seemed to think that one over. "Yes, I think so," she said. "Oh, of course it has its headaches, like everything else. We both get annoyed sometimes. But on the over-all picture—yes, I think she likes it as well as I do. You get kind of caught up in it all, you know."

The last starting gun had boomed, the last straggler slid across the line, and now the sails that had been bunched into a single, shifting pattern were silently and smoothly disjoining themselves, spreading the pattern wide across the mouth of the harbor and the Sound beyond. Betty turned the car around. "Maybe we can come back later and watch the finish."

She drove around the harbor to the yacht club. They sat on the veranda and watched children bathing inside the roped-in area of the beach and older children diving off the float. After a while they moved around to the other side, where they looked down on the tennis courts and out beyond to the yacht basin. Boats of all sizes and kinds were anchored there, their masts and antennas swaying lazily as the cumbersome launch wound its incessant way in and out among them and tiny dinghies with outboards scooted around it, like ducklings around a mother duck.

There were tennis matches going on down beneath them there, and they sat and watched them and chatted. And all the time, in the back of his mind, Noah was wondering what Natalie was doing now, what kind of thoughts were going through her head, what basis of thinking she would be using to approach this decision she was going to have made by five-thirty. She might, he supposed, be up in her bedroom, stretched out on her bed, with the shades drawn. She might be walking on the beach in front of the cottage, as he had done twice when he was here before and had had to have solitude to think—once in the middle of the night and once in the early forenoon. She might be in any number of places that he had never seen or heard of; there was so much of this place and her life in it that he knew nothing about.

3.

LATER Betty drove him up the Island to a high bluff with a light-house. They sat on a bench at the edge of the bluff, looking down at the surf breaking on the rocks far below. And minute after minute a clock in the back of Noah's mind was ticking off the minutes to five-thirty.

She chatted on amiably and aimlessly about their brother who was a broker in Chicago and their father and mother who were still living in St. Paul and their childhood summers on Lake Michigan, and for the first time in his life Noah began to understand that Natalie was as much a part of a family, the Parkes family, as he was of the Sibleys. All these things he was learning, he realized, were things that he had had no right not to know long ago.

Until Natalie had mentioned him earlier in the summer, he had forgotten that she had a brother. He had almost forgotten that she had a sister. He doubted that he had ever known that her father had been in the paper business until Betty mentioned the fact that Jeffrey had gotten his start in the advertising department of Mr. Parkes's paper company.

Always, when he had thought about being married to Natalie, he was realizing, he had seen her exclusively in the Sibley family context: an attractive adjunct to Sibley family dinners, a daughter-in-law whose manner with older people could be almost as charming as Louise's, a sister-in-law whom Barrett and Mark and Kate and Connie would like, another worshiper at the feet of the great William Huntington.

Now, as Betty got to reminiscing about earlier days, he was getting some idea of the continuity of Natalie's life, of its interrelation with her own family and with Jeffrey. Jeffrey, he learned, had been a high-school friend, a poor boy with a triple ambition to become a writer and a musician and a rich man, all three. There hadn't been any chance of his becoming a musician, but advertising had seemed a little closer to writing than any other kind of business where you might get rich.

Natalie had been interested in him because of his ambitions, and had gotten her father to give him a job in the advertising department. And when, five years later, her little back eddy of an interlude with Noah had come to an end, Jeffrey had been there, doing very well indeed at twenty-three as advertising manager of the company.

A few years after they were married, he learned, when Jeffrey had had a chance to go to New York with one of the big agencies, Mr. Parkes had been glad to see him go farther. Howard MacGarry had been another junior account executive in the agency. And later it was Mr. Parkes who had put up the capital they needed to start their own agency. They had worked very hard those early years—especially Jeffrey, Betty admitted, laughing. Jeffrey had written wonderful copy. But now for a long time, since they had gotten over the hump, he hadn't had time to write any copy at all.

Noah looked at his watch. It was four-fifteen. "I should be back at the cottage by five," he said.

"I'm thirsty," she said. "Let's go back to the yacht club and have something cold to drink. Then we can watch the finish of the races for a few minutes and go on back to the cottage. That should make it about right."

Back at the club they left the car in the parking area and walked around to the veranda. Betty went inside to order the drinks, and Noah placed a couple of chairs so that they faced the tennis courts and the yacht basin beyond.

She came out and settled into her chair and threw her head back and closed her eyes. "That's a nice breeze," she said. She opened her eyes and smiled at him, then turned her head slowly and looked out at the harbor. Suddenly she sat forward, staring. "Good heavens!" she said, rising from her chair as though she had had an electric shock, her body rigid, her eyes wide.

Noah stood up and raised his hand, ready to catch her. "What's the matter? Don't you feel well?"

"Look," she said breathlessly, "out there in the harbor."

He looked. The harbor was even fuller of boats than it had been.

"The big mahogany cruiser," she gasped, sounding as frightened as if it had been an enemy warship. "It's the Hittles." She stood still, stupefied, shaking her head. "I don't know what to do."

She looked up at him, her eyes vacant. Then quickly she turned and ran down the veranda and out onto the lawn. He followed her.

Shading her eyes, she studied the cruiser. "They're still aboard," she said, "but they look about ready to come ashore. I'll have to meet them at the dock."

She looked up at him again, breathless and limp and wilted. "This is the time they *did* surprise us. Look, Noah, you take the car and run out and tell Natalie the Hittles are here. Tell her I'm staying here to meet them and she'll have to figure out the rest. And hurry, Noah, please. This is awful. You haven't any idea how awful."

4·

NOAH hurried, in moderation, feeling amused, feeling more than ever that this man, on this strange island, somehow involved in the awful business of being surprised by a manufacturer of candy bars, couldn't really be Noah Sibley.

At the cottage he looked into the living room and Natalie was not there. He went upstairs and knocked on the door of her room and got no answer. He went back down and peered into all the rooms on the first floor. Finally he went out onto the veranda and saw her lying on a blanket on the lawn, out near the edge of the bluff. She had on the same sun dress, pale tan and dark brown, that she had worn that afternoon seven weeks ago when she had met him at the ferry dock, and she had a cloth over her eyes.

He walked out there, and she sat up, startled, and frowned at him and looked at her wrist watch. He watched her face, and because of the things he had learned during the afternoon, he found that he was seeing a new Natalie, neither the Natalie of his memories nor the Natalie of his dreams. There was a faint resemblance to the girl who had sat on hilltops with parted lips listening to wood thrushes, to the girl who had giggled an incongruous little giggle when he had cast a trout fly, to the girl who had walked around the lake with him on rainy days in her hooded raincoat, but it was only a faint one. And there was a resemblance to the woman he had been dreaming about all summer, the woman in the creamy white coat he had held in his arms one night down on this beach below them there, a woman who was troubled and melting and afraid she couldn't take it any more.

But the woman he was seeing now was neither of them. She was a middle-aged woman, beautiful in her own distinctive way, self-possessed and competent—competent, without a doubt, at the difficult and trying job of helping her husband entertain his clients, competent to handle the clashes of personality between her husband and her children, strong enough to hide her doubts and fears and disappointments.

"I said five-thirty, Noah," she said, pleasantly enough but still frowning down at her wrist watch. "It's only four-thirty."

Your dreams, he was thinking, could discount sixteen years of living, but— "I know," he said, smiling, "but the Hittles are here."

Her frown deepened. "What?"

"Betty wanted me to tell you that the Hittles are here, in their mahogany cruiser."

She stared, bewildered. "She's joking."

Noah smiled a little more broadly. "She didn't look like somebody who was joking," he said. "She looked as though she might be sick any minute. The Hittles seemed to be about ready to come ashore, so she stayed there to meet them and asked me to come out here and tell you that you'd have to figure out the rest."

She was on her feet, already starting toward the cottage, walking fast with her distinctive firm-muscled walk, dragging her blanket behind her. At the door she turned and looked at Noah, and her face was serious but self-possessed and determined. She didn't panic, Noah thought, the way Betty did. This was the expression of a woman rising to an emergency. "Will you run upstairs and call the maid, Noah?" she asked, her voice low and businesslike. "It's the door at the end of the hall. Tell her to come down quick—as fast as she can."

He went up and delivered the message, and when he came back down, Natalie was at the telephone in the hall. "I thought if anybody would know how to reach them, you would, Sid," she was saying. "I thought with their radio telephone . . . Yes, I thought of that . . . the Coast Guard? . . . I don't believe they'd have gotten very far; they were probably running under sail most of the day . . . that's right; if they started right back under power, they might be here in time for a late dinner. . . . That's wonderful, Sid. Thanks a million."

She hung up and looked up at Noah, concentrating, her mind obviously working fast. She picked up a pad and pencil from the telephone table. "Arnold Hittle doesn't like the dinners at the club," she said, talking, Noah could see, more to herself than to him. She went into the dining room and sat at the table with the pad in front of her, tapping on the table with the eraser end of the pencil. Then she heard the maid's footsteps and hurried out to the kitchen.

He could hear them talking, their voices urgent, and he could hear them moving things around on shelves, checking the larder.

She must have been out there for five minutes, and when she came back in she sat down and started to draw on the pad.

After a minute she said, "Look, Noah."

He stepped over beside her and looked. It was a map she had drawn. She used the pencil as a pointer. "This is the road you go into town on, and just before you get to the village you'll see this road turning off to the right. You can spot it by a little gray house with a big barn behind it, right there. Then when you get down here"—her pointer came to a fork—"take the left fork and keep going all the way to the end of the road. It will end at a dock, and there will be a shed right beside it, with a sign that says 'Carlton Hosmer.'" She wrote the name at the bottom of the map.

"Tell Mr. Hosmer that I've got to have enough lobsters for a dozen people—he'll know how much that is—chicken lobsters if he has them, but if not any size. If he has them now, you might as well bring them back with you, but if he hasn't, tell him I've got to have them by seven o'clock—without fail. And don't take no for an answer, Noah. Tell him to go out and pull all the pots in the Sound if he has to, but don't let him say that he can't get them for me. Tell him we've *got* to have them. Tell him it's the most important thing in the world. It's awfully important, Noah. You have no idea how important."

He stood still, smiling down at her. Suddenly, in these last few minutes, he had been experiencing a sensation that was completely new to him. It was a new kind of clarity, of clear-mindedness. There was an element of sadness in it, but there was also an element of release, of a new sort of freedom, of a final, complete release from long-held illusions.

She was looking through and past him, her mind still occupied with the problems of the dinner and the evening.

"I think I have a very good idea of how important it is," he said, and the tone of his voice made her look up at him, startled and bewildered. He was smiling at her. "It's more important than the little picnic we were going to have tonight, isn't it?"

She was still looking up at him, still looking startled and bewildered. For a long time her expression did not change. Then slowly her lips parted and she stared on into space beyond him. "I see what you mean," she said softly.

Then suddenly she was on her feet, looking a little hurt and a little angry. "But that's not fair, Noah. It's important to a lot of people beside myself."

"Of course it is. It's important to MacGarry, Humeston Associates, and therefore to Jeffrey and Howard and Betty and Pammy and Peter. I suppose it's important to a lot of people who are dependent on MacGarry, Humeston Associates for their jobs. It's important to everything you've lived with for these last fifteen years, to everybody who's been a part of your life."

He was surprised at how calmly he was talking, at how clearly thoughts came to him, as though these were thoughts that he had been over often in his mind. "I wasn't being unfair when I said that, Natalie, because I wasn't blaming you. I was merely recognizing the fact that you don't wipe out fifteen years of living, your own living or anybody else's, by coming around fifteen years late and trying to make the gesture you should have made long ago—without trying."

Her expression had changed as he talked. Now she was looking frightened. "You're making it sound awfully—awfully final, Noah. Such a little thing. I—that, my forgetting, that can't be the whole answer."

He nodded, feeling sorry for her. Whatever she might have been thinking as she lay out there on the lawn, she hadn't, apparently, reached the inevitable answer yet. But sooner or later she would have. She had almost said it this morning, when she had talked about spending fifteen years adjusting to a way of living.

He wished it hadn't had to happen this way, so abruptly, that she could have had time to work up to the realization more gradually, as he realized now that he had been working up to it all afternoon. And he wished that it could have come about over some other kind of incident, so that she wouldn't have to be feeling guilty. She was no more guilty than he was. But you couldn't go back now and start over.

"I'm not blaming you for forgetting, Natalie," he said. "Please believe me when I say that. I'm not mad at you for it. The forgetting in itself wouldn't have been the whole answer. But I'm wondering if it couldn't be a pretty neat symbol for the whole answer."

Now her expression had changed again. She no longer looked frightened. She looked puzzled.

"Perhaps it would be a good idea if I went and saw about the lobsters now," he said.

She was studying his face, scanning it as though there was something different about it, as though there was something in it she had to figure out. "Yes," she said. "I seem to be having a very odd thought, Noah. It's not very well formed in my mind yet. I'll have to work it out. Yes, you go see about the lobsters now. We'll talk when you come back."

He went, and on the way he was ashamed to find himself feeling calm. He had no right not to be devastated and crushed. But that, he could only tell himself, would probably come later—tomorrow morning when he woke up, or tomorrow night, when he said goodbye to Natalie and got on the ferry and headed back toward the mainland, or maybe sometime next week, when he was alone again in the house in Middlefield. This thing he was feeling now was probably numbness.

5.

WHEN Noah got back to the cottage, he heard Natalie talking to the maid in the kitchen. He went out there, and she was standing at the table counting drops of something into a bowl. He waited until she was through counting before he told her that Mr. Hosmer would have the lobsters ready for them at seven o'clock. He hadn't had them, but he wasn't going to let Mrs. Humeston down, no sir. They didn't come any nicer than Mrs. Humeston. He'd have them if he had to send a boat to the mainland for them.

"That's wonderful, Noah," she said, smiling at him. But she looked tired and her eyes a little puffy and he wondered if she had been crying.

"Is there anything else I can do?" he asked.

"I can't think of anything right now," she said. She hesitated for a moment, then picked up a little bottle and measured a teaspoonful into the bowl.

"I'll be out on the veranda," Noah said. "Call me if you think of anything I can do." He smiled at her, trying to make it a reassuring smile, and went on out.

It was perhaps five minutes before she came out. She sat in the chair next to his and looked out across the Sound. He waited.

When she finally spoke, her voice was friendly, almost casual. "Of course you were right, Noah. You were just quicker to see it than I was."

He watched her face. This, the moment when she accepted what he had already accepted, was, then, the final moment. And as his own mind looked at that fact, examining its full significance, he found that he was sad but still calm, sober but without any of that small sense of panic, that last-minute drawing back that so often comes with the realization of a finality.

She turned to look at him, curious for his reaction.

He smiled at her. "It's funny about that," he said. "Since my declaration of independence from the family, I seem to have become quicker-witted. I think faster than I did before."

"I know," she said. "That was the odd thought I had when we were talking in the dining room. I was thinking about the way you are now. It was something about the way you were talking—and about the way you talked this morning, down there on the beach. You really talked very well, with very good control of your thoughts and your language. I said that you were beating yourself over the head, but you really weren't. You were wondering how you could have been stupid for so long, but you were showing quite a lot of confidence in what you are now. Isn't that right?"

"I suspect it is."

She waited a while, and now when she began again there was a faint suggestion of amusement in her voice. "Don't they say, Noah, that women admire men for their virtues and love them for their faults?"

He looked at her out of the corner of his eye.

"The thought I had was about that boy I was so in love with up at that lake of yours. He was clumsy and tongue-tied and unsure of himself, and so blind to such obvious things and so sure that everybody was wonderful except himself and so very, very humble and well meaning and good. Of course some of those were things that I admired about him too, but—I loved that boy like the very devil, Noah. And the thought that popped into my head in the dining room there, when you were seeing this thing so quickly and stating it so clearly, was that that boy doesn't exist any more. He's gone."

He was nodding, following her thought, recognizing its rather astounding rightness.

"You had changed quite a lot when you were here before this summer, Noah. You had gained more confidence—at least on the surface. But there was still enough of that boy left for me to—well, enough so that I had a pretty uncomfortable summer. But now—even this morning, when you ran after that dog on the beach, you ran just as well as any other man your age could have, maybe better. You've even lost *that*."

He laughed, and they sat still looking out at the water. He was smiling to himself, a ruminative, nostalgic sort of smile, and he knew that if he turned and looked at her, he would find the same sort of smile on her face. It amused him to think that, having gotten all the way apart, having faced the final separation, they were now, for this moment, back together, sharing an emotion and a memory.

"I don't mean, Noah," she said, "that you're not a much better man. You undoubtedly are. You needed self-confidence, and you're getting it. You'll get more as you go along. You still have a long way to go before anyone will accuse you of being conceited. You're probably a much better man, but you're just not the same man." She laughed. "You're practically a stranger."

He was still smiling the ruminative smile. "That was the thought I had about you—at some time in the recent proceedings. I don't remember just when."

"And we're not blaming each other?"

"Of course not."

"It doesn't even hurt very much," she said. "I cried after you left, but I don't think I was crying for you. I was crying for that dream. I'd become quite attached to that dream, you know, living with it all these years."

6·

THEY were out on the Hittles' boat all day Sunday, cruising around the Sound, and when they got back Noah felt parched and dry but oddly relaxed. With two hours to wait before he had to be at the ferry dock, they had iced coffee on the side veranda, and as they sat there the fog started to come in again. It came in as it sometimes did at the Lake, actively, moving across the side yard like stealthy hurrying troops, seeming to pass across in front of the woods at the same time that it was blotting them out from sight.

Since the night before, a spirit of camaraderie had existed within the group who together had faced the crisis of the Hittles' arrival and conquered it. Noah was very much a part of that group. As the excitement mounted, he had shuttled around the Island, from the cottage to the yacht club to the liquor store to the grocery store to the lobsterman's to the cottage and back to the yacht club, where he had spent a final desperate half hour alone with the Hittles on their boat while Betty was home changing her clothes.

Also a part of the group were Jeffrey and Howard and Pammy and the Skinners, who had come boiling into the harbor while Noah was drinking Scotch with Mr. Hittle in the cockpit of his cruiser. Once, long ago, Mr. Hittle had heard William Huntington Sibley lecture. He was delighted to meet his son. "There was a man," he said, patting Noah paternally on the shoulder, "who really knew how to put it across. He'd have been a success in any line of business."

Pammy seemed to have forgotten the resentment she had felt toward Noah that day when she had failed at the piano. Her manner toward him was cordial and charming. With Donald Skinner in attendance—as he had been all evening and all day—she seemed to have lost entirely the little-girl quality that Noah had seen at odd moments that other weekend; she was playing, with considerable convincingness, the part of the sophisticated young lady. Noah had seen almost nothing of Peter; he had no idea whether he was still feeling resentment over Noah's presence at his failure at the cove or not.

Now, as they finished their iced coffee and moved in out of the fog, Pammy smiled at Noah. "Mr. Sibley," she asked, "do you play scrabble?"

He admitted that he did. She set up the table in the living room for the five of them, Noah, Natalie, Jeffrey, Donald, and herself. They all stood watching, and Noah noticed that Natalie had a very peculiar expression on her face. And as they all sat down and picked up their letters, she giggled—the incongruous, childlike giggle that Noah had wondered if she had lost forever.

"What's funny?" Jeffrey asked.

"Nothing," she said, and with an effort she stopped herself.

But twice in the next few minutes she giggled again, irrepressibly.

Jeffrey looked annoyed. "I wish I knew what was so damned funny," he said. "How about letting us in on it?"

Again with an effort she composed herself. "It's a little hard to explain, Jeffrey," she said. "It's just that"—she laughed—"it's just that I don't believe that when Noah came he expected to be spending his last hour playing scrabble with the family."

"I don't see anything funny about that. What's wrong with scrabble?"

"Nothing at all, dear," she said, looking open-mouthed at Noah. "It's a very nice game. Very good for the vocabulary."

By the time Noah and Natalie got down to the dock, the fog had settled in thick over the harbor, solid, no longer moving, a part of the
air itself. The ferry was not in yet, and they stood there in the fog,
chatting idly, smiling at each other, liking each other, closer, in one
sense, than they had ever been, in another sense infinitely remote.
They were like strangers who, by some odd circumstance, had shared
a personal and intimate experience and now knew that, the experience
ended, circumstance would probably never throw them together again.

From somewhere out in the Sound the ferry's foghorn sounded, and
they stood together, watching, no longer talking. The world seemed
to end in a gray nothingness out there at the end of the pier. Between
where they were standing and the end, the foot-thick piles stood out,
peculiarly isolated by the fog, peculiarly three-dimensional, the nearer
ones brown and wet, the farthest ones so wraithlike that they might
have been the ghosts of piles.

The foghorn sounded again and again, gradually nearer, gradually
placing itself straight out from the dock, and with it came the sound
of the bell. For an incredibly long time after that they could see nothing of the vessel as the horn and the bell came closer and closer. And
then, simultaneously with the loud churning of the water along the
hull, it appeared above them there, looming supernaturally large for a
moment before it slid in beside them and assumed its normal size and
normal appearance.

She kissed him lightly on the cheek and smiled at him and wished
him luck and turned and walked back to the station wagon. He
watched her go and felt a quick, sickening qualm at the thought that
he might never see her again. But then it was gone and he knew that
this was not going to be the moment when he was to feel devastated
and crushed. He felt strangely lighthearted, strangely free as he carried
his bags aboard the ferry.

He climbed the stairs and pushed his way through the crowded,
brightly lighted cabin to the sliding door that gave onto the starboard
deck. He pulled the door open and stepped out and closed it behind
him.

There were only three other people braving the fog outside there:
a middle-aged man and two younger women who turned and looked

as he came out, then turned back and looked out into the blankness, talking in low murmuring voices. He walked on along the deck a few steps and leaned his forearms on the railing and looked out too, feeling a little worried and more than a little puzzled.

He couldn't understand about that feeling of freedom he had had as he came aboard. He remembered that yesterday afternoon, in Natalie's dining room, when the realization that it could never be had come to him with such compelling certainty, his first feeling had been one of freedom, of release, and the memory worried him, making him wonder if throwing off the great love of his life so lightheartedly didn't prove some basic shallowness in his character.

The ferry was moving, but still backing, and now there was a ringing of bells in the engine room and a shuddering along the hull. He leaned over the railing and watched the wake as they churned about and headed for the mainland.

And while he was still watching, while the wake gradually ceased to be a churning and took on its flowing, curving form, he suddenly knew. He knew that it had not been a great love. It had been a dream, like Natalie's dream, and he was feeling released because for sixteen years he had been in bondage to a dream, as much in bondage to that dream of a girl he had never known as he had been to his family.

He stared down at the water, frowning, examining the thought, asking himself if this answer that had come to him was anything more than an apt phrase that his mind had borrowed from the things Natalie had said. But the more he examined it the surer he became that it was a simple, accurate truth. He thought back over those sixteen years, picking out incidents, conversations, things he had said and things he had done, and always it was true. Always his thoughts had been conditioned, his actions limited, his self held back from being quite his whole self, by the dream of Natalie, forever there in the back of his mind. And with the realization that it was true there came a far greater sense of release than he had felt before.

He stood up straight and stretched, breathing in the cool damp air, enjoying its flavor. Night had come in over the Sound suddenly, and the gray nothingness outside there had turned into a black nothingness. He smiled out into it, liking it.

He walked along the deck, away from the three people. Now for the first time in his life he was really free, free from every bondage. He had come all the way around the big circle again, completed one more cycle in the spiral of his increasing awareness.

Now he was ready to start again, on a new level. He could think about the future. It was amazing how easy it was to think about the future. The future meant Milburn and the history. He saw now why he had hesitated when he had thought about Milburn, and the reason was that his imagination had been unable to place Natalie in the Milburn setting. He had hesitated the other day, when Roger had stated his proposition, because he hadn't been able to see Natalie at Milburn, hadn't been able to imagine her enjoying the life there.

He mustn't forget to call Roger Wednesday night at that Connecticut shore resort. He went back over that conversation he had had with Roger, and he smiled when he remembered that he had asked him if he might someday bring back a wife.

He walked back up the deck and took up his position at the railing where he had been before, still smiling out into the soothing, enveloping blackness. Roger had said that it was high time he did find himself a wife, and now he saw that for the first time it was actually possible that he might someday find one. For the first time he could think of it as a possibility. Because now, for the first time, he was alone, without an imaginary girl at his elbow—and there was no more fear in the thought that he was alone than there had been in the thought that he was free.

He would never be vulnerable to the family because of his aloneness. That had been a silly fear, the fear he had had that day when he was driving away from New York. He would not be vulnerable for the very reason that he *was* free—free to order his own life, to choose his own friends, to find, if he wanted to, a girl he might marry.

There would be girls. There always had been girls: girls at the Lake, girls in Middlefield, girls at Milburn, the sisters of other masters, relatives of boys. But now he knew that he had never seen any of them clearly, in focus. The image had been distorted by the interposing image of Natalie, of the girl he had never known.

Of course, he told himself, he was thirty-eight years old—and not exactly the type that women swooned over. But it was still a possibility. Joan had said, that day at the Lake, that there were plenty of girls who would like to marry a man like him—and he had thought of Natalie and resented Joan's saying it. But Winifred had said something of the same sort the other day when they were driving up to Milburn.

He remembered that conversation, and the memory of it was, he admitted to himself, pleasing, soothing to his ego. He remembered that Winifred was going to be at Milburn, and the thought that she would be there pleased him too. And suddenly, without going through any preliminary thought processes, he knew that someday he would be marrying Winifred. He didn't know how he knew, but he knew—knew that it was something that could and would happen, that Winifred could want to marry a man like him, that she could love a man like him.

It was all possible. It was possible to imagine her in the Milburn setting, to imagine her living in one of those faculty houses on Woolcott Road, reading in one of those living rooms, sitting opposite him at the table in one of those dining rooms, eating dinner with him, eating breakfast with him. He could imagine going to bed with her—and that was something he had never been able to imagine with Natalie. It would be a double bed. If she was going to be married, she had said last week, she wanted to be—married.

He could imagine her sitting beside him at football games, walking around the field at track meets with her hand in his arm, walking with him out around the surrounding hills. He could see her with the boys, and with the other masters and their wives.

It was a lot more than possible. It was what was going to happen. And it was going to be very wonderful, very deeply and satisfyingly right.

He went over and over the thought in his mind. He reminded himself that she had spent those years in the sanitarium, and he smiled at the thought. There was no more danger of that now with Winifred than there would be with any other girl he might marry, probably less. That was not something he believed; it was something he knew. He had known it before he left the house on Proctor Street that afternoon last week, when he had seen in her the two things together—the inward fire and the perspective, the sense of humor. Either one, perhaps, without the other, would have left a doubt in his mind. Together, he had felt then and he felt again now, they added up to a sanity that was probably sounder, deeper rooted, than his own, sounder than that of most of the people he knew. And all the things she had said and done on their trip to Milburn, every expression that had crossed her face, had served to make him surer.

Yes, sir, it was right, and it was going to happen. And suddenly he thought of Mark's face when he told him that it was going to happen—and his mother's face, and Barrett's. And he laughed out loud into the black nothingness outside there.

The middle-aged man and the two younger women looked up, startled, and moved a few feet farther away, down along the railing. Noah looked at them and chuckled and stood still, smiling out into the fog.

[280]